A TIME FOR MURDER

A TIME FOR MURDER

TIME LOOP DETECTIVE
BOOK 1

PAUL AUSTIN ARDOIN

A TIME FOR MURDER

Copyright © 2024 by Paul Austin Ardoin

Published by Pax Ardsen Books

All rights reserved. No part of this book may be used or reproduced in any manner whatsoever without written permission from the publisher, except in the case of brief quotations embodied in critical articles or reviews.

This book is a work of fiction. Names, characters, businesses, organizations, places, events and incidents either are the product of the author's imagination or are used fictitiously. Any resemblance to actual persons, living or dead, events, or locales is entirely coincidental.

ISBN 978-1-949082-60-9

For information please visit:

www.paulaustinardoin.com

Cover design by Ziad Ezzat of Feral Creative Colony: feralcreativecolony.com

THE HANDOFF

I

WRAPPED IN A TATTERED RED-AND-BLACK TARTAN BLANKET, THE dead man lay on his back. The body rested behind a concrete bench in Lemon Hill Park. The forecast called for sun later, but the Sacramento morning was cold, the fog weighing heavily in the air.

Detective Luke Guillory, shivering next to his new partner, recognized the blanket. Then he saw the prominent Roman nose, the close-set eyes, and Luke's heart sank.

Detective Summer Symanski knelt next to the body. She wasn't squeamish, Luke noted. A good thing, since most of Luke's cases were overdoses.

With her hand encased in a latex glove, Symanski gently pulled down the blanket to expose the dead man's right arm. She pointed to a series of raised bumps. "Looks like heroin. This park is, uh, popular for drug use, right?"

Luke gave a brief nod. Symanski had only been with the Sacramento P.D. for a week, but already she knew this park saw more than its share of drug addicts.

Lemon Hill Park was designed in the 1920s by architect Frank Muñoz, one of the first Latino architects to make a name for himself in California. Some of Muñoz's most stunning features—the cable bridges, the covered walkway to the Santa Guadalupe Basilica, the hermitage in Grove Field—were secluded enough for users to experience their highs and lows in relative peace.

The dead man stared at the clouds with brown irises that had been intense and vibrant, showing both wisdom and damage, when he'd been alive. "I know him."

Symanski turned her head quickly toward Luke. "You know him?"

"Earl Shent. Three tours in Afghanistan."

Symanski frowned. "A vet?"

"Never the same after he came back, or at least that's what his sister said. In and out of jail, in and out of rehab. His sister finally kicked him out last year."

"How do you know him?"

"One of the few regulars at the park who'll talk to cops. Five overdose deaths at this park so far this year, and Earl helped me identify three of the bodies." Luke squatted on the other side of the corpse from Symanski. The world spun. "I talked to Earl last week. A couple days before you got assigned to me. Another—another heroin overdose. A kid, only seventeen. No ID, but Earl knew who he was." A flash in his head, the mother's face peering around the half-open front door in Del Paso Heights, a mixture of anguish and relief on her face. Luke blinked, coming back to the present. "Earl never would tell me the name of his dealer, though."

Symanski pointed at the man's ashen lips and skin. "Typical discoloration for an overdose."

Luke set his jaw. Earl was the sixth overdose death in Lemon Hill Park since January—and though the calendar had just turned over to April, the overdose deaths were already equal to all last year.

Luke had tried to get information about the park regulars from some detectives in Vice, but most of them ignored Luke's requests. When his mother was police chief—the first female police chief in Sacramento—most other cops viewed Luke getting the homicide detective position as nepotism; his mother's subsequent arrest and conviction for bribery and embezzlement had solidly cemented his status as a pariah. Never mind that Luke was still trying to prove his mother was innocent.

Symanski, in fact, was Luke's first partner in over two years who hadn't immediately put in a transfer request.

Luke pulled his attention back to the present. The recent spate of overdoses likely meant a new dealer had come into the park—with something cheaper, more potent, more dangerous.

Symanski pulled the blanket down to the dead man's hips, reached into the pocket of his jeans, and pulled out a nylon wallet. "A few dollars here." She took out a driver's license but said nothing. The name on the license obviously matched the name Luke had given.

Luke stood, his stomach roiling. "I'll be right back."

Stepping out from behind the bench, he ducked under the police tape and walked onto the main path. He checked his watch—then quickly pulled his sleeve down to hide it. He liked the Von Zeitmann that Ellie bought him for their anniversary a few years ago, but he felt ostentatious interviewing homeless people with such a pricey watch.

Luke made his way to the edge of the park, crossed the street, then pushed the door open to Basilica Coffee.

A few minutes later, a large coffee in hand, he headed to Puente de Inspiración, the impressive bridge at the park's center. Underneath the bridge, a man sat cross-legged, resting his chin in his left hand, his right arm listless at his side. His olive trousers were filthy, as was his jean jacket. His hair was getting long, like it hadn't been cut in three or four months.

Luke walked under the bridge and stopped. The man startled, then saw Luke's face and relaxed.

"Hey, Detective Luke." The man's voice crackled, thin and wispy.

Luke held up the coffee.

The man's eyes flickered with desire, and he reached his left hand up to take the paper cup from Luke. "Oh, the good stuff." He took a greedy sip, his eyes narrowing. "You must want something."

"Can't get anything past you, Hector."

Hector sighed. "Is it bad news?"

Luke nodded. "It's Earl."

Hector blinked. "Is—is he...?"

Luke hesitated. "Overdose, looks like."

Hector bowed his head and set the coffee on the concrete next to him. "Oh, man."

Luke took a step back. A stifled sob from Hector; Luke gave him a few moments.

Luke's phone buzzed, and he glanced at the screen. A call from Ellie—weird, she never called in the middle of her workday, especially from her firm's Boston office. He had to let it go to voicemail, though.

Hector took a deep, shuddering breath, and Luke spoke again. "Earl was a good guy. You remember Caleb Vargas, right? Only a kid. Earl's the one who identified his body. Got his mom some closure, even if it didn't end the way she'd hoped. Same thing with Tommy."

A sniffle from Hector.

"This year has been rough," Luke said.

"I don't touch heroin, Detective Luke," Hector said.

"I know," Luke replied. "But Earl did. And you and Earl, you looked out for the kids here, right? We've gotten some 9-1-1 calls and the paramedics got here in time to save a couple of them, right?" Those calls had been anonymous, but Luke knew Earl and Hector had likely been the callers.

Hector was silent. But his left hand snaked out and grabbed the coffee again.

"There's a guy," Hector said. Another sip of coffee—no, not a sip, a long drink. Hector set it down again and Luke waited. Hector smacked his lips and continued. "He works all over. The park, the clubs over on Fruitvale, even the rich bitches on the east side."

"The heroin dealer?"

"No, no, no." Hector bit his lip. "Look, this can't get back to me. I get Magic Star from K-Car, but he doesn't sell heroin."

Magic Star. The pills were everywhere, pink with a red star in the center. Marketing and branding had come to the drug trade. Good if you liked getting high but didn't like needles or bloody noses. Safer than heroin, too.

"So if K-Car doesn't sell heroin, why should I talk to him?"

"I bet he knows the heroin dealer. Maybe he'd give you a name." Hector glanced up quickly. "Oh—the heroin guy always wears a gold Oakland FC cap."

That was good info. Sports team gear had given more than one criminal away in Luke's past, and Oakland FC wasn't nearly as popular as other local teams. Might be easier to get a lead.

"You've seen him, then? Tall, short?"

"White guy, maybe in his thirties, medium height, I guess." Hector paused. "Tattoo on his forearm, though."

"How big?"

"Big enough I can see it from a ways away."

"Right arm or left arm?"

Hector lifted his right arm, then dropped it again, flopping against his side.

"Thanks, Hector." Luke paused. "Now that Earl's gone, you make sure these kids stay safe."

Hector raised the coffee in acknowledgment.

Luke trudged back toward the pathway leading to Earl's body. He stopped about twenty feet from the officer standing in front of the police tape and took his phone out.

A message from Ellie.

> We need to talk

He'd respond as soon as he was done here. Luke tapped the screen of his phone.

After two rings, Detective Aaron Rasmussen's hurried voice answered. "Hey, Luke, can this wait? I've got an interview—"

The one person in Vice who'd still talk to Luke, and he was always being pulled in ten different directions. Luke straightened up. "I've got a lead for you."

"On what?"

"I caught another heroin O.D. in Lemon Hill Park. This time, I've got a description of the dealer."

Aaron exhaled. "All right. I guess the interviewee can wait a few more minutes."

"White, medium height, big tattoo on his right forearm."

A chuckle. "Hey, that narrows it down to about a thousand guys."

"Wears a gold Oakland FC cap. My contact says that a Magic Star dealer named K-Car would know who he is."

"K-Car? Ah, okay, he's…" Aaron trailed off, as if chewing on his words. "Let's say he's more than willing to talk if it gets another dealer off the street and out of territory he wants. Thanks, man. This is helpful."

Luke hesitated for a second. "I knew the O.D., Aaron. Good guy but couldn't keep it together. If the dealer is cutting his stuff with—"

"We'll take care of it, Luke." Aaron paused. "I have to work with Broxley on this, and he won't, well, you know."

Yeah, Paul Broxley wouldn't have taken Luke's call. "Let's focus on getting the heroin dealer off the street. We can figure out who gets credit for the arrest once we catch the guy."

They ended the call, and Luke closed his eyes and took a deep breath.

II

Visitors' hours at Pioneer Mesa Prison were limited to weekends, holidays, and Wednesday evenings. After work, Luke drove up Interstate 5, past the Sacramento airport. The haze hung in the air of Sacramento Valley, keeping the worst of the sun's glare from his eyes.

Luke turned off the interstate onto Route 523, and ten minutes later, the five-story cement prison loomed on the flat plain in the distance, surrounded by razor wire and a twenty-foot fence.

He waited ten minutes in line, going through a metal detector—he'd left his gun in the safe at home—and sat at a beige plastic picnic table among families, girlfriends, lawyers waiting to talk to their clients.

And there was his mom, in Pioneer Mesa Prison's orange jumpsuit. Tall, commanding: her dark brown hair was halfway to a charcoal now that she wasn't dyeing it, and her large, wide-set eyes took in everything. A determination to her chin that Luke had, frankly, always been a little jealous of; he'd gotten his father's chin, which receded from the rest of his face. Hence the goatee.

Hold on—what the hell was *that*?

A bruise around Zepherine Guillory's right eye, half green already. Of course they wouldn't ice it in here.

"What happened to your eye, Mom?" he asked, rising to his feet.

"A precursor to going back to solitary," she answered. "It's good to see you, Lucien."

"It's good to see you too, Mom." He hesitated. "You heard from Uribe? He's still trying to set an appeal date."

Zepherine stared at her son. "You're doing your best, Lucien, but—"

"But nothing," Luke said. "I know you. You didn't do this. You were set up. And you need to cooperate with your own lawyer."

Zepherine smiled. "Knowing it and proving it are two different things."

Luke pressed his lips together. He could protest for his mother's innocence all he wanted, but the money trail, the hidden bank accounts, the city council votes furthering Zepherine's agenda—too much evidence to have any room for reasonable doubt. That's why the appeal was so important: they could introduce new evidence, show bias.

They both sat down at the table. "I still think you can win this," Luke said. "You want to get black eyes for the next five years?"

"Four years, seven months, six days." Zepherine folded her hands.

"But who's counting, right?"

"Lucien, it's never wrong to be accurate." She cleared her throat. "But enough about me and my appeal process. I haven't seen you in a week. How are you doing?"

"Pretty good," Luke said. "Got lucky on a case today."

Zepherine raised her eyebrows.

"Heroin overdose in Lemon Hill Park, and we caught the dealer." Luke suppressed a smile.

"Well. That's good, I suppose."

"And if we find he cut the heroin with fentanyl or rat poison, we might add homicide to the charge."

"That's good, Lucien. Maybe now Nancy will give you decent—"

"Nims, Mom. The captain transitioned—"

Zepherine held up her hands. "Right, right, sorry. She transitioned—"

"*They.*"

"They transitioned after I was sentenced." Zepherine's cheeks grew red. "I still think of them the way I knew them before. Sorry."

"It's fine. It took some getting used to. I screwed up a few times myself."

Zepherine straightened in her chair. "Still, you might get out of assignment purgatory, no?"

Luke shifted his weight on the bench. "My contact in vice brought in one of his people, and he's taking credit for the arrest."

Zepherine pursed her lips.

"Look, Mom, the important thing is that we got the dealer off the street. Not selling heroin to anyone else."

"I suppose." She straightened. "And how's Ellie? She came back from Boston, correct?"

Luke drummed his fingers lightly on the table.

Zepherine tilted her head. Waiting.

"I spoke to her today. She, uh, extended her stay through next week. She's working in the Boston office, and she's got a lot more depositions to prepare. Plus, she hasn't gotten any time to spend with her mom."

"I see." She paused. "Is everything okay between you two?"

Though an innocuous question on its surface, the layers of judgment and disapproval buried in the question nearly overwhelmed him. "Just work, Mom. And family." He grinned despite the gnawing in the pit of his stomach. "Besides, Ellie said she needed only one more week."

"I don't want to see you unhappy, Lucien."

"We'll be fine. Ellie Kaplan, junior partner. My wife is on the fast track."

Zepherine shook her head. "That girl works too hard."

Like you should talk. But Luke didn't say anything.

"How's Paul?"

"Paul?"

She rolled her eyes. "Your partner."

Oh. Paul Broxley. "He transferred." Luke didn't say that Broxley took credit for the heroin dealer's arrest.

"You go through partners like most people change socks, Lucien."

A gentle cough behind Luke, and Zepherine looked up—and her eyes sparkled. "Justine!"

Luke turned around.

With her midnight leather duster jacket, her coarse silver-and-black hair an inch past her ears, and her sharp cheekbones, strong chin, and piercing black-brown eyes, Detective Justine Blood looked like she stepped out the pages of a graphic novel. One of the few Black women on the Sacramento police force, hyper competent, and with her otherworldly ninety-five percent close rate, she was as close to a superhero as the cops got.

"Hey, Zeph," Justine said, taking a seat on the bench next to Luke.

Luke blinked. "I thought they had a one-visitor policy—"

"We're both cops, Luke," Justine said. "You like to follow the rules and all, but they make exceptions for us every once in a while." She winked, as if she and Luke were sharing a private joke.

"Well, uh..." Luke scooted over on the bench. "Welcome, Detective Blood."

"And how are you doing, Chief?" She pointed to Zepherine's eye. "I see you're getting a makeup tutorial in here."

Zepherine cracked a smile. "I gave a pretty good makeup tutorial myself. Blush, foundation, and lipstick, not just mascara."

Blood grinned. "I bet." She leaned forward. "Now listen, I'm officially out of here as of Friday—"

"Friday? Isn't your retirement party tonight?"

Blood rolled her eyes. "The new chief is too cheap to pony up for a bar tab on a Friday night. Wednesdays are two-for-one at the Blue Oak."

"You'd think he was spending his own money," Luke offered.

The smile hadn't left Zepherine's lips. "The more things change, right, Justine?"

Justine leaned forward. "But you can fight this, Zeph. You may have lost the battle, but you can win the war."

"I don't know." The smile left Zepherine's face, but the glint didn't go out of her eyes.

"You've been cooperating with Uribe, right? Getting prepped for the appeal."

Zepherine shifted her weight on the bench. "It's complicated."

"She can't tell us whether she's cooperating with her own lawyer," Luke said flatly to Justine, then turned to Zepherine. "I'm still paying his fees, Mom."

Justine pursed her lips. "I'd call you stubborn, but ain't no one more stubborn than me." She chuckled. "But I refuse to believe you're giving up—"

"Oh, come on, Justine, you know as well as I do that the cards are stacked against me."

"And I also know as well as you do"—Justine lowered her voice and leaned forward as if talking privately to Zepherine—"you didn't do this."

"That's what I've been saying," said Luke.

Silence.

Luke knew when he was a third wheel. Zepherine clearly wanted to chat with Blood, not talk to Luke about cases and lawyers. He stood. "I'll let the two of you catch up. I've got to get going, anyway."

"Good to see you, Lucien," Zepherine said. "You're going to Justine's retirement party, right?"

He hesitated. He hadn't planned on attending—he only knew Justine Blood through his mother—but he really couldn't say no. Besides, the rest of the department would be there.

Luke nodded. "Wouldn't miss it."

He walked back to his car in a daze. Broxley had taken credit for the arrest before Luke had even had a chance to file his part of the paperwork, and something in Ellie's voice this afternoon was worrying. Maybe work stress was to blame, but the two of them definitely needed to talk when she got back to Sacramento—just one more week.

Was he equipped to deal with any of this?

The gravel of the parking lot crunched under his feet. And now he'd have to slap on a fake smile for a few hours at Justine Blood's retirement party tonight.

III

Luke stepped into the Blue Oak Tavern a few minutes after eight o'clock, two hours after leaving Pioneer Mesa Prison. A huge white banner hung from the railing of the upstairs seating area. "Congratulations Justine—35 Years, 95 Percent!"

He hated that he was jealous of Detective Blood, but he couldn't deny it. He'd never get that kind of close rate dealing with drug users and sex workers who refused to tell him anything. But he'd heard the stories—she'd gotten all the shit assignments when she started as a detective, too. So, yeah, she deserved the accolades, the cover story in the *Sacramento Urbanite*, and the big retirement party. Sure, he was jealous, but who wouldn't be?

The Blue Oak Tavern was crowded with officers, detectives, and sergeants. Luke stood back next to an empty table, and his gaze wandered to Justine, standing at the bar ordering a drink.

A hard bump into Luke's right shoulder.

"Oops—sorry about that," Luke said.

In response, a clap on the bicep. "Come on, man, it's me!"

Luke turned around—a thin, balding man with gray eyes behind square wire-framed glasses and a clean-shaven face with a narrow, square jaw.

"Aaron!"

"You heard we got him, right?"

"I heard, yeah. And you think the charges will stick?"

"We won't get the tox screen back for a week, and another week after that before we can analyze the balloons we found in the dealer's apartment, but yeah, I think the charges will stick." He paused. "Sorry about Broxley taking credit."

"I get it, man. Not your fault."

"Broxley and Big Mike are close—"

"I said I got it." Oof, a little too sharp with that. Luke grinned. "All good. Bad guys off the street. And we do a few more of these, Big Mike can't get in the way of all of them, right?"

"Let's hope not." Aaron pointed toward the bar. "You want anything?"

"I'll get something in a minute."

Aaron headed toward the bar, and Luke folded his arms. After running into Detective Blood at Pioneer Mesa, he'd need to congratulate her at some point tonight. Should he mention the visit with his mom? Or would that be—

A man of about forty with a huge six-foot-nine pro-wrestler frame, wearing a tailored suit, walked in front of Luke: Detective Mike Moody. He held a pint of beer. "Better be careful, Lucy. Stand too close to someone with a track record like Justine Blood and you'll melt like the Wicked Witch."

"Good one, Mike," Luke said. "I get the feeling we're not in Kansas anymore."

Moody blinked. "What?"

"Never mind. You have a good night."

Moody barked a laugh and walked toward the pool tables. Luke had expected Moody to be there; after Detective Blood, Moody had the best close rate in the force, and her retirement would put him solidly at number one.

"You ignoring me, partner?"

Luke turned—Detective Summer Symanski stood with a smile on her face.

"How long have you been standing there?"

"Only a few seconds." Symanski crossed her arms and stuck her lower lip out. "Still, *rude.*"

Luke felt his shoulders relax—two friendly faces in a row. "I was about to grab a drink. You want one?"

"Sure." Symanski gestured with her head toward Big Mike. "What's with him calling you 'Lucy' all the time? You pull the football away from him or something?"

The image of Luke pulling the ball away and Big Mike flying up in the air flashed in Luke's mind, and he chuckled. "Nothing so comical. My given name is Lucien."

Symanski turned back to Luke. "Yeah, I figured 'Lucy' was a feminized version of 'Luke.' Why does he do it?"

"Once a bully, always a bully." Luke walked toward the bar, where Detective Blood still stood, back to him, engrossed in conversation.

Symanski followed and leaned closer to him. "Do you know Detective Blood?"

"Well enough that I should congratulate her on her retirement."

"Is she an asshole like Big Mike?"

Luke grinned. "Her heart's in the right place. Didn't get to a ninety-five percent close rate without doing something right." He tapped the bar and caught the bartender's eye. "What are you drinking?"

"Amaretto sour."

"Excellent choice." Luke glanced at Symanski. "Mind if I pick the bourbon?"

"Sure, go ahead."

"Kyle, one amaretto sour, Plum Luck Reserve, and an old fashioned with the same."

Kyle nodded, and Luke turned back to Symanski. "While Kyle's making our drinks, I see Miz Blood has rid herself of hangers-on. C'mon, I'll introduce you."

Symanski's eyes widened. "Wait—we're going to talk to her?"

"Don't worry, you'll be fine."

They took a few steps over to Detective Justine Blood, who was checking her phone.

"Detective Blood?" Luke took a step back so Symanski and Blood were facing each other.

"Hey, long time no see, Luke." Blood looked up from her phone.

"May I introduce my partner? This is Detective Summer Symanski. She's new to Sacramento, and we both wanted to wish you well in your retirement."

"The Cheatham case," Symanski gushed. "Fantastic work."

"Thanks." Blood guffawed, then addressed Symanski. "The only reason I'm leaving is the whole mandatory retirement thing. Thirty-five years, and they figure I'm making too much money to stick around, I guess."

"Pleasure to meet you," Symanski said, holding out her hand.

Detective Blood grabbed her hand with both of hers and firmly shook. "Nice to meet you. Don't let the stories about Luke here rattle you. Now, his mother, on the other hand—"

"I'm fine," Symanski said quickly. "Had a good first week. Luke's good at showing me the ropes."

Kyle set two glasses on the bar. "Your drinks."

Luke blinked; his old fashioned looked correctly made, but his partner's drink was clear. Detective Blood raised her glass. "To a successful partnership," she said.

Symanski reached for her drink—then cocked her head.

"That's not the right drink, is it?" Luke asked.

"I'm sure it's fine." Symanski picked up the glass, cleared her throat, and turned to Detective Blood. "To your retire—"

"Oh, for God's sake," Blood said, "don't choke it down to be polite on *my* account. Tell Kyle. Lord knows *I'd* have no problem sending it back."

Symanski hesitated, then nodded. "I'll just be a moment."

As soon as Symanski went to the other side of the bar to talk to Kyle, Blood turned to Luke. "She really mean that?"

"Mean what? That she's pleased to meet you? Of course. A ninety-five percent close rate—that's gotta be some sort of record. National average, fifty-two or something, right? Sacramento would sit in the low sixties if it weren't for you. I heard they offered you a publishing deal—"

"No, that's not what I meant. I meant if you're good at showing her the ropes."

Luke shifted nervously from foot to foot. "I'd like to think so."

Blood studied Luke's face. "I'll be blunt with you, Luke. Your mother would want me to be honest. You're not a good detective. You're dragging your precinct's numbers down. What happened with your mom was a big blow—"

"Hey, I got a drug dealer off the street today. If we're lucky, we can make a manslaughter charge stick."

"You getting credit for that?"

Luke hesitated for a moment. "Getting credit is nice," he said carefully, "but the important thing is getting that dealer off the street."

Blood rolled her eyes. "Why don't you set that to music and dance around in the forest with cartoon birds and squirrels chittering all around you?"

"It's true."

"Of course it's true. But that attitude makes you ineffective." She frowned. "You don't play the game, and that makes you a bad detective. I hear the stories your mom tells. Friend to children and animals, users and hookers." Justine raised a hand, palm out. "I'm not saying they don't deserve justice; I'm saying you won't be able to give them justice if you don't learn how to play the game. For fuck's sake, Luke, you've got the worst numbers of any detective on the force."

Luke bristled, but with effort kept his shoulders loose. His pulse was accelerating, but he could stay calm through this. "Well, if you think numbers are so important, I passed the detective exam with an eighty-five."

Blood rubbed her chin. "You want to play armchair psychologist? Maybe your mom's arrest makes you want to hide your face. Is that why you let others' negativity affect you so much? You sure let Big Mike walk all over you."

No wonder she was such a good detective; she probably annoyed all her suspects until they confessed just to make her stop. Deep breaths. "I don't—"

"Let me finish." She held up a hand. "You could improve your number. Mike Moody's an asshole but plays the game better than anyone. I know your captain, and Nims is great at clearing out the obstacles so you can do your job. If you let Big

Mike steamroll you, this will keep being a dead-end job you hate."

Luke took a deep breath. Despite his best efforts, Luke felt his hackles rise.

But Blood was right, dammit. The heroin dealer's apprehension would have been Luke's biggest arrest of the year. Luke's relationship with Hector—whom Broxley wouldn't have deigned to approach—led to a positive ID and the arrest.

And yet Broxley was taking the credit.

Luke stared at his shoes, gritted his teeth, and looked up. "Well, you've got a point, Detective Blood. Tough to hear it, but I bet in a month or two I'll be glad you said something." He took a drink of his old fashioned, not even savoring the bourbon.

Blood shrugged. "Wouldn't be doing my job if I told people what they wanted me to say."

Luke set the glass down. "Anyway, best wishes on your retirement." He held his hand out.

Justine Blood stared at it for a few seconds, a grin spreading over her face. "So formal, Luke." She reached out and shook his hand—

The lights went out.

A tingle, starting at his hand and running down his arm. A swirl of bright colors behind Luke's eyes, blinding—then darkness, then colors, then darkness in equal measure. All sound dropped too—he knew people were raising their voices, all around him, throughout the bar, concerned about the power outage, but the sensation was like pillows over his ears. Totally muffled. The tingling ran down his legs now; unpleasant, like bumping his funny bone or having a leg fall asleep. His body felt energized, awake, like his senses were discovering new directions, new feelings, flavors, sights.

The lights came back on.

The tingling stopped.

Justine was still gripping Luke's hand. Her jaw fell open, her brown-black eyes wide and unblinking, and, in an incredulous voice, said, "No." Justine's face erupted in a laugh. A big, throaty laugh, the leather duster shaking.

Luke froze. Had he missed something? "What is it?"

"I can't believe it's you," Justine said, still wheezing with laughter. "Of every cop in this city, of every law enforcement official I've ever met, it's you?"

Luke opened his mouth to say, "*What's* me?" But no sound came out. Just as well—he felt his blood pressure rise. This was the most confusing conversation he'd had in a long time.

Blood finally dropped Luke's hand and took a deep breath, her laughter stopping. "I mean, I can't believe it's you. Look, you're a nice enough guy. But like I said, you're a shitty detective. You let other people take credit for your wins and you keep all the failures for yourself. But since the universe has spoken—"

What was happening? Maybe Detective Blood was drunk. "The universe?"

Blood shook her head. "I don't expect you to understand."

Luke folded his arms.

She grabbed her purse, pulled out a business card, and grabbed a ball-point pen off the bar. "Okay, now, at some point in the future…" Blood wrote a phone number on the back of the business card. "Could be tomorrow, could be next week, or next month, or next year., but you'll want some answers."

"Answers about what?"

"About something that'll happen to you." Blood thrust the business card at Luke. "Something you can't explain. But I can explain it. I can tell you what's going on."

Luke stared at the card, uncrossed his arms, and took it. "What *is* going on?"

She shook her head again. "You wouldn't believe me if I told you. But when you're ready, call me." She pointed at the back of the card. "This is my private cell number. Three people have this number: my lawyer, my son, and now you."

"Not even my mom?" He had a trace of a grin on his face.

Blood didn't return the smile, fixing him with a piercing gaze instead. "Not even Zeph." She pointed with two fingers at his chest. "You spread my phone number around, you give it to a journalist or my precinct captain or my ex-husband, and I will hunt you down." She smiled mischievously. "And don't think I can't get the cops to cover it up for me."

"Uh..."

"Doesn't matter right now," Detective Blood said. "You'll find out soon enough. Keep the card in a safe place."

She strode away from the bar, her duster catching the air like she was in a Hollywood movie.

Symanski walked up. "Sorry that took so long. Kyle was remaking my drink when the blackout started. Weird, huh?" She held up her glass. "But I finally got my amaretto sour. And the bourbon you picked is *delicious.*"

"Glad you like it," Luke said, watching Justine Blood stride away.

What was *that* about?

CYCLE 1: WEDNESDAY, THREE WEEKS LATER

I

A GASP.

Luke sat bolt upright in bed, heart pounding.

He glanced at the bedside clock. 12:13 AM.

Was it a bad dream? Was it a noise outside? Or inside?

He listened carefully, searching his mind. No dream that he could remember. He'd had a couple of whiskeys, set his alarm. He'd planned to pick up Ellie from the airport, even though she said she'd get a FlashRide.

Three weeks ago, just before Detective Blood's retirement party, she'd told Luke she was staying one more week, then a few days later had extended her time in Boston another two weeks. After an entire month away, Ellie Kaplan was finally coming home to her husband.

Luke was looking forward to seeing her again. Things had been a little awkward when she'd left, and he'd called her almost every day, leaving messages. She'd been busy interviewing witnesses, preparing for depositions. Plus, visiting with her mom—who Ellie hadn't visited for almost a year.

Understandable that she was too busy to call back, especially with the time difference between Sacramento and Boston.

He was proud of her for making junior partner at such a relatively young age, and far from being bothered that she made more than he did, Luke felt relief that they no longer had to worry about money.

He looked at the clock. Now the time read 12:16. His alarm would go off in a few minutes.

He unplugged his phone from the bedside table, took his wedding ring from the ceramic bowl on the nightstand next to his watch, and tapped the AirSched app. Ellie's flight was landing exactly on time—12:27 AM. Perfect.

He'd have time for a quick shower.

Luke took off his clothes, dropping his battered Cricket Races T-shirt on the floor, hopped in the shower, lathered his body quickly. Some of his friends had hit thirty-five and developed a paunch, lost some of the muscle definition, but not Luke. He would be thirty-six in July—was that only three months away?—and he looked a little older, but still fit. He worked out four times a week: sometimes for an hour at Pure Life Fitness, sometimes a run around his neighborhood, sometimes a bike ride into the Sierra Foothills.

He'd fallen into a few bad habits with Ellie gone. He'd had a few too many nights where a beer with dinner turned into three, or one whiskey at the Blue Oak Tavern turned into four. Luke shook his head. A month didn't mean much, but he didn't want to be one of those cops who drank a six-pack every night. He was glad Ellie was coming home.

He dried off, ran into the bedroom to turn off the alarm that had been squawking for a few minutes, and reset the alarm for six fifteen. A little pomade for his hair, deodorant, a brief spritz of cologne—Ellie didn't like powerful scents, but she'd given him the bottle of *The Forest, It Echoes* for his birthday the year before. He debated for a minute before grabbing a fitted button-up shirt with a bold print, blue and orange swirls on it. Reminded him a little of his twenties, when he and Ellie would stay out at a dance club until three in the morning. Now, he was picking her up at the airport, as late as they used to arrive at Evoke on 15th and R.

He went down the staircase of their house to the foyer and called her number—12:31 AM. She should have deplaned by now. Ellie would have to wait for her bag for ten or fifteen minutes, and Luke only needed eight minutes to drive to the airport. She'd be impressed, and the best part was, Luke would look thoughtful without being desperate. They'd be back in bed by one fifteen, one thirty at the latest, and he'd still get a good six or seven hours of sleep—if you counted the two he had before he woke at 12:13.

The call went to voicemail.

He tapped her name in his *Favorites* again.

This time, she picked up. "Hey," she said, sounding flustered. "Sorry, I was grabbing my carryon from the overhead bin when you called."

"Yeah, no problem," he said, trying to be chipper. "I'm coming to pick you up."

A pause. "Oh, Luke, you don't have to do that. You've got work tomorrow."

"Hey, now, I'm already up and dressed. Gotta pick up my best girl at the airport, don't I?"

Silence.

"What is it?"

"Look—I, uh… I'm not coming back to the house."

The corner of Luke's mouth twitched. "You're not?"

"I—I need a little more time."

A little more time? Her weeklong business trip turned into a month. How much more time did she need?

"I rented a furnished apartment."

"A furnished apartment? I don't understand."

Silence on the other end of the line.

"You've had a month," Luke said. "And I didn't complain. You don't get to see your mom very often, and you work harder than anyone else at the firm. But I—" He almost said *I miss you*. But she didn't return most of his calls, going a few days between talking to him. And he'd been annoyed at her lack of communication. But had he missed her? He snapped his mouth shut.

"I thought I'd be able to work everything out in my head in a week, honestly I did. And then a week became—"

"Hold on," Luke said. "Work everything out in your head? Work *what* out?" But as soon as the words were out of his mouth, he knew.

"Luke," Ellie said gently. "Things have been rough for a while. Ever since…" She trailed off.

Ever since his mother was sentenced.

Maybe he shouldn't have talked about her so much at home. How his mother was innocent, how if she would agree to hire a private investigator, they might get some exculpatory evidence.

Oh. Ellie had brought up Boston several times in the weeks before she left. Now pieces of the past conversations made sense snapped: she'd been dropping hints that she wanted to move to Boston. Of course she did: she made junior partner, and that was where her career ladder was, not in the firm's satellite office in Sacramento.

Justine Blood was right: he *was* a shitty detective.

"Sounds like maybe you *have* worked things out in your head," Luke said.

She'd only returned two of his calls in the last week, and when they had finally talked, she'd been distracted, with stretches of awkward silences. Luke sat down heavily on the stairs. Could he have saved their relationship?

A lack of romance. Maybe he'd taken her for granted too much. He'd given her space for her job, but perhaps that made her think he was disconnected from her. "I get it," he said, even though he didn't. "Hey, now, this'll be okay. A separation might be good for us. Maybe we start slow. Me at the house, you at the apartment. I can come pick you up, we can go to dinner and a movie. Like we're dating again." She'd said nothing explicit about moving to Boston, so maybe Ellie would consider a separation where they both lived in Sacramento.

But she was silent.

"I guess," he said carefully, "I haven't been doing a great job of making you feel like you matter to me."

"That's not it, Luke." Ellie sighed. "It's after midnight. I don't want to get into this now."

"No, no," Luke said, "you don't have to explain right now. Listen, we'll talk tomorrow, all right? Sort this all out. You have a good night. Get some sleep and go kick ass at your job."

"Thanks, Luke. Good night."

After ending the call, he stared at the phone until his vision swam. He trudged upstairs. He'd wear the shirt tomorrow for work. Be a unique look. Big Mike would make fun of him, but that was nothing new.

He took his shirt and trousers off, hung them up, turned out the light, and collapsed on the bed.

But he couldn't sleep.

He put on an undershirt and went downstairs in his underwear. He stood in the kitchen for a few minutes, then walked to the liquor cabinet. A bottle of Plum Luck Special Cask. Almost full. For special occasions only—like their five-year anniversary coming in September.

He set the bottle on the bar, went to the cabinet and got a short water glass, put three ice cubes and two fingers of the whiskey in it.

Luke stared at the whiskey. He'd promised himself that when Ellie came home, he wouldn't drink as much as he had in the last month.

But if any situation called for a drink, this one did.

He drank the whiskey without tasting, before the ice cubes started melting.

He poured another two fingers.

II

The beeping started at six fifteen, and Luke hit the snooze bar. The alarm went off again almost instantly—ten minutes in the blink of an eye—and Luke hit the snooze button again.

The third time the alarm went off, he groggily sat up in bed, blinking in the early morning light. A flash in his brain as he remembered his plan to pick Ellie up, the phone call, the whiskey. He belched loudly and felt worse.

He'd sweated in his sleep and stank like alcohol. When he trudged into the shower, he held his head under the water for a full minute.

This was the worst he'd felt in a long time. Not only the hangover he had, but also the realization that his marriage might be over.

When the spray turned lukewarm, he shook his head. He'd be late if he dawdled any more. Luke got out and dried off, then stared at himself in the mirror and put a smile on his face. A headache started behind his right eye.

Shirtless, he went down to the kitchen, drank a glass of water. Four pieces of sourdough left. He toasted two of them and forced one of them down. Luke felt a little better, but the headache crept forward again. He took three ibuprofen with another full glass of water.

Luke went back upstairs, trying to distract himself from his hangover. He opened his closet. The blue-and-orange button-up shirt, the trousers from last night, a gray sport coat.

The house Ellie and Luke shared was on 53rd Street—"The

Fantastic 50s," as the locals were fond of saying. The houses were overpriced, the neighbors were nosy, and the traffic was mostly terrible, but there was a certain cachet important to Ellie. Though Luke didn't care for the vibe of the neighborhood, his commute to work was beautifully short: twenty blocks, five traffic lights, and no freeways.

He backed his ten-year-old Malibu out of the driveway. Ellie's Mercedes E-Class was in their single-car garage, and Luke drove down 53rd Street past his neighbors' Audis, BMWs, and Teslas. The headache ebbed and flowed, and the sun through the windshield wasn't helping. He braked for the stop sign at Alcatraz Avenue, putting his right-turn blinker on, and looked to his left. No cars coming. He hit the gas—then saw something out of the corner of his eye. He slammed on the brakes.

A cyclist, driving against traffic, going the wrong way. He'd almost hit the bike. The cyclist shouted something as he went past, and Luke was pretty sure it wasn't an apology. He looked again, both ways this time, and turned onto Alcatraz.

Ellie would have yelled at the cyclist.

III

The headache was in full force by the time Luke pulled into the parking lot of the eighth precinct at 20th and K. He parked, pulled down the visor, and slid the cover from the mirror. He looked worn out.

No, not worn out. Beaten down.

On the way to his desk, everyone ignored him. Most days, the shunning bothered him, but today, when he was fighting a headache, he was glad for his scarlet letter. Entering his bullpen, he was relieved to see Big Mike Moody and Vince

Babino weren't at their desks. Off getting a coffee refill—or maybe egging a teacher's house.

Luke looked at the fancy watch Ellie had bought him. A gorgeous Von Zeitmann. He wondered what kind of man would feel at home wearing such an expensive timepiece. Maybe the kind of man Ellie wished Luke could be.

He shut his eyes. The day would be difficult enough without spiraling into self-pity.

"Watch not working? Is that why you're late?"

Luke jumped in his seat and looked up—Summer Symanski. "Morning, detective."

"Not for too much longer," she said, smiling. "Nice shirt."

"Sorry for my tardiness." Luke could feel the color rise to his cheeks. "I had—I had kind of a rough evening."

Symanski arched an eyebrow. "Ellie came home last night, right?"

"That's right—I mean, she's in Sacramento. But she—" Luke felt the headache stab with pain again. "I'm sure you don't want me talking about my marital issues."

"I've complained enough to you about my ex. Turnabout is fair play." Symanski's ears turned red. "Not that you're—I mean, you two are still married—"

"I know what you mean, Symanski," Luke said. "Things are always better when we give each other a little grace."

Moody and his partner, Vince Babino, walked in from the side hall, holding coffee mugs. Babino, ten years older and a foot shorter than Big Mike, glared at Luke as he sat at his desk. "Bold choice for a shirt today, Lucy."

Big Mike guffawed. "I'd ask you to sit in on my next interrogation, but that shirt violates the Geneva Convention."

Luke chuckled and pointed at Big Mike. "Good one, Moody." Aaron Rasmussen in Vice would have made that joke as good-natured ribbing. But Big Mike's jokes always carried an undercurrent of malice. Luke wondered how much lunch money Moody had coerced out of his classmates in elementary school.

Symanski glanced at Moody and Babino, her face impassive. "We have to finish up the paperwork on that hit-and-run on Scarsbury and 9th."

"Right." Luke reached to turn on his computer.

"Whiskey?"

"What?" He knocked over his pencil cup, scattering a few pens, highlighters, and Sharpies on the desk.

Symanski smiled. "You're obviously hungover, and—what is that bourbon called? Peat Moss? That's your favorite, right?"

"Plum Luck." Luke grinned through the stabbing pain in his eye.

"You've never come in hungover before."

"Yeah, well, Ellie and I are, uh, going through a little rough patch. I might have made a bad decision to have a few drinks at one in the morning."

"Oh, Luke, I'm sorry to hear that." Symanski crossed her arms and bit her lip.

Luke grinned, not sure if his smile looked reassuring or unhinged. "Oh, don't worry about me. Once the ibuprofen kicks in, I'll be good as new."

Behind Symanski, a door opened. Symanski stood, as did Luke. Captain Nims Thoreau, their hair short and silver, their black police blazer crisp, stood in the doorway.

"Listen up, people," they said. "We've got a dead body in Lemon Hill Park."

"Let me guess—another junkie O.D.'d?" Babino said, chortling. "We should set up a conveyor belt between Lemon Hill Park and the morgue. It'd save time."

Luke ground his teeth but said nothing.

"Lucy and her girlfriend can take it," Big Mike said, sitting down at his desk, dwarfing the rolling office chair.

"Knock it off, Moody," Captain Thoreau said. "You talk like

that, I won't be able to stop the disciplinary committee from getting involved."

"Summer could take care of that just fine," Moody said under his breath. He winked at Luke.

Luke's stomach churned—was that a clumsy sexual reference to Detective Symanski? Discipline, bondage? Did he want to know?

Luke blinked and turned back to the captain. "Symanski and I can take it."

Thoreau nodded. "I'll send you the file. Officer is already onsite." They turned and went back into their office, shutting the door behind them.

"Told you the girls could handle it," Moody said to Babino. "Come on, they're bringing in that carjacking thug in five minutes."

Babino picked up his coffee and followed Big Mike out of the bullpen.

Symanski sat down and leaned forward. Uh oh. She was gearing up: Why do you let him talk to you like that? Why don't you defend yourself?

Or more accurately, perhaps, why didn't he defend her from that discipline comment?

"Sorry," Luke said. "I should have said something when he made that comment to you."

Symanski blinked. "Comment to me?"

"About the disciplinary committee thing. I'm not exactly sure what he meant, but it—it wasn't appropriate."

"Oh, hell," Symanski said. "You thought that was a sexual reference? Some kind of BDSM thing?"

Luke held his hands up in surrender. "He might have a good clearance rate, but he's not the most eloquent. I think he was trying to get under your skin, right? He winked at me—"

"Luke," Symanski said, "I've been here a month. Haven't you heard why I transferred to Sacramento?"

Luke spun his head around at the empty bullpen. "If you haven't noticed, Detective, the folks around here don't exactly keep me informed."

"Still, cops are the worst gossips."

"I don't want to know. What you do outside the office—"

"I went to Internal Affairs," Symanski interrupted. "I was getting harassed by my previous partner. I had enough. Recorded him doing it. Had emails, text messages, everything. He got a slap on the wrist, then made my life a living hell. So as soon as I passed the detective exam, I applied everywhere I could. Sacramento was the first department to accept me. For once, Big Mike wasn't making a crude joke. He was telling everyone that I went to the discipline committee. That I'm not to be trusted. That I don't have my partner's back."

"Oh." Luke pressed his lips together. "I'm sorry that happened to you."

"So you didn't know I reported a fellow officer?"

"No, I didn't."

Symanski narrowed her eyes. "If you don't want to partner with me, say so. I'll put in for a transfer somewhere else."

"I don't work like that, Detective." Luke blinked. "Now, come on. We've got a dead body in Lemon Hill Park."

IV

As Luke drove the cruiser toward the park, he was again struck by the beauty of the Puente de Inspiración, even with his headache. He maneuvered the cruiser next to a red curb on Muñoz Way in front of an old Lincoln and behind a green Nissan.

He and Symanski exited the car and walked a quarter mile to the covered walkway. The canopy of greenery kept the path cool in the summer, as well as providing a break from the wind in the winter months.

As the path widened, an officer stood about five feet in front of a sagging line of police tape. "Shit," the officer said under his breath. "Sacramento's finest."

Luke ignored him but made out his name tag: *Pressler*. "Morning, officer," he said. "What can you tell me?" Luke took out a pair of latex gloves; Symanski did the same.

"Got an anonymous call," Officer Pressler said. "Male, sounded like he was high. Said a man was dead." He motioned with his chin. "Be my guest."

"You haven't touched the body yet?" Luke pulled on his gloves.

Pressler shook his head. "Only to make sure he was deceased. Pretty obvious overdose. Figured I'd leave the clinical stuff to the professionals."

"Hmm." Luke stepped to the police tape and raised the center to shoulder height. Symanski ducked under the tape, pulling her gloves on.

The ibuprofen finally kicked in, and Luke's headache eased off.

The body was another twenty feet farther in behind the police tape. Face down, blue jeans, dress shirt. They both crouched next to the body.

"Doesn't look like our typical overdose case," Luke said. "Too well dressed." He peered at the dead man's face. He knew most of the regulars in the park, but this man wasn't a regular. His face was vaguely familiar, though. Luke had probably seen him in the park before, but never interviewed him.

The shirt collar concealed most of the dead man's neck, and the shadows shrouded his whole body in shadow, but—was that a red line?

"Symanski," he said, pointing to the half inch of skin visible between the top of the collar and the hairline.

"Am I seeing things," Symanski said, "or does that look like a ligature mark?"

"You're not seeing things."

Symanski reached out and pulled the collar down another inch and looked up at Luke, her eyes wide. "This wasn't an overdose. This man was murdered."

V

About an hour later, under the bridge in the center of Lemon Hill Park, Hector again sat cross-legged, head bowed. Same filthy olive trousers and jean jacket as three weeks before. But his hair was shorter, though ragged; possibly a rough haircut by another park resident. Luke held a hot coffee from Basilica Brews in his hand as he walked under the bridge and stopped.

Hector flinched. "What—what do you want?"

"It's me, Hector. Detective Luke. I brought coffee."

Hector narrowed his eyes. "Oh, man. The good stuff again. You always get me the good coffee when something bad happens." But his eyes flickered with desire, and he reached his left hand up to take the paper cup from Luke. "Nice and hot, too." With visible effort, he lifted his oddly twisted right hand to balance the coffee.

Hector raised the coffee to his lips, took a sip, then another. "Okay, Detective Luke, what can I do for you?"

"There's a man in the covered walkway. He's dead. You know anything about that?"

"I know it's not heroin." Hector smiled. "I haven't seen that cabrón in the Oakland FC cap since you were here last time."

"So what's the poison of choice now? Magic Star, right?"

"Magic Star." Hector shook his head. "It's like those fruity girl drinks, right? You think they're all sweet and nice because of the umbrellas and the strawberries, but those'll knock you on your ass faster than a shot of vodka."

"You've seen people use Magic Star here, I take it."

Hector leaned forward. "They call it Magic Star because it hits everyone different. Some people, they get happy, some get a ton of energy, other people zone out. But they always feel good doing it."

"Always?"

"So I hear." Hector smiled, a hard white blob of spit in the corner of his lip, his teeth yellow, his right top canine missing.

"I'd like to show you the deceased's picture. See if you recognize him. You up for that?"

"I'm surprised *you* don't recognize him."

"Honestly, I am too." Luke showed Hector the screen on his phone. The CSI team had helped pose the dead man so his face didn't look quite so terrifying. And they'd confirmed what Symanski had said: strangled. But no wallet, keys, or any kind of identification.

Hector's eyes widened. "Oh, man, that's C.D."

"C.D.?"

"Yeah, like a music CD."

"I was thinking initials," Luke said. "Charles David or Craig Donald. Something like that. How well do you know him?"

"He used to come here every so often. Six months, maybe a year ago? I don't remember. Mostly got his pills from K-Car."

"Right, K-Car. You gave me his name last time. He I.D.'d that heroin dealer and got him off the street."

"How 'bout that," Hector said. "My good deed for the month." He took another drink of coffee.

"Where can I find K-Car now?"

"No idea, man. I haven't seen him."

"When did you see him last?"

Hector paused. "Yeah, okay, he was here yesterday."

"And you haven't seen C.D. for six months?"

"I've seen him around the last few weeks. Right around the time Caleb and Earl… you know."

"C.D. is back off the wagon, I take it."

Hector shook his head. "Naw, just the opposite. He was trying to recruit people to stop using. Maybe he found God or wanted people for his cult, but that's what he was doing here."

"Anyone get mad at him for trying to stop? Dealers he pissed off, users who didn't want the lecture, anything like that?"

"He only came here in the morning. After everyone was trying to pick themselves up, feeling like shit." Hector took another sip of the coffee. "He asked me a couple of times if I'd stop using. I told him I'd think about it."

"You know anyone he had a run-in with? Anyone who was trying to hurt him?"

"Man, C.D. isn't from around here."

"Like, not from Sacramento?"

"Not from Lemon Hill. I expect if he had a lady—or a guy, I don't judge—they'd be pissed at him for hanging out in this park."

"Okay, thanks, Hector." Luke lowered his voice. "How's the hand?"

"Same as always."

"You see the physical therapist I told you about?"

Hector scoffed. "Man, when you haven't showered in a few days, nobody wants you in their waiting room, know what I mean?"

Luke nodded. After his last tour in Afghanistan, Hector had gotten a Purple Heart, after which he got hooked on painkillers. When the V.A. wouldn't give him anymore, Luke suspected he found Magic Star. And after the government abandoned him, he couldn't get a job with a messed-up right hand. So here he was, with nowhere to live, getting high in Lemon Hill Park.

"You got a place to stay?"

"At the shelter down on Z Street. Unless I'm here."

Luke took out a card from his wallet and a twenty-dollar bill, and handed them both to Hector. "Get yourself something to eat. And you think of anything else, call me. Enjoy the coffee."

"Thanks, Detective Luke."

Luke turned to go and scanned the park. No one else was around to talk to, and the CSI team was cleaning up, pulling the police tape down. Symanski was nowhere to be seen; she'd probably gone back to the cruiser. Soon, there'd be no signs that the man without identification had died on the canopied walkway. Luke pulled his phone out and after hesitating a moment, called Ellie's number. Almost noon. She'd be taking a break from her legal research soon—but Luke's call went right to voicemail. Maybe she was in the legal library. Ellie would often say the reception was terrible in there. He thought about leaving a message but instead ended the call before the beep.

Luke walked out of the park, got into the cruiser, and closed the door. Symanski, in the passenger seat, looked up at him from her phone.

"As Ben Franklin once said, 'Energy and persistence conquer all things,'" he said.

"You got something?"

"No one who saw anything, but Hector Corazón gave me a name. Well, initials, anyway. C.D." He started the car and turned on the air conditioning; the late April day was growing warm.

"That's something."

"It's not a lot. But Hector also said the guy had been at the park on a semi-regular basis. About six months ago, he stopped showing up. Now he's back—"

"Using again?"

"No, trying to get people to *stop* using. Throwing out some good into the world, Hector said."

"Who are the dealers in this area?"

"Hector gave me the name of that Magic Star dealer who helped get that heroin guy out of the park."

"Had a name like an 80s Dodge, right? Reliant or something."

Luke chuckled. "K-Car."

"Right, right." She screwed up her mouth in thought. "K-Car would have a reason to silence him. More people in rehab means less money for the dealers."

"We can talk to Vice, see if they know some of the players in Lemon Hill Park that I don't." Luke cocked his head. "Did you get anywhere with your interviews?"

"No one knew anything," Symanski said, "but the CSI guys said the ligature marks were likely made by a mixed-synthetic rope wound in a 'Multi W braid,' whatever that means."

Luke put the cruiser in gear, looked over his shoulder, and moved out onto Muñoz Way. "Does that get us any closer?"

"We'll see. The lab might say it's typical rope you can buy from any home improvement store, but maybe they'll find unique fibers on the victim's neck."

"The killer would have to be pretty strong, right?"

Symanski shook her head. "Nope. Not if our victim was drugged first. A seventy-pound kid could have done it."

"Wait—CSI thinks the victim was drugged first? Why?"

"Lack of defensive wounds suggests the victim was unconscious when he was killed. We'll know for sure when we get the tox screen back."

"With those clothes, though," Luke said, "C.D. wasn't a typical drug user. Maybe drove here from the suburbs or from a nice part of Sacramento. Someone must have noticed he was gone. Didn't come home last night or didn't show up to work today."

Symanski started dialing a number on her phone as Luke started the engine. "I'll check missing persons."

A minute later, Symanski ended the call. "No one with the initials of C.D. has been reported missing in Sacramento County," she said. "No one matching our victim's description has been reported missing in the last three days, either. I'll check neighboring counties when we get back to the precinct."

"Or maybe C.D. is a fake name or a nickname."

Symanski scratched her temple. "Maybe it's a name he only gave to his other friends who were users."

"Oh, yeah, I didn't think of that. Especially if he thought of himself as a big shot. Wouldn't want to give out his real name."

"Not necessarily a big shot. Could be a teacher or a social worker or something."

"With those clothes?" Luke responded. "Not on a teacher's salary."

Symanski's eyes swooped to Luke's wrist and the Von Zeitmann.

Luke pressed his lips together; she had a point. He turned his attention back to the road. "It's lunchtime. You want to stop for a bite?"

"I've been dying to try that new bistro on 5th."

"Ah, you think because my name is French that I'm up with all that hoity-toity stuff? I'm Cajun, not French, so my toity is decidedly not very hoity."

"Don't give me that," Symanski said. "I've paid attention to your lunch orders. You're secretly pretentious. And you can't get more pretentious than Le Bistro Cinq."

"I'm only pretentious about food." Luke chuckled. "But thirty dollars for a house salad is a little too much on a police detective's salary." Even one with a wife who made junior partner.

"Yikes. Thirty bucks? Never mind."

"You ever try Dae Bak? A Korean food truck. Best in the city."

She shrugged. "I had a phenomenal go-to bibimbap place in Fresno. Your food truck will have to be pretty damn good for me to like it."

"Oh, it's pretty damn good. Tell you what—you don't like it, I'm buying."

VI

Twenty minutes later, they sat in the cruiser with the windows rolled down, two Chilsung Ciders in the cupholders, and a Styrofoam bowl on each of their laps. Luke took a forkful of the bibimbap.

"Mmm, mmmh," he said, his mouth full. He chewed and swallowed. "Now see, I don't know what you all do in Fresno, but here, that's some good Korean."

Symanski swallowed her first bite; she'd ordered the chap chae noodle bowl. "All right, it's decent." She looked at him from the passenger seat. "I'm—I'm kind of surprised."

"By what? My outstanding culinary sensibilities?" He took another bite.

"That you didn't blink when I told you I reported my partner to internal affairs."

"Oh. That." He swallowed. "Look, I've got a famous mom who's in jail for bribery and embezzlement. And by now, you heard the whole 'nepo-baby' thing, right?"

Symanski was silent.

"Just because my mom was chief—"

"The first female police chief in Sacramento. That's a big deal."

"—that doesn't mean I didn't deserve to be promoted to

detective. And she might be in jail, but that doesn't mean I'm dirty."

Symanski smiled. "I don't think you're dirty." She took another bite of chap chae.

"I scored higher on the detective exam than Big Mike. And he's got the second-highest close rate on the force—"

"First-highest, now that Justine Blood has retired."

A ping in Luke's head. Justine Blood—he'd barely thought about her since the retirement party. She seemed to believe Zepherine Guillory was innocent of bribery too, but he was running out of ideas, and her lawyer was worse at returning his calls than Ellie. He still had Detective Blood's business card floating around in his wallet. True to his word—or to Detective Blood's request, anyway—he'd kept her private number private. Though he wasn't sure keeping his word counted, since he'd forgotten she'd given him the number three weeks ago.

"Earth to Luke." Symanski waved a hand in front of his face.

Luke grinned. "Sorry. My head was a million miles away."

"This case? Hey, Big Mike might be sorry he pawned it off on us. Not a homeless guy, not an O.D."

"I bet he tries to steal it back."

"Well, too bad. Captain Thoreau already gave it to us."

Luke hesitated, took another bite, and nodded.

Justine Blood hadn't been wrong: Luke's arrest record was terrible. High thirties, about fifteen percentage points below the national average, and way below Big Mike's numbers. Partly because so few of his fellow detectives and officers shared information with him, so his cases rarely went anywhere. Partly because he got all the cases of people no one cared about: the sex workers, the gang members, the undocumented, the girls of color who the other cops dismissed as runaways.

Luke stared out through the windshield. Detective Blood

would have dismissed those concerns as excuses. Maybe she was right.

Symanski took the last bite of her noodles, swallowed, and pointed at the clock on the dashboard. "M.E. said they'd run our victim's fingerprints right after lunch. They'll be done by the time we get back."

Luke took a final swig of Chilsung Cider and started the engine.

VII

The medical examiner's office was in the next building over from the eighth precinct, and after Luke dropped off the cruiser in the bay, he and Symanski crossed K Street.

Dr. Anna Koh was in an exam room, a body on a metal table covered in a blue sheet in front of her. About five years older than Luke, she had a willowy frame that made her look taller than her five-foot-two, and intense dark eyes that bore through everyone. Luke once assumed Dr. Koh hated him for the same reason everyone else did. Then six months ago, he realized she hated everybody.

"Ah, Detectives," Koh said. "I said I'd have the fingerprints on your John Doe after lunch, but the database called in sick. Gave me enough time to finish my pastrami on rye, though." She patted her stomach and belched. "You bring the paperwork to get started on the autopsy?"

"I thought you could tell us your preliminary findings when we got a positive ID."

"Tech support says it'll be six to twelve hours." Koh sighed. "Call back before you leave today. If I.T. has access to the database up and running by then, we'll see if we can figure out who your dead guy is."

They left the M.E.'s office and walked back across K Street.

Luke wanted to say something to Symanski, but after the conversation about his mother in the cruiser, he felt awkward. Symanski wasn't judgmental, so maybe he could trust her. He didn't want to appear desperate for a friend, although he was. He also didn't want to look like he was trying to hit on her. Symanski was an attractive woman, and she'd had men at work behave inappropriately before. Coffee, maybe. Something low-stress.

They got into the elevator. Symanski reached out and pressed the "3" button. The awkward silence stretched between them.

She was a co-worker and a potential friend, not his therapist. He needed to find a family law lawyer *and* a make an appointment with his counselor.

Couples' counseling. Maybe Ellie would agree to that.

"So," he said, "after work, you want to head over to the coffee place on 17th and complain about our co-workers a little more?"

Symanski looked up at Luke. "Uh—well, I'm meeting a woman from my book club for a run. Maybe another time?"

The doors opened on their floor, and a brunette white woman in a meticulously tailored light gray suit stood in front of the bullpen, a large manila envelope in her hand.

"Martha?" Luke said. "Oh—good to see you."

Luke walked out of the elevator—then he stopped. Martha was a hugger; they'd hugged every time Ellie's former maid of honor came over. But she did not step forward to embrace Luke. And Martha was *never* not in a hugging mood.

"I'm sorry," Martha said, handing Luke the envelope.

"You're—you're sorry?"

"Ellie couldn't do this herself, and she didn't want to pay a process server…"

Luke's stomach dropped. He opened the folder and glanced at the top sheet of paper.

Petition for Divorce, State of California.

"I see," Luke said. "I've been served." He was surprised Martha had handed him the papers; he figured Ellie knew a process server from her work. Maybe she didn't want news of her divorce going around the law firm. And was Martha authorized to serve Luke papers?

"I really have to get back to the office," Martha said. "Oh, hang on." She pulled her phone out and snapped a picture of Luke holding the papers. "So sorry, again." She stepped past Luke and Symanski into the empty elevator. Martha pushed a button, and the doors closed between them.

Symanski glared at the closed elevator doors, then turned to Luke. "I'll cancel my run."

Luke stared at the folder in his hand. "Give me a minute."

He sat at his desk, woke up his computer. An email had come in from Dr. Koh: the fingerprint database would be online tomorrow morning at the earliest. He opened a search engine. Wouldn't the divorce papers have to be given to him by either Ellie or a process server?

But no. The web page for the State of California appeared onscreen, and the statute was clear: friends and relatives of one party could serve papers to the other party. "Learn something new every day," Luke mumbled.

"What?"

"Nothing." He cleared his throat. "Okay. If the fingerprint database is down, we can canvass cars left overnight near Lemon Hill." Luke snapped his fingers. "And FlashRides. I'll see if anyone dropped off someone matching our victim's description last night near the park."

Symanski bit her lip. "Maybe you should take the rest of the day off."

"What?" Luke shook his head. "I'm fine. Besides, I'd rather stay busy than go home and dwell on it."

Symanski shook her head. "Divorce is a lot to process."

Justine Blood's words about him being a bad detective echoed in his ears. He should keep digging, especially since they didn't know the victim's identity. Hector had given Luke K-Car's name. Maybe the dealer could identify the victim. One call to Aaron might do it.

"No," Luke said, "we've got a murder victim, and I should keep working. The first forty-eight hours after a homicide are the most important."

"No need for the two of us to run a DMV search and a FlashRide information requisition."

Luke stared at the computer screen for a few seconds. "Okay, fine." He managed a small smile. "See if you can keep my situation quiet around the office. The last thing I need is Big Mike and Vince making fun of me."

"Yeah, no problem," Symanski said. "I'll tell Nims you're taking some personal time. I'm sure they'll understand. Or even if they don't, you'll be gone less than half a day."

"Right. Thank you, Detective."

VIII

Back in his Chevy Malibu, Luke rolled the windows down. He'd intended to take time this evening to go visit his mother at Pioneer Mesa Prison, but that was the last thing he wanted to do.

How long had Ellie been planning the divorce? No wonder she'd asked for more time—she was putting all the pieces into place.

Luke sat in the parking lot of the police station for fifteen minutes, clenching and unclenching his fists.

He was breathing faster and faster, so he forced himself to slow down his breaths. He had to go home. If he was losing control of his emotions, he'd rather do it at home where no one would see him instead of the middle of the precinct parking lot.

And while he couldn't stay at work and he couldn't go see his mom, the rest of the day stretched out before him, now an exercise in distracting himself so he didn't have to deal with his problems until he could fall asleep.

He looked at the clock on the dashboard. Two forty-five. Symanski had been right: not even a half day, so he shouldn't feel that guilty about leaving early. Besides, without identification of the deceased, what could he do? Symanski was already doing all the research.

Oh—Aaron might know where to find K-Car tonight, but Luke didn't feel like talking to anyone, not even Aaron.

Luke exhaled loudly. That's what text messaging was for. He took his phone out and tapped the screen a few times.

> Dead body in Lemon Hill Park this morning
>
> K-Car may know the victim's identity
>
> Can you put me in contact?

There. Now he didn't feel so bad about leaving early.

At least two hours before dinnertime, but his stomach was in knots.

He drove home in a daze, walked into the house, and set the divorce papers on the dining room table.

Huh. The house felt different. What had changed? Luke narrowed his eyes and looked around the room: two or three of the houseplants were missing, and a carving Ellie had purchased was gone from the mantle over the fireplace. He went upstairs and opened the closet. About half of Ellie's clothes were gone.

He went outside and crossed the breezeway to the garage: the Mercedes was gone, too.

Was this really happening?

A ping on his phone: a reply from Aaron.

> In the field rn, but I can contact K-Car tomorrow morning

Now there really was no pressing reason for him to stay at work. He sent a message to Detective Symanski that Aaron would contact K-Car the next day. He felt a small sense of accomplishment when he sent the message, even though they were no closer to catching the killer. Symanski texted back: no parking tickets last night issued to cars that were still in the area of Lemon Hill Park, and FlashRide was getting client information sent over the next morning.

Luke looked up from his phone to his empty garage.

He stared from the threshold of the side door at the vacant space where the E-series used to be. Luke chewed on the side of his cheek. He went back into the house and sat on the sofa. Maybe Ellie would be back this weekend and take the furniture, too.

This house: there was so much of Ellie in it. Luke hadn't made enough—or cared enough, honestly—to pick out the furniture. If Ellie wanted it and they had the money for it, she bought it.

He sat on the sofa for a long time. She'd loved this sofa when she saw it in the Jasper & Marquise showroom. Pricey but beautiful. He was fine with his old Nordic Furnishings sofa, though he had to admit the new expensive sofa was a lot more comfortable.

Luke waited. Would he scream? Stamp around the house, cursing Ellie's name? Cry, sob, dry heave with shame?

He took a deep breath and waited, but nothing came.

He took his phone out and opened the music app and put on *When We Fell in Love*, the song he and Ellie had danced to at their wedding. He squeezed his eyes shut, waiting for tears to come.

"I can't believe Ellie's leaving me." He felt like he was reciting the words. "She didn't even explain herself."

He thought for sure the sadness would overwhelm him. But still nothing.

He opened his eyes. "If you're some kind of emotionless automaton," Luke muttered to himself, "at least get off your ass and get a lawyer on the phone."

Luke stood, took his phone out, and called Anton Uribe. The receptionist said Uribe was out of the office and put Luke through to voicemail. But when Luke heard Uribe's voice telling him to leave a message, instead of asking for a family lawyer recommendation, Luke hung up.

He set the phone down, walked to the kitchen, and opened the refrigerator.

He needed to eat, but didn't want to go to a restaurant. He didn't want to cook, either. Maybe he'd get something pre-made from Davey's. The corner market had sushi and a decent Cobb salad. He could walk there. That would do him good, clear his head. His shoulders and neck were tight.

He left the house. Dave's Market was down two blocks.

Hmph. Blue Oak Tavern was also a short walk. Not like he'd be getting behind the wheel. And yes, he'd had too much to drink the night before—technically, early this morning. (*It's never wrong to be accurate*, said his mother's voice.) And if he were two or three drinks in, a gentle buzz might numb his feeling that he was a pathetic loser, eating a salad alone in his wife's house, watching a dumb TV show, without friends, a mother in jail, co-workers who went out of their way to avoid him.

A few drinks might drop his inhibitions, too. Maybe it would snap him out of this dead-eyed feeling and get him to process Ellie leaving him.

And suddenly, he was sitting at the bar.

"Evening, Luke," Kyle said. "What's your poison tonight?"

He stood with his hands on the bar. "Oh—before I forget, we got a bottle of Plum Luck Syrah Cask in yesterday."

Luke perked up. Sad that this was the best news he'd heard all day. "I always like the Plum Luck special editions—but I haven't heard of that."

"Bourbon finished in a Syrah cask, like the name implies."

"You tried it?"

Kyle leaned forward. "Don't tell anyone this, especially that prick Moody, but yes. And this whiskey is, uh, delicious. Might not be worth what we charge, but it's tasty as hell."

"Sounds like I better have it neat."

"Coming right up." Kyle stepped away from the bar, turning to reach up to the top shelf behind him.

A woman in a black leather trenchcoat plopped herself on the stool next to Luke, who jumped on his stool.

"Oh, relax," Justine Blood said. "It's only me. I was wondering when I'd see you again." She looked at Luke carefully. "Unless you've already seen me and didn't come talk to me on your last time through."

Luke blinked. "Last time through?"

Justine shook her head. "Never mind." She leaned forward. "Kyle, give me one of whatever he's having. And put it on his tab."

Luke wanted to protest, but didn't have it in him. "Nice to see you again, Detective Blood."

"I'm retired, Lukey-boy. You get to call me Justine. Because that's all I am now."

"Been keeping yourself busy?"

"Went to see my niece in San Francisco last week. I go for walks. Tried true-crime podcasts but kept yelling at the presenters. Didn't realize how boring life would be without the job."

"Lots of retired cops work private security."

Justine made a retching noise.

"A hobby, then. Maybe your memoirs."

Justine laughed. "As if anyone would believe me." She turned toward Luke. "So you're here to see me? Ask questions about what the hell's going on? You didn't keep my number, did you? I told you to keep it, but you probably thought I was a crazy old lady who missed the job and tore it up the first chance you got."

"Now Detect—uh, Justine. First, I would never call you a crazy old lady. If you're crazy, it's because you're touched by genius. A ninety-five percent close rate. That close rate may be crazy, but you, ma'am, are not."

Justine raised her eyebrows.

"And secondly, I'm in here because I wanted a drink."

Justine was quiet. A moment passed, and Kyle brought two old fashioned glasses with a generous shot of whiskey poured into each. "Two Plum Lucks, neat."

"Thank you, Kyle."

"My pleasure." And he turned and disappeared behind the swinging door.

Justine picked up the whiskey and sniffed. "This smells like pretty good stuff."

"Yep. My favorite whiskey, but a variety I haven't tried yet."

"What are we drinking to?"

Luke raised his glass. "To Ellie. May she find everything she's looking for."

Justine brought the whiskey to her lips and paused. "Ellie—that's your wife."

"Yes." Luke took a small sip—oh, that was heaven. He could only imagine how good it would taste if he were in a better mood.

Justine took a drink, too. "Oh," she said, "well, now, that's really quite good."

"Thanks."

"Thanks?" She chortled. "You distilled this or something?"

"I chose this. And continue to recommend it, despite everyone making fun of me."

"Oh, boo hoo," Justine said. "You don't know what it's like being the only woman detective in the department thirty years ago."

Luke took another drink. "I don't want to get into a game of one-upmanship. I had the shittiest day I've had since my mom was sentenced, and that's saying something."

He felt her pull back—not physically, but her body language raised a barrier. What had he missed?

When he took a mental step back, he saw the issue at once: she hadn't said *only Black woman detective,* but she'd implied the unspoken part, and he hadn't caught it. "I'm sorry. I'm sure you had more than your share of shitty days. Shittier than mine. I wish you hadn't gone through that."

Justine swirled the whiskey in her glass for a moment. "Words don't mean a whole lot, Guillory. When you've lived it, when your life depends on you solving the case in front of you and the universe is throwing everything in your way, then come talk to me."

"Now, I don't mean to be contrary, but you're the one who sat next to me."

She raised her glass. "That I did. I have no one to blame but myself." She took another drink.

He turned to her with a half-grin, an attempt at levity. "You know, if you need a hobby, I'm seeing all these Photoxio videos of retirees making great money selling those new artisan candles—"

Justine barked a laugh. "Yeah, sure, I'll be the cover model on their brochures soon." She drained her glass and set it down on the counter, then eyed Luke critically. "You sure you didn't come in here to ask me what's going on?"

"What's going on with what? You have info on my mother's appeal?"

Justine appraised Luke over the top of her whiskey glass and shook her head.

"I mean, it's good to see you, of course," Luke said.

"Kiss-ass," Justine said, a grin at the corner of her mouth.

"I came in here to have a couple of drinks, make me forget about how Ellie wants to divorce me, how she'll take the house —a house I don't like, by the way, and—"

Justine put her hands up, palms out in front of her. "Whoa, whoa, whoa there, cowboy. You don't want to confuse me with your shrink. The Sacramento P.D. has an excellent employee assistance program. Licensed professionals who get paid to hear you complain about your marriage."

"Yeah, yeah," Luke said. "Next time, first round is on you."

"I'll remember that," Justine said. She got up from the bar, smacking it twice with her open hand. "Kyle, you delicious human, you stay out of trouble."

"See you later, Justine," Kyle said as he walked over. "Luke, get you another?"

The Plum Luck Syrah Cask was too expensive for another glass, but maybe he could start spending the money Ellie would soon owe him in alimony. "Maybe downshift to the Plum Cask Reserve. I've paid for two of those expensive shots already."

Kyle leaned forward. "I gave her the Whiskey Lake Road Blend."

Luke recoiled.

"Yeah, it's rotgut," Kyle said. "But she drank it like it was unicorn blood, didn't she? And it's only four bucks a shot."

"In that case, yes," Luke said. "Give me another of the expensive stuff." After one more drink, he'd be ready to pick up the Cobb salad from Davey's Market and head home.

"Keep your tab open?"

"I'll close out," Luke said, opening his wallet. He pulled the credit card out and Justine Blood's business card was behind it. Justine Blood's private cell phone number. Supposedly. Should anything happen where Luke would say to himself, "The only person who can fix this is Detective Justine Blood, retired."

Detective Blood was excellent at getting Luke to feel bad about himself. Maybe she wasn't an asshole like Big Mike, but every interaction he had with her made him feel incompetent.

"Card?" Kyle asked, setting the glass of whiskey in front of Luke.

"Actually," Luke said slowly, "leave my tab open."

"You got it, boss." Kyle went back to get the whiskey bottle from the top shelf.

Luke took out Justine Blood's card from his wallet. He tore it in half, then half again, and half again. He put the torn pieces in a little pile on the bar and set Justine's whiskey glass on top of the pile.

The grocery store salad could wait a little longer.

Luke had a tiny amount of whiskey left in his first glass, so he tipped his head back and drained it.

Kyle set the second whiskey in front of him. He picked it up, swirled the whiskey a moment, and lifted his glass an inch.

"To better days ahead," he muttered.

CYCLE 1: THURSDAY

I

Ugh.

Cold on his cheek.

And the stench. Bile, maybe?

Luke blinked—yikes, the light was terrible. The headache he'd had yesterday morning was worse.

Oh, right. The bar.

He never made it to the grocery store, did he? No dinner for him. No Cobb salad. Maybe two thousand calories' worth of whiskey, though.

He pushed himself up—oh, gross. His mouth was dry and tasted like vomit. And he was on the tile floor next to the toilet in the downstairs bathroom. The guest bathroom.

Fortunately, he wasn't expecting any guests for a while.

Oh no. He hadn't had this kind of drunken blackout since—when? College? The Friday night after his Criminal Justice final? The whiskey was much cheaper ten years ago. And he'd never binged on a night when he'd had work or school the next day.

Vaguely, snippets of his phone conversation with Ellie came back. That wouldn't help things.

What time was it? From the quality of light streaming in from the bathroom window and stabbing his brain, he judged it was ten o'clock. And that meant he was already two hours late to work.

He still had his Von Zeitmann on, and he stared at his wrist until the watch came into focus. 9:42 AM. So not quite two hours late. Although he'd have to at least take a quick shower and brush his teeth before going in.

He blinked. Last night had been a succession of terrible decisions. Had he called anyone besides Ellie? He had a moment of panic: he hadn't called Summer, had he? Complained about Ellie not wanting to talk? God, that would have sounded so desperate and creepy, whining about his wife. He felt his left front pocket. Phone was still in there. He pulled it out—oh, boy. 6% battery. He tapped the *Recent Calls* tab. Just Ellie. Luke breathed a sigh of relief.

He pushed himself to a kneeling position and saw that while he'd made it to the toilet before he vomited, he hadn't flushed the last time he'd thrown up. There wasn't much in there—hopefully most of it *was* flushed down the toilet and not, say, on the expensive sofa in the living room.

He gingerly stood, the room spinning for a second but then righting itself, and after flushing the toilet, he walked around the house. No other signs of vomit, although he'd knocked a tower of coasters onto the floor next to the coffee table. In the kitchen, two cold slices of hard bread—the last two slices of sourdough—were in the toaster oven. A full glass of water on the counter next to a bottle of ibuprofen on its side. Drunk Luke had tried to take care of Future Luke; that was nice of him.

He opened the bottle, shook out three pills into his palm,

and popped them in his mouth and drank. Slowly, slowly. Don't overdo it. But drink the full glass.

He went back to the guest bathroom and picked his phone up off the floor. He went to *Favorites* and tapped *Captain Nims Thoreau*.

"Luke?"

"Sorry, Captain," he said, as his phone chirped with a low battery warning. "I guess you heard I got served divorce papers yesterday, and I made—well, I didn't realize I'd wake up this late."

Captain Thoreau sighed. "You have an active investigation."

"I apologize, Captain. I'll be in shortly."

"Don't let it happen again."

"I don't think Ellie will serve me another round of divorce papers today. Although if she does, I'm more emotionally prepared."

"Get in here. The fingerprint database is back online, and the M.E. is running the fingerprints of your John Doe. Symanski will start without you if you're not here when the report comes in."

They hung up without saying goodbye.

Luke went into the kitchen and plugged his phone in.

And now, he had to go upstairs, get a fresh change of clothes, and get in the shower. He could clean the guest bathroom when he got home.

II

Luke walked outside and saw his Malibu in the driveway—oh, no, he hadn't driven home drunk, had he?

No—he'd walked to the Blue Oak Tavern, intending to get dinner from the grocery store. Whew. His headache was bad enough without another bad decision weighing on him.

He drove to the office, sunglasses on, though the day was cloudy. He parked in one of the last spaces in the lot, which made his walk to the building longer than usual. Served him right for being over two hours late.

He pushed the button for the elevator and looked at his wrist—aw man, he'd left his Von Zeitmann on the bathroom counter. Not a huge deal, he supposed, but he'd feel naked all day. As if the hangover wasn't bad enough.

The elevator dinged and he winced with the high-pitched sound as he stepped inside.

He got out on the third floor and flinched at the bright overhead lights. At least Big Mike and Vince Babino weren't there.

Symanski sat at her desk, a manila folder spread open in front of her.

"I'm sorry I'm late," Luke said.

"No crazy shirt today?" Symanski tilted her head. "You okay?"

Luke smiled despite his headache. "Can't say for sure. Never been served with divorce papers before."

Symanski looked up. "We all get a mulligan sometimes."

Luke nodded. "You do anything stupid when you got divorced?"

"Opened a bottle of champagne with a couple of my college friends, but they ended up drinking it all. My stomach was still in knots. Took a couple days to get back to normal."

"I'll be lucky if I'm back to normal in a couple days." He rubbed his forehead. "I hope I don't repeat last night, anyway."

Symanski looked around the empty bullpen and leaned forward. "You okay? Really?"

Luke sat at his desk. "I just need a handful of ibuprofen and a quart of water."

"Because when a spouse leaves you, it can really mess with your head." Symanski studied Luke's face. "It's like someone died, only no one lets you grieve. We throw parties instead. My best friend in Fresno wanted us to go on a cruise."

Luke leaned back in his chair and gave Symanski a smile. "You don't need to worry about me, Detective Symanski. Hey, I've been living on my own for the past month. It's not like ripping a band-aid off. This is everything I've done for the last four weeks, but now longer."

Symanski hesitated. "If you need to talk, I'm here."

"I appreciate it." He paused a moment, then pointed at the manila folder. "Is that the M.E.'s report?"

She pushed the folder forward toward Luke. "Yes, it's the M.E.'s report. Well, the fingerprint report anyway. Pye Domino."

"Pie—like the dessert? Or like the geometry number?"

"P-Y-E. Don't know what his parents were thinking."

"What's his middle name? Carl? Caesar? Chanticleer?"

Symanski furrowed her brow. "Morley."

"Huh. You tell people to call you 'C.D.,' I'd expect a C and a D in their name. D could be for 'Domino,' but..." He trailed off.

"What?" Symanski said.

"I asked you if Pye referred to the dessert or the number. I think it was the number. Pi equals circumference divided by diameter. C over D. C.D. Pye."

"You might be overthinking it."

"With this headache? I doubt that."

"And he was a big deal in Sacramento," continued Symanski. "Maybe that's why he gave fake initials. Care to take any guesses who he was?"

Luke tried to think, the stabbing pain behind his eyes threatening to block the way, then in his mind he saw the *For Lease* signs were all over downtown Sacramento. "Domino-Barkley Properties." He also remembered a cover story with two smiling white men—one of them might have been Pye Domino—on the cover of *Sacramento Business Monthly*.

"Right." Symanski rubbed her chin. "So we talked to everyone in the park this morning. He was fond of proselytizing to people, but if he got someone angry enough to snap, no one told us."

"Any news on the rope?"

"Oddly enough, yes." She pulled the folder toward herself. "Ligature marks came from a type of rope wound in what's called a Multi W Braid. And there were traces of a synthetic fiber that's only available in one brand of rope—Canfield."

"Canfield?"

"If you want me to get specific, Canfield Pro Polymer A. It's only for commercial use. So not a home improvement store. You'd need a business license to get it."

Luke thought for a moment. "Could it have been Domino's rope? The property company must have access to places that carry that brand."

Symanski's eyes lit up as she looked at Luke. "We're looking at the three commercial dealers. See who ordered this rope in the last six months."

"Did Mr. Domino have a record?"

"An arrest record, starting roughly two years ago. Charges always dropped. But no arrests since, uh…" Symanski flipped a few pages in the file. "September of last year."

"So seven months since the last incident."

"And there's a Mrs. Pye," Symanski continued. "Angelina Domino. We'll go to her house at four o'clock."

"Anyone else?"

"The other half of Domino-Barkley Properties. But in Fresno, we always interviewed business owners without notice. They tend to be a lot more honest when they're trying to rush cops out of their place of business. I say we go see if he's in the office today."

Luke got to his feet, a little shakily. "You drive," he said. "I need to get some water, maybe a coffee."

"I expect you'll let me do most of the talking, too," Symanski said, a smile playing on the corners of her mouth.

"You can be both good cop *and* bad cop today." Luke walked toward the bathroom. "Barkley won't know what hit him."

III

They stopped at Java Jim's after they left the precinct. Though the morning was heating up, Luke wanted a coffee, and he kept it simple: a medium black coffee. Summer, in contrast, ordered an iced blended cappuccino with two pumps of hazelnut.

Luke raised his eyebrows. "I hear your coffee order tells you a lot about a person."

"Don't judge," Symanski said.

"I would never." He took a drink of coffee and felt a little better.

While they drove to the offices of Domino-Barkley Properties, Luke searched online for Calvin Barkley. Mostly professional information. He'd been co-founder and president of Domino-Barkley for fifteen years. On the board of three Northern California tech companies, two in Silicon Valley and one in a Sacramento suburb. No personal information on his ProfLinks bio, and no photos with a partner or children. He clicked on Pye Domino's bio: co-founder and CEO of Domino-Barkley for the same amount of time. If they spent most of their working days together for the last decade-and-a-half, perhaps no one knew Domino as well as Barkley did.

As Symanski turned the corner onto 16th Street, Luke's head pounded in pain. He rolled down the window and took a deep breath. A few blocks later, they arrived at the corner of 16th and H.

Domino-Barkley Properties had its headquarters on the top floor of the Braley Tower, a twenty-story building in the heart of midtown Sacramento. The lobby, on the ground floor of the tower, was all glass and marble in gray and silver, low couches and coffee tables. It could have been a black-and-white photograph if it weren't for the security guard behind the black lectern with the Braley Tower logo emblazoned on the front.

Luke and Symanski both flashed their badges to the security guard, and when they stepped in the elevator, the LED sign above the doors flashed *PH*. Domino-Barkley Properties wanted to announce its status.

When they got off the elevator, the glass-and-marble theme continued in a large, empty reception area; the two sofas and end tables were duplicates of the furniture in the lobby, and the art on the wall provided the only splashes of color: muted olive greens, indigos, and maroons. Austere and expensive, if a bit dated. The office, despite the acoustically live walls, was quiet, somber.

Symanski strode to the long reception desk with a single person, young with long hair and a gray floral top, reading a paperback. "May I help you?"

Symanski flashed her badge. "We'd like to speak to Calvin Barkley."

The receptionist put down the book—*Poverty in America*. "Do you have an appointment?"

Luke stepped forward. "I think you'll find the badge means we don't need an appointment."

A frown. "Mr. Barkley is in a meeting."

"Would you tell Barkley the police need to speak with him?"

The receptionist hesitated. "Of course."

Luke looked around the office. An open-office plan, to minimize both money spent on cubicle walls and employee privacy. That meant a straight-shot view into the rear offices, also glass-encased, and Barkley—whom Luke recognized from his ProfLinks photo—was in the corner office on the left, standing in a charcoal gray suit, earbuds in, gesticulating forcefully. Possibly negotiating a deal. Luke looked at the receptionist's desk: a photo of a white dog with large black splotches, one encircling its right eye. A metal placard: *They/Them.*

"Cute dog," Luke said, gesturing to the photo.

"Uh, thanks," the receptionist replied.

"I know how this goes," Luke said. "Your boss is on the phone, and he'll ask us to come back later. But we have a serious matter to discuss with him, and I don't want to get you in trouble. So we'll walk in there and interrupt his call, and you'll say you told us to stop, but you weren't able to physically stop two cops from talking to him, okay?"

The receptionist pursed their lips.

Luke walked past the reception desk through the open office, Symanski on his heels.

"You can't go back there," the receptionist said, voice quiet, without enthusiasm.

Luke knocked on the glass of Barkley's office—the pinging of his knuckles on the floor-to-ceiling window was shrill in his ears—and held his badge at shoulder height. But Barkley didn't look up, instead waving his hand as if shooing a fly. Luke sighed and knocked again.

Barkley looked up, annoyed, then saw the badge. His demeanor changed instantly. He spoke briefly, took his cellphone from the top of his desk, tapped the screen, and walked across his office to open the door.

"My apologies," he said. "I thought you were my controller with the projections—well, look, it doesn't matter. Come in and sit."

"Thank you," Symanski said. Two black leather guest chairs sat at a slight angle, both facing the large glass desk. Barkley's office was an exercise in minimalism: few wires, clean surfaces. *A cluttered desk is the sign of a cluttered mind*, his mother used to say. Barkley's desk was empty except for a thin laptop.

They sat; Luke was annoyed at how comfortable the chairs were. Better than anything he had in his office.

"To what do I owe the pleasure?" Barkley said, taking a seat in the tall-backed charcoal-gray leather chair behind his desk. Clearly, news of Pye Domino's death hadn't reached the office yet.

"We have some questions about your business partner," Symanski said.

Barkley rolled his eyes and sighed. "What's he done now?"

"Now?"

Barkley cocked his head. "I assume he's in some kind of trouble. Does he need to be bailed out? Can't get ahold of his wife?"

"What kind of trouble is he usually in?" asked Symanski.

Leaning forward, Barkley put his elbow on the glass desk. "Look, I don't want to put my nose where it doesn't belong. But he had back surgery about three years ago, and he had an issue getting off the pain medication. He hoarded the prescription stuff for a while, but I heard he switched to some stuff he got off the street."

"Stuff?" Symanski asked.

"Drugs. Pills. Has a girly name, like one of those horse dolls."

"Magic Star," Symanski said.

Barkley snapped his fingers. "Yep. That's it."

"Do you know the name of his dealer?" Symanski asked.

Luke leaned forward; maybe Barkley could confirm what Hector had already said.

"No idea." Barkley gave Symanski a sad smile. "He hid his addiction from me, but it messed him up. Angelina almost divorced him because of his drug use. And the cops picked him up a couple of times. Twice for public disturbance. I'm sure there were other incidents."

"Arrested, but never charged?" Symanski asked.

Barkley nodded. "As far as I know, yes."

Luke sat back in the comfortable guest chair. Had Symanski said how many times Domino had been arrested and never charged? The rich live a different life.

"Mr. Domino hasn't had a run-in with the law in several months," Luke said. "Why do you think that is?"

"He told me he swore off the stuff," Barkley said.

Symanski nodded. "We heard he not only got clean, but tried to get others to quit using."

"Good. I was ready to go to the board to ask for his dismissal."

"Did Mr. Domino get any threats in the last few weeks?"

Barkley shrugged. "If he got threats, Pye didn't tell me."

Symanski nodded.

"Wait," Barkley said. "Did Pye get hurt? Is he in the hospital somewhere?"

Luke glanced at Symanski, and indecision crossed her face. Was it too early to tell Barkley his business partner had been murdered?

"I'm sorry to tell you this," Symanski said carefully, "but Mr. Domino was attacked last night. Unfortunately, he didn't make it."

Barkley blinked rapidly. "I'm sorry—you mean to tell me that Pye is *dead*?"

"That's correct," Symanski answered.

"And that's why," Luke said, "we're asking if there's anyone who might have wanted to hurt him."

Barkley's eyes dropped to the floor. "I, um, I don't know." He bowed his head for a moment and looked back up. "I didn't think about the drug dealers wanting to hurt him," Barkley said. "I mean, the people at that park are bad news."

"Drug dealers?" Luke asked.

"Uh—well, you said he was trying to get other people to

quit drugs. I just figured the dealers might, you know..." Barkley shrugged.

Luke leaned over to Symanski and whispered in her ear, hoping his breath didn't smell as bad as he felt. "A drug dealer wouldn't garrote—"

"I know," Symanski murmured and leaned forward. "Can you think of anyone *specific* who might want to do Mr. Domino harm?"

"Like who?"

"Often, murders are committed by the victim's intimate partner," Symanski said, shifting in her seat and crossing her legs. "You said Mr. Domino had trouble in his marriage?"

"I shouldn't say this," Barkley muttered. "But Pye wasn't always, uh, faithful."

"I see." Symanski rubbed her chin. That might expand the list of intimate partners. "Who else was Mr. Domino seeing?"

Barkley pressed his lips together. "I suspect Pye was involved with one of our former admins here—well, the person in the receptionist role before our current employee."

"Do you have a name?"

"Vesper Montpelier. But she comes from a good family."

Luke and Symanski were silent.

After a moment, Barkley kept talking. "Vesper and Pye—well, they were closer than I was comfortable with. If I suspected something romantic between the two of them, perhaps Pye's wife did, too."

"Where can we find Ms. Montpelier now?"

Barkley shook his head. "I don't know where she ended up. But—uh..." He rolled his eyes. "Look, I don't know if I should say anything. I don't want to hear from the Labor Board."

"Well, now, Mr. Barkley," Luke said, "as you've gathered, we're from the robbery and homicide unit. It's not our job to report anyone for gray-area business practices."

Barkley seemed to debate for a moment, then finally spoke. "We fired Vesper *strictly* for sleeping on the job."

Luke tilted his head. Strictly?

Symanski nodded, probably putting two and two together. "But you suspected Ms. Montpelier had a substance abuse problem."

"I don't know that for a fact," Barkley said hurriedly.

Luke finally connected the dots: if Vesper had a substance abuse problem, the state would consider it a medical condition, and it could be difficult to fire her. But if she did something that was a fireable offense—like sleeping on the job—the company would likely be in the clear.

"She showed up late constantly," Barkley continued. "Pye was willing to overlook it, but I wasn't. And one afternoon, our head accountant found her asleep in our supply closet."

"And you suspected that Mr. Domino and Ms. Montpelier were still, um, romantically involved when she was let go?"

"I believe so. I didn't ask him, not directly, and I pretended I didn't suspect anything. Much less awkward to fire your business partner's lover if your business partner believes he's kept the relationship secret." He blinked and stroked his chin.

"He have any other affairs?" Symanski asked.

"I don't know." Barkley pushed his tall chair back. "Now, if you'll—"

But Symanski cut him off. "You've been in business over a decade, Mr. Barkley. You must have had some clients who were dissatisfied with your services. Or business relationships that didn't go as others wished."

Barkley shrugged. "Nothing springs to mind."

"How was your working relationship with Mr. Domino?" Luke asked.

Barkley pressed his lips together. "The drugs, sadly, were an issue, but when Pye was on the wagon, he was great to work with."

"Where were you on Tuesday night between eleven P.M. and two A.M.?" Luke asked.

Barkley narrowed his eyes.

"Covering our bases." Luke smiled. "Otherwise my boss will ask why I didn't ask."

Barkley folded his arms. "Asleep in bed."

Luke nodded. "And can—"

Barkley waved his hand dismissively. "I was negotiating a deal with one of our partners when you came in. I really must get back to it, or it could cost me literally millions. I'm sure you understand."

Luke didn't, but Symanski was leading the show here—and she'd already interrupted one of Barkley's attempts to exit the conversation. But this time, she relented. "We'll come back at a more convenient time," she said, standing and reaching out her hand for him to shake.

Barkley's phone already was against his ear, his back to the detectives. "Gabe?" he asked. "So sorry about that. Yes, I've finished. Now, if you—" He turned over his shoulder. "Brev can show you out."

Symanski dropped her hand to her side and walked out ahead of Luke.

The receptionist looked annoyed as they put the paperback down again.

"Hi," Luke said, smiling and trying not to let his headache affect his demeanor. "Did I hear your name was *Brev*?"

Brev nodded.

"Mr. Barkley wanted us to ask you if Mr. Domino had problems with any clients or partners recently."

Brev paused. "Mr. Domino hasn't been in today," they said carefully.

"Do you know anything about that?"

"Well," Brev said, "Maybe you should speak with Mr. Vargas."

"Who is that?" Luke said.

"Solomon Vargas," Brev said.

"Is he one of Mr. Domino's clients?"

Brev paused, sighed, and crossed their arms. "I thought this place was different when I came to work here. The housing project was something I was proud to be part of. I mean, I'm the receptionist, but it's better than working for an oil company that wrecks the environment, right?"

Luke nodded.

Brev stole a glance at Barkley's office; he was on the phone, waving his arms. His muffled voice could be heard through the closed office.

"Solomon Vargas is a civil engineer who designed a process to change commercial offices to housing."

Symanski shrugged. "Don't they do that already?"

Brev shook their head. "Lots of people think converting commercial space to residential is super-easy. But it's not."

"It's not?" Symanski asked.

"Offices aren't meant to be lived in. Ripping the guts out of an office building and getting the plumbing and electrical up to code is a nightmare. It's cheaper to knock the whole building down and start over."

"You know a lot about this."

Brev nodded. "I asked Mr. Vargas all kinds of questions when he was waiting in the lobby for a meeting. I was an architecture major at UC Davis."

"So—Vargas was one of Domino's clients?"

"Not exactly." Brev's ears reddened. "Vargas has patents on three types of materials. A composite with copper-like qualities for pipes, a pre-built electrical conduit, and an inexpensive drywall replacement. Property companies like ours can take his material and convert the buildings way faster—about a quarter of the time and a quarter of the cost. Suddenly, converting office buildings to residences makes sense."

"Were Vargas and Domino working on a project together?"

"Sutter Block Towers." Brev leaned forward. "Vargas used to be homeless, and he agreed to lease the patents cost-free if he could head up the project."

Symanski shot a questioning look at Luke.

"The Sutter Block Towers," Luke said. "Twelve stories, two towers with a half-moon design, mirroring each other."

"Beautiful," Brev said. "And empty."

Symanski nodded. "Yeah, I've seen the buildings. Just didn't know what they were called."

Luke nodded. "Finished construction right at the start of the pandemic. A few of the storefronts on the ground floor were rented out for a year, but no one ever moved in."

"Have you read the Walters-Rodriguez study on the unhoused population in Sacramento?"

Luke shook his head.

"Sixty-three percent of unhoused people had full-time jobs when they lost their primary residence. Loss of primary residence often means a loss of their job. It's a vicious cycle."

Luke furrowed his brow, trying to will his headache away. "So—you're telling me Solomon Vargas convinced Pye Domino, a multimillionaire real estate investor, to convert one of his major holdings into housing for the homeless."

Brev pressed their lips together and nodded.

"Would that kind of project make as much money as..." Luke searched for the right words. "As his usual real estate deals?"

"Not even close. But a project like that makes a big difference. It's why I work here."

"And why do you think Vargas has something to do with Domino's—" Luke caught himself just in time—Brev didn't know Domino was dead. "With Domino not coming into work today? Domino reneged on the deal?"

"His end of the deal was negotiating with the city council to change the zoning in that block to residential."

"Let me guess. The neighbors balked?"

"An abandoned building like that? It already had all kinds of property crime around there. And the homeless camps are in the River East area. That's only a couple blocks away. The neighborhood association was *for* it."

"And still the zoning change didn't pass?"

Brev shook their head.

"Did Vargas blame Domino?"

"I think so. *I* blamed Mr. Domino. He couldn't get the zoning approved." Brev leaned forward. "He was zeroed out on the material cost, basically in exchange for a job building this. He'd already gotten pre-approval for the government grants." Brev shook their head. "This could ruin him. He worked for the last five years to get back to a place where he wouldn't be unhoused, and the zoning vote pulled the rug out from under him."

"Ah. So Vargas could blame Domino not only for the loss of the project, but for him losing his—what? His apartment? His job?"

"All of the above," Brev replied. "If I were Vargas, I'd be pissed off."

"One more thing," Luke said. "Do you have rope here?"

Brev blinked. "Uh, yeah. We keep some on hand for projects, promotions, stuff like that. Why? Did Mr. Domino—"

"Do you know what brand?"

"I don't do the ordering. That would be Janice."

"Where's Janice?"

"Cabo. On vacation."

Symanski asked Brev a few more questions, evading Brev's questions about the rope. An hour later, Luke and Symanski took the elevator down and stepped out onto the sidewalk onto 16th Street.

"Where to next?" Luke said.

"Let's get you some more water," Symanski said. "We'll go back to the office where we can do some background research on Solomon Vargas and Vesper Montpelier. I get the feeling we'll be conducting a lot of interviews today."

IV

Luke bought a bottle of water from a corner store—overpriced—and he drank the entire bottle on the way back to the precinct. His headache was getting better.

"So I want to make sure I have the timeline right," Symanski said in the precinct's elevator. "According to Barkley, Pye starts his affair with the receptionist about a year ago."

"That's when Barkley first became aware of it."

"And during this time, Pye was having an issue with drugs."

Luke nodded. "With Magic Star, it sounds like."

"After that, about six months ago, Barkley fires Montpelier. About the same time Domino stopped using."

"According to Hector Corazón."

"And trying to get people in Lemon Hill Park to stop using."

The elevator dinged, the doors opened, and Luke followed Symanski down the short hall and through the double doors into their bullpen.

"I wonder if Vesper getting fired was some kind of wake-up call for Pye," Symanski mused. "He stopped using drugs, he starts a work project to house the homeless. Maybe he stopped his affair, too?"

They walked across the bullpen to their desks, and Luke scratched his head. "We should see if Mr. Domino had any hospital visits."

Symanski sat at her desk. "You mean, if he was treated for an overdose?"

Luke pulled out his chair and sat, picking up the phone.

"Who are you calling?"

"Aaron Rasmussen in Vice. He knows the Magic Star dealer." But the call went right to voicemail. "Aaron, this is Luke Guillory from Robbery Homicide. Following up on K-Car, the dealer in Lemon Hill Park. Any information you have—where he was Tuesday night, Wednesday morning. Thanks." He hung up.

The elevator doors opened and Big Mike Moody strutted over the threshold, elbows out. "Lucy, I'm home," he cracked in a bad Cuban accent. Vince Babino followed him into the bullpen.

"You got some 'splainin' to do, Lucy." Big Mike dropped the accent. "I heard the dead guy in Lemon Hill Park was someone important."

Across the desk from Luke, Symanski bristled and folded her arms.

"You weren't hiding a high-profile case from me, were you?"

"Following the evidence," Luke said coolly, but his stomach sank.

"I've officially requested to get the Domino murder reassigned to me," Moody said.

"You didn't want it twenty-four hours ago," Symanski seethed.

"I'm only thinking about the optics," Big Mike said. "Our captain doesn't want to make waves by putting the son of the disgraced police chief as the lead investigator on a high-profile murder."

Luke gritted his teeth. "Look, Detective, the captain wanted to give you the case. You said you didn't want it. You said it was beneath you. Now, Symanski and me, we were happy to take it."

"And now I'm taking it back." Big Mike grinned. "I'd have

never declined the case if I knew the visibility this would have with the media. If you keep it, reporters will ask why we don't have the best on the force working on it. I'm the guy who solved the Anderman case. How will Captain Thoreau justify giving this murder to the guy with the lowest close rate in the precinct?"

"In the whole county," Babino piped up.

"You had your chance," Symanski said.

Big Mike pressed his lips together. "I'm doing you a favor, Symanski. You think anyone in this department will have Lucy's back? Or yours? You mess up on a high-profile case like this, you'll be directing traffic in the graveyard shift."

Luke glanced at Symanski. The tips of her ears were crimson, but she said nothing. His headache pulsed.

"I expect you'll have about three-and-a-half more minutes on this case," Big Mike said, miming a look at the nonexistent watch on his left wrist. Luke thought of the Von Zeitmann he'd left on the bathroom counter. "Might want to start putting notes together for me."

Big Mike strode to the captain's door, Vince Babino on his heels. He knocked, and with the "Come in" from the other side, walked in and closed the door behind him.

Symanski sighed. "I'd be lying if I said I was surprised."

"I'm only surprised it took him so long to find out. He's got friends in CSI. One of them must have had access to the fingerprint results." Luke opened his top drawer and took out a small bottle of ibuprofen, holding it up in front of his face and shaking it. "I think I'm rid of my hangover. My headache is now solely the result of Big Mike Moody."

Luke pushed himself to his feet and walked into the break room. He was hot, flustered. Why did he stay in this job? Maybe he should call Ellie, tell her he was willing to move to Boston. That might save his marriage.

He shook out three pills into his hand, dumped them in his

mouth, and drank. The water was so cold it made his teeth hurt.

Two years since his mother's arrest. Over a year since her sentencing.

The other detectives and officers hadn't talked to Luke during the trial, but things had improved—a little—since then. With Moody as the exception, the harassment and silent treatment of the other officers had become—well, not better, but tolerable. He'd kept a friend in Aaron Rasmussen. Summer Symanski had come along a month ago, and she seemed like the first partner of his in Sacramento not to be itching to get away from him.

He threw the paper cup away and walked back to the bullpen.

Captain Thoreau stood in front of Luke's desk. Big Mike and Detective Babino were nowhere to be seen.

"Sorry, Luke," Thoreau said.

Luke held up a hand. "I get it."

"No," Thoreau said. "I need to talk to you." They motioned with their head toward their office, and Luke followed the captain inside.

"Shut the door," they said.

Luke closed the door behind him.

"You're going through a rough time," Thoreau said, indicating the chair in front of their desk.

Luke nodded, sitting down.

"Officially, I'm giving the case back to Moody and Babino because I can't have a new detective like Symanski on such a high-profile case."

"Or one with the baggage I have," Luke said.

Thoreau cocked their head. "Solving a big case like this would go a long way toward restoring your reputation."

Luke smiled sadly. "It'll take more than one arrest."

"Certainly. You'll get there."

"And look, Big Mike is a bully—" Luke began.

"He's not—"

"Please." Luke held up a hand. "Everyone knows Detective Moody *is* a bully. But I see his close rate, and I get why you're giving this case to him. I'm not stupid, Captain."

"No, you're not," Captain Thoreau said. "Zepherine wouldn't have promoted you if she didn't think you had it in you." They smiled. "In fact, I think Zepherine was *harder* on you because you were related."

"Maybe." Luke sat back in the chair.

"And I can go to bat for you," Thoreau said. "But not when you come in late two days in a row. Not when you have a sub-forty percent arrest rate."

"I don't have the resources—"

"I know," Captain Thoreau said. "I understand CSI, Vice, Trafficking—very few of those officers and detectives will share information with you. Very few of them will help you out on cases. Not the way they do with Moody and Babino. But that means you need to get creative to close cases. I had to get creative in my career. You think management is happy I came out as non-binary *after* I was promoted to captain? Maybe you think other departments are keen on helping an enby out?"

"I guess not."

"So get that close rate up," Thoreau said. "You have it in you."

Luke ran a hand over his face. Some kind of miracle, really, that he closed thirty-six percent of his cases. The number had ticked up in the last month with Symanski partnering with him, though Vice had taken the Earl Shent case away from him.

"I heard you were at the Blue Oak Tavern last night talking with Justine Blood," Thoreau said.

"Uh, yeah." Of course his conversation with former Detective Blood had gotten out; a cop bar like Blue Oak had no secrets.

"Good," Thoreau said. "Blood's the best there is. If you're getting advice from her, you better follow it. Can only help you be a better detective."

Luke nodded. Thoreau sounded like his mother.

"We have an excellent employee assistance program, too," Thoreau said.

Luke was silent.

"Getting served divorce papers in the office can really screw with your head," Thoreau said. "I get why you came in hungover today. But you're not doing yourself any favors. Call the EAP number. Get a therapist."

"I have a therapist," Luke said. Hadn't talked to her in months.

"Then for God's sake, make an appointment," Thoreau said. They stood up. "Dismissed. I've got to give Chief Dyson an update on this case."

"Symanski and I have made some good headway," Luke said, rising from his chair.

"Outline what you've learned and send it to Moody and Babino," Thoreau said. "When they make an arrest, I'll make sure you and Symanski get proper recognition."

"Thank you," Luke said, although he doubted proper recognition would come. He turned the door handle. "Closed or open?"

"Open. I'm on my way to the sixth floor."

Luke trudged back to his desk, Thoreau passing him on their way to the elevator. As he sat down, Detective Symanski stopped typing, and he felt her eyes boring into the top of his head. He glanced up.

"You okay?" Symanski asked.

"Sure."

"Did you get written up?"

Luke's brow furrowed. "For what?"

Symanski pressed her lips together. "For being late this

morning. For being hungover. For the two of us having the lowest close rate in Robbery Homicide."

"I got a talking-to. Get my act together. Rise above. Figure out how to work around our problems. And we need to send all our notes to Moody and Babino ASAP."

Symanski nodded and went back to typing.

Luke looked around the empty bullpen. "Where did Big Mike go?"

"'Gotta get my ass to Lemon Hill,'" Symanski said, imitating Big Mike's voice. "I told him we had a full list of suspects—the wife, the former mistress, the jilted business guy. But he went right to the park. Called the wife and canceled the interview."

"Big Mike has the best close rate in the precinct," Luke said, opening his laptop and getting his notes out. "He must be doing something right."

"Assumes facts not in evidence, Detective."

Luke looked up at Symanski's face. A hint of a smile.

That was nice. She wasn't blaming him for losing the case to Big Mike. He hadn't had camaraderie with any of his co-workers for a long time. He barely recognized it.

V

At half-past four, both Luke and Detective Symanski got their notes to Big Mike and Vince Babino. Forty-five minutes after that, Luke and Symanski were shutting their laptops down.

Big Mike and Babino threw the double doors of the bullpen open.

"The victors have returned with the spoils of war," Big Mike announced as he strutted through the double doors.

"You made an arrest?" Symanski asked.

"No thanks to you," Babino said. "What were you thinking? The business owner? The wife?"

"A rich asshole was killed in a park where ten bucks will either buy you a blow job or get you high," Big Mike said. "I can't believe you let the junkie go."

Luke furrowed his brow. Who had he let go?

"A simple dispute between addicts," Babino said.

"Who are you talking about?" Luke asked.

"Hector Corazón," Big Mike said. "Had your business card in his pocket—along with our victim's cell phone. Beats me why you didn't arrest him yesterday."

"Now, hang on a minute," Luke said. "The victim was garroted—"

"And our killer used to be an Army Ranger," Big Mike said.

"Means, motive, opportunity," Babino said.

"He can't—" Luke started, but Big Mike interrupted.

"If we'd been on this from the beginning, we'd have solved it before lunch yesterday. See? The captain knows how it works."

Luke crossed his arms.

"I'd have the two of you write up the paperwork," Big Mike continued, "but I'm afraid you'd screw that up, too."

Babino chortled and the two of them sat at their desks on the other side of the bullpen.

Symanski leaned forward. "I didn't talk to Hector. How come you didn't suspect him?"

"Because he can't use his right hand at all. IED in Afghanistan. No way he could have garroted the victim."

"And the phone in his pocket?"

"He could have taken it off the corpse after he was killed. And didn't want to tell me. He could sell the phone and get a couple of hot meals, a couple of pills of Magic Star, maybe more."

"We need to tell the captain. We don't want this to get to trial. It'll embarrass the department."

"Or worse," Luke said, "some overwhelmed public defender who's too busy to find out Hector couldn't have physically been the murderer, and Hector gets twenty years or life." He turned and stared at the door. "When do you think Thoreau is coming back?"

"It's past five," Symanski said. "At this point, they'll probably leave as soon as the sixth-floor meeting is over."

"In that case," Luke said, putting his laptop in the bottom drawer and locking it, "maybe we should also put this day behind us. Start again tomorrow. If they let Hector go now, he'll never get a bed at the shelter."

"Right," Symanski said. "And once we free Hector, maybe we can get a new case that's so uninteresting Big Mike won't want to steal it."

"I'll drink to that," Luke said, standing up and stretching.

Symanski paused. "Do you want to go get a drink?"

"Only metaphorically. No alcohol for me tonight. I need to get my head on straight." Tonight, he'd actually purchase—and eat—the Cobb salad at Dave's Market. After which he'd call Uribe and get a recommendation for a divorce lawyer.

And after that, he could mindlessly zone out to some dumb TV show. Or read a book—he hadn't done that in a while.

Tomorrow was Friday. The week was almost over.

CYCLE 2: WEDNESDAY

I

A GASP.

Luke sat bolt upright in bed, heart pounding.

He glanced at the bedside clock. 12:13 AM.

Again?

He fell back on his pillow. He ran his tongue over his teeth. Why did he feel like he'd had a couple of drinks the night before? He'd expressly refused to drink.

Maybe his current misery was the residual effect of the hangover yesterday. He didn't want to end up like one of those people who got divorced and poured alcohol on the problem. Time to stop feeling sorry for himself.

He rolled on his left side. Huh. He could have sworn he'd worn a different T-shirt when he went to bed.

And weird that he woke up at the same time as he had the other night.

Okay, focus on getting back to sleep. Breathing exercises, in for a count of twenty, out for—

His alarm went off and he flinched.

What the hell? 12:20 AM? He thought he'd turned off his second alarm. It hadn't woken him up yesterday.

Oh, that's right. He'd passed out in the guest bathroom on the tile floor yesterday. He probably hadn't heard the alarm go off at 12:20 AM on Thursday morning since he was unconscious next to the toilet, reeking of his own stale sweat and vomit. Ugh. Embarrassing. And gross.

He turned the alarm off and made sure his alarm was set for six fifteen.

All right. Back to the breathing exercises.

His mind wandered. He still hated Big Mike, but there was a small, hopeful spark for the first time. Maybe he would meet with Justine Blood again; Captain Thoreau thought talking to her would be good for him.

Oh, crap. He'd ripped up her card.

But she was a regular at Blue Oak Tavern. He'd go there; she was sure to show up. If not the first time he went, for sure another time. He'd say Nims had recommended he talk to her. Maybe she'd realize how bored she'd be in retirement and take him on as a pet project.

And he was asleep two minutes later.

II

The alarm went off at six fifteen. Luke's hand hovered over the snooze bar, but his head was relatively clear. He wanted to make a good impression today. After screwing up so badly on Thursday morning, there was no harm in trying to be a better employee. He'd show the captain that he'd taken their words to heart.

He got up, turned on the light, and walked over to the closet.

He blinked. Hadn't he worn that orange-and-blue shirt on

Wednesday? What was it doing hanging in his closet? He scratched his head. Did he have two shirts like that? Had he done a load of laundry when he'd blacked out from drinking on Wednesday night?

He grabbed another shirt, laid it on his bed with slacks and a sport coat, grabbed a clean set of underwear and headed into the shower. He'd go to Pure Life Fitness after work—it had been two days, after all.

He turned the water on and looked at himself in the mirror.

He had on the Cricket Races T-shirt he'd had on two days ago. How had this happened? He frowned. Had he put it on again without realizing it? Hadn't he put it in the hamper Wednesday? Or maybe not. Had it still been on the floor? And had Ellie come home and passive-aggressively cleaned up after him and done laundry?

When the thought formed in his head, it sounded insane.

He shook his head. He couldn't explain the reappearance of his T-shirt, and he didn't *think* he was dreaming. Weird. Had he been sleepwalking? That sometimes happened when people were confronted with a new stressful situation, right?

He turned on the shower.

After getting dressed, he felt better than he had the last two days. Today was the end of the week, he had the weekend to look forward to, and he was turning over a new leaf.

He picked up his phone and saw a message from Ellie.

> I'm not coming home tonight
>
> I'll call you later and we can talk

Of course she wasn't coming home. She'd rented a furnished apartment.

He went downstairs to the kitchen and looked at the clock on the microwave. Still had plenty of time before work. Maybe he'd make himself a real breakfast.

The date on the milk was Thursday, but it smelled okay, and he mixed a splash of it into two eggs. He thought he'd eaten the last of the sourdough bread, but he must have misremembered.

After his breakfast, he glanced at the clock again. Ugh—it was past time to leave. At least he'd only be a couple of minutes late.

He backed his ten-year-old Malibu out of the driveway and put the car in Drive.

He drove down 53rd to Alcatraz Avenue, the way he'd go to downtown, looked to his left. No cars coming. He hit the gas—then saw something out of the corner of his eye. He slammed on the brakes.

A cyclist, driving against traffic, going the wrong way. He'd almost hit the bike.

Just like Wednesday morning.

The cyclist yelled at him.

An intense feeling of déjà vu. Same biking outfit, same bike, same yelling. Luke shook his head. This whole day felt off.

A few minutes later, Luke pulled into the parking lot of the eighth precinct at 20th and K. He parked, pulled down the visor, and looked at himself in the mirror. He looked much more rested than the last two mornings. Couldn't explain his tardiness, but he wasn't that late. Although this made three days in a row.

Everyone ignored him in the halls on the way to his desk. Going through the double doors to enter the bullpen, he was surprised to see Moody and Babino weren't at their desks.

He looked at his watch. A pang of pain—it reminded him of Ellie.

"Watch not working?"

Luke looked up. "Good morning, Detective Symanski. Sorry I'm late. I know that makes three times this week."

"Three times this week?"

Luke furrowed his brow. "Uh, yeah."

She arched an eyebrow. "I figured you'd come in a little late today. Ellie was coming home last night, right?"

"Uh... well, no. In fact, she texted me and said she wasn't coming."

"Did she get stuck in Boston?"

Luke furrowed his brow. "What?"

"That's where she was, right? Some work trip?"

"Well, yes, but that was a couple days ago."

"Are you sure?" Symanski asked. "I could have sworn it was last night."

"No, she got back Tuesday night. Technically, early Wednesday." *It's never wrong to be accurate.*

"Uh—last night *was* Tuesday."

"What?"

Symanski turned toward Moody and Babino, who walked in from the side hall, holding coffee mugs. Babino glared at Luke as he sat at his desk. "Nice of you to join us, Lucy. Or did you forget your mommy can't cover for you anymore?"

Symanski glanced at Babino, then turned back to Luke. "We have to finish up the paperwork on that hit-and-run on Scarsbury and 9th."

"Didn't we do that already?" Luke reached to turn his computer on.

Symanski cocked her head. "All right, what's going on?"

"What do you mean?"

"That's only the third weird thing you've said today."

"What do you mean?"

Symanski held up her index finger. "First of all, last night was Tuesday, which you seem to have forgotten. Second, you were talking about Ellie coming home all day yesterday, and you acted like I was crazy for mentioning it. Third, last night we both agreed we'd finish the hit-and-run paperwork when we got in today." She leaned forward, a concerned look in her green eyes. "Everything okay? You and Ellie all right?"

Luke blinked. "What are you talking about?"

"What are *you* talking about?"

Behind Symanski, a door opened. Symanski turned around, then stood, as did Luke. Captain Thoreau stood in the doorway.

"Listen up, people," they said. "We've got a dead body in Lemon Hill Park."

"Another one?" Luke asked.

"Let me guess—another junkie O.D.'d?" Babino said, chortling. "We should set up a conveyor belt between Lemon Hill Park and the morgue. It'd save time."

Luke blinked. Hadn't he said that two days ago?

"Lucy and her girlfriend can take it," Big Mike said, sitting down at his desk, dwarfing the rolling office chair.

"You need some new material, Mike," Luke said. He turned back to the captain. "Symanski and I can take this one. Is it related to the Domino case?"

"The what?" the captain asked.

"The dead body from two days ago. And I need to tell you something about the suspect Moody and Babino arrested."

Thoreau stopped. "Arrested? Guillory, what the hell are you talking about?"

Luke stopped. Was this a joke? A joke everyone else was in on but him? "I—I'm not..."

He looked around. Everyone stared at him.

"We can take this case," he said weakly.

Thoreau nodded. "I'll send you the file. Officers are onsite." They turned and went back into their office, shutting the door behind them.

"Told you the girls could handle it," Moody said to Babino. "Even if Lucy can't remember what day it is. Come on, they're bringing in that carjacking thug in five minutes."

Babino picked up his coffee and followed Big Mike out of the bullpen.

Symanski sat down and leaned forward. "Are you okay?"

Luke blinked. "I—I don't…"

"Look, Guillory, Ellie hasn't been home for a month, and if the two of you are going through a rough patch—"

"Is that what you're calling it?" Luke said.

Symanski blinked. "Sorry, I don't mean to overstep. Forget it."

Luke leaned forward in his chair. He didn't know what was going on. If someone was playing a trick on him, they'd gotten everyone in on it.

"All right," Symanski continued, "you heard the captain. We've got a dead body in Lemon Hill Park. Let's get moving and see if we can get our arrest rate up."

Luke stood, his head swimming.

"And," Symanski continued, "maybe I should drive."

III

Symanski parked the cruiser on Muñoz Way in a metered space. The two of them walked a quarter mile to the covered walkway. Everything was the same as two days ago: the weather, the traffic. Fifty feet in front of the metered space was a red curb, an old Lincoln on one side and a green Nissan on the other. Same cars as before. Weird.

Officer Pressler stood in the middle of the walkway, about five feet in front of a sagging line of police tape. "Shit," he said under his breath. "Sacramento's finest."

"Officer Pressler," Luke said. "What can you tell us about the body this time?"

Pressler looked at Luke in confusion. "This time?"

"You were here two days ago," Luke said. This couldn't be a dream. What was happening to him?

Pressler shook his head. "You must be thinking of someone else."

Symanski pulled out a pair of latex gloves, and Luke did the same.

"Got an anonymous call," Pressler said. "Male, sounded like he was high. Said a man was dead." He motioned with his chin. "Be my guest."

"And, let me guess, you didn't check for signs of foul play." Just like two days ago. Luke pulled on his gloves.

Pressler blinked. "Hey, people overdose in this park more often than your mom steals from the police. You want to tell me how to do my job, I can get the union involved."

"That's a no?"

Pressler looked away.

Luke held up the police tape, and Symanski stepped under it before Luke followed.

"I see you're reading *How to Win Friends and Influence People*," Symanski said under her breath.

"Tell me you're not messing with me, please."

"What?"

"This day is on repeat," Luke said. "This whole morning, everything anyone has said, the cyclist I almost hit this morning—it all happened two days ago."

"What are you talking about?"

"This dead body," Luke said. "Big Mike only said he didn't want to take it because he thinks it's an overdose. As soon as he finds out it's one of the richest people in the state, as soon as he finds out the guy's been murdered, he'll step up and steal the case from us." He shook his head. "But that was Wednesday, and this is Friday."

Symanski blinked. "What the hell are you talking about? This is Wednesday."

"It is not. You and I already…"

Then he saw the dead body. Same as the dead body as Wednesday morning.

He took his phone out of his pocket and tapped the screen.

9:17 AM. Wednesday, April 23.

"What the hell," Luke muttered. Luke's head spun—how did it become two days ago? Or two days before, or whatever?

"What?" Symanski asked.

"It *is* Wednesday."

"Yeah."

The body was another twenty feet farther in behind the police tape. Face down, blue jeans, dress shirt. Symanski crouched next to the body.

"He's pretty well-dressed for an overdose case," Symanski said.

"Lower his collar and look at his neck," Luke said.

"Why?"

Luke blinked. He must be dreaming. It was the only possible explanation.

Symanski looked closer. "Am I seeing things, or does that look like a ligature mark?"

"You're not seeing things."

Symanski reached out and pulled the collar down another half inch. "Those are ligature marks, definitely." She looked up at Luke. "You saw these from that distance?"

"I—" Luke paused. "I had a hunch."

Everyone would think he was crazy—assuming this wasn't a dream.

And if this was a prank and everyone came out and laughed at him for being gullible—well, he'd been through worse. "I need to interview Hector Corazón." He glanced at Symanski's face; Hector should be in jail. But Hector's name didn't seem to register.

Luke made a beeline for the bridge in the center of Lemon

Hill Park. A man was sleeping there, and Luke recognized the filthy olive trousers and jean jacket.

Hector wasn't in jail. If this was a prank, had Big Mike lied to Luke about arresting the one reliable ally he had in the park? Or had the police realized their mistake and released him?

Luke took a few steps back from Puente de Inspiración, then turned his gaze toward the Basilica Brews across the street from the park.

Ten minutes later, a large coffee in hand, Luke returned.

"Morning, Hector." Luke's voice was gentle but firm.

"I got you a coffee," Luke said. "The good stuff."

The man stirred.

"I don't mean to startle you," Luke said, "but I need to ask you some questions. Figured a little coffee would be a decent way for you to start the day."

"What—what do you want?" the man asked in a thin, wispy crackle, pulling himself into a sitting position. "Oh, Detective Luke."

"Want some coffee?" Luke held out the large cup.

"You must have some bad news." The man's eyes flickered with desire, and he reached his left hand up to take the paper cup from Luke. "Nice and hot, too."

The déjà vu was killing him. "Yep. So, listen, Hector, there's a dead man under the canopy." *Again,* he almost said.

"I had nothing to do with it, man."

"If I search you right now, will I find a cellphone that doesn't belong to you?"

"What are you talking about? You have no probable cause to search. Just because I'm homeless doesn't mean—"

"If you have the dead guy's phone, you'll want to give it to me."

Hector shook his head.

Luke took a twenty-dollar-bill out of his wallet and palmed it in his latex glove. "I know you have C.D.'s phone,

Hector. Turns out C.D. is a multimillionaire, a pretty important guy, and the other cops will want to make an arrest. You sure you want to get caught with his phone when that happens?" He almost asked Hector if his scenario played out last night with Big Mike, but he thought he might sound crazy.

Hector licked his lips, not making eye contact. Then he set the coffee down on the asphalt, fished the phone out of his pocket, and handed it to Luke. Luke passed the twenty-dollar bill to Hector, whose eyes widened.

"I didn't dig it out of his pocket," Hector said, putting the bill away. "It was lying next to him."

"What time did you discover the body?"

"I'm not sure. Late."

"After midnight?"

A shrug. Hector picked up the coffee again and took another sip.

Luke folded his arms. Was the universe giving him another chance to put this right? Were the last two days some strange dreamlike premonition? Was this a complicated prank meant to drive him insane? All those possibilities seemed equally unlikely.

"I appreciate you giving me the phone, Hector." Luke shifted his weight from foot to foot. "What day is today, Hector?"

Hector narrowed his eyes. "I think it's Wednesday, right? Unless I slept through it."

Luke blinked. Nothing made sense.

"So you got your phone, Detective Luke. Is that it? Can I enjoy my coffee in peace?"

"Let me ask you some questions about C.D. He was into Magic Star, wasn't he?"

"Magic Star? I wouldn't touch the stuff." He smiled, his teeth yellow, his right top canine missing.

"Now, Hector, I'm trying to help you out here. You can get a hot meal with that twenty bucks, right?"

Hector gave a brief nod.

"So don't lie to me."

Hector was quiet for a few seconds. "Yeah, all right. What do you want to know?"

"I heard C.D. was getting people off drugs."

"Yeah, that's right. Maybe he found God or something."

"But that would piss off the dealers, right?"

Hector guffawed. "Man, K-Car wouldn't get mad at C.D. I heard he introduced K-Car to some of his rich friends in the good neighborhoods. More money, more respectability. Has to put up with the rich people and their entitled ways. Once they realize they're doing something illegal, it tends to shut down the entitlement quick."

"You sound like you go out with K-Car on runs."

Hector grinned. "I don't clean up good enough."

"And when is K-Car here?"

"Tuesday nights and Saturdays too. You just missed him."

"Tuesday night? So was he here with C.D.?"

Hector shook his head. "I didn't see them together."

"Where can I find K-Car now?" Luke remembered that Hector had said he hadn't seen K-Car two days ago—or whatever that was—but this day, this hour, was different. But today, now, whether it was a dream or if he was taking a mulligan on the last two days, maybe he'd get a different answer.

Hector chewed his bottom lip then spoke. "Okay, all right. He's selling in the rich neighborhoods when he's not here."

"They let a drug dealer walk down the street in a rich neighborhood, do they?"

Hector shook his head. "It's not like he *looks* like a drug dealer when he goes there. Clean-cut. Shirt and tie. You wonder if he's gonna ride up on his bike and tell you there's another testament of Jesus."

"Got it. What's K-Car look like?"

Hector shifted uncomfortably.

Okay, no description of K-Car. "Thanks, Hector." Luke started to turn away, then remembered his conversations at Domino-Barkley's office. "C.D. ever talk to you in the last month about a—uh, an option for housing?"

Hector shook his head. "Naw, man. I figured he had somewhere to stay. Rich guy, like you said, gets high before he goes to work, pretends everything's okay."

"You sure he didn't mention anything?"

"No, man."

Luke took out a card from his wallet and handed it to Hector. "You think of anything else, you let me know. Enjoy the coffee. And spend that money on food, okay?"

"Thanks, man."

Luke turned to go and pulled an evidence bag from his pocket, slipping the phone in there. If he could get back to the body before the M.E. took it away, maybe he could unlock it—fingerprint, face recognition.

He looked at the phone and pushed the side button from outside the clear evidence baggie. It powered up. Luke held the phone up—there it was again, *Wednesday, April 23*. And *Face ID not recognized.*

Well, it would be soon.

Luke ducked out from the cover of the bridge, squinting in the sunlight, and racewalked to the canopy.

No corpse.

Luke went out the other side of the canopy. Ambulance pulling away from the curb. The body was already in there.

Luke swore under his breath.

He still wasn't sure what was going on, but he wondered if he should treat this like an old-school video game where he'd lost a life and went back to the last saved spot. Previously, he hadn't known victim's identity until the next day. Maybe this was his subconscious trying to be a better detective. Captain Thoreau had said to talk more with Justine Blood.

Justine Blood.

There's going to be a point in the future. You'll want some answers. Something you can't explain. But I can explain it. I can tell you what's going on. You wouldn't believe me if I told you. But when you're ready, call me.

Well, shit. He'd torn up her personal number in a fit of pique.

But Justine Blood, retired detective, was always at the Blue Oak Tavern. She'd be there this afternoon, wouldn't she? He could ask when he saw her.

Could he wait that long? Would anyone believe him?

Blood's voice in his head: *You wouldn't believe me if I told you.*

One thing was certain in Luke's mind: no one would believe what was happening to him.

He pulled his phone out. He hadn't put Justine Blood's number into his phone, had he? No, of course not. But he scrolled through his list of contacts anyway.

No listing for Justine Blood.

And before he turned the phone to sleep mode, he remembered the message from Ellie.

> I'm not coming home tonight
>
> I'll call you later and we can talk

If this was Wednesday, Ellie's message wasn't about coming to pick up clothes from their shared house. It was about Ellie coming home from Boston; how she hadn't come home after landing at the Sacramento International Airport.

Oh. He should call Ellie. Make sure she knew he had gotten the message.

But he stared at the message from his wife. Were the

previous two days a premonition of what was happening today? If so, would he get divorce papers later today?

He shook his head. Big Mike and Vince Babino were interviewing robbery suspects. They'd be busy for most of the day, so that would give Luke and Symanski a few hours to show enough progress to convince Thoreau to keep the Domino murder assigned to them.

Symanski walked up next to him. "You look like you got a lot of information from that guy."

"Victim's name," Luke said. "Pye Domino, the real estate guy."

"Wait," Symanski said, furrowing her brow. "The Domino in Domino-Barkley Properties?"

"That's right. And I got the name of his dealer, but that guy said our victim found religion or something. Been trying to convince users not to use."

"That must piss off the dealers."

"Apparently not this dealer. Pye introduced him to his rich friends. I got a street name of the dealer. Aaron from Vice knows him."

"Well, Pye Domino—we'll be able to search DMV and get an address, next of kin."

"I think I read an article that mentioned he was married," Luke said. "We should talk to the wife."

Symanski pointed to the phone in the evidence baggie in Luke's hand. "Where was that?"

"Oh. The witness over there had it."

She turned to look at the bridge. "And you don't think he's a suspect?"

"Right arm was badly injured in Afghanistan. He can't grip —no way he could garrote anyone."

"So he says."

"It's not what he says. I've known the guy for a few months.

I've seen his hand. One look at that, and any jury will see he wouldn't be able to grip the rope enough to garrote anybody."

Symanski nodded. "We've got some more interviews to conduct."

Luke hesitated. He knew from two days ago—if, in fact, he was reliving these last two days, whether in a dream or a premonition—that no one else in the park would provide information.

He ran his tongue over his teeth. When he asked for information two days ago, he didn't know who the victim was. Hector had given different answers—and given up Domino's phone—when confronted by the truth. This time, maybe Luke would solve the case.

IV

Luke spoke to others in the park for the better part of an hour but got no more useful information. Not a surprise: the killer had been there, but after killing Pye, had probably fled. The only people who were still in the park after being there all night were addicts who were too high to strategically garrote anyone.

So Luke had lost precious time; time he could have been interviewing Angelina Domino, Pye's widow. Symanski had called in the victim's identity, and dispatch had sent over Pye Domino's address—in Beckman Highlands. Of course the richest neighborhood in the city.

Symanski drove the cruiser, and Luke stared out the window. Everything looked the same: the landscape, the car, the atmosphere. There was nothing dreamlike about this day. And as far as the premonitions: everything Luke had found out in the first go-around was happening again.

His mouth felt dry, and he wished he had some gum. Luke

turned from the window and studied Symanski's face. She didn't seem any different than she had two days before. Had everything that transpired in the last two days affected her at all?

Would Luke be served divorce papers today? Was Martha already waiting for him at the police precinct with a manila envelope full of bad news and a sympathetic look on her face? If this were a prank, that would be cruel.

"You okay?" Symanski asked, making brief eye contact.

"Sure," Luke said. He wanted to tell her he was repeating the last two days. After all, he and Symanski were both outcasts. And she'd said she'd be there for him if he needed to talk. If anyone would believe him, maybe Symanski would. "Actually, no. I'm not okay."

Symanski looked at Luke full in the face. "I could tell something was wrong."

"Right," Luke said. "See, today, the whole day has been totally off-kilter. Today is…"

But Luke made eye contact with Symanski, and in her eyes, he saw she wouldn't believe him. Not right now, anyway. It was one thing to bond over being outcasts in the department. It was quite another thing when your partner said something that defied the laws of science, of physics, of the space-time continuum.

Unless this was a complicated prank she was in on. That could explain why the ambulance took the corpse away before Luke could use the dead man's face to unlock his phone—because this whole day might be an elaborate ruse.

"Today is," Luke repeated. "Today is weird. Like I'm walking around in a haze." His mind spun; how could he save this without mentioning that he was repeating Wednesday? Oh—of course. "I think Ellie's going to divorce me."

"What?"

Luke shrugged. Maybe he'd go along with this still being

Wednesday—for now, at least. "She came back to Sacramento, but she didn't come home."

"What do you mean, she didn't come home?"

"I woke up to a text from her. She never planned to come home—she rented an apartment. She said she'd call me later and explain everything."

"That doesn't make any sense."

"Maybe not, but I have a bad feeling in the pit of my stomach."

"Where is this coming from?"

A honk behind them. Pretty ballsy move to honk at a police cruiser at a green light. Symanski turned her attention back to the road and pressed the accelerator.

"My first clue should have been when she spent a whole month on a business trip," Luke said. "And only returning my calls once or twice a week."

"Do you think there's somebody else?"

"Huh." Luke ran his hand over his goatee. "Could be someone in Boston. Or someone she works with, who *also* went to Boston for a month." He pressed his lips together. "Or Ellie's getting a promotion and wants to move to Boston."

"You wouldn't move to Boston for Ellie? Get away from your terrible situation here?"

Luke smiled sadly. "She and I haven't really talked about it, but maybe she knows I wouldn't. My mom's incarcerated here. I visit her every week. I can't do that in Boston."

"A fresh start might be good for you." Symanski looked at him out of the corner of her eye. "And some people might say you were choosing your mother over your marriage."

"No, that's not what's happening." Luke shook his head. "My mom doesn't want to help with her appeal. If I move to the other side of the country, she'll never get a new trial."

"That's tough. I'm sorry." Symanski cleared her throat. "You want to get some coffee or something before we interview the widow?"

Luke shrugged. An expensive-looking breakfast place appeared on the right, with an elegant sign reading *This Morning*. He thought he read the word *mimosas*, which sounded both delicious and like a terrible idea. "No, let's see what the wife has to say."

Symanski nodded, turning into the Beckman Highlands neighborhood. "So you don't know if Ellie is coming home tonight?"

"She said she'd call me. Maybe she'll come to pick up her stuff." The closet full of her clothes, the Mercedes in the garage.

"I see." Symanski pulled the cruiser in front of a huge two-story house with rock gardens, a balcony overlooking the large front yard, a four-car garage, and Italian villa-inspired architectural accents. The Domino residence was the most ostentatious house Luke had ever seen—and he lived in a bourgeois neighborhood himself.

"Does she know her husband is dead?" Luke asked.

"Angelina Domino is the next of kin. She had to make the official identification, since he didn't have ID on him." Symanski pursed her lips. "Saw the marks on his neck, so she knows he was murdered."

"And we didn't interview her at the station?"

"She was pretty upset, so I told her we'd be by this afternoon." Symanski turned the engine off. "I don't know how this will go."

They got out of the car and went up the winding flagstone walkway to the front door. Symanski reached out and rang the doorbell next to the large mahogany door. She pulled out her badge, and Luke did the same.

After a moment, the door opened.

The woman who answered the door was about five foot four, her long hair bleached a white blonde. Perhaps early thirties. Long fingernails, expensive maroon linen casual pants, a white silk blouse. Her hair was in disarray—not in an artful way, either. She had no makeup on, and her gray eyes were rimmed with red.

"Angelina Domino?" Symanski said. "I'm Detective Summer Symanski with the Sacramento P.D., and this is my colleague, Detective Lucien Guillory."

Luke realized he'd given no thought to what to ask the wife. Wow—though he'd scored well on the detective exam, a few years investigating the deaths of people whose families abandoned them had dulled his senses to spouses and family members as suspects. He had no time to berate himself.

"Detectives," Mrs. Domino said, opening the door wider. "Please come in. You said you had some questions for me."

"That's right," Luke said. "And we're sorry for your loss."

"I can't believe he's gone," Mrs. Domino murmured. She walked into the living room, tastefully decorated with leather couches in a buttery-soft tan color, art adorning the cream-colored walls. Expensive but a little sterile; the artworks were the only signs of personality. Mrs. Domino sat on the sofa; Luke and Symanski remained standing.

"When was the last time you saw your husband?" Luke asked.

"Yesterday morning," the widow said. "He gave me a kiss before he left for work."

"And he didn't come home after work?"

"He often worked late. I didn't think anything of it. Not until I woke up this morning and Pye wasn't next to me. His side of the bed hadn't been slept in at all."

Like Ellie. Luke swallowed hard and continued. "When did you go to bed Tuesday night?"

"Around ten thirty."

"And you slept straight through?"

"That's right."

"And no one else was in the house, correct?"

Mrs. Domino blinked. "No."

Luke saw a touch of suspicion in Angelina Domino's eyes that he was fishing for an alibi. He quickly spoke. "What was your husband doing in Lemon Hill Park?"

Mrs. Domino took a deep, shuddering breath. "I don't know—he knows how I feel about that place. He told me that was over."

"When you say 'that,' Mrs. Domino—"

She steeled herself and continued. "A few months after his back surgery, the doctors wouldn't prescribe him more pain pills. So he found a dealer. Started in Lemon Hill Park, I think." She crossed her arms, a sneer on her face as the name of the park left her lips. "I mean, I suspected *something*. That park has been a blight on the city for decades. Drugs, alcohol, people getting killed."

"You suspected your husband of using drugs?"

She paused. "That or an affair."

"And his bad behavior stopped when? About six months ago?"

Mrs. Domino looked up at Luke. "Yes, right after the plane crash."

Luke's eyes widened. "The what?"

"Pye crashed his plane about six months ago," she said. "Only minor injuries, considering how bad it could have been."

Barkley hadn't mentioned any plane crash when Luke and Symanski had interviewed him yesterday. Or tomorrow. Whatever.

"Yes," Mrs. Domino said, "it gave Pye a real wake up call. He started acting *better*. More attentive, more interested in making the world a better place. At first, I thought it was great."

"Sorry—you said earlier that you suspected an affair?" Luke asked.

Mrs. Domino crinkled her nose. "It was drugs. Pills. And he

swore them off after the crash. Said he had a few friends who needed help, too."

"Many people can't quit cold turkey like that," Symanski said.

"He had meetings. Friends. He had me, although I was—" Her voice caught. She paused and continued. "I was so angry at him for keeping his drug use from me that I wasn't—I wasn't as supportive as I could have been." She looked down at the floor and folded her hands in her lap. "As I *should* have been."

"Had you and he fought about his drug use?" Symanski asked.

"We fought about him staying out all night, looking like hell when he got home. I hired a private investigator to figure out where he was going. Then he had the plane crash near Lake Tahoe."

"And that was when he told you the truth about the pills?"

"No," Mrs. Domino said. "I found a bottle in the trash that I didn't recognize. He tried to play it off like it was from a friend of his. But the bottle was unlabeled—and it was clearly a pill bottle. That's when he finally confessed he'd been an addict, but he'd thrown all the pills into the toilet and had thrown away the bottle."

"Who's his dealer?" Luke asked.

Mrs. Domino took a deep breath. "I honestly don't care."

"Have you heard the name K-Car?"

Her brow furrowed. "No. Is that his dealer? I thought he was done with all the drugs, but if his body was found at Lemon Hill Park, I guess he was using again."

"Not necessarily," Luke said. "Many of the people we talked to said he was trying to get some of the addicts at the park to stop using."

Mrs. Domino barked a laugh that turned into a half-strangled sob. "That's Pye. Making friends everywhere he goes."

Luke blinked hard, trying to recall the name of the former

receptionist at Domino-Barkley Properties. Victoria. Valentina. No, and no. Her name was more unusual. Veda. Veda? That sounded right.

Oh—not Veda. *Vesper*. And the last name. Something a little fancy—ah, yes.

"Does the name *Vesper Montpelier* mean anything to you?" he asked.

Mrs. Domino blinked. "Um, I think she was the company's admin assistant."

Symanski looked at him square in the face, but Luke didn't return her stare. "That's correct. She was let go right around the time of the plane crash."

"That's news to me." Angelina's lower lip quivered, then stopped. Ah, she knew about the affair but didn't want to say anything.

Luke paced back and forth between the coffee table and the archway separating the living and dining rooms. "Are you sure you don't know about Vesper and your husband?"

"If you're implying they had a relationship beyond secretary and boss—"

"I'm afraid, Mrs. Domino, that I am doing more than implying it. Witnesses put—" Luke paused. Shit. If this was really Wednesday, he wasn't supposed to know about this. Out of the corner of his eye, he saw Symanski open-mouthed.

"Witnesses put Miss Montpelier and your husband together outside of work on several occasions."

Angelina bowed her head. "I—I suspected. I didn't want to believe it."

"Is that why you hired the private investigator?"

Angelina nodded. "But then Pye crashed his plane, and he was in the hospital for a few days." She briefly sucked in air through her teeth. "He came home an entirely changed man. No more disappearances overnight."

"Other things changed too, didn't they?"

"He was more focused on helping others. He encouraged me to start a charitable foundation with some of our money. A million dollars at first. I gave money to food banks. There's a museum downtown that needed restoration. I paid for a few college scholarships."

"He had a deal to get a building downtown converted for housing, too, right?"

Angelina nodded again.

"Did Mr. Domino keep a home office?" Luke asked. "A library? A study?"

"Yes," Angelina said.

"It's possible there are clues in there about who may have wanted to hurt him," he said. "Mind if we take a look?"

Angelina stood and led them through the kitchen into a fifteen-foot by fifteen-foot room behind the butler's pantry. Luke stuck his head in. Dark walnut wood: bookcases, the desk, two low file cabinets. A monitor on the desk and an empty docking station for a PC laptop.

"This is his office?"

"That's right."

"Where is his laptop?"

Angelina shrugged. "Work, maybe?"

Luke and Symanski stepped forward. Symanski looked in the desk; Luke opened the file drawers. To the side of his desk, a small stainless-steel refrigerator. He opened it: full of bottles of diet cola.

"Ever since the accident, he's been drinking diet soda like crazy. I can't keep it in the house. I guess if it's a choice between diet soda and drugs, I'll pick the soda."

Symanski leaned toward Luke. "How did you know about the receptionist?"

"Research," Luke said.

"When?"

"Earlier this morning." He wanted to ask Symanski questions too, like why she was pretending this was Wednesday. Or if it really was Wednesday. Or whether Big Mike had put her up to this elaborate prank. But nothing made sense. And his questions wouldn't make sense, either.

Luke went through the first drawer, bills and receipts mostly. Looked like personal stuff. In one of the folders, an envelope from Kadema First Bank. It was thick; Domino must have liked to have the papers of cancelled checks and statements he could hold in his hands, rather than getting everything online. The envelope had been opened but not emptied. And yes, cancelled checks, but only four of them. An auto body shop for eight hundred dollars. A housekeeping service—two of those. Must be biweekly.

And a check for twenty-three hundred to Kadema Gardens Luxury Apartments, in another ritzy neighborhood, not too far away. "Mrs. Domino," Luke said, "did your husband have any properties in Kadema Gardens?"

"Not that I'm aware of. Those are all residential properties, aren't they? Pye dealt in commercial real estate."

Luke nodded, looking at Symanski out of the corner of his eye. She was struggling with one of the drawers in the desk.

"You okay, Symanski?"

"What?" Symanski looked up. "Oh, yeah, I'm fine. The drawer stuck a little."

"I can help," Angelina said.

"No need," Symanski replied, jostling the drawer and closing it. "I'm done."

Luke opened the bottom drawer. He leafed through several folders until he came to one labeled *Sutter Block Towers*. "Does the name Solomon Vargas mean anything to you?" He caught Symanski's head pop up slightly. Another name he'd heard yesterday or tomorrow.

Angelina raised her head. "Yes. Do you know where Solomon is?"

Luke pulled the folder out and placed it on the desk, on top of one already there. "I was hoping you could tell me."

Angelina motioned vaguely with her arm. "Pye brought Solomon over to the house on a couple of occasions. The last time, they hauled a bunch of wood out of an old pickup truck and put it in the garage. I barely have enough room left for my Mercedes."

Luke looked through the rest of the drawer as Symanski perused the contents of the Sutter Block Towers folder.

Luke stood. "Can you show me?"

Angelina released the door frame and went down the hallway. Luke started to follow, but Symanski grabbed his elbow.

"Did you see the folder I took out?" Symanski whispered.

"No."

"You put that Sutter Block folder on top of it. It holds a lease agreement for an apartment. It was in the false bottom of the top desk drawer."

"In Kadema Gardens?"

"Yes. That's why I thought you might have seen something. Because you asked about Kadema Gardens."

"I found a cancelled check. Signed by Domino."

"The lease agreement says *Vesper Montpelier*. That's the woman you said was his mistress."

"And the former receptionist at Domino-Barkley Properties." Luke walked through the butler's pantry, back to the kitchen.

Symanski fell into step next to him. "Where exactly did you research that?"

"Don't you remember?" Luke said, searching Symanski's face as they walked through the kitchen, past a pocket door, and out a larger door to a porte cochère.

"No, I don't."

They walked toward the garage. Luke still couldn't figure out if this day was a prank, a dream, or a repeat, and he didn't know how to respond. He changed the subject. "Anything else in the drawer?"

"Some documents for his company. A signed agreement between Domino and the other guy."

"Barkley?"

"Yeah. Seemed like standard contract stuff."

They opened the side door to the garage and stepped inside. Luke's eyes widened: half the four-car garage was packed with pipes and wood in pallets five to seven feet high. Maybe ten or twelve of them.

Well, no, they weren't pipes and wood. It was material Luke had never seen before. "Solomon's new building material," Luke whispered. "This must have cost a fortune to produce."

"What did you say?" Symanski asked. "New building material? When did you find this out?"

Luke cleared his throat. "I read an article about this new type of building material that can save a ton of time and effort converting offices to residential housing. The city council had a meeting about a project that used the new material—Monday night."

"They're doing that here? In Sacramento?"

"I think Pye Domino was spearheading the pilot project. And Solomon Vargas created this new material." Luke pointed to the pallets. "And, apparently, storing it in Pye's garage."

"Again, how do you know this?"

The gears in Luke's head spun. "Article in the *Sacramento Business Monthly*."

Symanski crinkled her nose and looked at Luke. "Okay, it's a ton of material, but is it material or immaterial?"

Luke grinned. "Why, I appreciate the play on words, Detective Symanski."

"Figured you'd like it."

"I think Solomon Vargas staked his future on this building material, and Domino failed to hold up his end of the bargain. At the city council meeting, the project was voted down."

"Ah." Symanski put her hands on her hips. "And what should we do with all this material?"

"Well, it's not our problem, but maybe it'll give us an excuse to talk with Mr. Vargas."

Luke stepped forward, gears turning in his head. "Mrs. Domino, would you mind if we asked Mr. Vargas to bring his pickup truck and get all this out of your garage?"

"Be my guest." Angelina stepped over to the side door and pushed a button. The garage door opener rumbled, and the sectioned door raised.

Parked in the driveway was a Jeep. And Big Mike Moody was behind the steering wheel.

V

"Well, how about that," Big Mike said, jumping out of the doorless Jeep. "Surprised to see you here actually doing detective work, Lucy. I guess a broken clock is right twice a day."

Angelina stepped out of the garage. "I'm sorry, who are you?"

Big Mike's face registered surprise for a half-second, then his demeanor transformed. "Mrs. Angelina Domino?"

"I didn't ask who I was," Mrs. Domino said. "I asked who *you* were."

He pulled his badge out. "Detective Michael Moody, ma'am. We shuffled things around at the precinct, and I'm taking over this case."

Big Mike. Something popped inside Luke's head.

Today was all a prank.

Of course it was. This day had the signs of his bullying cruelty all over it. Making Luke think he could make more headway on the case. Lying to Luke that he'd arrested Hector last night—probably paying him off to pretend Luke hadn't talked to him two days before. Luke had read about remote mobile phone management too; that's how Big Mike could have forced Luke's phone to show that it was Wednesday, not Friday. And Detective Symanski—well, threats to make her life hell could be very persuasive. He had to hand it to her, and Big Mike, and Captain Thoreau: they were all great actors.

And in today's scenario, Moody had taken the case from Luke a whole day ahead of time. Just when Luke was getting hope that he could keep and solve this case, no matter how crazy the explanation for the repeat was.

Luke exhaled loudly, ran his fingers through his hair, looked up at Big Mike—and saw red. "Moody, what the hell is wrong with you?"

Moody jumped as if he'd been electro-shocked.

"You didn't want the case this morning." Luke's pulse sped up. "You didn't want this case two days ago. I get that humiliating me is how you get off—"

Symanski shot Luke a warning look. *Not in front of the victim's wife*, the look said. Luke pulled his phone out of his pocket and called Captain Thoreau.

"Thoreau." They obviously hadn't looked at the screen before answering.

"It's Guillory." He was breathing heavily, agitated and ashamed.

"Oh, Luke, I'm glad you called. Listen, once we discovered who the victim was—"

Thoreau was still acting off like today was Wednesday—like it was real. "How did Moody put you up to this?"

Silence. "I'm sorry, Detective. Put me up to what?"

"How long has he been planning this? Was arresting Hector fake?"

"What? Arresting who?"

"The guy in Lemon Hill Park."

"For what?"

"For murder. Yesterday."

"What are you talking about?"

"I don't know how you did it," Luke said into the phone, striding down the driveway past Moody's Jeep. "But you've all been screwing with me."

Thoreau sounded perplexed. "Screwing with you?"

"Tricking me. Setting everything up. Did you send an 'update' to my phone that reset the date? And for what? You think I *like* getting the rug pulled out from under me? Again?"

"Luke," Thoreau said, and there was soothing in their voice, but with an undercurrent of concern. "No one's been messing with you."

"I've been investigating this murder," Luke said. "You know it, I know it, Symanski knows it, and Big Mike knows it. I'm already screwed up because Ellie already served me divorce papers two days ago. Why would you think pranking me to make me relive this day would be funny—"

"Luke!" Thoreau barked. "You need to calm down and start making sense."

"I know it's Friday, Captain. Symanski and I interviewed the victim's business partner yesterday. We found out about the mistress. We found out about the business deal with Solomon Vargas. And I swear to God, if Moody arrests Hector Corazón again…" His head spun and his eyes watered. Corazón had been in the park that morning, in the exact same spot.

"Today is Wednesday," Thoreau said carefully.

And the body of Pye Domino had been in Lemon Hill Park, too. Or was it him? This time, Luke hadn't gotten nearly as close to the body as two days ago. Maybe this corpse was fake. They wouldn't pull Domino's body out of a refrigerated drawer in the morgue to screw with him, would they?

Luke set his jaw. He remembered the cold shoulder he'd

gotten from everyone when his mother was on trial. That had taken planning and foresight. So maybe this was the kind of prank *everyone* would pull.

"Where are you?" Thoreau said.

"Getting kicked off the case by Moody. Again."

"Again? Luke, I gave you the case not five hours ago—"

"Stop it, Captain. Consider me punked, okay? There, I said it. I'm a shitty detective and I'm gullible as hell. I thought I'd gotten things back on track yesterday, but that was all to trick me, right? To make me think I'm going crazy?"

"Luke—"

"Maybe you think this is how you'll get me to quit the department. To avoid legal wrangling with the police union. To save money on a payout. Get me to quit before I qualify for a pension."

"You need to stop, Detective Guillory."

Luke found himself several doors down, walking on the edge of the road. He spun around—

And almost ran into Symanski.

"What the hell are you doing?" Symanski hissed.

"Don't pretend you don't know what I'm talking about," Luke said. "I was starting to trust you. All that talk about how you'd be there for me if I needed to talk about the divorce."

"Of—of course you can talk to me—but I thought you were just worried something was off with Ellie."

"Don't give me that, Symanski. You *saw* Martha serve me divorce papers. You and I worked on the case yesterday until Big Mike convinced Thoreau that I was too much of a liability to work on it. We found the victim's mistress. Domino's new receptionist told us about a deal that went south. And that asshole"—Luke jabbed his finger in Moody's direction—"arrested the homeless guy at the park because he had Domino's cellphone, even though he can't use his right arm."

"You sound—" began Symanski. She stopped and pressed her lips together.

"You're all trying to make me think I'm going crazy."

Symanski knotted her brow.

"I've gotta go." Luke turned and too late realized the cruiser was the other direction—and that Symanski had the keys.

No matter. He'd walk. He could use the exercise anyway.

VI

He was out of the neighborhood in five minutes. Luke turned right on John Sutter Boulevard and walked on the sidewalk, the heavy traffic zooming by him, for another ten minutes. And there it was: the American River Parkway ahead of him.

A concrete walkway led down to the Parkway Trail, and he walked along the banks of the river for a while. They'd had a lot of rain in Sacramento over the winter, and snow in the Sierras—the first good snowpack in a few years—and the river was high, the current strong, and the rushing sound of the water made Luke stop thinking about how he might be going crazy.

Roberts Island, in the middle of the river, was home to an old stone house that had been built in the 1800s but abandoned for over a hundred years. He and Ellie had taken their engagement photos there, but Ellie hadn't liked how they'd turned out. Further on, the river went under the interstate.

He pulled out his phone and called Ellie. She couldn't be part of this game, could she? He could see Moody and Babino staging all of this. Maybe getting Thoreau and Symanski on board. He didn't think Symanski had any kind of cruel streak, but he had only known her for a few weeks.

Ellie's phone went right to voicemail.

Of course it did. During work hours, Luke always got Ellie's voicemail. Always in depositions, or in the law library, or researching something.

And maybe Big Mike and the gang were all waiting for Ellie to leave him. The manila envelope with the divorce papers was —uh, where was it? Had he left it in the office? In his car last night?

He ended the call before the beep.

Wednesday seemed to be repeating. That was impossible, right?

The weird thing—well, one of the many weird things—was that he was making different decisions than the previous Wednesday. So things happened in a different order. As soon as it was made known that the murder victim was someone important, Big Mike swooped in and took the case away. Last time, it was on Thursday. Today, it was on Wednesday.

Hold on. That was crazy. He *couldn't* be repeating the last two days. Even though his phone said it was Wednesday, even though Pye Domino's dead body had still been in the park. There must be another explanation.

Had Big Mike or Thoreau figured out a way to send the wrong date to Luke's department-provided cell phone? That seemed possible. Big Mike would have loved a prank like that—

But wait. Luke would still have his call history. They couldn't delete that remotely. Or could they? He had called Ellie on Tuesday night—well, Wednesday morning. Twice, right around twelve thirty. Luke remembered it went to voicemail the first time. He'd called back and Ellie had picked up.

He tapped on the call log. He'd called Ellie at 2:51 PM.

He blinked. No other calls to Ellie. And none on Wednesday morning.

In fact, no calls at all on Wednesday or Thursday.

And Tuesday's calls were ones he had made on Tuesday. He clearly remembered those.

What happened? Luke searched his mind for answers. What had he done on Thursday night that was odd?

He'd tried to mellow out. He was angry about losing the case to Big Mike, but he was oddly numb about Ellie leaving. He'd gone to Dave's Market and gotten the Cobb salad. He'd eaten it in front of the TV and washed it down with a sparkling water. He read a book for the first time in months, and though he'd only gotten through two chapters before stopping and putting the book on his bedside table…

Luke paused. When he'd gotten up this morning—first at 12:13 AM and again at 6:15—had his book been on his bedside table?

It must have been. A book didn't just careen off a nightstand.

He could have knocked it onto the floor and not noticed. Or maybe he placed it precariously on the nightstand and it fell. He could have slept through that.

He'd have to look when he got home.

Luke kept walking. Away from Angelina Domino's house, away from the interview. The phrase *dereliction of duty* sprang into his head, but if Big Mike had come to rip the case out of his hands, there was no duty left.

He was a long way from the precinct—at least four or five miles—and that's where his car was. But he didn't want to go back yet.

He had to see something for himself.

Luke climbed up a cement staircase at the overpass for Greenridge Boulevard, pulled his phone out and tapped the FlashRide app.

VII

Twenty minutes later, Luke got out of the FlashRide car at the Braley Tower on the corner of 16th and H Streets.

Luke entered the lobby, taking in all glass and marble. He saw the security guard behind the black lectern with the Braley Tower logo emblazoned on the front.

Luke walked up to the security guard.

"Did I see you yesterday?"

The security guard looked up from the lectern, his eyes moving from Luke's face to the police badge he held out.

"I would remember a cop."

Strange. Luke put his badge back, his mind trying to wrap his mind around the possibilities. "I need to interview the owner of Domino-Barkley Properties."

"Top floor," the security guard said, nodding as Luke walked past the lectern. In his head, Luke saw the button labeled "PH" before he stepped into the elevator.

On the penthouse floor, more déjà vu: the same glass-and-marble theme from the lobby. He'd been here before; the last two days hadn't been a dream.

Aha: behind the long reception desk, the young enby with long hair was *not* wearing the gray floral top they had on yesterday. Instead, a pale blue Oxford dress shirt.

"May I help you?"

Luke searched his mind for the receptionist's name. It had begun with a B. Not Brad, not Bev, but something like that. "Sorry—was it *Brave?*"

The receptionist grinned. "Brev," they said, cocking their head. "I'm sorry, have we met?"

Luke decided to go with a lie. "Well, we must have if I'm familiar with your name. Did you go to UC Davis?"

Brev nodded.

"Ah, that must be it. When I started, I was investigating

some bike thefts from the architecture department, I probably interviewed you."

Brev narrowed their eyes.

Oh, shit. Like with Captain Thoreau, perhaps Brev had only transitioned recently and had gone by their deadname at UC Davis.

"That's not it, is it?" Luke said.

"No."

"Well, maybe it'll come to me," Luke said brightly. "In this line of work, you meet all kinds of people in all kinds of places, and I forget I met someone at a coffee shop or a dinner party." He forced a grin onto his face. "I need to speak with Calvin Barkley."

"Do you have an appointment?"

"Oh, right." Luke pulled his badge out. "My wife says I look like a cop. Makes me forget people sometimes need to see my badge."

"Oh—the police."

"I have a few questions I need to ask. Regarding his business partner."

"Mr. Domino?" Brev frowned. "He didn't come into work today. Is he okay?"

"I just need to talk with Mr. Barkley."

"He's in a meeting, but it's scheduled to wrap up in a few minutes. Would you like to wait?"

"Sure." Luke glanced up across the open space and into the glass-enclosed office of Calvin Barkley. Another man was in with Barkley, sitting in the comfortable guest chair in front of Barkley's desk. He rose. The man was tall, perhaps six three. White, close-cropped salt-and-pepper hair, Roman nose, strong jawline, clean-shaven. In his shiny light gray suit, his broad shoulders and stiff posture were evident. Former military, maybe. He shook hands with Barkley, who stepped in front of him, opening his office door. The two of them walked through the open floor to the reception desk, chatting.

"It's a good price," the man in the shiny suit said. "And you'd be doing a great service for your country."

A broad smile from Barkley. "Let's continue this conversation tomorrow."

"Seven?"

"Sounds perfect."

The man in the shiny suit walked out. Barkley turned to Brev. "Get us a table at Le Bistro Cinq tomorrow night at seven."

Brev paled. Le Bistro Cinq—with the thirty-dollar house salads—was a reservations-only place. On the weekends, the place was packed. Saturday night would be impossible to get a table.

"Mr. Barkley," Luke said, pulling his badge out. "I need a word."

"You'll need to arrange it with—" Barkley started.

"Just a few minutes. It's about Mr. Domino."

Barkley stiffened for a half-second. "What's he done now?"

Luke examined Barkley's face closely. The man seemed to have no recollection of their interview from yesterday. Admittedly, he had paid significantly more attention to Detective Symanski, but he expected a flicker of recognition.

Something weird was happening. The only thing that had made sense was a coordinated, long-game prank on Luke, with the precinct, the medical examiner, even witnesses in on the joke. Such a prank had seemed unlikely, but now, with the vacant looks from the security guard, from Brev, from Calvin Barkley, it seemed impossible.

Was Luke actually reliving this day? The last two days?

He cleared his throat. "Can we go into your office, Mr. Barkley?"

Barkley's nose twitched. "I suppose."

Barkley walked quickly toward his office, Luke following him. This time, Luke didn't bother sitting down, standing in front of Barkley's desk.

"I know you're a busy man, Mr. Barkley, so I'll get right to the point." He paused. "Did we speak yesterday?"

Barkley's brow creased. "I don't think so."

Luke nodded. "Very well. Would anyone want to hurt Mr. Domino?"

"Pye? No, he gets along with everyone." Barkley paused. "He didn't show up to work today."

"That's correct."

"Did Angelina report him missing?"

"We've already spoken with Mrs. Domino." Luke smoothed his goatee. "I understand that he's been having an affair for most of the past year."

"Oh. Uh, yeah." Barkley walked around behind the desk. "Our previous receptionist. Vesper Montpelier. She comes from—"

"A good family," Luke finished. "We'll be talking with her next. You understand, we must leave no stone unturned."

"Yes, I understand." Barkley hesitated. "Is Pye all right? Is he in the hospital or something?"

"I'm not—"

"I don't know if you know this, but Pye had a little trouble with prescription painkillers. He went to some street stuff when the doctors wouldn't give him more prescriptions."

"Yes, we're aware."

"Well, if you want my opinion, you should be asking the drug dealers and the other addicts in that park he hangs out in."

"Lemon Hill Park?"

Barkley shrugged. "I don't know the name of it. He said that's where he met his dealer sometimes."

"You don't have a name of the dealer, do you? I only know him as K-Car."

Barkley blinked. "Wow. You guys move fast."

"Mr. Domino's an important man," Luke said, a serious look on his face. "We have our best people on it."

"Yes, yes, I'm sure you do."

"Now, Mr. Domino has made a lot of deals over the years. Anything go sideways recently?"

Barkley nodded. "Not that I can think of."

"You're sure?"

Barkley took a step back. "No one is leaping to mind."

"Solomon Vargas?"

"Oh—no, not Vargas. I wouldn't consider that going sideways."

"What about the city council vote earlier this week?"

Barkley blinked. "At the meeting Monday night? I didn't hear about any vote. What happened?"

"The project was voted down," Luke said. "The project Pye convinced Vargas to push forward." Wow, so this is how it felt to keep a witness on his back foot, unsure of what narrative to spin. Barkley had had control of the conversation yesterday. Today, it was all Luke. Never ask questions in the courtroom you don't know the answer to—and that same advice sometimes applied to police interviews. In this case, he knew already. And Calvin Barkley—who'd been in control of everything in his business—wasn't in control of this interview. And if Calvin was in on Big Mike's day-swapping trick, he wouldn't be reacting like this.

So maybe it *wasn't* a day-swapping trick.

Maybe this really was Wednesday. Maybe he really was repeating this day.

That would mean that the day he had interviewed Barkley and talked with Brev in the lobby—that was actually Thursday. Tomorrow. Both Brev and Barkley might know more on Thursday.

"Where were you last night?" Luke asked.

"Me?" Barkley asked. "I don't see what that has to do—"

"No stone unturned," Luke repeated.

Barkley crossed his arms. "Home by myself."

"Can anyone vouch for that?"

"Not since my divorce."

Luke nodded. "And how did you get along with Mr. Domino?"

Barkley sighed. "For over a decade, he and I were not just business partners, we were best friends. Before he got addicted to those pills. It put a real strain on our relationship. If he hadn't gone cold turkey about six months ago, I'd have pushed him out of the company."

"He must have hated that."

"As far as I know, he had no idea he was on such thin ice. And I intended to keep it that way." Barkley put his hands flat on the desk. "But that would provide a motive for him to kill me, not the other way around."

Luke paused.

"Is there anything else?" Barkley asked.

"Contact information for Solomon Vargas."

"I told you, he had nothing to do with this."

Luke smiled. He'd get Vargas's contact information anyway. "All right, then. Thank you for your time."

He was out the door before he realized he hadn't told Barkley that Pye Domino had been murdered—or even that Domino was dead. Barkley had asked if Pye Domino was in the hospital, but after Luke's non-answer, he hadn't followed up. Of course, Barkley had been flummoxed that Luke knew so much about the players already.

He walked to the reception desk and smiled at Brev. "Mr. Barkley asked if you'd give me the contact information for Solomon Vargas."

"Oh. Sure." Brev eyed Luke warily. It wasn't the easy interaction they'd had the day before. *That's what being too ahead of things gets me,* Luke thought. Brev scribbled a phone number on a notepad, tore the top sheet off, and handed it to Luke.

"Thank you kindly," Luke said, a lilt in his voice.

Brev gave a curt nod and went back to their computer.

VIII

Though he had to wait almost ten minutes for his FlashRide, Luke didn't mind. He ran over everything in his head, standing on the corner of 16th and H. No additional possibilities occurred to him. He was either reliving the last two days or he was going crazy. It might be both.

He wanted to go home. The book he'd put on the bedside table last night—would it still be there? He knew Big Mike and Thoreau and Symanski couldn't mess with that. Even if they'd been able to change the day on his phone, get to all the witnesses, the officer in the park, even make it look like a dead body.

And why? What possible motive would they have for doing it? Yes, Big Mike went out of his way to make Luke's life miserable, but the level of planning and detail that went into this would be exorbitant. And Big Mike would never expend that kind of energy on Luke.

His phone buzzed. His FlashRide was here.

As he got into the backseat, he remembered his car was still at the precinct. A deep sigh. He'd have to get it later. Another FlashRide. Or he could walk the twenty minutes and forty blocks to get there.

He closed his eyes. Pinching himself would be stupid, right?

Well, he'd done a lot of stupid things. He grabbed a hefty bit of skin on his left arm and pinched, hard.

Ouch.

He opened his eyes. Still in the back seat of the FlashRide.

He looked at the lock screen on his phone. Still Wednesday, April 23.

Luke stared out the window, the scenery familiar, but the day feeling more and more like it was slipping away from him.

He leaned back in his seat and closed his eyes again.

From behind his eyelids, Justine Blood's face appeared.

He remembered tearing up her number—he'd torn it into eight or twelve pieces and left the pile of torn paper on the bar in the Blue Oak Tavern.

But if he were really repeating these two days, the card would still be whole. Not even Big Mike could make *that* part of the prank.

He pulled out his wallet. There it was: Detective Justine Blood's business card. He flipped it over. She'd scrawled her personal cellphone number on it, and that scrawl was staring him in the face.

This was totally screwed up.

He wouldn't call Detective Blood in front of the FlashRide driver, but would as soon as he got home. Maybe he'd check the book on his bedside table first, just to make sure.

Ten minutes later, the FlashRide pulled up in front of his house.

There on the front step stood Detective Summer Symanski. The corners of her mouth were turned down, her hands on her hips.

This wouldn't be pleasant.

IX

"I don't know where you've been," Symanski said, "and I don't know what your shouting was all about. But everyone thinks you've gone off the deep end. And it was embarrassing."

Luke walked up to the porch. "Good afternoon, Detective Symanski."

"Don't 'good afternoon' me, Guillory."

"Oh, come on now, don't dispense with pleasantries just because I'm losing my mind." Luke unlocked the door and went inside. He'd cleaned on Tuesday in anticipation of Ellie coming home, right? Oh—the vomit in the guest bathroom. He made a beeline for the bathroom—

But it was spotless.

Like he hadn't thrown up all over the toilet seat two nights before.

He walked out of the bathroom. "Make yourself at home."

"I don't think you deserve pleasantries." Symanski sat on the loveseat, angled toward both the TV in the living room and the corner of the kitchen.

In the kitchen, Luke grabbed two cans of beer from the fridge and cracked one open. He'd had nothing to drink the night before—Thursday night—but losing one's mind was a reason to have a beer. "You want one?"

"Sure." A note of wariness in her voice.

He gave a beer to Symanski and plopped down on the couch across from her. Luke snapped his fingers. "All right, Detective Symanski. I'll put myself out there on this one. I want to see how you regard the situation I find myself in. See if you can think of something I haven't."

Symanski looked at him suspiciously.

"Maybe you're wondering why I'm not freaking out anymore. Or why I'm not denying that I might be going a little cuckoo."

"Maybe."

"I don't believe it myself." Luke took a drink of beer. Cold, smooth, it felt *very* good after his walk and the meeting with Barkley. "I'm living the last two days over again."

Symanski sat and took a drink of her beer.

"Well, technically," Luke said, "it's not the last two days. It's Wednesday and Thursday. Today and tomorrow."

"You're reliving the last two days? How many times?"

"Oh. Only once. I don't know if it'll happen again."

"What happened on Wednesday and Thursday last time?"

Luke chuckled. "We found the dead body, but didn't know who it was. Thursday morning we found out it was Pye Domino."

"Twenty-four hours later?"

"The fingerprint database was down."

Symanski gawped. "I found out the fingerprint database was down when I was on my way here."

"I know. I told you, I'm repeating this day." Luke paused. "Actually, no, I don't think I'm repeating this day. I'm going off the rails."

Symanski leaned forward and rested her chin in her hand.

"I woke up this morning at 12:13 AM, like I did two days ago. Or anyway, what I *remember* about two days ago. I got ready for work and almost hit the same cyclist on the way to work I did the first time." He set the beer down on the coffee table, taking care to put it on a coaster. "Actually, that first Wednesday, I drank a few shots of whiskey and woke up hungover. Today, no hangover. Oh—and I wore a loud blue and orange shirt to work. But I didn't today."

"You wore a blue and orange shirt to work?" Symanski asked.

"Two days ago. The today that was two days ago."

"I don't follow."

Luke grinned. "No, I don't either. Anyway, after we found out the murder victim was Pye Domino, we went to interview his business partner. The receptionist there gave us a *ton* of information about Pye's mistress and about Solomon Vargas."

Symanski screwed up her mouth. "I thought you got that

information from research. An article in the *Sacramento Business Monthly*."

"Hector Corazón gave me a little more information today than he did on Wednesday. Uh, the Wednesday two days ago. And he gave me Pye's phone today. Last time, Big Mike found it on Hector and arrested him for murder."

"Last time?"

"Right, like I said, I'm repeating this day. And last time, Big Mike arrested Hector for murder."

Symanski pursed her lips, like she didn't know which part of the conversation to respond to first. Finally, she cleared her throat. "If Hector had the murder victim's phone on him, don't you think he *should* be a suspect?"

"He doesn't have use of his right arm, remember? He can't pull the rope tight enough with one hand to strangle him."

A crease formed in the middle of Symanski's forehead.

Luke pointed at her. "Oh. And Ellie's friend Martha served me divorce papers in the office, but that was Wednesday, not Thursday."

Her jaw dropped. "What?"

"Yeah. I haven't been in the office this afternoon, so I guess she missed me there."

"So let me get this straight. You experienced today and tomorrow, and now you're reliving them?"

"Well, that's my perception. Physically impossible, I know. Space-time continuum hiccup, maybe. I don't know, I got a C in Physics."

"So what's happening tomorrow?"

Luke frowned. "A lot that happened tomorrow already happened today. Last time, Big Mike didn't steal the case from us until Thursday, but he did it today. We didn't figure out the deceased's identity until Thursday, but since I already knew it from last time, I gave us a little boost."

"So you *didn't* recognize Pye Domino from the *Business Monthly*."

"No. But since I knew who he was, why not use my knowledge and jumpstart the investigation? You know how the first forty-eight hours are the most important?"

Symanski took another drink of her beer and set it down. "So you think you're going crazy."

"I haven't run my symptoms through the Internet or anything, but maybe getting the divorce papers triggered some sort of dissociative disorder. I could be dreaming this whole thing."

"Or you dreamed it all yesterday."

Luke shook his head. "It would be more difficult to explain all the things I thought happened over the last two days still happening today. Or things I learned in my dream that are true of the world today." He rubbed his goatee. "I thought maybe I'd had some sort of traumatic event and I'm lying in a coma somewhere."

Symanski nodded. "I can see how you'd come to that conclusion. Doesn't change the fact that I'm right here."

"But are you?" Luke said. "And if you are, what happened to the you from yesterday?"

The doorbell rang.

"You expecting anyone?"

"No. But I wasn't home at this time on the last Wednesday I experienced." Luke rose from the sofa and walked into the front hall.

He opened the door.

Martha, trepidation in her eyes, holding a large manila envelope.

"Hi, Martha," Luke said, pointing at the envelope. "Those Ellie's divorce papers?"

Martha flinched. "Uh, yeah—listen—"

"I'm sorry, Martha." Luke took the envelope. "I can't talk

right now. Tell Ellie I'll look at these and have them back to her as soon as I can."

"Wait, Luke—"

"No, Martha, I'm sorry. I'm not quite myself. I'm… I'm on a case."

"Oh."

"I know it seems like I'm not acknowledging the seriousness of the divorce papers," Luke said. "Truth is, I've been expecting it for a while now." If the two days he was possibly reliving counted as *a while*. "Now, I'm sorry, Martha, but I have to get back to my investigation."

Luke started to close the front door, Martha looking shocked—as shocked as Luke felt two days before when Martha had served the papers in his office. Suddenly he stopped. "Martha, hold on for one second."

Martha had turned and was down two steps from the porch. "What is it?"

"I've got my partner here—I … uh, I want a witness. Someone who sees that I've been served divorce papers."

"For what?"

But Luke had already gone back to the living room. "Symanski, come here for a minute."

Symanski followed Luke to the front door.

Luke stood back. "Detective Summer Symanski, Martha Underwood. Martha is Ellie's best friend. Martha, will you tell Symanski what you're doing here?"

"What? I'm not—"

"You're not in any trouble. I wanted Symanski to hear it from you."

Martha crossed her arms. "I'm serving Ellie's divorce papers."

Symanski furrowed her brow. "You're what?"

"I'm serving Ellie's divorce papers. To Luke."

Symanski looked at Luke. He shrugged. She turned back to Martha. "Did you try to serve him earlier today?"

"I went to the precinct, but he wasn't there. I waited for an hour or so, but I had to get back to work."

Symanski blinked. "Are you allowed to be a process server?"

Luke nodded. "Yes. The California statute is clear. Friends and relatives of one party can serve divorce or separation papers to the other party."

Symanski dropped her shoulders.

"Thanks, Martha. Sorry about all that. You can go." Luke watched her turn, then stopped. "Oh, wait—don't you have to take my picture with the papers?"

"Oh," Martha said, color rising to her cheeks. "Yes. I almost forgot." She took her phone out and quickly snapped a picture.

"Have a good night." Luke shut the door and turned his head to look at Symanski. "Now do you believe me?"

"You could have heard from the captain that she was there to serve you divorce papers earlier today."

"Yeah, that's true. And for what it's worth, I *don't* think I'm repeating these two days. I think there's another explanation. Maybe I'm having a schizophrenic episode. An out-of-body experience."

Symanski took a step back and ran her hands through her auburn hair. "I'm not sure about that, Luke."

"What, you think I'm really reliving the last two days?"

"I know *I'm* not a fever dream. And the only way your explanation works is if I'm not really at your house and you're hallucinating all of this."

"You're telling me you're not a hallucination, but that's exactly what you'd say if you *were* a hallucination."

Symanski laughed. "I can't argue with that."

They walked to the living room, Symanski on the loveseat, Luke on the sofa, and both took another swig of their beers.

Luke set the can down thoughtfully. "I mean, I don't *feel* like

I'm having any kind of episode. No pain, no confusion—except for the obvious. I'm not seeing weird migraine lights or hearing voices. I just know what I found out on Wednesday and Thursday. This version is different, but I don't have any other explanation."

Symanski furrowed her brow.

"Anyway," Luke said, "did you stick around? Did Big Mike find anything?"

"He went into Domino's office again. Looked at the three folders we'd taken out. Said he needed to talk to Solomon Vargas."

"Big Mike looked at both folders?"

"Yep. Watched it with my own eyes."

"So he saw Vesper Montpelier's folder, but said nothing. Now, that's a little suspicious."

"I would have brought Vesper's name to his attention, but you know how Big Mike is."

Luke took another drink, stared at the label, and let his eyes go out of focus. "Why would Big Mike ignore a woman who's clearly getting her apartment paid for by Pye Domino?"

"Maybe he didn't want to say anything in front of the victim's wife."

"No, that's not it. Big Mike doesn't have an empathetic bone in his body. He'd want to see the wife's reaction, see if she knows about the mistress."

"Maybe he didn't think Vesper Montpelier was important."

Luke scoffed. "Big Mike might be a bully who makes my life a living hell, but his close rate doesn't lie." Close rate—that made him think of Justine Blood. *I can explain it. I can tell you what's going on.*

Luke exhaled loudly. He'd have to see Justine Blood. "What else did Big Mike do?"

"He kicked me out after that. Told me to go find an Internal

Affairs agent and—well, he had some suggestions of what I could do with him."

Luke nodded. "That sounds like Big Mike." He shook his head. "I could report him to H.R."

Symanski shook her head. "After your episode this afternoon, you're on thin ice. I don't know how much longer Thoreau can protect you."

Luke shrugged. "Nothing happened to me yesterday. Or, uh, tomorrow. Well, we got kicked off the case, but that's already happened."

Symanski stood. "I'd stick around, but I'm late meeting a friend."

"Going for a run with your friend from book club, right?" Luke stood.

Symanski frowned. "As a matter of fact, yes."

"You told me that two days ago." Luke followed Symanski to the front door. "I'll see you tomorrow."

"Will do."

He closed the front door after her and stood in the darkening foyer, listening to the seconds tick by on his watch, before pulling out his wallet. He dug out Justine Blood's card, pulled his phone from his pocket, took a deep breath, and dialed her number.

X

One ring. Two rings.

A click. "This better not be a damn sales call."

Luke paused. "Justine? This is Lucien Guillory."

"Lukey-boy! I was wondering how long I'd have to wait for your call."

He paused. "You don't remember running into me in the Blue Oak Tavern two days ago, do you?"

Justine cackled. "Well, of course not. What did we talk about?"

"You called me an idiot."

"That's on-brand for me." Justine exhaled. "So how many times is this?"

"How many times is what?"

"That you're repeating this two-day cycle?"

Luke's breath caught. Maybe he wasn't going off the rails. "What the hell is happening to me?"

"Remember when I said you wouldn't believe me if I told you what happened the night of my retirement party? When the lights went out?"

"Yeah."

"Okay, let me ask you again: how many times have you repeated this two-day cycle?"

"This—uh, this is my first time repeating it."

"Okay. I was heading to the Blue Oak Tavern. Meet me there in half an hour."

The Blue Oak Tavern was a ten-minute walk, so he had twenty minutes to kill. He figured he'd need a stiff drink or two to get through the conversation with Justine. Especially if she'd explain what was happening to him.

He paced around his house until he couldn't stand it any longer, so he walked the five blocks to 50th and McKinley. He looked at his Von Zeitmann watch: still fifteen minutes before Justine Blood said she'd get there.

He took a seat at the bar—the same seat he'd had two days ago. He caught Kyle the bartender's eye.

"Evening, Luke," Kyle said, walking over and a setting a short stack of cardboard coasters down. "What's your poison tonight?"

Luke furrowed his brow. "I heard that Plum Luck released their Syrah Cask. You don't have a bottle of that, do you?"

"You're in luck."

"I'm in Plum Luck, right?"

Kyle acknowledged the terrible pun by slapping the bar lightly. "We got a bottle of the Syrah Cask yesterday." He leaned forward. "Between you and me, it's delicious."

"Sounds like I need a glass of that. Neat."

Once Kyle retrieved the bottle from the upper shelf, he poured a generous helping into an old fashioned glass. Luke watched him, his eyes out of focus, trying to keep his breaths slow and steady. He was freaking out a little. What would Justine say? Would she be able to explain what was happening to him, or would she think he was crazy too?

Oh no. What if Justine *couldn't* explain? Maybe Luke had a medical condition: a brain tumor, an aneurysm, a stroke? What if Luke was dead or lying in the hospital in a coma?

Kyle set the glass down in front of Luke. "Enjoy."

"Thanks."

A woman in a black leather trenchcoat plopped herself on the stool next to Luke. Luke didn't startle this time.

"Evening, Justine," he said.

"Oh, we're on a first-name basis now?" Blood asked.

Luke grinned. "Well, two days ago, you told me to call you Justine, because 'Detective Blood' was retired and was no more." He turned to her, glass in hand. "Now I think you're just a curmudgeon."

"Guilty as charged," Justine Blood said. "You know, only this morning, I was wondering when I'd see you again." She looked at Luke carefully. "So you're repeating? Right now?"

Luke blinked. "Uh, maybe? There was a Wednesday and a Thursday, and I woke up this morning, and it was Wednesday again."

Justine stuck out her lower lip. "Wow. It took me five or six repeats before I asked for help. I guess I'm more stubborn than you are." She leaned forward. "Kyle, give me one of whatever he's having. And put it on his tab."

Luke watched Kyle out of the corner of his eye—two days ago, he'd said he'd given Blood the rotgut whiskey. Sure enough, he reached for the Whiskey Road, blocking his view from Justine, then bringing the glass over and setting it in front of her.

Luke raised his glass. "To the wonders of the space-time continuum."

Blood guffawed, but raised her glass, clinked with his, and downed her drink in one gulp.

"Hey now," Luke said, "that's no way to treat a Plum Luck Syrah Cask."

"Oh, that's right," Blood said. "You're one of those pretentious whiskey drinkers. You pretend you don't drink to get fucked up like the rest of us just because you drink something ten times the price with your pinkie out like you're having tea with royalty." She bowed on the stool. "Terribly sorry, m'lord. 'Twere a pity to sully such a refined liquor on a wench of questionable upbringing like me-self."

"Yeah, yeah," Luke said, motioning to Kyle. "Garçon, another for the lady. And make sure the whiskey doth befit her palate."

"Tennessee Canyon," Justine said. "And make it a double." She turned to Luke. "Drink up. You won't be getting out of these two-day cycles any time soon."

"I'm sorry, Justine, but you'll have to explain this to me. I don't get what's going on."

Kyle put the double whiskey in front of Blood, who picked it up and stared through the side of the glass at the bar in front of her. "Let's start with a simple question. What exactly do you *think* is going on?"

"I don't know. I feel like someone's playing a trick on me." Luke swirled his whiskey. "But it's not a trick. The amount of planning and coordination to make this all a prank? No one has that level of skill. And no one would go to those lengths just to screw with my head." He took a sip. Well, if this was a fever dream, the Syrah Cask tasted delicious. Luke was impressed with his subconscious. "I think this might be a dream. Or maybe a dissociative break from reality." He looked at Justine out of the corner of his eye. "My wife wants a divorce. I found out today. Well, two days ago. Maybe that was the catalyst for all the hallucinations I've had since." A bubble of rage started in his stomach. He frowned. Maybe the rage *wasn't* better than being an emotionless automaton.

"Interesting," Justine said, then took a gulp of her whiskey. "I never thought it was a prank."

"You told me to call you up if I couldn't explain what was happening."

"Right."

"You could have told me three weeks ago at your retirement party."

Blood chuckled. "You'd have thought I was delusional. Hell, you thought you were being pranked." She blinked a few times. "Funny you thought that first. I wonder why."

"I'm sure it won't surprise you that I was a real goody-two-shoes when I was a kid."

"It does not."

"And I wasn't a real popular kid." He sat back. "One day, fifth grade, I was out on the playground at lunch, and every kid made me believe we had a half-day—teacher conferences or something. I knew my mom had a meeting that afternoon, and I didn't think I had any choice but to walk home. It was about four and a half miles, and you know Sacramento in late August."

"Pretty damn hot."

"That day especially. About a hundred thirteen in the shade. And me carrying a thirty-pound backpack. I passed out from the heat two blocks from my house and a neighbor recognized me and took me to the hospital. IV fluids, ice. I was okay, but my mom? Boy, she was madder than I'd ever seen."

Justine picked at the top of her paper coaster.

"That experience taught me two things," he continued. "One: verify stories like this. Sounds too good to be true? Probably is. Sounds like it distorts reality? Probably does. And I don't believe today is Wednesday."

Justine nodded, staring at her drink.

"And the other thing I learned," Luke continued, "is that those kids might've been mean, but my neighbor was kind. Kind enough to save me, you know? A kid she'd seen down the street a few times, didn't know my name, but she scooped me up and drove me to the ER at Capitol West like I was her own flesh and blood."

"I guess there are worse things than being a goody-two-shoes."

"So I'm a goody-two-shoes who's asking you for help. So help."

Justine settled herself on the barstool. "This could take a while. You want to grab some food?"

"Let's finish our drinks first."

"Fair enough." Justine took a deep breath. "Okay—um, well, look, I've never had to explain this before. Bear with me."

Luke arched an eyebrow but said nothing.

"You said you woke up and it was Wednesday. When did you wake up?"

"A little after midnight. 12:13 AM."

Justine swirled the whiskey in her glass. "And that day, were you assigned a murder case?"

"Yes. The big-shot real estate developer. Pye Domino."

"I'll assume your cycles work the way mine did. Mine always started when the murder occurred." Justine took another drink.

"Like the minute the murder happened?"

Justine nodded. "And if I was asleep at the time of the murder, I'd always wake up. It was always when the victim died, not when the fatal blow was given. One of my cycles started when a man in a coma died in the hospital, even though he'd been beaten to a pulp nearly a month before."

Luke's eyes bugged out. "That was the Uptown Jack's case."

"Yes."

"That was huge. The gay community in Sacramento didn't think the police cared about—"

Justine held up her hand. "Don't give me credit where it's not due, Lukey-boy. I solved it because I had to escape the cycle. I wish I had done it out of a sense of justice or equality or some shit that was more altruistic, but no. I didn't want to be stuck in August 2013 forever."

"And how many times does the cycle repeat? Is it once—" Luke grimaced. "No. You said 'stuck in August 2013.' So you're stuck? Until when?"

"Oh, Lukey-boy, I'm not stuck anymore. *You* are. The night of my retirement party, when you shook my hand and the lights went out?"

Luke blinked. "You mean you had some superpower that magically transferred to me during a power outage?"

Blood shrugged. "That same thing happened to me thirty years ago, in this very bar—it was called Romano's back then—and the detective who shook my hand couldn't believe he was transferring the power to a *woman*. And a Black woman at that. Roscoe Dunbar was that old motherfucker's name. That's why I didn't want to reach out to him. He hated me being a detective, he hated everything about me. He only helped me as much as he had to. Gave me just enough info to survive."

"And you're—I mean, I'm stuck? Until when?"

"Until you catch the killer."

Luke slumped on his stool.

"I know," Blood said. "You don't think you can do it. You have a shitty close rate. But you have to."

Luke closed his eyes. He wished he *were* dreaming.

"All right, let's see," Justine mused. "What questions did I have… Okay, well, for one thing, I don't think you can die."

"Like, I'm invincible?"

"No—just the opposite. If you think you can die and come back to wake up the minute of the murder, I don't think you can. I haven't tested it, but one thing ol' Douchebag Dunbar told me was 'don't die.' I don't know why, but I took his words to heart."

"Okay. Well, I try not to die. On a regular basis."

"Don't be a smart-ass. That's my job." A slight smile on Justine's mouth as she took another drink.

"So I have to solve this murder before I can get out of this repeating-day cycle."

"Yes. Either arrest or kill the murderer. Oh—the murderer can also die from other causes. Like if you're chasing him and he gets hit by a bus." Justine cackled. "The Phoebus case. 2018."

"I thought that was an open case, still. The killer was never caught."

"Right. Because Greg Gekkie ran out in the street in front of the 27B."

"Didn't Gekkie's family sue for wrongful death?"

Justine shrugged. "Not my monkeys, not my circus."

"So you're okay with anything as long as you escape the repeating days?"

She finished her drink and motioned to Kyle for another. "Listen, newbie," she said, a slight growl in her voice. "You might be acting all high and mighty since you're on your first repeating cycle. But I'd repeated Phoebus for a lot of cycles. Maybe a hundred, maybe more. I lost count."

Luke stared at his half-full whiskey. "This won't be my only cycle?"

"Oh." Justine chuckled. "No, no, not even close. I went through—I don't know, hundreds of cycles. Thirty years of cycles. Maybe four or five every year. Sometimes more, sometimes less."

"That's over a hundred twenty cycles."

"Good at math, too." She swirled the whiskey in her glass. "I did what I had to do. Come talk to me in ten years when you've tried everything you can think of, and you still haven't solved the case." She gritted her teeth. "Or worse—you know who the killer is, but you can't prove it. Let's see how high and mighty your attitude is then."

"Why didn't you arrest Gekkie anyway?"

She shook her head. "You think I didn't try that? Yeah, I arrested him. My captain was pissed off that I'd arrested him without enough evidence to hold him for more than forty-eight hours, but I figured I'd worry about that once I escaped the cycle. But I never did."

"Do I have to be the one to arrest or kill the murderer?"

Justine furrowed her brow.

"This murder—Pye Domino—Big Mike stole the case from me. If he makes the arrest, will I still escape the cycle?"

Justine blinked. "You'd think I would know the answer to that, but I don't."

Luke was silent.

"That's it? No more questions?"

"I'm sure I'll have more questions," Luke said.

"Like, who's behind the repeating cycles? Did some mad scientist come up with a way to warp the laws of the universe to bend the arc toward justice?"

Luke looked at Justine out of the corner of his eye. "Do you know the answers?"

"Hell, no."

"So you don't know why this is happening, why I shouldn't die, whether I have to make the arrest—"

"I know what I know. I'm willing to share it with you, unlike Douchebag Dunbar."

"Where's Dunbar now?"

"Dead. I didn't go to his funeral, either." Justine nodded at Kyle when he set another drink in front of her. "All right, well, since you don't have any more questions, let me tell you what I think you need to know. And some things that will allow you to keep your sanity."

"Okay." Luke took another sip.

"I got assigned a lot of murders, but not all of them were the 'solve-it-or-get-stuck' variety. More than half, though. Maybe two in three. I didn't keep a spreadsheet or anything, but I think that's about right."

Luke's shoulders slumped.

"And you'll remember everything that happened, but you won't have a record of anything. If you write something down, you won't be able to reference it later. If you get a piece of evidence and bag it up, it won't be entered into evidence after your days reset. And I bet you've figured this out already, but no one will remember anything except you."

"Right, I got that so far."

"So if you convince someone that you're repeating a cycle, they won't remember when you reset."

"But if they're convinced you're repeating and then you solve the murder…"

Justine shrugged. "Let me know if that works for you. One time, I convinced my husband. Once, I convinced my partner. There were two different times I convinced my captain. But I never convinced anyone I was repeating during a cycle where I also solved the murder."

"Ah. So no one knows about the repeating cycles but you and me?"

"That's right." Justine took another drink, this one slower, and set down the glass. "A few times, I solved the case on the first couple of repeats. And a few times, I was stuck for thirty, forty, a hundred cycles."

Luke's eyes widened.

"And let me tell you, it can be tempting for you to just say *screw it*. Walk into the Sacramento airport and take the next flight to Mexico. Get on a cruise. Take a few days off. Or not show up to work. Lie in bed, catch up on your reading, spend your time eating at fancy restaurants on your credit card since you won't have to pay them off when the cycle resets. But whenever I did that—especially if I took time off a case for a few cycles in a row—then I forgot most of the stuff I learned. Not because of time loop magic or anything, but after ten or twelve days away, I forgot the details. I forgot interviews. Sometimes, I had to start over at square one. I hated myself for wasting so many of those cycles."

Luke nodded.

"Sometimes you need the time off, I won't deny that. Sometimes you're so deep into it, pushing so hard to get through the cycle and out the other side, that a couple days off is just what you need." Justine got a faraway look in her eyes. "And sometimes…"

Luke was quiet. Finally, after half a minute: "What?"

"Sometimes you need to take advantage of the situation to do things you'd never let yourself do before." Justine clamped her mouth shut.

Luke furrowed his brow.

A deep breath. "Big Mike is an asshole," Justine said, "but he sure is *pretty*."

Luke blanched.

"Yep, I banged him," Justine said. "I know I'm fifteen years older than him, but I had to have him—but only once. And once became a couple of times." She smiled. "Or ten."

"When you were married?"

Justine shrugged. "What happens in the cycle stays in the cycle."

Luke picked up his drink and finished it.

"He was absolutely terrible in the sack the first time," Justine said. "But after I figured out that he wanted someone to dominate him—"

"Whoa, whoa, whoa," Luke said. "I do *not* need to know the details."

Justine stuck her lower lip out. "Man, I've been holding that in for years. I've finally got someone to talk to about all this shit."

Luke inclined his head forward an inch and stared at his whiskey glass.

"It's not like Big Mike remembers it," Justine said. "We only did it when I knew I wouldn't be catching the killer that cycle." She raised her eyebrows. "Come on, now, don't tell me you're not thinking the same thing."

Luke raised his head and looked at Justine.

"Not about Big Mike, you idiot. About Summer Symanski."

"Detective Symanski?"

"I see the way she looks at you. Maybe it's a newbie thing. She's only been here, what, two weeks?"

"A month."

"And I've heard about her whole thing with internal affairs down in Fresno. You and Summer, against the world. It would almost be romantic if you weren't married to someone else."

"Now way. I won't screw anything up by sleeping with my partner."

"And with your judgmental tone, you're not the kind of person who'd cheat on his wife. Even if the day resets."

Now it was Luke's turn to be silent.

"Aha," Justine said. "So you *are* thinking about it."

"Well—I got served divorce papers."

Justine raised her eyebrows. "Before the cycle, or in the cycle?"

"In. Earlier today, in both the first Wednesday and today."

Justine nodded. "If you want, you can try to save your marriage. Maybe. You might have time."

Luke turned the idea over in his mind. "I don't think I can. I think it's too late."

Justine nodded. "Yeah. I couldn't do anything about my divorces either. Too much had happened."

"Even if I were emotionally ready to date someone else," Luke said, "Detective Symanski and I are partners. We couldn't get romantically involved."

"Well, not on a day when you catch the murderer," Justine said. "But on a day when you know you'll reset, why not? She's cute. She's into you." Blood grinned. "I don't regret anything I did in the cycle when I knew it would reset. I always wanted to try a line of cocaine, so one cycle, I did. I wanted to bang Big Mike, so I did. Why would I regret anything? The cycle is the ultimate mulligan. I don't have any guilt, because those other days never happened. *I didn't do it.*"

Luke knotted his eyebrows. In the cycle or not, he *would* have done it. He'd know if he did drugs or slept with someone —and Justine Blood knew what she'd done. Luke wasn't sure he could let go of what he'd done in previous days in a cycle. "What's the worst thing you've ever done?" The words were out of Luke's mouth before he realized he was speaking.

Justine Blood laughed, a long, loud bray of a laugh. "I don't think we know each other well enough yet."

"Something worse than sleeping with Big Mike?"

Blood grinned.

"I'll get to know you a lot better than you know me," Luke said. "I'll try to get advice from you when I'm stuck in the cycle, maybe every day. I might open up to you. But you'll never know it unless I solve a crime that day."

"Sucks to be you," Justine muttered. "And I'm not just saying that. It sucked to be me. Yeah, I've lived five or ten more years in total, repeating days. I never kept track. Maybe you'll want to."

"Why didn't you quit?"

Justine blinked. "What do you mean? Quit my job? And not had access to the resources I need to get out of the time loop?"

"Wouldn't you shake hands with someone at your goodbye party, some unsuspecting schmuck like me, and boom, lightning bolts and tingling body parts, and you'd be able to get out of the repeating cycles?"

Justine laughed. "Oh man, I forgot. I *did* quit once. Without notice, too. Right after my divorce. I couldn't take it anymore. Man, quitting felt fantastic. And a murder came in—not thirty seconds after I screamed at my captain and got out of his office."

"And you had to repeat those two days?"

"Sure did. Man, that case was rough. I was so burned out, I must have taken fifty or sixty cycles to solve the case."

Luke's shoulders slumped.

"It's not all bad," Justine said. "I've had a lot of life experiences I'd never get otherwise. Expensive meals, days at the beach, telling off my boss, my sexcapades with Big Mike—"

"Okay, I get it," Luke said. He could have gone his whole life without hearing the word *sexcapades* associated with Big Mike.

Justine's eyes twinkled with mischief. "The last time Big Mike agreed to let me tie him up was only because Vesper had recently dumped him for some rich, married guy."

Luke was about to object again—then stopped. "Vesper?"

"Yeah, Vesper. His girlfriend. He kept it quiet, of course, but when you can do a deep dive on someone's background without anyone finding out about it? Kind of a thrill."

No, it couldn't be. But how many women were named Vesper? "What was Vesper's last name?"

Justine's face grew pinched. "Uh—I don't remember it off the top of my head. French-ish. Something a little snooty."

"Montpelier?"

Justine cracked a smile. "Oh, Lukey-boy, maybe you'll be better at this than you think."

"Well, I don't know about that."

"Not like you have a choice." The smile faded from Justine's face. "I've got two failed marriages and a kid who won't talk to me because of this damn *gift*." Justine's face turned sour. "Hard to remember you promised to pick your kid up from the airport on Friday when you made the promise on Monday, and you repeated Wednesday and Thursday thirty-five times."

Luke turned back to his whiskey. "Just when I thought my life couldn't get any worse."

Justine leaned forward. "You know, your mother thinks she's innocent."

Luke flinched. "She sure doesn't act like it."

"Yeah, she doesn't. Maybe she thinks it's hopeless. Or maybe there's something she's afraid you'll find. But you'd like to know for sure, wouldn't you?"

Luke was quiet.

"You could use your repeating days to figure out if she's telling the truth," Justine said. "Maybe this isn't the curse you think it is." She drank the rest of her whiskey and looked up, her eyes sparkling. "Or maybe you need to view it differently."

He exhaled, long and slow.

"Buy me another drink," Justine said, setting the empty glass on the bar. "Not like you'll have to pay for it."

CYCLE 2: THURSDAY

I

LUKE BLINKED AT HIS WATCH.

To celebrate their one-year anniversary, he and Ellie had dinner at The Oven, the only Michelin-star restaurant in the area. The meal was outstanding; Luke was happy. Zepherine had been with them, and she tried to insist on paying, but after a quick trip to the ladies' room with Ellie, Zepherine had come back and allowed Ellie to pay. The bottle of wine alone was more than Luke's monthly car payment.

When they arrived home, a lacquered mahogany box with a blue bow sat on the kitchen counter. Inside the box was the Von Zeitmann.

Luke wore it nearly every day. When he didn't wear it, Ellie asked why. The alligator leather band was showy; he didn't want to wear it going for a run or taking a trip to the garden center or Marks-the-Spot. Maybe Ellie wanted someone who liked flaunting an expensive timepiece.

Right. He was looking at his watch. A little out of focus. He blinked, once, twice, three times. He opened his eyes as wide as he could. Ah, there it was. Two minutes past midnight.

He lifted his head. Oh, boy, the bar was spinning.

"How you doing?" Kyle asked.

"Good, good, good," Luke said. "Did you know I'm reliving this day and the next day, today and tomorrow, over and over?"

"Oh," Kyle said. "Like that movie with the time loop."

Luke nodded. "Only that was only one day. *This* is two days."

"Impressive," Kyle said. "Twice as good as the movie."

Luke sighed. "No, it sucks."

"I can see how that would be bad," Kyle said. "How about some water?"

"I could have another Lucky Plum Bastard Service."

"Plum Luck Syrah Cask?" Kyle asked.

Luke pointed at Kyle with his right hand and touched his nose with his left. Well, his hand ended up below his eye, but Kyle got it.

"I'll get you another one right after you finish the water. You don't want a hangover tomorrow, do you?" Kyle set a glass of ice water in front of Luke.

"I guess not."

"Here." Kyle reached underneath the bar and emerged with a small white plastic bottle. He popped it open and shook out two pills into his hand.

"What's that?" Luke squinted. "I'm investigating a murder with a guy who took pills. You trying to compromise my investigation?"

"It's ibuprofen. It'll help with the hangover. You'll be hating life tomorrow morning, but a little less if you take this."

"Yeah, yeah, okay." Luke reached his hand out unsteadily, and Kyle dumped the two pills into Luke's palm. Luke pulled his hand to his mouth, miraculously getting the pills into their intended target, then drank the water. Felt good.

He set the water down on the bar. "Where'd Detect-tech-tative Blood go?"

"She called it a night. About ten minutes ago."

Luke slumped on the stool, and stood, wavering, but keeping his balance by holding the bar. "I guess I should head out, too. I have work in the morning." He frowned. "I really shouldn't have drinken so much. Drunken so much. Not good, Kyle."

"We all have to blow off a little steam," Kyle said. "Especially with what you're going through."

"You, my friend, called it a time lap." Luke cackled. "A time loop. And yeah, it blows."

"I meant what's going on with Ellie."

"Right," Luke said. "Right, right, right. Ellie." He'd talked Kyle's ear off for the last hour or two, hadn't he? "Hey, Kyle, I know you know my mom's in jail and that she did some super bad stuff. And Ellie's leaving me. But you still talk to me. You still treat me like a person. A person, you know? And I appreciate that. You don't know how much I appreciate that."

Kyle shifted his weight uncomfortably. "You're saying that because you're drunk, Luke."

"No, man." Luke took his hands off the bar. He could stand on his own. "I mean, okay, yeah, maybe I'm saying it because I don't have much of a filter now, but I feel it every time I come in here. I've *wanted* to say it every time."

"Well, that's nice, Luke. You're a good guy." Kyle tapped the bar. "You're not driving, are you?"

"Walked here."

"Good. Be careful going home. And finish your water before you leave."

Luke gave a wide smile. "Looking out for me, dude."

Kyle gave a curt nod and stepped away to take an order at the other side of the bar.

Luke drank the water slowly, focusing on a knot in the wooden bar, and thinking how he could solve the case.

The first thing Luke had to do was to keep Big Mike away from taking over the case. Well, not the first thing, because he'd already taken over the case. But on the next repeat.

If the cycle repeats were all a delusion, everything was otherwise normal. None of his acquaintances were morphing into demons before his eyes. He didn't hear voices in his head. And Justine Blood had given him an explanation that matched perfectly with what he was experiencing.

He really had no choice but to ride the wave of this time loop and try to get out of it.

Luke finished the water, found his way across the bar, and opened the door to the outside.

The April day had been warm, but the night was chilly, and Luke hadn't brought a jacket. He thought he'd be talking to Justine for a little while, grabbing some dinner, having an early night.

Though really, what was the point? He'd made a fool of himself in front of Detective Symanski and Big Mike—and the murder victim's widow, too.

He'd learn all he could tomorrow and use that knowledge when the cycle reset.

Justine had called it a *cycle*. That made sense, like a wheel that spun from Wednesday morning to Thursday night and back again. Like he was driving down the road, going the speed limit, then encountering a roundabout. Usually he'd drive onto the roundabout and exit at the clearly marked street where he wanted to go. But once or twice, he'd gotten confused in a roundabout, missed the exit, and had to loop around again. It was like that. Like a roundabout in time.

He looked up. Aw, crap. He'd walked too far on McKinley and was now at 55th St. He turned right.

55th was a much nicer block than 53rd. These houses were

all well over two million dollars; three or four thousand square feet, more than twice their cute Tudor house on 53rd. Well-manicured gardens. Ellie had often expressed her envy at the houses on 55th.

Luke furrowed his brow. He'd never really cared about how fancy his own place was. He wanted to be safe, but the location always mattered more to him. Walking distance to cool stuff was ideal. Restaurants, bakeries, bars, places he could see live music. His former apartment on 18th in Midtown had been a perfect location. But Ellie hadn't ever wanted to spend the night there. Too loud—it was close to the railroad tracks, although Luke had gotten used to the noise after a week.

He found himself on Alcatraz Avenue and turned right again. Now two blocks away from home.

Five minutes later, he walked up to his house and tripped over the top cement step, catching himself just in time. He held out his key unsteadily and miraculously found the lock.

Luke entered and stood in the foyer, then closed the door behind him. He tapped his foot, thinking.

He walked toward the garage, holding onto the walls as he went. He opened the door to the attached garage and turned on the light.

No Mercedes. She'd picked it up earlier.

He clicked off the light and let the garage door close on its own, then walked in the house and into the living room, closing the door behind him. He stared at the expensive sofa. And suddenly the bubble of rage came back up. He was yelling, swearing at Ellie, though she wasn't there. It wasn't fair. She'd left him, and he couldn't respond. She was the one who hadn't returned his calls. She was the one who'd kept postponing her return. And it wasn't *fair*.

How long had he been yelling? Long enough for his voice to be hoarse and his throat raw. Maybe he should have done more to save their relationship. Maybe he should have fought. But how was he supposed to know?

He spat his anger out some more. He was angry because he was alone. He was mad at the missed opportunities to convince Ellie to stay. He was pissed off because maybe Ellie knew his marriage was doomed from the minute Zepherine Guillory had been arrested for embezzlement and bribery.

And Luke was so, so tired.

II

Ugh.

Luke's eyes were closed, but the room was clearly bright. With sunlight, not artificial light.

His mouth tasted terrible.

Where was he?

He opened his eyes. Living room floor.

Right. His life was falling apart, and he was reliving the two days when it was all crumbling around him.

Oh. Sunlight. It wasn't six fifteen. The quality of light meant the sun was much higher in the sky.

He looked at the expensive watch on his wrist.

10:23.

Shit. That was later than the last cycle.

He scrambled to pull the phone out of his pocket. He called Captain Thoreau.

They answered on the first ring. "Detective Guillory."

"Nims—Captain Thoreau. I apologize. I've had..." How would he play this?

Luke stopped. Did it matter? If Justine Blood was right, these two days would repeat.

"I've had a rough couple of days. Ellie served me divorce papers. I don't have an excuse, but I hope you understand that my personal life has pretty much exploded over the last forty-eight hours."

Thoreau was silent.

"Captain?"

"Luke, I've always appreciated your positive attitude, even when things are at their worst. I've always appreciated your willingness to take on the cases no one else wants. I like your ability to stick up for the people who otherwise have no advocates."

Luke sensed a *but* coming.

"With Detective Symanski, I thought you'd finally found a partner who'd be able to work with you. But after your antics yesterday…"

"Symanski and I talked afterward, Captain. I apologized for my behavior. We're good. Or—or I think we're good, anyway."

"You acted in an unprofessional manner around the widow of our murder victim," Thoreau said. "You left the scene. Moody returned and said you'd abandoned the job. And I couldn't get ahold of you."

"No, I get that. I was—"

"Let me finish, Luke. I asked Symanski what happened, and she tried to cover for you. I appreciate the loyalty. But she had no answers." A deep sigh. "I like you, Luke, but I can't protect you anymore. And after yesterday, I don't want to expend the energy to do it."

"It won't happen again, Captain."

"I had Chief Dyson in here demanding your suspension."

Luke blinked. Wow. This was worse than his worst-case-scenario in his head. "Chief Dyson? Why was he involved?"

"The wife of the victim lodged a complaint, and Moody's report didn't exactly paint you in the best light."

"Chief Dyson can't suspend me."

"But he can demand that I do it. And I couldn't give him a good reason why I wouldn't. So you're on suspension."

Luke's jaw dropped open. "For what? For taking a walk to clear my head?"

"For a Category C violation," Thoreau replied.

"What's Category C?"

The sound of a page rustling. "Violations that have a pronounced negative impact on the operations or reputation of the department or on relationships with employees, other agencies, or the public." Thoreau sounded like they were reading from the policy handbook.

"I didn't—"

Thoreau sighed. "You had a verbal altercation with two members of the police force in front of a member of the public." They cleared their throat. "A member of the public with powerful public connections. If you lose your temper in front of a drug user at Lemon Hill Park, no one says boo. But do it in front of a rich murder victim's widow, and it's another story."

"But a suspension? I've never gotten any kind of disciplinary procedure against me."

"As I said, Dyson insisted. You can go to your union rep if you feel strongly about this."

"I've never even been issued an official warning."

"Ordinarily, for a suspension," Thoreau continued, "we'd ask you to come in and turn in your firearm and badge. But Dyson made it clear that you are not to enter the precinct. We're sending an officer to your home. You will provide your badge and gun to the officer. You will sign a form acknowledging your suspension."

Luke was stunned into silence.

"If you wish, you can ask your union representative to travel to your home when you are to meet with the officer."

Luke blinked. Even if he appealed the suspension, he wouldn't be able to use police resources to do any more information gathering today.

"I can't stress this enough, Luke," Thoreau continued. "Do not come to the precinct. Do not attempt to contact any employees of the department. If you have any questions, either contact me by phone or go through your union rep."

"Big Mike is exaggerating."

"I don't doubt it, but Chief Dyson gave me a direct order. This isn't a democracy." Thoreau was silent. "Maybe you want to refute Detective Moody's claims?"

"I—uh, no." Luke rubbed his eyes. If Justine Blood was right, tomorrow would be a new cycle anyway. "When will the officer be here?"

"We'll contact you when we have a time," Thoreau said. "Sometime in the next few hours."

"Yeah."

They paused. "I have to get to a meeting, but take care of yourself."

"You too, Captain."

They hung up.

Luke stared at the phone. If his throat hadn't been so raw from screaming after he got home from the bar, he'd have screamed again.

He had no idea he'd been skating on such thin ice. That one incident in front of Big Mike could result in suspension. He was angry at that, too.

Luke pushed himself to his feet. For the first time, he was glad that the cycle would reset at the end of today. He hadn't gotten suspended during the first cycle, so that was good. As long as he solved the murder on a day when he didn't piss off Dyson—or Big Mike. And he'd need to rehabilitate his image.

He walked into the kitchen, opened the fridge, and poured himself a glass of orange juice. It felt cool going down. He turned to the coffeemaker. Would he really make a whole pot for one or two cups?

What the hell, the coffee would be back in two days.

As he made the coffee, he thought about his image. He'd been mistrusted ever since he made detective. Charges of nepotism followed by his mother's arrest.

If he could go back further in time—five years—maybe he wouldn't take the detective job in the Sacramento department. He'd put in his application in many other cities around the state. His mom wouldn't have liked it, but she'd be in jail in a few years anyway. It might be hard to have to drive a few hours to see her in prison, but would his mental health be better?

He walked into the guest bathroom downstairs.

Oh—he had a headache, but it wasn't that bad. And he hadn't thrown up this time—plus, he hadn't blacked out. His hangover wasn't as bad, either. Luke silently thanks Kyle for the ibuprofen and the water. He'd only nursed one whiskey the last hour at the bar, which must have helped. Not great that he'd gotten drunk again, but compared to the first cycle, it was infinitely better.

He sat on the toilet, his head in his hands. Part of him hated his situation, but he had to look at this from a positive perspective. Justine Blood saw this as a curse, and so far, Luke did too. But Justine's close rate was obviously due to the cycles, and Luke could use the cycles to improve his close rate, too.

With a start, Luke remembered he hadn't seen his mother during visiting hours yesterday. He *always* saw her on Wednesdays. He sighed. Well, it's not like she'd remember he missed visiting her when the cycle reset.

He blinked. What happened to everyone else when he reset? Were these different dimensions or different universes where a version of himself—and another version of everyone else—were continuing this version of their lives?

He'd have to ask Justine Blood the next time he saw her.

Luke could do more than solve cases in the cycle, too: he could work on his mother's appeal. Perhaps uncover evidence that would convince Zepherine to help her lawyer.

There were worse ways he could spend his time.

III

Two hours later, Luke turned off on California Highway 523 toward Pioneer Mesa, the prison five miles farther. Not official visiting hours, but he could use his badge to get into see his mother. Zepherine would probably give him hell for not showing up yesterday, but he could deal with it.

He exited at Justice Center Way and maneuvered his Malibu into the prison parking lot.

Less haze today. The midday sun was beating down through a clear sky. Luke hadn't thought about wearing his usual tie and sport coat today. His mother would notice. Cross that bridge when he got there.

The line was shorter at midday, and after a five-minute wait, he went through the metal detector. Once again, he'd left his gun in the safe at home—

Oh, crap. The officers were coming to his house. Captain Thoreau had said to expect them in the next few hours—and here he was, about to talk to his mother, a forty-five-minute drive from his house.

Nothing to do about it now. The guard motioned him to a beige picnic table, the same one he'd sat at in the last cycle.

A guard brought his mother, dressed in a Pioneer Mesa Prison's orange jumpsuit, to sit at the table.

She gave Luke a condescending smile. "And here I thought my only child had forgotten about me."

He cleared his throat. "I caught a case."

"Oh, you did? Are you undercover? Is that why you're dressed so shabbily?"

He ignored that comment. "Pye Domino was killed. The real estate developer."

Zepherine smiled and folded her hands in front of her. "Oh, that's big. Is Nancy finally giving you decent cases?"

"Nims, Mom."

"Right, right. I'm sorry, she transitioned—"

"*They* transitioned. Yes, before you were sentenced. I know, you're not used to it yet." He screwed up his face. "Listen, I've been talking with Justine Blood—"

"Oh, good. She's the best detective in the department."

"Right. Well, she's retired now."

"That's excellent. She has time to take you under her wing—"

"Hang on, Mom, let me finish."

"Sorry, sorry."

"She thinks you're innocent."

"Of course she does."

"No, Mom, not 'of course she does.' That isn't a popular sentiment in the force. Everyone thinks you did it. Everyone thinks that makes *me* dirty, too."

"What? Surely Nancy doesn't—"

"Nims, Mom. Nims."

"Sorry. Surely—"

"Say it, Mom. Say 'Nims.'"

Zepherine folded her arms. "I don't have a problem with trans people."

Luke paused. He pursed his lips, staring at his mother's crossed arms. He ran his tongue over his teeth, then spoke softly. "His name was Caleb. Heroin. A couple of the regulars in Lemon Hill Park looked after him, but when his family didn't —" He swallowed hard, started over. "He'd been on the street since May. I went to the funeral; I thought it was the right thing to do." His voice was getting louder, but he tried keeping his tone calm, even. "It wasn't Caleb's funeral, though. They put his deadname on his headstone. They buried him in a wig and Mary Janes. They didn't bury a teenager, Mom, they buried a doll. I saw that kid every few days for half a year, and I stared at that casket for the whole ceremony." He balled his hands into fists, barely noticing his fingernails digging into his palms. "I can't change that headstone. I can't fix his death certificate. But I put away the asshole whose bad drugs killed him, and I sure as hell can call him Caleb." He raised his head to meet his mother's eyes. "And you sure as hell can call them 'Nims.'"

Zepherine stared at Luke for a moment, then dropped her eyes. "I'm sorry."

"Don't be sorry. Just start using their name. Say their name. Get yourself used to it."

Zepherine dropped her hands to her side. Luke relaxed his hands, trying to will the tension out of his shoulders.

"When you were little," Zepherine said, "you used to love that movie *E.T.* You wore the videotape out and I had to go to a million places to find the DVD. I don't know why you loved a movie that came out when *I* was a teenager, but anyway."

Luke knotted his brow.

"You loved that this little boy was fighting for this stupid little alien who no one else understood. And you continued that when you joined the police. Fighting for the little guy. You care, Lucien." Zepherine cleared her throat. "That's what I saw in you. That's why I wanted you to be a detective."

"I'll fight for you, too," Luke said. Why was he saying this now? Zepherine wouldn't remember this conversation in the next cycle. "But you need to help Anton Uribe with your appeal." He leaned forward. "Help *me* out with your appeal."

Zepherine was quiet.

"Don't you think I can do this?" Luke asked.

She pursed her lips, but whether in denial or frustration, Luke couldn't tell.

"I got an eighty-five on the detective exam, remember? Everyone thinks I was a nepotism hire, but I know how to find things out." Maybe not get credit for his work, maybe not play the game. But he knew how to get to the truth. "So don't you think you should help me out with your appeal?"

"I think that's enough for today," Zepherine said. She turned, motioned to the guard, and stood, turning her back on Luke.

Luke shook his head. He'd have to try that differently in the next cycle.

IV

Luke got back into the Malibu. His mother was stubborn, but refusing to help her own lawyer was odd, even for her. He started the engine, backed out of the space, and turned out of the lot onto Highway 528.

Zepherine wouldn't be mad at him tomorrow, though. Tomorrow would be Wednesday number three, after all, and he'd get to try again.

His phone rang—Captain Thoreau.

"Captain," Luke said, answering.

"Officer Pressler is on their way to your house. About ten minutes."

"Yeah—uh, sorry about this, but I'm not home. Maybe he could stop for lunch first?"

"You're not home? Where the hell are you?"

"I went to visit my mom."

"You're at Pioneer Mesa? Dammit, Luke, I told you—"

Luke raised his voice. "My wife left me, I got suspended, and you're giving me grief about driving to see my mom?" He scoffed. "What are you gonna do, fire me? I'll be home in about a half hour." He ended the call without saying goodbye.

Huh. That was a little uncharacteristic.

Oh well. What happens in the cycle stays in the cycle, right?

He thought for a moment as he took the on-ramp from 528 onto the interstate.

Le Bistro Cinq. He'd wanted to go since it opened. And he wouldn't have to pay the credit card bill. He grinned. Maybe this was his chance.

Officer Pressler was parked in a cruiser in front of his house when he pulled into the driveway. He put the car in *Park* and exhaled slowly. Pressler was already standing on Luke's front porch by the time Luke got out of the car.

"Sorry, Officer Pressler," Luke said. "I had to go see my mom. I'm sure you've heard of her."

"I get paid by the hour," Pressler said, folding his arms. "You can keep me waiting all you want. Badge and weapon?"

"Sure thing," Luke replied. "I'm going in the house, grab the gun from my safe, put it in a packing envelope. Unless I can't find one, and then I'll get a box or something. You want to come in and get some water or anything?"

"Not necessary," Pressler said.

Pressler was civil, but the undercurrent of hostility was palpable. Pressler didn't like Luke, didn't like Luke's mother, and didn't like having to come to Luke's house. He must have derived some satisfaction from the suspension, though.

Luke went inside, upstairs to his safe, and pulled out his gun. His badge was in his pocket in a badge holder, and he grabbed a puffy envelope from Ellie's home office before he went downstairs.

"There you go," he said, handing the envelope to Pressler. "You have a good day."

Pressler looked inside the envelope, grunted, and walked to the cruiser. He unlocked the trunk, put the envelope inside, then got in the cruiser without looking at Luke. He started the engine and drove off.

Luke sighed and walked through the front doorway. He

took his phone out of his pocket, tapped Contacts, and tapped *Det. Summer Symanski*.

"Luke?"

"Hey, Summer. Sorry for putting you through all this."

"You shouldn't be calling me."

"I'm suspended, not dead."

A pause. "Gimme a second." A rustling, footsteps, a door opening, an echo of a door closing, more footsteps. "Okay."

"You somewhere you can talk?"

"Now I am."

"Anyway, I wanted to say that I appreciate you trying to cover for me yesterday. I know it's my own fault I got suspended."

"Well, now they've got me working with a temporary partner."

"Yeah. Sorry about that."

She sighed. "It's fine."

"So… look, you're the first person in Robbery Homicide who's treated me like a human being in a really long time." He hesitated. "First friend I've made in the force since Aaron."

"Yeah, well, look where it got us."

"I'm saying, I don't want us to stop…" Ugh. *Being friends* sounded so trite. He sighed. "I know I got blindsided by this divorce, and I got suspended—"

"And you think you're repeating the last two days over and over," Symanski said. "That's actually the scariest part."

Luke snapped his fingers. "Oh—and I found out a reason Big Mike might not want to follow up with Vesper Montpelier. Vesper is Big Mike's ex-girlfriend."

A pause. "Are you serious?"

"Unconfirmed, but people in other precincts know." Well, at least one former detective from another precinct.

"That's a conflict of interest."

"Yes, it is. Maybe you'll get back on the Pye Domino case after all."

"Maybe so." Symanski hesitated. "Thanks, Luke. I'll see you when you're back."

"See you."

And she ended the call.

He walked to the living room and sat on the sofa. The two open beer cans from the night before were still on the coffee table.

Luke shook his head. Is this how he'd left things when Ellie was there? Leaving his trash all over the place, having her to clean up after him after working a thirteen-hour day at the law firm? No wonder she thought she was better off alone. He grabbed the cans, took them into the kitchen, rinsed them out, and threw them into the recycling. A little hard than he'd intended.

Had he been messy like this when he'd lived in his apartment on 18th?

Who was he angry with? Ellie? Or himself?

Luke went back to the living room, opened the browser on his phone, and typed *Le Bistro Cinq*. He tapped the phone number that appeared.

"Le Bistro Cinq." The woman's voice was high, clipped, and professional.

"I'm looking for a reservation for tonight."

"I apologize, sir. We book out two to three weeks in advance."

"It's just one. I'm… I'm only in town for tonight."

"One moment."

The woman put Luke on hold for a moment, then came back. "We do have a single seat at the bar available at 5:30. No later. I'm afraid you'll be limited to an hour and a half."

"That works for me." Luke gave his name and number.

And now he had about three hours to wait before he had to leave for Le Bistro Cinq.

He sat back on the couch, folded his arms, and thought about why Ellie hadn't told him she was unhappy.

V

He arrived at Le Bistro Cinq a few minutes early. He drove but fully expected to take a FlashRide home. His car would be back in his driveway when he woke up.

The host led him to a seat at the bar, next to a couple who were in the new-relationship-energy phase. They stared into each other's eyes, they ran their hands over their backs and shoulders, they kissed on the lips a few times. Luke stared straight ahead. He'd figured out that he was mad at Ellie, and the smooching couple made him seethe. After a few minutes, the couple's name was thankfully called for a table.

The bartender doubled as his server, and she was friendly. He ordered a pinot noir, seven years old, and over three hundred dollars.

Hard to be mad with an expensive bottle of good wine, right?

A tuxedoed sommelier presented the bottle, going through the motions of a well-rehearsed ritual in the crowded bar area before pouring a taste into a glass. Luke swirled, stuck his nose in the glass to get a good sniff, took a taste, and proclaimed it delicious. Like he had any idea what he was doing; he might have been pretentious about food and whiskey, but he knew little about wine.

Another couple sat at the bar for a few minutes, waiting for a table.

The tuna tartare appetizer and the shallot-infused ribeye

steak were both listed as market price. Yeah, this would be an expensive meal.

The food came promptly but Luke never felt hurried. He ate slowly, savoring every bite. He didn't look at his phone, he didn't have a conversation with anyone. Just him and the food.

The ribeye left him stuffed, and he was too full for dessert. He poured the last of the wine into his glass as yet another couple next to him heard their name called for dinner. He caught the eye of his server and made a signing motion with his hand.

And then Calvin Barkley sat next to him.

VI

Another man took the seat next to Barkley.

"You'll love the steak here," Barkley said to the other man.

"I appreciate you taking care of dinner," the other man said, "but I'm here to move the project forward."

"We've still got to eat, right?"

"We've got to eat, not wait hours for a table. This morning was crowded, and I don't want a repeat here. I want to get down to business."

Luke froze. Should he try to get information out of them?

He pressed his lips together. Of course he should. What happens in the cycle stays in the cycle, right? He turned to face the two men.

"I thought I recognized you," Luke said.

The other man looked at him, no recognition in his eyes. Barkley turned as well, then cocked his head. Yes, Luke looked familiar, but it was clear that Barkley couldn't quite place him.

Luke held out his hand. "I interviewed you regarding Mr. Domino's—" He almost said *death,* but at the last minute, Luke remembered he hadn't informed Barkley that Domino had passed. He could use that to gauge Barkley's reaction, perhaps. "Mr. Domino's disappearance. Luke Guillory."

Barkley stared at Luke's proffered hand, then cautiously took it. "Nice to see you again. My apologies, but I'm having dinner with a client."

Luke paused. What would be the better way forward? Continue to pretend he hadn't been suspended and ask subtle but penetrating questions? Or admit he was on a forced leave—maybe as a disgruntled detective—and try to gain their trust?

"I didn't realize," Luke said. "I'm sorry for your loss." He turned back to his wineglass.

The other man popped his head up. "What loss?"

"Oh—Mr. Domino," Luke said. "He was found dead yesterday."

The other man cocked his head. "Calvin, why didn't you tell me?"

"I—I'm just finding out myself," Barkley sputtered, then turned to glare at Luke. "Not very professional, Mr. Guillory."

"My apologies," Luke said. "I thought you knew."

The other man folded his arms. "Keymind's deal is with Mr. Domino."

A click in Luke's head. The other man had been leaving the Domino-Barkley Properties office when he'd gone there yesterday.

"Respectfully, Mr. Wexler," Barkley said, "your deal is with Domino-Barkley Properties. Even without Mr. Domino, we have more than enough expertise to move the deal to a satisfactory conclusion for you."

"Respectfully, Mr. Barkley," Wexler said, a note of disdain in his voice, "I believe you need to let me be the judge of that."

"You've been talking to me as your main point of contact," Barkley said. "And I've—" He turned to look at Luke. "We're having a private conversation."

Luke cocked his head. "I just ate dinner," he said. "I'm waiting for my check."

Barkley glared.

The server appeared and dropped off the check. Luke took out his credit card, but the server had already disappeared. "Sorry," he said to Barkley. "I thought I was quick enough."

"Let's take this conversation elsewhere, Gabe," Barkley said. "You and I can certainly iron out the details over dinner and sign on the dotted line tomorrow."

"I recommend the shallot-infused ribeye," Luke said.

Barkley and Wexler stood and walked past the host stand, stepping to the side of the foyer.

After signing the credit card bill, Luke got up from the stool. Four glasses of wine: not quite drunk, but too much to drive.

The sun was still out—still before seven thirty.

The evening was cool and crisp. He hadn't walked all the way home from Midtown in a couple of years. About thirty blocks, twenty minutes or so. When he got home, what would he do? Go onto the Internet and do research into Gabe Wexler and Vesper Montpelier?

Well—yes. That's exactly what he should do.

But he could find information from the browser on his phone as easily as he could from his computer.

And he could do that in a bar as easily as he could do it from his house.

And the Blue Oak Tavern was five blocks closer than home.

The walk felt good, particularly after so much time away from the gym. Then, three blocks away from the Blue Oak Tavern, Luke shook his head. Why was he going back? There were other bars. Bars that weren't frequented by cops. Bars where no one knew he'd been suspended.

But he didn't know any of those bars. He knew the Blue

Oak Tavern. He knew Kyle. He wondered if he'd run into Justine Blood again. He pushed the door open. About half-full.

And standing at the bar was Ellie.

Luke let the door slam behind him as he stood rooted to the spot. The woman turned—and no, it wasn't Ellie after all. Different nose. Taller than Ellie, hair a shade darker, and shoulder length instead of Ellie's professional bob.

But, wow, they could have been sisters. And a remarkably similar shade of strawberry blonde.

And Justine's voice in his head. *What happens in the cycle stays in the cycle.*

Ellie had been gone for a month. The divorce papers were sitting on his kitchen counter, waiting to be signed. Then what —was it a six-month waiting period? Whatever. Ellie had obviously been planning this for weeks—if not longer.

He'd never so much as looked at another woman since he'd fallen in love with Ellie, but had she cheated on him with a co-worker in Boston?

She hadn't returned most of his calls. She hadn't told him she wasn't happy. And yes, he was angry with her.

So maybe he'd dip his toe back into the dating pool. And if the woman looked like Ellie, maybe he'd be a little cooler, a little more confident. Just see if he could have a conversation without making a fool of himself.

Luke walked up to the bar, conscious to keep a few feet between him and almost-Ellie.

"Evening, Kyle," he said.

"Luke," Kyle said, setting down a drink—was that a martini in a coupe glass?—in front of almost-Ellie. "Kind of surprised to see you in here." He must have heard about Luke's suspension.

Luke shrugged. "This place is still three blocks from my house."

"True enough," Kyle said. "You want the Syrah Cask?"

"Uh, no. Let's do a ginger ale."

Kyle nodded. "Of course." He stepped to the bar and bent toward the refrigerator.

Luke turned to the woman next to him. "Good evening." Oof. Real smooth.

"Hi." She took a sip of her drink.

A horde of terrible pick-up lines popped into Luke's head. Oh, he was out of practice. Maybe dipping a toe in the pool wasn't such a great idea. "Waiting for someone?"

She glanced over her shoulder, quickly looking Luke up and down. "Yeah. She'll be here soon."

"Excellent," Luke said. Kyle set the ginger ale in front of him and Luke handed Kyle his credit card. He raised his glass. "I'm Luke."

"Kimberly." Her eyes dropped to his left hand. No ring—he hadn't put it on Wednesday morning.

"Nice to meet you."

"So, Luke," she said, "what do you do?"

"Ah," he said. "I'm a homicide detective. I've recently gotten myself into a position where I will be a man of leisure for a few days."

"A man of leisure, huh?"

"I don't have a yacht or anything, before you ask."

Kimberly smiled.

Luke smiled back. Maybe the anger was dissipating. This was, unfortunately, the most positive interaction he'd had with a woman with romantic intentions in—well, at least a year.

No, that wasn't fair. He and Ellie had some romance thrown in there in the months before she'd gone to Boston. He cleared his throat. "You live in Sacramento?"

"Midtown."

"What brings you to this side of the city?"

Kimberly shrugged. "My friend lives in the neighborhood."

"I live in the neighborhood too."

Kimberly stood. "There she is."

Luke turned. An Indian woman, about five foot six.

"Hey. Kimberly," the woman said, giving her a side hug. She glanced at Luke. "Guillory."

"Hey, Detective Damanpour."

"I heard a rumor you were let go," she said.

Kimberly's eyes widened.

"Suspended," Luke said. "You can't get rid of me that easily." Yikes, that sounded terrible.

Damanpour turned to Kimberly. "Ready to go?"

"Yeah." Kimberly followed Damanpour out the door of the Blue Oak Tavern, leaving her almost-full drink on the bar.

Luke sighed and ran his hands through his hair. He sat on a stool and drained the glass.

Kyle walked over. "Refill?"

Luke ran his hand over his face. "You know, Kyle, let me close out. I remembered I have a few things to take care of."

He should be at home. Researching, studying, trying to figure out who had motive and opportunity—the bar was an excuse and a distraction. If only he could be in Lemon Hill Park when the murder happened. When the evidence was minutes old, not hours.

He paid the bill and left.

CYCLE 3: WEDNESDAY

I

A GASP.

Luke sat bolt upright in bed, heart pounding.

He glanced at the bedside clock. 12:13 AM.

He fell back on his pillow. He had no hangover. Like the Wednesday mornings before, he felt like he'd had a couple of drinks, but no headache.

Ellie's plane would land in about fifteen minutes.

If you want, you can try to save your marriage. Justine's words from the last cycle.

He knew Ellie had divorce on her mind. She might have had the papers with her on the plane. But he could try.

He unplugged his phone from the bedside table, then saw his wedding ring in the ceramic bowl on the nightstand next to his Von Zeitmann. With a sigh, he slipped the ring back on his finger.

He'd still have time for a quick shower if he hurried.

He got up and went into Ellie's home office. She'd done a

project last year, and Luke remembered... yes, there it was, behind the bookcase: a two-foot square piece of posterboard.

He took it downstairs and rummaged through the kitchen junk drawer. A single permanent marker in blue ink. Good enough.

He sketched out the letters in pencil first, then thick outlines for the letters.

Welcome Home, Ellie!

And in smaller letters below: *I missed you!* The exclamation point maybe was a little much.

Luke ran back upstairs to take a quick shower. Deodorant and a brief spritz of *The Forest, It Echoes*. No bold print today, just a black polo. The cut of the shirt made him look a little slimmer and gave good definition to his biceps. He hoped.

An eight-minute drive to the airport. He should be able to get to Ellie as she was walking from the gate area into the main terminal. If she saw him putting in an effort—beyond cleaning the house the last few days before she came home—she'd stay. Or she'd at least come home with him. They could talk.

He grabbed the sign and was out the door.

The lights were green on his way to the airport, and there was a parking space right next to the walkway toward the Terminal A. He didn't run—he didn't want to be all sweaty when he saw her, but his brisk walk across the skybridge to the terminal was a fast one.

Luke glanced at the information screen above his head: the connecting flight from Denver had arrived at the gate only a minute before.

After another few minutes, people began walking through from the gate area toward the terminal. A few looked chipper, but most looked haggard, no doubt from a long day of traveling.

Twenty, thirty, forty people passed.

Then he saw her. Ellie. The strawberry blonde bob, her

round face and soft features. She looked tired, too, but still beautiful. She wore dark blue jeans and a teal blouse, a purse over one shoulder and a laptop bag over the other.

Luke raised the sign over his head.

Ellie saw. Her eyes grew wide. She set her mouth in a line.

Oh. Not the reaction Luke had wanted. He shouldn't have been surprised, and he kicked himself because he *was* surprised. He thought this gesture was grand enough to—

To what, exactly? Get Ellie to like him again?

Still, Luke forced a smile onto his face as she got closer. "Welcome home, babe."

"You didn't have to come get me."

"I know. I wanted to."

She nodded. Unenthusiastic.

"We haven't seen each other a month. I figured a little celebration was in order."

"The sign is very nice. Thank you."

Luke put the sign down as they walked toward the escalator toward baggage claim. "Okay. Look, I guess it's clear that you're not happy."

"Well…"

"No," he said, stepping onto the escalator behind Ellie. "You don't have to sugarcoat it. You kept delaying your return. I'd be an idiot if I thought everything was good between us."

"It's not you," she said.

"Now you and I both know that's not true," Luke said. "Maybe it's not all on me, but we both know my mom's incarceration has been hard on me. It's strained our relationship."

Ellie was quiet as they got off the escalator.

"They're giving you another promotion at work, aren't they?"

Ellie hesitated, then nodded.

"But you have to move to Boston."

Another hesitation, another nod.

"And you know I'll insist on staying here where I can visit my mom."

"I wouldn't ask you to move."

"Because you know what the answer would be."

"My issue is not just your mom being in prison," Ellie said. "I hate the way they treat you at your job. You're miserable, and you won't even acknowledge how miserable you are."

"Give us another month together. Things can be different."

"Things could be different if you'd get a job in Boston. A place where you'd actually *like* going to work every day."

Before the repeating cycles, Luke might have insisted on staying because of his mom—but he might have moved for the sake of his marriage. But now, he knew if he left, he'd never be able to escape the next cycle of repeating days.

"Please think about it," Luke said. "Our marriage is important to me. Other couples have survived worse."

Ellie stopped in front of the baggage carousel, dug in her laptop bag, and pulled out a manila envelope.

"You don't have to do this, Ellie. Things can be different. Better."

Ellie held the envelope out to Luke.

Luke took it. "I know what this is, Ellie, and you're not giving us a chance."

"The problem," Ellie said, "is that I gave us too much of a chance." She stepped forward, grabbing a gray suitcase off the carousel.

"You're not planning on staying at the house tonight."

Ellie shook her head as she pulled up the handle on her case. "I'm sorry, Luke."

"At least I can drive you home so you can get your car."

"No. I don't want to sit in the car with you for twenty minutes. It's been a long day."

"Yeah," Luke said. "A long couple of days, indeed."

II

Luke drove in silence after Ellie got in her FlashRide. He knew what the future held once he got out of this cycle: he couldn't stay in the house on 53rd Street, he knew that now. Maybe Ellie could buy him out of his half of the house, and he'd have a nice windfall. Maybe move back to an apartment like the one he'd had on 18th Street.

Of course, he'd have to improve his reputation at work. The first step would be to solve the murder case—which was also the only way he'd get out of this cycle.

Wait. Something Justine had said. He'd wake up at the time of the murder. The *minute* the victim died. He looked at the Von Zeitmann watch on his wrist. It was past one o'clock. If he left for Lemon Hill Park, he'd be able to discover Pye Domino's body hours before the anonymous caller. He'd get assigned the case immediately. He could get Detective Symanski down to the park, too, and with the extra hours of investigation—and knowing about the mistress, the potentially jealous wife, about Solomon Vargas, they'd be able to get much further in the investigation. Plus, even if they couldn't identify the killer today, they'd be able to eliminate some possibilities. And they'd do it all while Big Mike was still asleep. Luke could get down to the park within twenty minutes when the cycle reset. This could be his best chance to get out of the cycle.

He drove past his exit and went another five miles south. Luke arrived at Lemon Hill Park at half past one.

He parked next to the curb where they'd found the body and hurried to the covered walkway. He turned on his phone's flashlight and readied himself to see Pye's dead body.

And there was already someone rummaging through the pockets.

"Hector!" Luke called.

Hector Corazón looked up—then ran.

To the other end of the covered walkway. Luke ran after him.

Hector was slow and possibly high, and Luke made up half the ground by the time the covered walkway ended.

"It's Detective Luke, Hector. Stop."

"I didn't do it," Hector blubbered, doubled in two, catching his breath, hands on his knees. "I was trying to find stuff, yeah, but I didn't kill him."

"I know, I know, Hector," Luke said. He slowed to a walk and stood next to him. "You okay?"

"Is it really you, Detective Luke? What are you doing here?"

"Man, you wouldn't believe me if I told you."

"I didn't do it."

"I know, I know. You couldn't even if you wanted to. Someone garroted him."

"He was what?"

"Strangled with a rope. You can't grip a rope with your right hand."

Hector was silent and stared at the ground.

"Now, listen, give me the phone and we won't have any trouble."

"I don't have any phone."

"You have the dead man's phone, Hector, and that doesn't look good."

"I don't."

"Give me the phone and I'll give you twenty bucks. And I won't arrest you."

Hector scrunched up his face, but he dug in his pocket and pulled the phone out.

Luke took a twenty-dollar bill out of his wallet, handed it to Hector, and took the phone.

"All right, Hector. Go get yourself a hot meal tomorrow morning. And I wouldn't stay in the park tonight if I were you."

"You know that guy?"

"C.D.," Luke said. "His real name is Pye Domino. Pretty important guy. Police will be looking for the phone."

Hector hesitated. "Thanks, Detective Luke. Sorry." He hurried off.

Luke walked slowly back to the dead body. He woke the phone up and aimed the screen at Pye Domino's face. It unlocked.

Luke tapped the screen and brought up recent calls.

Angelina, 12:01 AM, 3:03
Unknown number, 11:54 PM, 16:32
Solomon Vargas, 6:41 PM, 2:11

A good night call to his wife, a sixteen-minute call to an unknown number. And a brief call with the man who had dumped his hopes, dreams, and all his money into a failed Sutter Block Towers upgrade.

As far as Luke was concerned, they were all suspects.

He turned the flashlight off on his own phone and took a picture of the call log. Then he tapped the home screen and called police dispatch.

III

Officer Pressler stood over Pye Domino's body. "What time did you say you found the body, Detective?"

"About one thirty," he said.

"And where was the victim's phone?"

"A few feet away in the bushes. I saw the phone before I saw the body, so I didn't use gloves. Sorry—I know that screws things up."

Pressler frowned. "And who is this guy?"

"Pye Domino. Co-founder of Domino-Barkley Properties.

You see their signs all over downtown. I should be leading this investigation."

"Let's not get ahead of ourselves," Pressler said. "How did you know the victim?"

"I didn't. I recognized his face from an article I read a couple months ago."

"Were you meeting him here?"

"No." A moment of panic. How would he explain why he was in the park—and why hadn't he thought about that before? He'd been so excited about getting ahead of the Domino investigation, he hadn't considered how his appearance in the park would look to outsiders. Stupid, stupid, stupid.

He couldn't say he was there to break up a drug deal; he was a homicide investigator, not on Vice. And though he was on okay terms with Aaron Rasmussen, Aaron wouldn't lie for him.

He ran through possibilities in his head. A late-night taco truck? That was an idiotic idea. A friend's apartment? No. He didn't know anyone in the area, and he had few friends.

Would they believe he was here on a drug bust? Maybe. If he said it was to rehabilitate his terrible reputation. That might work.

"Seriously, Guillory, how do you know the guy?"

"I don't," Luke said.

"You know," Pressler said, "forty percent of all homicide victims are killed by the person who found the body."

"I'm a cop, Pressler."

Pressler narrowed his eyes at Luke. "I hate to do this, because I don't want to get the reputation your partner has. But I have a feeling Big Mike will think this is funny."

"Will think *what's* funny?"

Pressler took out his cuffs. "Turn around and put your hands on your head."

"What?"

"You heard me. Turn around and put your hands on your head."

"This is ridiculous—"

Pressler took a step forward and glared at Luke. "You want to add resisting arrest?"

Luke hesitated but turned around and placed his hands on top of his head.

So far, the day was going swimmingly.

IV

The police were certainly in no hurry. He sat on a bench, handcuffed, inside the first precinct for over an hour, then they took his wallet, his phone, even his Von Zeitmann. Then back to the bench, where we waited for a long time before an officer led him to an interrogation room. No windows, so he couldn't tell what time it was, but the station was busier than when he'd arrived. Probably after eight o'clock, now. Six or seven hours waiting already.

Luke hadn't been on the wrong side of an interview table before. The fluorescent lights were glaringly bright. The cuffs dug into the skin of his wrists. Not pleasant at all. This was a misunderstanding, although Luke was stupid for not thinking this through.

He wouldn't be held for the murder, though. They'd find that Pye Domino had died an hour before Luke arrived.

At least Luke had time to think of a reason to be in the park. He came up with different scenarios and explanations. If he'd been thinking straight, he wouldn't have simply driven to the park from the airport; he would have created an external reason to go. A stop at the eighth precinct, maybe a web search of the clubs near Lemon Hill Park—something that would establish a foundation. Unfortunately, his lack of foresight meant he needed to have an *internal* reason to go to the park: one that would make sense to a police detective.

Every cop had intuition, right? An itch in their brains that something was off?

Blaming his impromptu park visit on a gut feeling wasn't great, but it was the best he could come up with.

He continued to wait, hearing the bustle of police business outside the door. Luke's stomach rumbled; he'd had nothing to eat, and he figured the breakfast hour ended long ago. Maybe lunchtime had passed, too.

A detective Luke didn't recognize finally came into the room, setting folders on the table on his side. He bent over the table, opened the folder, and read the first page.

"Detective Lucien Guillory." He glanced up at Luke, a serious look on his face. "I heard your mother's a dirty cop, and I've heard the rumors going around that you might be too. But I never in a million years expected you to kill anyone."

"I *didn't* kill anyone," Luke said. Should he know this detective? "Have we met before?"

"I'm out of the first precinct," the detective said. "I saw you at Detective Blood's retirement party."

"Oh. Sorry, I don't remember."

The detective cleared his throat, tapping the page in front of him. "Your mother was convicted of accepting bribes, although my paperwork here doesn't mention who she took bribes from. Would you care to enlighten me?"

"Why are you asking me about my mother? That's not why I'm—"

The detective leaned forward. "I'm the one asking the questions here."

Luke felt the bile rise in his throat and waited for a moment to calm his nerves. "My mother never took bribes. And she never embezzled any money from the department."

The detective looked Luke full in the face. "Since she was

convicted by a jury of her peers, I don't have to use the word *allegedly*. It's a statement of fact. Now, I'll ask you again: who did she take bribes from?"

Luke was quiet, gears turning in his head. He was here to answer questions about the dead man in the park, right? Was the detective trying to catch Luke wrongfooted, or did he think Pye Domino's death was somehow connected to his mother's conviction?

"As I said," he said slowly, "she didn't take bribes. But if I'm wrong, I don't know anything."

"That's too bad," the detective said.

"Not if she's innocent."

The detective pulled the chair out on his side and sat. "You know, I don't make the accusation of you being a dirty cop lightly, Guillory."

At least the detective wasn't calling him *Lucy*.

"But they've done studies," the detective said. "If you have a parent who's a criminal, you're three times more likely to be a criminal yourself."

Luke was quiet.

"And the strongest correlation in those studies is between mothers and sons," the detective continued. "There's only three reasons people are in that park at one in the morning. One, they're getting high. But you don't have any of the indications of a drug user."

Luke didn't like where this was going.

"Two, you're looking for a prostitute. A cop like you, looking for a little strange on a Tuesday night—not out of the realm of possibility. But you didn't have any cash in your wallet, and you don't look like you'd just had a, uh, an encounter. So we're ruling that out, too."

The detective was quiet for a minute, probably waiting for him to ask what the third thing was.

But the detective got tired of waiting. "Three, you were

accepting a bribe."

Luke cocked an eyebrow. "You just said I didn't have any money."

"And you wouldn't have, if the deal had gone south. Here's what I think: Mr. Domino said he'd bribe you to look the other way on a case, destroy some evidence, what have you. You get there and he doesn't have the payment. Maybe he got cold feet, or maybe you were just negotiating your fee."

"That's ridiculous."

The detective shook his head. "If you were on the take, that explains what you were doing in the park."

"I'm not on the take."

"Then why were you in Lemon Hill Park? We're looking into Domino's financials, seeing if he made any large withdrawals or any large payments. If we analyze your bank statements and find deposits that match Mr. Domino's withdrawal, it won't look good. So talk, Guillory. Even if the story is hard to believe."

Luke put his hands flat on the table; it was story time. "You ever wake up in the middle of the night and think something's wrong?"

The detective folded his arms. "I've been a cop for twelve years. Who doesn't?"

"Right. Like you forgot to lock the front door, or you left the stove on. This year, I've been dealing with a lot more overdose deaths in Lemon Hill Park than normal. And I woke up at about a quarter after midnight and immediately thought something was wrong." He paused. "No. I *knew* something was wrong."

The detective kept his arms folded and twitched his lips.

Luke took a deep breath. "I've got a few contacts in the park. People who trust me enough to give me a little info. I lost one of them to an overdose last month—Earl Shent. I didn't want to lose any more. I knew I wouldn't be able to get back to sleep anyway, so I figured I'd head down there. Worst case, I'd be too late. Second worst case, I'd go down there for nothing."

"So you went down to the park."

"Actually..." Luke paused, and the detective frowned. "I had to pick up my wife from the airport. She landed a little after midnight. But after I—" He hesitated again; Ellie hadn't come home with him. How would he explain that?

"After you what?" the detective prodded.

"After I met my wife at the airport," Luke said, "I kept having that terrible feeling, so I drove straight to Lemon Hill Park."

"You didn't drop your wife off at home first?"

"I—uh, she didn't come with me. Handed me divorce papers." Luke internally winced; the detective would think Luke would have been angry or unhinged. He had no choice, though; if the police talked to Ellie to confirm Luke's story, she'd mention the divorce papers. He'd had hours to come up with an explanation for being in the park—and this was the best he could do?

"She served you divorce papers at the airport?"

Luke nodded.

"Man, that's screwed up," the detective said. "That would have pissed me off."

Luke recognized a trap when he saw it. "I'd seen it coming for a while. Kind of resigned to it, actually."

"So you're saying that your wife just told you she wanted a divorce, and instead of going home and getting angry, or going to a bar and getting shit-faced, you went to Lemon Hill Park to make sure your contacts hadn't overdosed?"

"I know it sounds strange," Luke said carefully, "but like I said, I knew something was wrong. The feeling was so strong, not even the divorce papers could get that premonition out of my brain."

The detective sighed. "Guillory, you're a detective. Put

yourself in my shoes. If a guy gets surprised by divorce papers in a public place, then drives to a park known for drug activity, then reports a dead body, what would *you* think?"

Luke kept his mouth shut. Is this the point he should ask for a lawyer? Or a union rep?

"Most people in that situation would be surprised," the detective continued. "Angry. Maybe embarrassed. Maybe a little humiliated." He rubbed his chin. "I find it hard to believe you weren't pissed off. I bet you're also pissed off that your arrest rate is in the toilet. You've been assigned Lemon Hill Park ever since you got the detective job here, but the overdoses, the violence in that park—you feel overwhelmed." The detective glanced into Luke's eyes. "Maybe a little impotent."

Well, now, that was just designed to push Luke's buttons, given the divorce papers. Luke kept calm.

"Who knows?" The detective continued. "You could be telling the truth that you had a bad feeling about someone overdosing." The detective cocked his head. "I'd bet, if we asked around, that there's a dealer who you can't get off the street, right? And you get to the park, angry about your wife, and you're itching to *get* someone. Maybe you have someone in mind, but maybe you're so pissed off, anyone will do."

Luke folded his hands again.

"So if one of these junkies or dealers—maybe one of the bad guys—gets beat up or killed, there's a good chance they'll never find out it was you who did it."

Luke slumped his shoulders. His explanation was weak. If Luke had been the detective, he would have thought the same thing.

The detective bent forward and flipped a few pages in the folder. "Pye Domino is a rich asshole, isn't he? Maybe he's dealing, maybe he's making business deals that keep your friends in the park homeless. Or maybe he was in the wrong place at the wrong time."

"Mr. Domino was trying to stop other people from using," Luke said, his voice shaky.

The detective drummed his fingers on the paper. "What this report is telling me is your numbers drag the whole department down. That's one reason I thought the murder was a bribery negotiation gone wrong." He leaned back and scratched his scalp. "But now? Hearing your story? Maybe you snapped."

"Snapped?" Luke said. Ugh. He needed to keep his mouth shut.

"You snapped, and Domino lay dead at your feet. But you start feeling remorse. Guilt, maybe. This Mr. Domino, he doesn't deserve to be found in a few hours, treated like another O.D. case. So you call 9-1-1. Maybe you plan to confess, maybe you don't know what your plan is. But after you make the call, you think, 'Hey, I'm a cop. This park is my beat.' So you concoct this story about having a dream about someone overdosing in the park."

Luke looked down. The detective's story sounded plausible —more plausible than Luke's story.

"Anything you want to tell me?"

Luke shook his head. "You've got it wrong. Like I said, we never met before."

"But you said he was trying to keep other people off drugs. How do you know that if you've never met him?"

"My contact at Lemon Hill Park. He knew Domino." Luke leaned forward. "But look, no matter what my state of mind was about my impending divorce, no matter what my reason for going to Lemon Hill Park, I didn't get there until one thirty. I have the parking stub from the airport. It's in my wallet, which you have with my other personal effects. I left the airport at about one o'clock, maybe later."

"Getting there at one thirty still gives you plenty of time to kill him before making that 9-1-1 call."

"I found the body as soon as I got there. And he was killed at least an hour before."

The detective tilted his head. "How do you know?"

"Because—" Shit. How *would* he know?

"Body temperature," Luke blurted. "When I checked for a pulse, his body was already cooling down." He couldn't remember the equation off the top of his head for time of death versus body temperature dropping. Was an hour long enough to tell the difference by touch?

"Body temperature," the detective repeated. "Is that what you're going with?"

"It's the truth." Luke stared down at the table again. "I bet you'll find the parking stub in my wallet."

The detective sat back in his chair, rubbing his chin. "Okay, let's assume for the moment that you're telling the truth. What's your theory of the crime?"

Luke raised his eyes. "You want to hear what I think?"

The detective put his palm up in front of him and made a swooping movement. *Yes, let's hear it.*

"Okay, I saw the body, and I got the victim's phone—" Luke stopped. He'd have to organize his thoughts more clearly. Something *else* he should have done in the hours he was waiting. He folded his hands and started over.

"I knew Mr. Domino tried to get others off drugs. My first thought was a drug dealer who viewed Mr. Domino as a threat." Whew, okay. His pulse had been racing, but now it was slowing. "I found his phone, thinking perhaps he had made a call to a dealer, but I only saw his spouse and a business partner. However, his call log had a sixteen-minute call to an unknown number just before midnight." He kept his tone calm, his breathing even. "I've been a detective long enough to know that when a married man makes a long call to an unknown number, he's usually having an affair." He looked up at the detective, who seemed to take him seriously. "I don't have a theory yet, but I would find the names of the dealers who work the park, then talk to Mr. Domino's wife, business partner, and mistress—I mean, whoever owns that unknown number."

Should he say he suspected that the number belonged to Big Mike's ex-girlfriend? Luke rejected the idea—how would he explain having that information?

"All right," the detective said. "We're still looking into any relationship you might have had with the dead man. You both hung out in the park a lot, which doesn't look great. If there's any financial connection between you two—"

"There's not."

"*If* there's any financial connection between you two," the detective repeated, "you should tell me now. Things will look a lot better for you if you do."

"There's nothing to tell."

The detective closed the folder, picked it up, and stood. "I'll be back."

V

After the detective left, Luke sat for a long time in the interrogation room. At one point, an officer came in and gave him a sandwich and a soda and let him use the facilities. He still didn't know what time it was; maybe the afternoon now, but whether early or late, he couldn't tell. He was exhausted, and he almost nodded off a couple of times, but the uncomfortable sitting position—and the handcuffs—kept him awake.

He'd spent the entire day in this room. His legs fell asleep a few times, and he kept rearranging himself in the chair.

He hadn't asked for a lawyer yet, or his union rep. But that would be next.

They'd find no connections between him and Pye Domino.

And surely the parking stub would prove that he wasn't in the park when Domino was murdered.

Finally, the door opened, and Luke glanced up, expecting to see the detective. But Big Mike walked in instead. He held a blue folder in his hand.

"Where's the, uh, other detective?" Luke asked, regretting it as soon as the words were out of his mouth.

Big Mike blinked. "No idea."

Luke pressed his lips together. Big Mike had taken the Domino murder case in this cycle, too.

Big Mike's grin showed his eyeteeth as he sat down. "I used to think I never wanted to share an interrogation room with you, Lucy." He chuckled. "But I was wrong. I'm kinda enjoying this."

Luke was quiet.

"I gotta admit, you're more clever than I thought." Big Mike opened the file folder. "We had to look all day before finding the connection."

"The connection?"

"Pure Life Gym."

Luke wanted to correct him and say *Pure Life Fitness* but thought better of it.

Big Mike was quiet. "Well, if you won't answer my question…"

"There was no question."

"Oh, yeah, being a smart-ass will work for you."

Luke fought to not roll his eyes and mostly succeeded. "Okay. Pure Life Fitness. What do you want to know?"

"Is that where you met with the murder victim?"

Luke blinked. What tack was this? Luke shook his head and started to say no—but realized it was a trick question. If he'd said no, Big Mike would ask if they didn't meet at Pure Life, where had they met? Luke would be on his back foot right away. Yes, it was childish, but Big Mike's interrogation techniques were often effective.

"I've never met with the victim," Luke said.

"No?" Big Mike pulled two photos from the folder. "Here's a picture of you walking into Pure Life last week." He tapped the other picture, but Luke couldn't see it well. "And here's the murder victim walking in ten minutes later."

Luke tilted his head. The two photos made an extremely tenuous connection, but it might be enough to hold him in jail for a couple of days. "Pure Life shares the building with other businesses. He could have been visiting any one of them. Pure Life has electronic check-in. I'm sure you'll find that I entered the gym shortly after your picture. Did Domino go into the gym, too? Is he even in workout clothes?"

"Pure Life has locker rooms," Big Mike said.

"No matter what Domino was doing in that building, he and I never met."

Big Mike closed the folder. "That's your story?"

"That's the truth." Luke folded his hands on the table.

"As true as you having a dream of the murder victim overdosing?"

Luke bristled; he hadn't said his premonition was of the murder victim at all. But he didn't have the upper hand with Big Mike. "View the footage from the parking garage at the airport. I drove in at twelve thirty or twelve forty-five, I picked up—I met with my wife, I drove straight to Lemon Hill Park. I bet there's a security camera somewhere that'll prove I wasn't at the park until half-past one. And I'll also bet the M.E. comes back with a time of death before one thirty."

"Nice of you to tell me how to do my job," Big Mike said. "Remember, you have a close rate that's half of mine." He leaned forward. "You're forgetting something, Lucy. If the murder was committed before twelve forty-five, you don't have an alibi."

Luke's nostrils flared. Right. He hadn't left the house for twenty minutes after he'd woken up—after Domino died.

"All right, Detective Moody. What else do you want to know?"

He leaned forward again. "I heard you had a theory about the murder."

"It could have been the wife or—" Luke stopped. Oh no. How would Big Mike react to his ex-girlfriend being the fifteen-minute call before midnight? "Or maybe a disgruntled client," Luke finished.

Big Mike leaned forward, glaring at Luke. "You have something else to say, say it."

Luke swallowed hard. Would it be better to feign ignorance or tell Big Mike that he suspected the unknown number was Vesper Montpelier?

He was getting nowhere this cycle, so he might as well see how much Big Mike knew about it.

"Mr. Domino called a woman I believe to be his affair partner."

Big Mike shook his head. "That doesn't align with our evidence." He pointed at Luke. "There's no record on the victim's phone last night of any phone call except to his wife and business partners."

Luke averted his eyes. Big Mike had obviously deleted the number from the call log.

"Look at me when I'm talking to you, Lucy. You're in a world of trouble, you know. Found with a dead man who made a large payment somewhere we can't trace yet."

Luke looked up; that was new information.

"But I think your mommy taught you well. Bribes, embezzlement, who knows what else. At least you do a better job than she did covering your tracks. Too bad your plan to kill Pye Domino and pin the murder on one of your Lemon Hill Park buddies didn't work."

Luke's heart pounded—fear, anger, maybe both—but if this cycle wouldn't get him closer to finding the killer, maybe he'd see how far he could push Big Mike. "Oh, come on, Mike. You deleted the record of the call to Vesper Montpelier?"

Big Mike's face fell—then quickly returned to its previous snarl.

"That's tampering with evidence," Luke continued. "Once a defense lawyer finds out the call log doesn't match the cell phone company's records—"

"And who'll tell the defense, asshole? You gonna do it from jail? Who'll believe you, anyway?"

Luke blinked. "Come on, Mike, we both know I didn't do this."

Big Mike closed the folder. "And I say maybe you did. We've got enough to hold you. And knowing you're spending two days in a holding cell? I'll love every minute of it." He rose from the table. "Lucy—oh, sorry. *Lucien* Guillory, you're as crooked as your mother, and you're under arrest for the murder of Pye Domino. You have the right to remain silent. Anything you say…"

As Big Mike finished reading Luke his Miranda rights, a white blob of spittle formed in the corner of his mouth.

Like Hector Corazón.

VI

Another long time passed before two officers came to lead Luke to holding. Two hours? Three? More?

"Don't I get a phone call?"

"Detective Moody said that's a post-magistrate thing."

Ah. A loophole his precinct rarely used. Technically, they could hold him without officially filing charges for forty-eight hours—and that was only because of California laws. Most other states, the cops could hold people without charge for three days, sometimes longer. And some states were lenient about how their district attorneys could reset those clocks, too.

The two officers pushed Luke ahead of them, down three labyrinthine corridors. He'd never been down this way, and finally they pulled on his shoulders until he stopped in front of a large cell with a man in dirty jeans and a ratty polyester jacket who was sleeping on one of the three benches in the cell.

"Where's Rocky?" one of the officers asked. Then yelled: "Hey! Greg! Where's Rocky?"

A guard popped his head around the corner. "Keep your voices down, guys."

"Yeah, well, we asked you a question, Greg."

"And I'm on the phone."

"So where's Rocky?"

"Charges dropped. We turned him loose about a half hour ago."

"Huh." The first officer glared at the other officer. "You gonna tell Moody we can't put Guillory in a cell with Rocky?"

"What he doesn't know won't hurt him." The second officer dipped his chin at the sleeping man. "Put him in with Bruce."

The first officer opened the cell as the second officer unlocked Luke's handcuffs. As soon as the handcuffs were off, he pushed Luke forward into the cell, and he tripped and nearly fell headlong at the steel toilet.

The cell door clanged shut behind him. Bruce—Luke assumed that was the sleeping guy's name—snuffled in his sleep, kicked his leg out twice, and stilled. Bruce smelled like he hadn't showered in a week, maybe longer.

Luke had no idea what time it was. The cell had no windows to the outside world.

The longer Luke was in the cell, the worse Bruce smelled. Nothing a shower and a washing machine couldn't fix, but Bruce was obviously homeless. And considering that in the first cycle, Luke had awakened next to a toilet full of vomit, this wasn't the worst smell he'd experienced in the world of the repeating cycles.

But this was a terrible waste of a cycle. No phone, no research, no way to move his investigation forward. All he knew was that Big Mike was capable of tampering with evidence to fit his narrative. Maybe *that's* why his arrest rate was so high.

He sat down on one of the open benches and stared into space.

After a while, he lay down.

And closed his eyes.

CYCLE 3: THURSDAY

I

Metallic clanging startled Luke awake.

Was it Wednesday morning?

His eyes focused and his hips ached. Oh, that's right. He was in the holding cell in the Sacramento police department. And this was only Thursday morning. Another day.

And a laugh behind him.

The guard had run his nightstick—or flashlight, or something—along the bars.

Luke stared into space for a few minutes before going back to sleep.

Another set of clanging a little later.

The holding cell door opened some time after that, and a skinny man, about six foot five and wearing a shiny silver shirt and tight skinny jeans, shouted at the officers.

"I don't know what you're talking about. I want my lawyer! I want to talk to—I don't think you know who you're messing with! I've got friends, you know! Friends!"

The skinny man yelled for a while, then he screamed, got

hoarse, and finally curled up into a fetal position on the floor. After a moment, he passed out.

Luke was able to fall asleep a few minutes later.

When he woke up, the drunk man was gone.

The lights came on. "Wakey, wakey, assholes," the guard said, running his flashlight along the bars again.

Luke pushed himself into a sitting position and blinked. The other man sat on the bench, still like a stone statue. Maybe he'd been in that position for hours. Luke raised his hand in greeting. "Morning."

The man nodded, not smiling, but not frowning.

"I'm Luke."

The man narrowed his eyes at Luke, then relaxed. "Bruce Vee."

"Vee? Does that stand for anything?"

"V-E-E," Bruce said. "My ancestors were Dutch and the people processing them were lazy."

Luke nodded. "What are you in for?"

"Being homeless."

Luke nodded again. Technically not a crime, but Sacramento had outlawed almost everything homeless people needed to do to survive. The California statute on disorderly conduct, for instance, was often used specifically to categorize "wandering" and "loitering"—two activities often associated with homeless people in the judgement of officers—to arrest people for, essentially, being homeless under the guise of "preserving the quality of public spaces."

He knew better than to ask why Bruce hadn't been in a shelter.

Vee looked as if he couldn't figure out whether to talk to Luke or not, but finally spoke. "And you?"

"I found a dead guy in the park. They say I killed him."

"Well, that sounds like a bullshit charge."

"It is."

Bruce stretched. "Mine too."

"Ah."

"As if I could simply choose to not be homeless." He stared at the floor. "I need a chance, man. Thought I was gonna get it, but I was wrong."

"What happened?"

"Sol said I wouldn't have to stay in the shelter much longer. Thought he'd get me a job."

"Doing what?"

"Man, anything that would allow me to get off the street would be great. This was an entry-level position at some construction job on those empty towers downtown."

Something clicked into place in Luke's head. "Wait—Sol. You mean Solomon Vargas?"

"What is he, some sort of celebrity?" Bruce chortled. "Sol called me on Tuesday and said the job wasn't happening, and I kind of wandered around in a daze. I missed my chance to get a bed last night, so I made myself comfortable somewhere. And now I'm here."

"You were going to work on retrofitting the Sutter Block Towers?"

Bruce shrugged. "That's right. Apartments. HVAC, plumbing, electrical, the works."

"And they'd give you an apartment there?"

"That was part of the deal. You finish your apartment, you live there. You work on everyone else's apartment, you get a break on your rent, plus you make some money. Not enough to buy a BMW or anything, but, you know, enough not to have to sleep under an overpass."

Luke nodded. "And the city council voted no on the zoning."

"I don't know what happened. I don't keep up with cable news like I should." Bruce grinned; his teeth weren't in bad shape. "Sol said it wasn't happening."

Something clicked into place in Luke's head. "Hey, do you know if Solomon has a relative named Caleb Vargas?" The funeral where his family hadn't even used his name. "Maybe his son?"

Bruce shook his head. "Aw, man, Caleb—he passed."

"I know," Luke said. He didn't want to go into details on catching the heroin dealer. "So Solomon and Caleb—they're related?"

"Sol's sister's kid," Bruce said. "I don't know how close they were, but Sol wasn't himself for a couple weeks."

Another guard appeared. "Bruce Ronald Vee?"

The man looked up.

"You're free to go."

The guard opened the door, and Vee walked out. "Maybe I'll see you around."

"Maybe," Luke said.

Alone in the holding cell with nothing to do but think, Luke's mind kept wandering off. He couldn't remember everything he'd learned the cycle before. He put his head in his hands and tried to remember who he'd interviewed and what he learned. The wife. Veda—no, Vesper, the mistress, Big Mike's ex. Solomon Vargas, who got screwed over by the zoning vote. The business partner who ate at Le Bistro Cinq.

What was his name? Something with a B? Bankman? No, Barkley. The name after Domino on all the *For Lease* signs.

Luke sighed. Detective Blood had been right: he wasn't a very good detective.

II

Another clang behind him made him jump.

"You've got a visitor," the guard said, slapping the baton into his empty palm.

"When do I get to call my lawyer?"

"Soon," the guard said, stepping back.

Aaron Rasmussen appeared behind the guard, then stepped up to the bars. Luke stood quickly.

"Man, Aaron, it's good to see a friendly face."

"Shit, are you okay?" Aaron kept his voice low.

Luke shrugged. "No one's beaten me up yet. And holding is surprisingly unpopulated for this time of year."

"Yeah, well, Captain Thoreau might have had something to do with that."

"Oh." Luke pressed his lips together. In one cycle, Thoreau suspended him; in the next, they were making sure Luke didn't have anyone violent sharing his holding cell.

"I told Renfrow you weren't good for this," Aaron said, "but Paul Broxley has him in his back pocket. I think Broxley called Moody."

"Renfrow. That was the detective's name, huh?" Luke sighed. "You don't know when I'm getting out of here, do you?"

Rasmussen tightened his jaw. "They can hold you for forty-eight hours without charging you."

"And without giving me a phone call to my lawyer?"

"I can call if you want."

"Anton Uribe," Luke said.

"Isn't he the guy who lost your mom's case?"

"Well, beggars can't exactly be choosers, now, can they?"

Aaron nodded. "True enough." He cocked his head. "Why *were* you in the park at one in the morning, anyway?"

Luke opened his mouth, then shut it. Aaron wouldn't believe the truth, so Luke's brain raced. "Man, you won't believe me, but I woke up in a cold sweat, *knowing* that something bad had gone down."

Aaron frowned. "You mean like a premonition?"

Luke shook his head. "I don't believe in supernatural stuff like that. In fact, I think that with all the O.D.s in the park over the last few months, my brain was making stuff up. But still, I couldn't get back to sleep."

Aaron blinked. "Weren't you picking up Ellie at the airport Tuesday night?"

"Yeah, in fact, I *did* go to pick her up, but she was waiting for me with divorce papers."

Aaron sucked in a breath. "Oh no."

Luke grimaced. "Maybe that fed into it. I invented some crazy O.D. story in my head so I could distract myself from dealing with…" He waved his arms vaguely. "But when I got there, Domino was already dead. He'd been dead for maybe an hour."

"You told Renfrow this?"

"Yeah. But he left, and Moody was the next detective I saw."

"Okay, I'll see if I can get you out of here," Aaron said. "Or maybe Thoreau can do something. This is a B.S. charge and everyone knows it, but the wheels of justice spin slowly."

"Thanks, man."

Aaron raised his hand and made a fist. "Stay strong, Luke."

A dumb gesture, but Luke appreciated it all the same.

III

The food was terrible. He didn't expect Le Bistro Cinq or Dae Bak, but the jail food was awful. The oatmeal was lukewarm and slightly rancid. The ham and cheese sandwich at lunch was served on stale white bread with no mayo or mustard: just ham and American cheese. Dinner was a stew with some kind of ground meat and lentils. And it was all bland and gross.

He asked three times to make a phone call, denied each time. The first time, he thought of call Anton Uribe. The second time, he thought of calling Justine Blood. The third time, he wanted to call Detective Symanski, but he'd screwed everything up with her.

Oh, wait. He hadn't seen her during this cycle.

When they finally turned the lights out, Luke was relieved. He'd been alone in the holding cell all day. He was glad that Captain Thoreau had pulled some strings to make sure he was alone, especially since Big Mike wanted someone to come in and beat the hell out of Luke.

He stared at the dark cinderblock wall for a long time, searching his brain for what he'd done to damage his marriage.

Back in the real world, Martha was probably visiting Luke at work and at home, not finding him in either place. Ellie let her friend do her dirty work for her.

Oh, wait. In this cycle, Ellie had given Luke the divorce papers at the airport. The manila envelope was still in his Malibu parked at Lemon Hill Park. At least Martha wasn't wasting her time.

If he could go to sleep, he'd wake up in his bed yesterday morning. But his eyes were wide open.

He'd barely moved all day. He'd expended no energy. That's why his body was so wired.

His cheeks were wet.

How pathetic. In jail, and he had no one to call but his mom's lawyer, his partner, or the detective who'd had his stupid superpower before him.

He concentrated on a spot on the cinderblock wall. Was that a shadow, or maybe a stain from water damage? A dead insect, maybe. He squinted. It wasn't moving. Didn't look like a shadow.

How long had it been since lights out? An hour or two? And when had that been: ten o'clock? Ten fifteen?

His vision blurred, and the distant sounds of the police station seemed to suck out of his ears.

CYCLE 4: WEDNESDAY

I

A GASP.

Luke sat bolt upright in his own bed, in his own house, heart pounding.

He glanced at the bedside clock. 12:13 AM.

New piece of information: when he was awake—at twelve minutes past midnight on Thursday night, or rather early Friday morning—the forty-eight-hour cycle still reset. Good to know how the rules work.

He took a deep breath and turned on his bedside lamp.

Luke had been suspended, then he'd been arrested. So going down to the scene of the crime early hadn't gotten him clues any sooner, and it hadn't gotten him more time to be ahead of Big Mike.

Pye Domino had died in the last sixty seconds, and whoever killed him would leave the scene shortly. Not enough time to catch the murderer. Plus, Luke would have the same problem explaining why he was there. He didn't feel like spending another two-day cycle in jail.

Luke turned off the 12:20 AM alarm and lay back on his pillow, hands behind his head, staring at the ceiling.

If he couldn't go to the murder scene, maybe he could at least work on taking Big Mike off the case. And that meant digging up more info on his ex-girlfriend.

He grabbed his phone from the nightstand and launched his Photoxio social media app. He had to log back in—it had been months since he had used it. Okay—*Vesper Montpelier*. There were three users with that name, but only one from California. He tapped on her account. As he expected, she was beautiful; Big Mike would never date anyone who wasn't magazine-cover-model pretty.

His finger tapped on "follow." There—that would let him know whatever Vesper Montpelier posted. Then he winced; the follow could be traced back to him. He hoped that wouldn't bite him later. Oh well; if it did, the cycle would simply reset in two days' time.

Luke sat up and stared at Vesper Montpelier's Photoxio profile. He scrolled through her feed. When did Justine say they had broken up? Six months? Three months? That was a lot of scrolling. He was wired, although he knew he hadn't gone to bed very early on Tuesday. Running on two hours of sleep or less right now.

There.

Seven months previous: a photo of Montpelier and Big Mike together outdoors. Looked like a nature trail somewhere. Another picture of them—was that a concert? A distant stage behind them, dark lights and thin lasers aimed above the audience. Eight months: a restaurant, along with pictures of their food. A week before that, they posed in front of a go-kart at an indoor racetrack. And one more: they were kissing. Luke took screenshots of all of them.

He'd figure out how to use those later.

Oh—he had an idea. He went to the latest photo in her feed

—a picture of Vesper Montpelier in front of the Sacramento Hall building.

He tapped the photo and typed in the comment field:

Hey, you look familiar - did you ever date a cop named Mike Moody?

His finger almost tapped the *Post* button, then he realized he was logged in as himself. Nope. A follow was one thing, but a comment was too risky.

He walked downstairs. Setting his phone down on the kitchen counter, he grabbed his personal laptop from the end table, then opened a VPN app to obfuscate his location. He picked a connection in Phoenix.

He initiated a new Photoxio account, typing in *VinceBabino* as the username, but thought better of it. The name would have been taken anyway. Finally, he settled on *GreatMinds3036*—the song title of one of his favorite tracks as a teenager, plus the street number of his first rental half-a-duplex in Cordova Ranch when he'd first moved out of his mom's house. Couldn't be easily traced back to him. Luke shifted in his chair, typed the message again, and hit *return.*

His phone dinged from the kitchen.

He blinked. Ellie. She might be expecting him to pick her up —no, that didn't make sense. She hadn't called or texted him in the previous cycles. Had she?

Oh, to tell him she wasn't coming home. Maybe this was that message.

He sighed and rose from the sofa, walking into the kitchen. He grabbed the phone, expecting a message from Ellie, but instead saw a notification from Photoxio.

A Photoxier you follow, @VesperMont98, has posted a new Photoxio Video.

Oh, right: the constant notifications that couldn't be turned off. Now he remembered why he'd gotten rid of the Photoxio app in the first place.

He went to dismiss the notification and tapped on it instead.

A new photo appeared. A club: colored lights, a dance floor, otherwise dark. Vesper three-quarters in frame with a clear drink in a clear plastic cup. A lime wedge. A vodka tonic, if Luke had to guess.

Nothing better than dancing to your favorite songs

And the hashtags: #partygirl #fashionablylate #sactown #clubcollective #bffs

Luke shook his head. He felt old, and he was barely a decade older than her, if the number in her username was her birth year.

She probably wouldn't respond to the comment, though.

He looked at the hashtags again. Huh: #fashionablylate. He looked at the timestamp on the photo: 12:46 AM. He opened a map app and searched for Club Collective. Ah, only a few blocks from Lemon Hill Park—the old Evoke nightclub location.

Vesper Montpelier could be a suspect. She would have plenty of time to get to the club after meeting Domino in Lemon Hill Park. The murder had been bloodless, too, so no need for a change of clothes. And if Pye Domino and Vesper Montpelier had been lovers, he would have trusted her. Maybe enough to let her give him drugs before she garroted him.

Now that he was at his laptop and not on his phone, it would be easier to do a few web searches.

He searched for Montpelier's name but found nothing more interesting than her Photoxio feed. Her name didn't show up on ProfLinks, so he couldn't search her job history.

Luke stood and paced around the living room. He had enough evidence on his phone—the photo of Big Mike and Vesper Montpelier kissing—to make sure Big Mike would stay off the Domino case.

Now he could research other people. Like Solomon Vargas.

He found a treasure trove of information. Luke was surprised that Solomon Vargas was a CEO as well: the company made building materials called Vargastic. Luke made a face: a terrible name. The Vargastic website had a somewhat cute story of how Solomon *Vargas* had created a *fantastic plastic*. Hence the eponymous name.

The pictures of the Vargastic looked exactly like what had been in Angelina Domino's garage.

An obituary for Caleb Vargas didn't mention his real name, his overdose, or his gender. Calling him "a beloved daughter and niece," the obituary didn't give a hint of the Caleb that Luke had met. Solomon's name appeared in the "survived by," but he couldn't tell from the obituary if they'd been close. A search for *Caleb Vargas and Pye Domino* returned no matches—not even when Luke replaced *Caleb* with his deadname, but the web wouldn't likely reveal if Magic Star was the connection.

Solomon Vargas's ProfLinks page showed a man with tightly curled black hair, a bushy mustache, and—was that a tweed suit? His bio still listed his CEO job at Vargastic as current. From everything he'd heard, Vargas had hinged his whole career on this building project. Just because his title was CEO didn't mean he was getting a salary. If he'd had to front the money to make the product, he might very well be in a tenuous financial position.

Vargastic was privately held. No real way to look at its financial information. Not from Luke's home laptop, anyway.

He started a new web search, this one on Angelina Domino. She was on the board of directors of three local charities: an art therapy group, an animal shelter, and a homeless foundation.

Hmm. That was interesting. *Lost Way of Sacramento County.* He hadn't heard of that foundation before. He searched for *Solomon Vargas Lost Way*, but no results. Just to be thorough, he searched for *Bruce Vee Lost Way*. No matches there, either.

He went back to the other charities Angelina was involved with and clicked around their websites but saw no names that clicked in his head.

The suspects were coming together in Luke's mind. Pye's mistress, Vesper Montpelier. Angelina. Solomon Vargas—if Pye had double-crossed him on the building materials or if he'd somehow blamed him for his nephew's death.

Those were the people he wanted to focus on for now. Luke grabbed a notepad from the kitchen and wrote a list. He'd find out where every one of his suspects was at the time of Pye Domino's death.

He wanted to find Solomon Vargas's financial situation. He wanted to know what Pye Domino did to blow up the Sutter Block Towers agreement. Maybe he could get Calvin Barkley to give him that information. He wanted to know if Angelina Domino knew about her husband's affair.

He yawned. He should get back to bed; being out and about this early would only get him into trouble.

II

The alarm went off at 6:15.

Luke opened his eyes. He *had* been able to go to sleep. Maybe it was because he wasn't sleeping on a concrete bench like the night before.

He debated with himself, then hit the snooze bar. After spending a night and a day in jail, the sheets and the pillow felt great. He dozed and hit the snooze button once more.

The third time the alarm went off, he sat up. Okay, that was enough. He was riding a thin line for losing his job, and he needed to be a model employee.

He picked up the phone from his nightstand. There was the message from Ellie that she wasn't coming home.

He showered, put on sweat shorts and an undershirt, and went downstairs. He made a pot of coffee and ate breakfast— two eggs to go with two of the last four pieces of sourdough. Back upstairs, he opened his closet and found the blue-and-orange swirl shirt, though it would be more at home at Club Collective in Vesper Montpelier's Photoxio feed than the precinct. He chose a white Oxford instead and finished getting dressed.

He felt good: no headache. His stomach was pleasantly sated but not stuffed. A cup of coffee, but not the whole pot, so he was awake without buzzing. His head was clear, and he wanted to get moving on the case he knew would be assigned to him.

He backed the Malibu out of the driveway. Putting the car in Drive, he drove down 53rd to Alcatraz Avenue. He looked to his left, no cars coming, and pushed the accelerator.

Thump.

Luke slammed on the brakes.

Oh, no. The cyclist.

That same cyclist was still driving against traffic, going the wrong way in the Alcatraz Avenue bike lane, and this time, Luke *had* hit him.

Well, technically, the cyclist had caused the accident; Luke had started pulling onto Alcatraz Avenue and the bicycle hit Luke's right fender.

Ugh.

Luke got out of the Malibu. The bike was on its side—it had been going fast and had been traveling the wrong way. The cyclist was already standing, though an angry red road rash was on his right knee and lower leg.

"What the hell were you doing?" the cyclist shouted.

"You were going the wrong way," Luke said.

"I'm on a bicycle. I always have the right of way."

Luke felt his stomach sink. The confidence of the cyclist was annoyingly strong. If this had been a car accident, Luke would have given his insurance information to the other driver. As it was, Luke thought the cyclist was at fault. But the paperwork for this accident could be ignored for two days.

"All right. Uh… I'll get my insurance."

"No, man, no. This isn't an insurance situation. I want a police report."

Luke rolled his eyes. "Look, I know the procedure on this. The police won't do anything. This is a civil matter. You want to take up a complaint with my insurance company—"

The cyclist folded his arms. "I'll wait for the police, thanks."

Luke gritted his teeth.

"I saw the whole thing!"

He turned: a gray-haired woman in a white minivan had parked on 53rd and was out of her vehicle. "That biker was riding the wrong way in the bike lane and smashed into your car," she continued. "Didn't even try to stop."

"I had the right-of-way, lady," the cyclist said. "I'm calling the cops."

"All right," Luke said. "Ma'am, I'd really appreciate if you stuck around for the police."

"You know what I think? I think he"—the woman jabbed her finger in the cyclist's direction—"is running some sort of insurance scam."

"Let's not jump to conclusions. Tell the officers what you saw when they get here."

The cyclist had his phone out and was shouting at the person on the other end, possibly the police dispatcher.

Luke walked to the Malibu and opened the door.

"Hey!" the cyclist squawked. "I'll report you for leaving the scene of an accident!"

"I'm moving my car to get it out of the way." Luke said. "Maybe you want to do the same with your bike?" The bicycle was still in the crosswalk, blocking traffic from 53rd Street from making a right turn.

"The police need to take pictures."

Luke gave the man a gentle smile, got in the car, put it in reverse, and parked on 53rd Street at the curb. He called Captain Thoreau and left a message that he would be late. He was glad Thoreau wasn't around to pick up the phone; they might have had an awkward conversation.

After hanging up, Luke stared at his phone and sighed. He wanted to get to work quickly—he had to be there when Big Mike didn't want to take the case. He started to dial Detective Symanski's number.

Oh, wait.

What would he say? That he knew there was a report of a death in Lemon Hill Park, and to make sure Symanski took it when Big Mike didn't want it? Luke shook his head. How would he explain that?

Maybe he could use the accident. He looked at his watch.

How many days had it been without Ellie? Not just the time cycles, but the month of her being in Boston? The Von Zeitmann looked ridiculous on his wrist, like a tiara on a construction worker.

He shifted in his seat. He hadn't registered what time it was and looked at his watch again.

8:26 AM.

In the first two cycles, he'd gotten to the precinct by quarter after eight, and Captain Thoreau had handed Big Mike the case file almost as soon as he'd walked in. With a start, he realized that the reason Captain Thoreau hadn't been at their desk was because they'd gotten the case file.

He didn't have time to think of a better ruse; he dialed Symanski. The first time, it went to voicemail. The second time, she picked up.

"Where are you?" she asked in a whisper.

"I left a message for the captain. I was in an accident."

A sharp intake of breath on the other end. "Are you okay?"

"Everyone is okay. Bike rider going the wrong way hit my car as I was turning. We're waiting for the police."

"So you'll be a while."

"Right." He cleared his throat. "Listen, I'd really appreciate a way to take my mind off things this morning." Oh, of course—the bike accident was only the tip of the iceberg. "Ellie didn't come home last night, and I need a distraction."

"She didn't come home? Is she okay? Is she stranded in an airport somewhere?"

"No, nothing like that." Luke closed his eyes and pinched the bridge of his nose. They were getting farther afield from what he wanted. "I'll tell you when I get in. If there's any case that can get us out of the office. Maybe a robbery another detective doesn't want to follow up on. Or"—he opened his eyes and cleared his throat—"a drug overdose somewhere. In fact, that would be ideal."

"Too bad you didn't call earlier. Thoreau just gave an overdose case to Big Mike."

Luke hesitated. "And he took it?"

"He said he had to finish up a carjacking interview first, but yeah, he took it."

Wow. So Big Mike had only complained about getting the case specifically to antagonize Luke. He said his goodbyes to Symanski, ended the call, and tapped his phone to his chin.

He'd have to do something about the Domino case when he got to the precinct.

III

Throughout the next hour, the cyclist kept muttering that Luke was making him late for work. After giving Luke her contact information, the witness in the minivan went back to her vehicle, glancing at her watch.

Luke, tired of the invective from the cyclist, returned to his car, then spent the next half hour calling his insurance company and opening a case. After hanging up, Luke wondered why he bothered; this cycle was unlikely to end in a solve.

Finally, at a quarter after ten, a cruiser pulled up and two officers in short-sleeved dark blue uniforms got out. Luke didn't recognize either of them, and he took his driver's license out of his pocket and his registration out of his glove compartment. One of the officers, a thin Black man of about forty with a mustache and a strong jaw, walked up to the side of the Malibu.

"You involved in the accident here?"

"Morning, officer. Yes, that's right."

"License and registration?"

"Sure." Luke handed both to the officer. "That woman in the minivan across the street saw the whole thing, and I think she's a little impatient to get the rest of her day started."

The officer stared at the license for a minute. "Lucien Guillory? You're the detective who—" The officer stopped.

"Yes, you got me. I've heard it all. Mama's boy, only got the job because she was chief, and if she's dirty, I must be too." He cleared his throat. "I hope that doesn't affect your assessment of the situation here."

The officer gave Luke a small smile. "Man, other cops get into an accident, they want me to make sure I say they're not at fault even when they clearly are."

Luke nodded. "Do you want to hear my version of events after you speak to the witness?"

The officer turned to glance at the minivan. "Sure." He walked across 53rd Street, and the woman in the minivan visibly relaxed—she'd finally be able to get out of there.

Luke stared through the windshield at the cyclist who was talking to the other officer, a white woman with her brown hair pulled back into a severe bun. The cyclist was pointing at the Malibu and kept increasing the volume of his voice. Luke's window was down, and he could hear everything.

"Somebody's paying for my bike. And it won't be cheap. You can't buy it just anywhere. I go to a specialty bike shop. Don't think you'll be replacing this with some cheap shit you can get at Marks-The-Spot."

Luke blinked. *You can't buy it just anywhere.*

The rope. Luke closed his eyes—two or three cycles ago, Symanski had told him it was a special brand. Not a rope anyone could buy at the home improvement chains—people needed a contractor's license. Can-something. Canwater? Canlake? No.

And the rope had a special kind of core, right? Some special synthetic name. Professional something-or-other.

Then the name of the rope sprang into Luke's head: Canfield Pro Polymer A.

But Luke had to sit and wait.

By this time, in the first two cycles, Luke and Symanski had already interviewed most of the people at the park. If he'd been able to get to the precinct, he could have returned to the office by now and casually dropped the hint that the murder victim was having an affair with Big Mike's ex-girlfriend. That alone would likely have been enough to keep Luke and Symanski on the case.

It took ten minutes to talk to the first witness, then the officer took Luke's statement. The officer stoically wrote his notes on an electronic tablet. Maybe Luke would be at fault, maybe not. If the day reset, it wouldn't matter. Next time, Luke would get his ass in gear a little quicker and be at work before the cyclist took that turn onto Alcatraz Avenue.

The officers cleared Luke to go at a few minutes past eleven o'clock. Three hours out of his life.

That was about the time that Luke and Symanski had returned from the park in the first two cycles. Maybe Big Mike would return, crow about catching a big murder case once he found out the victim was a big shot.

He got to the precinct fifteen minutes later, frustrated and in need of coffee. Symanski looked up at him from her desk. "Everything okay?"

Luke shrugged. "No one's hurt. The cyclist kept saying he wanted to sue me."

"Did he know you're a cop?"

"I didn't tell him. Some people hear that, they get scared, but some people double down and decide to sue the whole department. I didn't want to give him any ideas." He motioned his chin toward the captain's closed door. "They in there?"

"Prepping a report." Symanski picked up a file on her desk. "And Thoreau gave me this five minutes ago. A woman got mugged last night in Red Town. I thought we could go interview her."

"Oh." Luke's shoulders slumped. How could he get Big Mike off the murder case now? "Yeah. We can do that."

"I thought you wanted something to distract you."

"I did." Luke looked up. "I do. Anything to take my mind off the bike accident."

"I'll drive, if that'll help."

Luke looked up and smiled at Symanski. "Yes. Thank you." He cleared his throat. "Any word on the overdose in Lemon Hill Park?"

Symanski cocked her head. "Big Mike's case from this morning?"

"Right."

"Uh, no. I haven't heard anything." Symanski stood up, grabbing her purse. "Ready to go?"

Luke needed to at least talk with Thoreau about the Lemon Hill Park case. As of now, Thoreau still thought the death was an overdose. If he could just stay in the precinct until Big Mike returned and announced the murder, Luke could elbow his way into the conversation, make sure everyone knew that Big Mike's ex had been involved with the dead man, then show the photo of Big Mike and his ex kissing. Luke still had a glimmer of hope that Thoreau would reconsider and reassign the case to him. Perhaps this cycle wouldn't be a complete waste of two days.

"Tell you what," Luke said to Symanski. "Can you give me ten, maybe fifteen minutes? I haven't had any coffee yet." Well, not since the two cups he'd had before leaving his house.

"I guess so."

Luke went to the break room. At a such a late hour in the morning, the coffee pot was off. About two inches of coffee remained in one of the pots.

He could brew another full pot. That would take another five minutes. Big Mike had been gone a couple of hours; would he be back in the next thirty minutes? But Luke was deliberately wasting time, and Symanski would be annoyed.

He dumped the cold coffee out, got another packet of ground coffee, and started a fresh pot.

Symanski walked in, her purse over her shoulder. "You're not done?"

"Coffee was burnt," Luke fibbed. "I had to start a fresh pot."

"We couldn't stop at a Java Jim's?" Symanski folded her arms.

"I'm okay with the coffee here. What's the rush?"

"The victim is waiting for us."

"Oh." Luke scratched his head. Wow, it was so much easier to be an asshole when everything you did on this day would be forgotten. "I certainly don't want to keep the victim waiting, but I want to be on my toes when we do the interview. Right now, I'm a little, uh—"

"Distracted?"

"Discombobulated, I was going to say." Luke reached up to the open shelves above the sink and grabbed a mug with the Sacramento Police badge on it. "I just need ten more minutes, I swear."

Symanski frowned.

"Ten minutes," Luke repeated.

Symanski sighed and dropped her arms to her side. "Okay, look, I don't want to be here when Moody and Babino get back, all right? They'll insult the overdose victim; they'll make fun of you for being in a car accident. I don't need that. How about you put that mug back and *I'll* buy you a cup of coffee from Java Jim's?"

Ah. That was a problem, since that was the opposite of what Luke wanted. If they left before Big Mike arrived, Luke would never have the opportunity to mention Vesper Montpelier.

Or the Canfield Pro Polymer A rope, either.

But the situation was causing Symanski distress—and Luke didn't have the heart to continue. He'd have to come back later and see if there was any hope of bringing the case back under his control.

Luke nodded and put the mug back. "Lead the way, Detective."

As they exited the break room, the elevator dinged. The doors opened, and walking out with smug faces were Big Mike and Babino.

"Oh, Lucy," Big Mike said, "nice of you to join us."

Luke nodded. "Too bad I wasn't around this morning. You like to pawn off the overdose cases on me."

The captain's door opened, and Thoreau stuck their head out. "Moody—update on the case?"

Big Mike grinned. "This isn't a drug overdose case at all," he said. He strode to his desk and dropped the case file on top of it. "I don't suppose any of you know who Pye Domino is. He's a big deal in Sacramento."

"The real estate developer?" Luke saw his chance. "Isn't he dating your ex, Moody?"

Big Mike flinched. "*What* did you say?"

Luke shrugged. "I know Domino is married, but I could have sworn I saw pictures of... uh, sorry, I don't think I remember her name. Veda Mont-something."

"Vesper Montpelier," Big Mike said automatically.

Luke snapped his fingers. "Yeah, that's right. I'm sorry, man. I thought you knew. I think his wife *must* know, but maybe Domino and Montpelier convinced her it's a professional relationship." Luke blinked. "Wasn't she Domino's admin assistant?"

"Where did you find that out?"

"You meet all kinds of people in this job," Luke said. He glanced at Symanski's face. She grimaced, looking down at the ground. "I must have run into Vesper somewhere."

Big Mike's upper lip curled into a half-snarl.

"Come on, Detective Guillory, let's go," Symanski said.

"Hang on," Thoreau said. "Detective Moody, you know the victim's affair partner?"

Luke pulled his phone out and scrolled until the Photoxio photo of Big Mike kissing Vesper appeared, then turned the screen toward Big Mike. "This is her, right?"

"I—" Big Mike stuttered, shooting Luke a withering glance. "I didn't know they were romantically involved."

"Still," Thoreau said. "Any appearance of impropriety and

you'll get roasted by defense on the stand. If they did have an affair, we won't get the conviction."

Big Mike puffed out his chest. "I've already made an arrest."

Luke tilted his head. "Really?"

"One of the tweakers in the park. He killed Domino for his cell phone. Probably selling it to buy drugs to last a day or two."

"Good work," Luke said. "What's the killer's name?"

"His name is Shut the Fuck Up If You Know What's Good for You," Big Mike said.

"Detective Moody," Thoreau said, "I would make a sizable wager that's not his real name, and might I remind you that you're in a police precinct, not a frat house. Speak with respect. Now, *I* will ask you for the killer's name."

Moody furrowed his brow.

Babino piped up. "Hector Corazón. Real piece of shit."

"Is that the way you talk about military veterans?" Luke said. "He was in Afghanistan. Lost the use of his right arm in an IED explosion that killed a bunch of soldiers in his battalion. Piece of shit, huh?"

"That's enough, Detective Guillory," Thoreau said. They walked to the desk and picked up the file folder, opened it, and scanned through the handwritten notes. "Garroted?"

"That's right."

Thoreau glanced at Luke. "You sure it's the same Hector Corazón who lost use of his arm in Afghanistan?"

"Is there a picture?"

Big Mike looked uncomfortable.

Thoreau held their hand out. Big Mike pulled out his phone, tapped the screen a few times, then placed his phone into Thoreau's hand. Thoreau glanced at the screen and showed it to Luke.

"That's him," Luke said.

"How do you know Hector Corazón?"

Luke shrugged. "I work the park all the time. Hector

pointed me in the right direction so we could arrest the heroin dealer last month."

Thoreau looked at Big Mike. "Explain to me how someone without the use of his right arm could garrote an adult."

Babino spoke up. "He could have stood on the rope, pulled it with one hand."

"Is that what happened? Do the garroting marks on the neck support that assertion?" Thoreau flipped through a few more pictures on Big Mike's phone. "Oh, I see you took pictures of the victim's neck. And it does not look like the ligature marks support a foot-on-the-rope theory. You've already arrested him?"

Big Mike raised his head. "He could have done it. PTSD. Wanted to steal stuff off the victim to support his drug habit. He had the victim's phone. He lied to me several times."

"Because he doesn't trust cops," Luke said.

Thoreau threw Luke a warning glance, then closed the folder. "Moody, we're going to release Mr. Corazón, and we'll get another detective on this case."

Luke's heart leapt. Yes. This was the way to go.

"We'll get Friedman and Damanpour on it."

Luke's mouth dropped open. "Symanski and I are right here, Captain."

"I see you," Thoreau said. "But weren't you over three hours late this morning?"

"I understand blocking me from taking the case if I were late because I was hungover or if I'd overslept, but I was in a traffic accident. You don't think—"

"I'm not docking you for today, and that's not the reason." Thoreau pointed to the file folder in Symanski's hand. "You've already got a case."

"But..." Why did Thoreau mention his lateness if they didn't intend it to be punitive? But Thoreau's argument didn't have to make sense; he and Symanski weren't getting the case.

Luke glanced at Moody. A tiny smile on the corner of his mouth. He was annoyed about losing the case, but he was delighted that Luke wanted the case and wasn't getting it.

"Luke?"

He raised his head and turned toward the elevator. A blonde woman in an impeccably tailored gray suit exited, holding a manila envelope in her hand. She walked purposefully out of the elevator, holding the envelope in front of her. As she stepped into the light, Luke saw it was Martha—really, who else could it be? His stomach sank.

She handed Luke the envelope. "Luke, I'm really sorry about this."

"Divorce papers," Luke said. "I've been served."

IV

After Martha had given the packet to Luke and had taken his picture, Symanski took a step closer to Luke and lowered her voice. "Maybe you should take the rest of the day off."

"I'm fine."

"You got served divorce papers. You need time to process this."

"I was expecting this."

"I don't care how mentally prepared you think you are for this. When it actually happens, you're going to find out you're never ready."

"I really am fine."

Thoreau cleared their throat. "All right, if you're still up for it, go take the robbery victim's statement."

Symanski and Luke gathered their things and walked out of the bullpen. Luke pushed the button for the elevator.

They got a police cruiser, and as they drove, Detective Symanski gave the victim's name and a brief background, then she went quiet. Luke glanced at her face: her jaw was tight, and her eyes focused intently on the road ahead. She obviously didn't know what else to say. He'd been handed divorce papers, and he'd been in a traffic accident earlier that day. To an outside observer, Luke's life was falling apart.

A twist in his gut. Not just to an outside observer. Luke's life *was* falling apart..

Every time Martha handed him the divorce paper packet, he felt different. He wasn't shocked and confused like he'd been the first time, he was sad. He blinked—were those tears forming in his eyes?

Sure, when he was at home by himself, trying to will himself to feel something, he was blank, empty. But now, driving in the cruiser next to Detective Symanski, about to interview a mugging victim, he was losing control of his emotions.

His eyes focused again. The cruiser made a right turn into the Beckman Highlands neighborhood.

This was the same neighborhood where Pye Domino lived. Oh—was that the street they'd turned to go to the Dominos' residence a couple of cycles ago?

"What is it?" Symanski asks.

"No, no, it's nothing."

They pulled up in front of a large house that appeared to be the mirror image of the mansion owned by the Dominos, walked up, and rang the bell.

The woman who answered the door, at first glance, looked to be in her early thirties, with light brown hair that touched her shoulders. She wore an elegant cream-colored shift dress and had large diamond studs in her ears. Luke let Symanski lead with the questions. The woman was distraught, leading them to the living room to sit on their immaculate furniture. She wavered between not talking at all and offering a ten-minute explanation to a yes or no question.

"I know all they want is money for another high," she said, looking to Luke for affirmation. He looked back at the woman and gave her a sympathetic sad smile, then stared at a point on the wall above her head.

Luke blinked—he wasn't paying attention to a crime victim. What was wrong with him? Justine Blood had said he wasn't a good detective because he didn't know how to play the game. Now he found himself zoning out in an interview. Had he done this in previous cases—and had it affected his arrest rate? He focused on the victim now, listening.

She'd gotten mugged south of downtown, walking to her car after dinner with another couple at an expensive restaurant in Red Town, three blocks north of Lemon Hill Park. The neighborhood was considered hip but still had more than its share of property theft. "My husband is beside himself. He's promised he won't work late again." He'd been so late that they had to travel separately.

She couldn't describe her attacker. "But I'm sure he was on drugs."

"Why do you think that?" Luke asked, trying to keep the edge out of his voice.

"Everyone knows there are drug dealers on every corner. And that terrible park is only a few blocks away. Why else would he be in that neighborhood?"

To have dinner with friends, Luke almost said. "Could you tell if your assailant exhibited signs of drug use or withdrawal?"

She sniffed. "I don't know. I don't know anyone who—" Then she snapped her mouth shut.

"I'm sorry," Luke said as kindly as he could. "I didn't catch that. You don't know anyone who…?"

Symanski leaned forward.

"I, uh," the woman said. "Nothing."

"No, no, please, finish your thought. It might very well help us find—"

The woman scoffed. "No, it won't."

Luke raised his eyebrows. "If we don't have a complete picture—"

"Because," the woman snapped, "the people I know don't go down to that area."

"The people you know," Luke mused. "Are you saying you know people who use drugs? But they get their drugs somewhere else?"

"Guillory," Symanski said softly, a note of warning in her voice.

Yes, Luke's question was rude, but this woman was hiding something, and Luke would be damned if he didn't pick at this. He didn't want to be a pathetic detective who ignored odd statements because the interviewee was rich or powerful. "*Do* you know people who use drugs?"

"I meant," the woman said carefully, "I don't know anyone who goes to the Lemon Hill Park neighborhood."

"Ever?" Luke put a surprised look on his face. "There are a couple of theater venues right there. Didn't they do a performance of *Aida* there last year? That's only a few blocks away from the park."

"They don't go there for their drugs." Then the woman stopped—perhaps realizing what she'd just admitted to.

"Oh." Luke turned her statement over in his mind. "Where do they get their drugs?"

The woman cocked her head. "Don't be obtuse. You're twisting my words."

But the look on her face told him he was close to the truth. Luke put his hands on his knees and remembered what Hector has said about K-Car: a drug dealer in a shirt and tie. "The dealers come to them, don't they? In *this* neighborhood. And you don't complain about it to the police because the dealers look presentable. They don't smell, they don't look different, they don't bring property values down."

"Guillory," Symanski said more sharply this time, admonishment in her voice.

He looked at Symanski, then back at the woman. What an idiot he was; he didn't remember her name. "I want you to remember, though, that the people who sell those pills here are working for the same people as the ones who work Lemon Hill Park. There's a direct correlation between what you allow in Beckman Highlands and what happens to people downtown."

"Are you lecturing me? After I was attacked?" The woman folded her arms. "Is this the way you treat people who report crimes?"

Luke grimaced. Pathetic, as Detective Blood might say. He'd gone too far. Luke turned to Symanski. "Best if I go wait in the car."

Symanski nodded, eyes shooting daggers through him.

Luke got up and left the house.

V

In the cruiser, while Symanski still spoke with the mugging victim, Luke called Thoreau. The captain was none too pleased with Luke upsetting the witness; they demanded that Luke take the rest of the day off. Luke texted Symanski, got out of the cruiser—Symanski had a key as well—and walked three blocks out of the Beckman Highlands community and ordered a FlashRide.

He went back to the precinct, got in his car, and drove out to Pioneer Mesa Prison.

After waiting in the line and checking in, the guard motioned him to a beige picnic table, the same one he'd sat at in the last cycle.

A guard led Zepherine Guillory out to the table.

He cleared his throat. He hadn't been straight with his

mother before. Let's see how this worked. "Ellie came back from Boston."

"Good. Now she can finally—"

"She served me with divorce papers."

"What?" Zepherine's eyes went wide. "Doesn't she realize—"

"I haven't asked her why yet, Mom. But I expect she's got a great opportunity she can't pass up at work to transfer to Boston, and I'm not going with her."

"Boston? But—"

"There's a ton of public sector work for lawyers here in Sacramento," he said, "but Boston is where the money's at."

"Did she *ask* you to go?"

Luke shook his head. "No, but I wouldn't want to go. I'd only be able to see you a couple of times a year at most. And I think Ellie knows that."

Zepherine stared at the table. "You know, I always wished I'd had a closer relationship with Ellie. She seemed so standoffish."

Luke sighed. He didn't feel like defending Ellie to his mother. "Anyway, I was talking with Justine Blood—"

"Detective Blood? You've been talking with her?"

"She told me I was a terrible detective."

Zepherine blinked. "What? You're not."

"I am. I was in an interview with a mugging victim today, and I couldn't keep my mind focused on the case. I was thinking of another case—one I'm not even assigned to. And I can't seem to remember details."

"You can always write details down."

Luke shook his head. "I can't refer to my notes when I'm talking to a suspect and don't want to push them away since I get all the sex worker and drug overdose cases. No one wants to talk to cops, and if I pull my notebook out, everyone runs away." He tilted his head. "You have a lot of handwritten notes?"

"Of course I do. I had to refer to them occasionally when I was a witness."

"Did you have any notes from the case against you? Like where you were on the nights they accused you of taking bribes?"

"Just because I wrote that certain things took place doesn't mean I could prove they really happened." She gave Luke a tight smile. "Especially if, as the prosecution said, I was trying to establish an alibi. Uribe tried to get my notebooks submitted, but the judge deemed them inadmissible."

Luke sat up. "That could be the basis of our appeal. Not allowing exculpatory evidence."

"It won't work, Lucien."

Hmph. Was his mother being intentionally evasive?

He stroked his goatee. Luke was renting out Zepherine's house right now on a month-to-month lease to a software engineer who commuted into the Bay Area—a two- or three-hour drive each way. He'd put boxes and boxes of her papers and personal files into a storage unit. He could go through those files to find the evidence he'd need to set her free—and she'd be none the wiser.

Hmm—and if the renter left, Winona Mills was more his speed than the Fabulous Fifties. Maybe once Ellie bought him out of the house...

Luke drummed his fingers on the table. "All right. Well, listen, I've got to get back to work."

"I can have Anton Uribe recommend a good family lawyer for your divorce."

He opened his mouth to tell her he'd already called Uribe about a divorce lawyer, but that had been in another cycle.

"A good lawyer might minimize the amount of alimony you have to pay." Zepherine shook her head. "I knew that girl was a gold digger from the moment I saw her."

Luke chuckled. "Mom, Ellie makes five times what I do. She'll be giving *me* alimony."

"Oh."

He stood. "I love you, Mom. I'll talk to you again soon."

VI

Trudging across the Pioneer Mesa Prison parking lot, Luke sighed. Why had he tried so hard with his mother when he'd have to do it all over again in a couple of days? He reached his car, got in and started the engine, letting the air conditioning blow over his face for a minute. He put the car into reverse, backed out of the parking spot, and drove home.

Traffic was terrible crossing the Sacramento causeway, and the forty-five-minute drive took almost two hours. He replayed the conversation with his mother in his head.

Could Uribe use the box of notes in his storage facility?

Maybe. But Luke didn't want to waste time taking the box over to the lawyer now—plus, this cycle was likely to reset. He had a murder to investigate.

And he was hungry.

He shuddered, remembering that he'd gone to the Blue Oak Tavern and never got dinner—and got suspended Thursday morning. Today, this time, he was going to actually eat something.

He got off the freeway a couple of exits before his turnoff and stopped at Jake Dandy's, a hole-in-the-wall burger joint with a sign reading *Since 1933* and with a grill that looked like it been there as long. The burgers were the best in the city, and if he was going to repeat the cycle, he'd eat as unhealthily as he wanted to.

He sat at the counter. The ancient grill was right out in the middle of the back wall, visible to everyone who walked in. A thin white woman, perhaps in her late fifties, stood in front of the grill, cleaning it with water that sizzled as she poured it on. A Black woman behind the counter wiped a place clean in front of an empty stool.

"Come and set yourself down, hon."

Luke sat.

"Get you a drink?"

"You have beer?"

"Bottles. The Twin River Stout is our special this week."

"Sounds good."

"Get you a menu?"

Luke paused. "You know, I've always wanted to try the Southern Dandy." That was a double burger with a Louisiana Hot Link, topped with fried onions and coleslaw.

The woman cocked her head. "One of our most popular items. Fries or rings?"

"Fries."

She nodded and turned away.

Luke sat, his eyes unfocused. He was sure his mother was innocent—but was that blind devotion talking? He scratched his goatee. Was she really guilty? Is that why she wasn't helping her lawyer with the appeal?

He snapped back to reality when the server put the burger in front of him. Oh wow; it smelled delicious. He took a bite—heavy, meaty, and greasy, but phenomenal. He could feel his arteries hardening.

As he ate, he went over everything in his head. Solomon Vargas and his building material.

He blinked. Varg—something. It was related to his name: Vargas Plastic? No, it had been one word. He pulled his phone out; hadn't he found it online before?

After tapping around in the browser for a few minutes, he found it: Vargastic. As he took another bite of hot link burger, his heart dropped. If he couldn't remember the hard-to-forget dumb name of Solomon Vargas's building material, what chance did he have of remembering important things like what suspects said when they were interviewed? If something the killer might have said in an interview in the last cycle didn't jibe with the response in the next cycle?

He finished his burger and paid, then drove home through the maze of downtown streets. Five thirty: the middle of rush hour. The drive took twenty minutes to travel a mile and a half. He could have walked faster.

As he pulled into the driveway, Luke rummaged through the center console of the Malibu and found the garage door opener. As he expected, the Mercedes E-class was gone, and the garage was empty. He drove his car in. Might as well take advantage of this while he could.

He didn't want to walk into an empty house.

Belly full of greasy food, he walked out of the garage, closing down the door with his remote. The Blue Oak Tavern was calling.

VII

"Evening, Luke," Kyle said. "What's your poison?" He stood with his hands on the bar. "Oh—before I forget, we got a bottle of Plum Luck Syrah Cask in yesterday."

Luke sat down and looked at his watch. A few minutes after six o'clock.

"Waiting for someone?" Kyle asked.

"I was hoping Justine Blood would be in here."

"Not a bad place to look for her."

He turned his attention back to Kyle. "The Plum Luck Syrah Cask sounds excellent. Neat, please."

"Good choice."

He sat, sipping his whiskey slowly. This would be his only drink of the evening: he wanted his faculties about him.

Out of the corner of his eye: a black leather trenchcoat.

"Detective Blood."

"Detective Guillory," Justine Blood said. "I wondered when I'd see you again." She looked at Luke carefully. "Unless you've already seen me and I don't remember."

Luke nodded, picking up his whiskey. "I've seen you a few times now."

Justine cocked her head. "Oh. So, uh, how many cycles have you been through?" She leaned forward and raised her voice. "Kyle, give me one of whatever he's having. And put it on his tab."

Luke took another sip and set down his drink. "How's your niece?"

"She's fine." Justine narrowed her eyes. "I told you about my niece, huh?"

"Two or three cycles ago. I don't remember." He cleared his throat. "So that's what I'm here to ask about. How to remember stuff between cycles. Obviously, I can't write it down."

Justine nodded. "Ah, so, we've talked a few times before."

Luke held up two fingers. "Twice. The first time, I didn't realize I was about to repeat these two days. The second time through, you gave me a crash course." Luke grinned. "And you told me you did the horizontal mambo with Big Mike Moody while you were in the time cycle. Though you wouldn't say if he was deserving of his moniker."

Justine rolled her eyes. "Crap on a cracker, I must have been drunk."

"I don't think so. I have one of those faces people think they can trust. They say more than they intend to."

"You'd think that would make you a decent detective."

"I know. Too bad I'm still shit, right?"

"If you can figure out how to get out of this cycle—and how

to take credit for your solves—people will think you're a *brilliant* detective." She rummaged in her purse, found a pen and handed it to Luke. "And you've already said the thing that'll help you get out of this."

"Which is?"

Justine held up the pen. "Write it down, dumbass."

"Why? I won't be able to reference it later." Not like the written notes of Zepherine's in the storage locker. "I could type my notes, but saved documents disappear, too, don't they?"

Justine glared at Luke. "Where did you get your fancy criminal justice degree?"

"Uh… San Francisco Polytech."

"That school is too damn expensive for you *not* to remember anything you took in your foundational psychology class."

Luke's eyebrows knotted.

"About fifteen years ago, these two researchers did a study where they had half the students take notes by laptop and half of them write it down by hand. Which set of students do you think had a better understanding of the material and did better on tests where they had to apply those concepts?"

Luke shifted his weight on the barstool. "Well, since you told me I was an idiot for not writing things down, I guess the group that wrote stuff down."

"That's right. And another study figured out why. Turns out there was a lot more brain activity with the writers than with the typists. Precisely because you can't write as quickly as you can type. So writers actively engage with the material, prioritize information, consolidate it—they built on their knowledge instead of regurgitating everything with their fingers."

Luke lifted his glass again, but didn't drink. "So you're saying I can remember things that happen simply by writing it down?"

"That's right." Justine took a sip of her whiskey—Kyle had

set it down without her noticing. "But you have to engage your brain—don't simply vomit it out onto the page. Think about what you're writing. Think about how it relates to other things you've learned about the case. I always tried to start my two-day cycle out by writing down everything I remember. Then I write it down again just before the cycle reset."

"And that helps?"

"I got out of every single one of the time loops I started, didn't I?"

"I suppose so."

Justine drained her glass. "Want another?"

"You go ahead."

She turned to Kyle and lifted her glass. Kyle nodded.

Justine set the glass back down on the bar. "How are you doing otherwise?"

"Other than these two days repeating? Could be worse. I could be in jail like I was during the last cycle." He took another small sip of his whiskey. "Oh, right, you don't know in this cycle. My wife is divorcing me." He pointed at Justine. "You think my mother is innocent."

Justine shrugged. "That's no secret."

"And you think I have a shot with Detective Symanski."

Justine folded her arms. "Huh. I guess you do have one of those faces."

"What I'm trying to do is get Big Mike off this murder case. Every time he figures out that the victim is Pye Domino, he goes to Captain Thoreau, who kicks me off the case."

"Can you blame them? Moody's got the best close rate in—"

"Yeah, yeah, I know. But he's arrested the wrong person twice now. Once during my first time through, and once this morning."

"You said this is your fourth time through. What happened the other times?"

"Last cycle, I got arrested for the murder. I guess that means he arrested the wrong person three times. And the other time, I got suspended. So I never found out what happened to the case." Luke looked up as Kyle appeared with a new glass of whiskey. "So I also need some advice on how to keep this case."

Kyle set the new glass in front of Justine. She took a drink, then set the glass down thoughtfully. "A good question. You have any leverage against him?"

"His ex-girlfriend is the dead guy's mistress. Vesper Montpelier."

Justine gave a start. "Damn, how did you figure that one out?"

"You told me. Right after you admitted you and Big Mike—"

"Right, right. That name sounded familiar."

"I think I have to be in the precinct when the captain gives the case to Big Mike. He tells me he doesn't want it because it's a homeless person overdosing, but now I think he's just trying to annoy me."

Justine nodded. "Yeah, he's good at annoying people."

"Perhaps the biggest understatement of all time." Luke drummed his fingers on the bar. "Every cycle, though, I have to figure out how to tell the captain that Big Mike was involved with a potential suspect."

Justine narrowed her eyes. "How confident are you that Vesper is a real suspect?"

"She's a definite possibility." He counted on his fingers. "First of all, she was in the area when Domino was killed. And secondly, our victim paid for her apartment and maybe won't anymore."

"A fairly weak motive."

Luke scratched his nose. "Maybe he wouldn't leave his wife for her. That's a motive."

"Gotta be more than a maybe. Does she have a record? A history of assault?"

Luke was silent.

"Oh, you've got to be kidding me. You don't know? Go back to work and get everything you can on her. Find out what you're dealing with."

"But it's not my case anymore."

"You've already been suspended. And you said you went to jail. So what happened? The cycle reset. You've got your job back and you're out of jail, right? It doesn't matter what your captain does. The cycle will reset. Get the info you need."

"And write it down."

Justine took another drink of whiskey, finishing half of it in one gulp.

Luke shifted in his seat. "So can I ask you—do you know what happens to all the other people?"

Justine blinked. "The other people?"

"Well, yeah. When I loop back to the minute of the murder, what happens to everyone else? What happens to *me*? Are there three parallel universes out there? One where I got suspended, one where I'm in jail awaiting arraignment on murder charges?"

Justine laughed. "I've never thought about that before." She downed the rest of her whiskey.

"Want another?"

"Sure. Not like I have to work tomorrow." She looked at Luke out of the corner of her eye. "But you, on the other hand, have work to do. Maybe you should head back and start writing things down."

"You're right." Luke stood from the stool and stretched his arms above his head. He signed in the air to Kyle, who nodded and stepped to the cash register. "Thanks, Detective Blood."

She shook her head. "I'm retired—"

"I know. But I can't call you *Justine* yet." Luke smiled. "I'll see you in a day or two."

"And I won't remember a thing."

CYCLE 4: THURSDAY

I

Luke's alarm went off at six fifteen. He tapped the snooze button and sat up in bed. He looked at the bedside table. A notebook, ten pages taken up by everything he could remember about the case. He'd stayed up until midnight trying to remember everything he could.

Suddenly, a name popped into his head: *Brev*. The receptionist at Domino-Barkley Properties, who wanted to move on to bigger and better things. He flipped a couple of pages until he found where he'd written things he remembered Calvin Barkley saying. He scrawled *receptionist = Brev* in the margin. His brain was whirring, so he got up.

He should have gotten up earlier and been at the precinct with a few hours to himself, where he could have dug into the records of everyone involved with the Pye Domino investigation. He hurried into the bathroom and took a quick shower, threw clothes on, grabbed a granola bar on his way out the door, and made it out to the driveway—where he realized he had parked in the garage.

Yeah, he hadn't written *that* down.

He went back in the house, opened the garage, and drove to the precinct. He left much earlier. No cyclist to hit today.

A shade past seven. He'd have an hour to himself, give or take.

He logged into the state criminal records system and searched for *Vesper Montpelier.* She'd lived in California all her life. A drunk and disorderly at Calabasas University ten years before.

Oh, and look at that. An arrest three years ago. At a dive bar in South Sacramento. Arrested with two other people who were charged with battery. The other two got the weekend in jail, sentenced to thirty days, sentences suspended upon completion of an anger management course and a year's probation.

But the charges against Vesper Montpelier had been dropped.

Maybe that was when she'd been dating Big Mike, and maybe he pulled some strings. Wouldn't be the first time a cop had asked for a favor.

He noted her contact information. Address in Kadema Gardens, like he'd seen on the real estate paperwork when he and Symanski had gone through Pye Domino's home office. And a phone number, which he scribbled down on the notepad in front of him.

He picked up the phone, but it was too early to call her.

Luke searched for Solomon Vargas in the database. Six years ago, a disorderly conduct charge—Luke suspected Vargas had been arrested for being homeless. He frowned and looked at the name of the arresting officer: it was Pressler, the cop who'd been onsite at the murder scene.

Vargas had been arrested for nothing violent, but Luke knew from experience how disorderly conduct was often interpreted by juries and laypeople. The cards had been stacked against him, and he'd come through the experience with a job and a dream. He'd started his own company, created building materials to help other homeless people, and his plans were yanked from him.

Luke would have been pissed if that had happened to him.

And there was the matter of Caleb Vargas, Solomon's nephew. Did his death have anything to do with Pye Domino?

"You're in early."

Luke jumped in his chair. Captain Thoreau. He looked at his watch: a little past seven forty-five.

"You start the coffee?"

"My apologies, Captain. I was going to start it, but I figured I'd get caught up on some paperwork first. Next thing I know, you're in here, scaring the pants off me."

Thoreau laughed, a touch of nervousness in their voice. "All right, I've got a call. If you start the coffee and you have it in your worker-bee heart to pour me a mug, I'd be eternally grateful."

Grateful enough to give the Domino case back to Luke? No, not a chance.

Thoreau opened their office door, then turned and addressed Luke. "So you're okay today?"

Luke blinked. "Captain?"

"After what happened yesterday." What had happened the day before? Oh, right; he'd been served divorce papers in the office.

"I'm fine, Captain. The divorce was something I'd been—"

"Not that," Captain Thoreau said sharply. "I need to address your treatment of Alannah Zimmer."

Luke tilted his head. Alannah Zimmer?

"The mugging victim you and Symanski interviewed yesterday."

Aha. Something he *hadn't* written in his notes: insulting the mugging victim and lecturing her about classism. That's why the captain sounded nervous: they needed to admonish him about his behavior the day before. He sucked in air through his teeth. "I'm sorry about that. I was unprofessional. First thing, I'll contact the victim and apologize."

"She, understandably, doesn't want to talk to you. I've already dealt with it." Thoreau crossed their arms. "And don't think coming in and doing work early is going to magically fix everything. You left a big mess for Symanski to clean up. You apologize to anyone, apologize to her."

"Yes, Captain."

Thoreau paused. "I know divorce is hard, Guillory. Go get yourself to a therapist before you take your frustration out on anyone else."

Thoreau turned, went into their office, and closed the door.

Luke sat back in his chair.

He hadn't remembered the mugging victim's name. That was the hallmark of a bad detective. He had to learn to get better if he was going to rehabilitate his image. And if he was going to escape the cycle.

Oh—but Zimmer had implied there were people in the rich Beckman Highlands neighborhood who used drugs. Maybe the same drugs that the homeless in Lemon Hill Park did. The Magic Star dealer—K-Car, right?—worked in both areas.

Maybe Aaron could help connect the dots. He dialed Aaron's cell phone.

Three rings.

"All right, who are you, and why are you at Luke's desk?" Aaron said when he answered.

"Uh—sorry?"

"It's not even eight o'clock. You never roll in before eight."

"Oh. Well, I'm doing some research. Wanted to be in before anyone else got here."

Aaron chuckled. "That sounds suspiciously ambitious. Or that Thoreau's got you on a short leash these days."

"Maybe a little of both." Luke couldn't help but grin. "Listen, we had a homicide a couple nights ago."

"Man, I heard. Pye Domino, right?"

"Yeah, Lemon Hill Park. And I heard—"

"Hang on," Aaron said. "You're not working the case, are you?"

"Well, Big Mike was assigned to the case, but he used to date one of the suspects."

"Right, Friedman and Damanpour got it."

News traveled fast. "Well, Big Mike arrested someone who physically could not have committed the murder, and I want to make sure—"

"Coloring outside the lines in the name of justice," Aaron said. "I don't think I can help you, but I haven't seen you in a while. Tell you what—let's meet for coffee."

"Uh, I'm a little busy this morning."

"You can make time."

Luke grimaced. "Yeah, sure. It'll be good to see you too. Java Jim's on 15th?"

"Let's do Basilica Brews."

Luke hesitated. That would be a ten-block walk. Or a drive, and parking in that area was terrible. "I'm not sure I can get away for that long."

"You got in early, right? I'll have you back in thirty minutes." A slight pause. "I insist."

II

The midtown location of Basilica Brews was in the shadow of the Basilica of the Beloved Sacrament on 20th Street. Luke ordered an iced coffee and sat at a small round table with a fake marble top. The coffee shop was half full of people sitting and working on their laptops, and the coffee line stretched to about ten people, almost at the front door.

Aaron walked through the door. His gray eyes darted back and forth, taking in the entire interior. His eyes passed over Luke, taking an overview of the rest of the shop. His shoulders relaxed, and he took a seat at the small table across from Luke.

"Good to see you again, man."

Luke took a sip from his iced coffee. "Can I get you anything?"

"No, I'm good." He ran a hand over his face. "Look, the reason I asked you to come here is that you were calling me on your work phone."

Luke's brow furrowed.

"You were soliciting information from me on a case that you weren't on. That's not smart, Luke."

"Oh."

"I don't think we've got recording devices on the phones, but Sacramento wouldn't be the first police department in the country to record their officers."

"So why not meet at Java Jim's?"

"Because that place is crawling with other cops." Another glance over his shoulder, then Aaron leaned forward, elbows on the table. "Now that I'm reasonably sure we're not being recorded or watched, what can I help with?"

"You remember that dealer, K-Car?" Luke lowered his voice. "The one who got the heroin dealer out of Lemon Hill Park?"

"He works for tips," Aaron said with a smile.

Luke narrowed his eyes. "What?"

"Sorry—that's something we say in Vice. Magic Star users have their fingertips turn a slight shade of magenta. If you're not looking for it, you might not notice. So we say the Magic Star dealers work for tips—the fingertips that turn color."

"You'd think an E.T. joke would work better." Luke held a finger up. *"Elliott."*

Now it was Aaron's turn to look confused.

"E.T.? Movie from, I don't know, the early eighties."

"Before my time."

"Mine too." Luke cleared his throat; he didn't want to go into how he and his mom would watch the video when he was little. "Okay—so I'm pretty sure Pye Domino's Magic Star dealer worked in Beckman Highlands, but Domino's body was found in Lemon Hill Park. After the heroin dealer in Lemon Hill Park got arrested, do you think K-Car expanded his territory?"

Aaron straightened. "I wouldn't put it past him." He tilted his head. "But most heroin users won't switch to Magic Star right away."

"No, but if K-Car isn't competing with a heroin dealer, and if he's the first one in there…"

"Yeah, yeah, I can see that."

"Can you get me a meeting with K-Car? If he was in Lemon Hill Park on Tuesday night, maybe he saw someone with Pye Domino."

Aaron shook his head. "I'm not setting up a meeting for a case you're not assigned."

"No problem," Luke said. "I think K-Car may be involved in a robbery I was assigned yesterday. A woman who lives in Beckman Highlands but was attacked near Lemon Hill Park."

Aaron exhaled. "You're not stretching the truth, are you?"

"I don't think so." Luke tapped the side of his cup thoughtfully. "The robbery victim is hiding something. She has friends who use drugs. Maybe K-Car has information."

"A fishing expedition."

"Didn't you say he helps the cops out?"

"He's an informant from time to time, although I'm starting

to suspect it's only when he wants to get his competition in trouble."

"Does he have a non-street name?"

"Ashton Carruthers."

"Wait—Lincoln Carruthers' kid?"

"Yep."

"The state senator from L.A., right?"

"Chair of both the housing and the military committees. His kid came to help out in his office one year and never left. He's got a condo in midtown, a lowered BMW, and so much clout with the cops, he might as well have diplomatic immunity."

"Does he have a reputation for violence, anything like that?"

Aaron laughed. "Better than that. He's got the local HOAs in his back pocket."

Luke furrowed his brow.

"Some drug dealers, you stiff 'em on payment, or you try to rip 'em off, they'll break your legs. K-Car, he looks like such a weakling, some of his rich clients think they can get away with ripping him off."

"And he doesn't break their legs?"

Aaron sat back. "This one rich guy, one of the tech bros from East Brannen Hills, he figured he'd go over K-Car's head and get his Magic Star directly from K-Car's supplier. Next day, he finds his mailbox on the lawn and a thousand-dollar fine from his HOA. The next day, he walks out to his garage and finds it wide open. His car is parked on the street, leaking oil. Another thousand-dollar fine. Gets home from work that day and his garbage cans are in front of his privacy gate."

"Let me guess, another thousand-dollar fine?" Luke chuckled.

"Gets a letter the next week that his house color is out of compliance, and he has five days to paint it an approved color or rack up more fines every day. He checks the bylaws, and sure enough, his color is out of compliance. In a panic, he calls up every house painting company he can. Only one can do it in the time frame he has, and the price is *exorbitant*. They get on site, and the head painting guy walks up to him and insists on payment up front. The homeowner says, 'Don't you know who I am?' And the painter says, 'Yeah. You're the one who can't pay K-Car per your agreement.' Never had another issue with on-time payment after that."

"So K-Car's not the kind who'd garrote a client he had a disagreement with."

"His method of strangulation is only with the red tape of bureaucracy. Maybe it'll land him on the business end of a stolen .38 one day, but he and his family have way too much power right now."

"So how can I talk to him?"

Aaron scratched his head then sighed. "He works in Beckman Highlands on Tuesdays and Thursdays."

Luke blinked. "He doesn't stand on a corner in that fancy neighborhood, does he? He goes to his clients?"

"Beckman Highlands School is a K-to-eight. They start early on Thursdays—a 'zero class,' they call it. Jane drops little Timmy off before her husband Jack leaves for work, and K-Car delivers to all the Jacks who need a little something to get through the week. About an hour later, all the Jacks have left for work, then K-Car goes back and sells pills to all the stay-at-home Janes who *also* need a little something to get through the week. He just bought himself a silver Jaguar."

Luke shook his head. "I'm in the wrong business."

"K-Car does the evening commute too. He sells to Jane when Jack is taking little Timmy to soccer practice. I can't set up a meeting, but if you show up in Beckman Highlands this afternoon, you might find him." Aaron stood. "Now, if you'll excuse me, I need to get back to work." He clapped Luke on the shoulder and walked out the door.

Luke stood and moved toward the door, stopped, then got

back in line. He finished his iced coffee just as the person ahead of him finished their order.

"Welcome to Basilica," the barista said. "What can I get you?"

"Medium iced blended cappuccino," Luke said. "Two pumps of hazelnut."

III

Luke walked out of Basilica Brews back to the precinct. It was almost ten o'clock now, late enough to call Vesper. She might be at work, but if the database system had given Luke her cell number, maybe she'd pick up when he called.

He turned things over in his head. What would he say to her? If she'd gotten Domino involved in drugs, she might be more willing to give up information on her dealer to stay out of trouble. Or maybe she'd think Big Mike would keep her shielded from legal consequences.

Back in the bullpen, there was no sign of Big Mike or Vince Babino. Summer Symanski sat at her desk, staring intently at her computer screen and typing. Luke set the frozen cappuccino in front of her.

Symanski looked up. "What's this?"

"A small and insufficient way to apologize for my behavior with…" Luke searched his mind for the mugging victim's name. "With Anna Zimmer."

Symanski crossed her arms and sat back in her chair. "Alannah Zimmer."

Luke cursed softly under his breath. "Of course. Alannah Zimmer."

Silence.

"Well?" Symanski asked.

Oh. The apology. Luke took a breath. "I'm sorry for the way

I acted with Ms. Zimmer. I put you in a terrible situation, and it won't happen again."

"And how will you make it up to me?"

"Well, there's the frozen cappuccino."

Symanski cocked an eyebrow.

"And I'll..." Luke's mind raced. "I'll do all your paperwork next week." As the words left his mouth, he felt bad about making the offer when he wouldn't actually follow through.

"The whole week? I guess you *must* be feeling bad about it." Symanski grabbed the drink and took a sip, and tilted her head, looking at the side of the plastic cup. "Oh, you went all the way to the good place."

"Plus, two pumps hazelnut."

"You remembered I like my drink with two pumps of hazelnut syrup, but you can't remember the name of our mugging victim?"

"I guess not. Any chance you'd believe I'm working on getting better?"

Symanski leaned forward, elbows on the desk. "Don't ever do that shit again, Luke."

"I won't," he said quickly.

"All right." She took another drink from the frozen cappuccino, shook her head, and—was that a hint of a smile? "Good thing you went to Basilica. The Java Jim's drink doesn't cut it for an apology." She took the top form off the stack of papers in front of her, then slid the rest of the papers onto Luke's desk. "There you go. You can get a head start on these."

"Any leads on the mugging case?"

"No."

Luke rubbed his goatee. "You know, I bet Alannah Zimmer knows the dealer of Magic Star in her neighborhood."

"She wasn't *in* her neighborhood when she was mugged. And chances are, the perpetrator was a drug user, not a drug dealer."

"But," Luke said, "I talked with Aaron Rasmussen."

Symanski's brow furrowed. "Your friend from Vice?"

"Yes." Luke leaned forward. "The dealer is an informant. The son of a politician. He thinks he's untouchable, and Aaron said he only informs on dealers when he wants to take their territory. Like he did with that heroin dealer last month."

"Great. So Sacramento P.D. is doing his work for him."

"Maybe," Luke conceded. "But it's worth checking if K-Car—"

"Sorry—did you say 'K-Car'?"

"That's his street name."

Symanski rolled her eyes.

Luke pressed on. "K-Car is great at working the families who live in Beckman Highlands. Because the heroin dealer in Lemon Hill Park got arrested a few weeks ago, Vice thinks K-Car might have expanded his Magic Star distribution there."

"Into Lemon Hill Park?" Symanski asked. "Are you insane?"

"Only one way to find out. Alannah Zimmer is hiding something, and K-Car might know what."

Symanski narrowed her eyes. "Okay, that *can't* be the reason you want to talk to this K-Car person."

Luke cleared his throat. "Well, we know Vesper Montpelier is a user of Magic Star, and that she's bought from the dealer in Beckman Highlands *and* she's frequented Lemon Hill Park."

"We do? When did we find that out?"

"I—uh, talked to Vesper's old boss." Ah, crap, that was in a previous cycle. Still, it was true. "She got fired for falling asleep on the job. Calvin Barkley strongly implied she was high on Magic Star when he caught her." Not exactly the way he'd explained it, but good enough for Luke's purposes.

Symanski chuckled. "So—you get Big Mike kicked off the case because he used to date the dead guy's mistress, and now you want to get her involved in this mugging investigation? Do you think she fenced Zimmer's valuables or something?"

Luke shrugged. "I want to go where the evidence points. I doubt Friedman and Damanpour asked her the right questions."

Symanski took another drink of her frozen cappuccino. "You're working an angle to get back on that murder case. You think if you can solve a rich guy's murder, you'll start fixing your reputation."

"I just want to see what K-Car knows. And one of his top customers can give us info."

She still looked skeptical.

"We don't have any other leads, right?"

Symanski exhaled loudly. "Fine, let's put the squeeze on Big Mike's ex. That'll piss him off." She turned to her computer. "Now, let's see where she works."

IV

The office park of American River Realtors was a set of two-story office buildings across Exposition Parkway from CalExpo. The vast expanse of solar-panel-covered asphalt parking lots contrasted with the tree-lined streets of brutalist-architected office buildings on the north side of the parkway.

The realty company was on the ground floor, and as they entered the office, with its charcoal gray carpet and light gray cubicles, Luke had a glimmer of gratitude that he wasn't stuck staring at these sterile walls all day. He was helping people get closure. Usually, for his assignments anyway, the victims' friends and families thought the police didn't care. Half the time, Luke couldn't give the victims' loved ones any closure. But half the time, he could.

"Vesper Montpelier?" Symanski said next to Luke, and her voice was so confident and firm that Luke jumped.

The receptionist looked up. "Yes?"

Symanski pulled out her badge. "Is there somewhere we can talk?"

"I—I, uh, can't leave my desk. I need coverage."

"We'll give you time to find someone."

"Can this wait until my lunch break?"

Symanski paused. "I'm sorry we're bothering you again, but I'm afraid we can't wait."

Montpelier's brow furrowed. "Again? I don't remember you."

Luke piped up. "Not us, but Sacramento P.D. I believe two of our detectives contacted you yesterday?"

"Uh… no. Should I know what you're talking about?"

"Bobby Friedman? Minha Damanpour? Those names ring a bell?"

Montpelier shook her head.

Symanski gave Luke a sideways glance.

"We're here to discuss a robbery," Luke said. "Alannah Zimmer was—"

"Alannah?"

"You know her?"

"I worked for a temp agency late last year, and they assigned me to cover for her admin who was on maternity leave. Vision Care Systems over in Cordoba Ranch. I was there for about three months."

Luke nodded. He'd done his research into Vesper's criminal record, but, he realized, he'd neglected to research her job history. Not remembering victims' names, not thoroughly researching suspects—no wonder Thoreau gave the high-profile cases to Big Mike and Vince Babino.

"Alannah was robbed two nights ago," Luke continued, "and she believes the assailant was someone who frequently purchased Magic Star at Lemon Hill Park."

Montpelier nodded, the muscles in her neck tense. "Okay."

She picked up the phone. "I'll get coverage at the desk. Give me a minute."

Symanski and Luke took a step back and let Montpelier talk on the phone. When she set the receiver back on its cradle, her hand was shaking.

"I got coverage," she said.

A moment later, a young man in a shirt and tie walked up to the desk and nodded at Montpelier, who rose.

"There's a coffee shop in the next building," she said.

Symanski and Luke followed Montpelier, who walked stiffly out of the office. Across the plaza, a Java Jim's was on the ground floor of another office building.

The Java Jim's was empty of customers, and they sat at a small round table by the glass doors. Montpelier glanced around.

"We're trying to find who attacked Ms. Zimmer," Luke said. "Perhaps she was in the wrong place at the wrong time, but we need to determine if the Magic Star dealer who sells in Beckman Highlands is targeting his high-value clients for additional ways to get money."

Montpelier looked confused.

"Look, Vesper, we know you left your last job. One of the co-owners says you had a problem with Magic Star."

Montpelier crossed her arms.

Hmm. Luke might be losing her. Maybe bringing in the big guns would work. "Where were you Tuesday night, around midnight?"

Vesper was quiet.

Luke pulled out his phone. "You want me to bring up your Photoxio feed?"

"Yeah, okay, I was at Club Collective."

"When did you get there?"

"Around eleven. And I left at, I don't know, two thirty, maybe."

"Did you exit the club for any reason between eleven and two thirty?"

"I—" Montpelier glanced from Luke to Symanski. "I went outside around midnight."

Bam. This had the potential to break the Pye Domino case open. "And where did you go?"

Her eyes darted again. "No—nowhere."

"Lemon Hill Park?"

"I—I maybe met someone a couple blocks away from Club Collective."

"Which is, what? Six, eight blocks away from Lemon Hill Park?"

"I don't know."

Luke shook his head. "You do, Vesper, because K-Car only goes to Beckman Highlands, what, twice a week? And when you need a fix, you have to go somewhere else."

"I—I don't know what you're talking about."

"Can we see your hands?" Luke said.

Montpelier's brow furrowed. "My hands?"

"Your hands."

She pressed her lips together. "I don't want to talk to you anymore. You want more information, you talk to my lawyer." Montpelier stood, cleared her throat, brushed her hair behind her ears, and walked out of the coffee shop.

"Sorry," Luke said.

Symanski frowned. "You screwed that up. Whoever killed Domino garroted him, right? So if it was her, she might have marks on her hands from the rope digging into it. She refused to show her hands, so—"

Luke shook his head vehemently. "I was looking for signs of drug use. Magic Star discolors your fingertips. She could have been trying to hide her drug use. And—"

"You aren't trying to solve the mugging. You're trying to elbow your way into the Pye Domino murder."

Luke sat back in the chair and rubbed his goatee. "I wanted signs of her Magic Star use—that's why I asked to see her hands. You heard her—she knows Alannah Zimmer. Maybe Vesper worked with the robber and sold Zimmer's valuables for some Magic Star."

Symanski pursed her lips.

"Okay, I *also* think the Domino case is being mishandled. Pye Domino used to be a Magic Star addict. I think Vesper still *is*. Domino's business partner suspected they were having an affair. But Friedman and Damanpour haven't interviewed Vesper yet. You were there—everyone in the bullpen heard me say she was Pye Domino's mistress, but no one is interviewing her?"

"You think Big Mike is covering something up."

Luke nodded. "And Friedman and Damanpour are going along with it." He smacked the table. "Vesper has no alibi—she admitted she went outside the club around the time of the murder. She works for a real estate office, and they must have rope for all kinds of things—I've seen those all those open house signs tied down in the backs of pickup trucks. Her real estate office can get the right kind of rope."

"The what? The right kind of rope? How do you know—"

Oh no. That was another detail he'd learned in a previous cycle. But he should roll with it. "I have friends in the crime lab. They got a fiber from Domino's neck wound that's unique to one brand of rope only sold for commercial use. Canfield Pro Polymer A."

Symanski blinked. "Quite resourceful."

"And Vesper is Domino's affair partner—he was paying for her apartment. Maybe Pye didn't want to leave his wife for her, or maybe he wanted her to get clean and wouldn't take no for an answer." Luke snapped his fingers. "

Symanski narrowed her eyes. "How do you know all this?"

Luke opened and closed his mouth. He and Symanski had

gone through Pye Domino's home office and had found the paperwork for Montpelier's apartment, but that was a couple of cycles ago. "I—I have my sources," he said.

"You've been researching this case," Symanski said. "I bet you never had any intention of solving this mugging. You're trying to make Big Mike look bad. And it's not even his case anymore."

Luke hesitated.

Symanski stood. "I get it. He's constantly making fun of you. He makes fun of me, too. You want to put him in his place. But this isn't the case to do it, Luke."

"I think he's purposely interfering with the police to make sure Vesper isn't considered a suspect." Luke felt his pulse speed up; Big Mike had deleted Vesper's call from Domino's phone last cycle, and he'd somehow convinced Friedman and Damanpour not to interview his ex. "I'd be angry about that if I were you."

Symanski set her jaw. "Just because I reported *one* person to internal affairs doesn't mean I'm keen to report Big Mike. I've got a reputation to rebuild." She put her hands on her hips. "And so do you. If Thoreau catches wind that you're investigating someone else's murder case instead of the robbery we were assigned, they'll have your head."

Luke sighed and pinched the bridge of his nose. "Yeah, yeah, you're right." He sat back; he had half the day left to solve this Domino murder, and he had very little to go on. Vesper Montpelier was a person of interest, if not yet a suspect.

He'd have to find a way to stay on the case after Pye Domino was identified in the next cycle.

"Now, look," Symanski said, "if you're serious about getting this mugging solved, let's get the list of the stuff Alannah Zimmer said was stolen in the robbery. Maybe it'll show up at one of the pawnshops near Lemon Hill."

"I hate to do this to you—"

"I know that tone," Symanski said. "You will *not* the divorce papers as an excuse today. Thoreau is pissed off, and they've got every reason to be. Get your shit together and come with me. If you can't keep it together, shut your mouth and wait in the cruiser. But don't do anything that will jeopardize our partnership. Yeah, no one likes you, but no one likes me either, and at least I know you have my back. At least when your head isn't up your own ass."

Luke knew when he was beat. "Fair enough," he said. He'd waste the afternoon on this robbery case, but maybe that was okay.

V

"She already put in the insurance claim on these items," Luke said, staring at the photo on his phone of the emerald necklace on his phone. "She wore this to dinner at a hipster restaurant?"

"She did say she expected her husband to go with her." Symanski pulled the cruiser next to the curb in front of *Baubles & Treasures*. "And the other couple said she was overdressed. Maybe she expected more of a Michelin-star restaurant."

"Maybe." Luke stared at the storefront. Nicer than the last three pawnshops they'd been to, for sure. They got out and walked into the store, the bells tied to the front door jingling.

The owner, who said he'd been behind the counter for the last two days, hadn't purchased an emerald necklace, a diamond-encrusted watch, or a Bianchi Milano handbag.

"You might try Morotto Gems," he said, squinting at Symanski.

"That's over in Beckman Highlands, isn't it?"

"It is," the owner said. "You think my customers are interested in a fifteen-thousand-dollar watch? Maybe a Bianchi Milano knockoff, but not this. I wouldn't be able to pay anyone what these pieces are worth, anyway. Too risky trying to sell them."

So twenty minutes later, they pulled into a high-end shopping center in Beckman Highlands and walked into Morotto Gems. A man, medium height, in his sixties, dressed in an impeccably cut Italian suit stood behind the glass counter. He looked up.

"Welcome, my friends!" He strode out from behind the counter, his hand stretched out to Luke in greeting. "What brings you in today, sir? An engagement ring, perhaps?" He waggled his eyebrows at Detective Symanski.

Symanski pulled her badge out.

"Ah," the man in the suit said, frowning at the badge. "Well, I hate to see that you're here on business, but I'm sure there's hope for both of you in the future. Now, what can I help you with?"

"An emerald necklace, a diamond-encrusted watch—"

He nodded. "Oh, yes. Fine pieces."

Luke raised his eyebrows. "Unfortunately, those items have been reported stolen."

"Stolen?" The man straightened his tie. "Oh, my, no. Mr. Zimmer purchased both those items himself. The gentleman who came in here yesterday morning had the bill of sale. Those designs have been discontinued, and I have two clients coming in to look at the necklace this weekend. Hoping for a bidding war!" He chuckled.

Luke frowned.

"I'm the owner," he said. "Jay Morotto, at your service. Thirty-seven years in business."

"Someone sold you these items?" Symanski asked.

"And I do *not* deal in stolen goods. I can show you the bill of sale if you like. Private party, of course, but Ms. Zimmer signed it over."

"Ms. Zimmer? I thought you said *Mr.* Zimmer purchased the items."

Morotto nodded slowly. "Jewelry is a common gift between spouses. It's not uncommon for wives to return or exchange gifts."

"Right." Luke cleared his throat. "How much did you pay for it, if I may ask?"

"I convinced the seller to return it for what Mr. Zimmer originally paid for it, although I believe my clients will pay double. Perhaps more."

"Sorry—did you say 'return it'?"

"Of course. The necklace was originally purchased here."

Luke took out his phone, opened a browser, and searched for *Ashton Carruthers*. A photo popped up of him in a suit and tie on his father's state senate web page. Luke turned the screen toward Morotto. "This the guy who returned the necklace?"

"Ah, yes. Mr. Carruthers. I've done a fair amount of business with him over the last year or two. He has excellent taste. Always brings in valuable pieces that can generate real interest with my clientele." He frowned. "Look, if these items were reported stolen, there must be some mistake. Perhaps Mr. Zimmer wasn't aware his wife sold the pieces. But California is a joint property state, and if Mr. Zimmer—"

"Can you hold on a moment, Mr. Morotto?" Luke smiled. "This may be a misunderstanding. Let me consult with my colleague."

"Certainly."

They took a few steps back into the corner by the front door.

"Fraud," Symanski said flatly.

"Yep. We should have checked Alannah Zimmer's fingertips to see if they'd changed to magenta."

Symanski scratched her scalp in thought. "So Ms. Zimmer goes to dinner with her friends in a bad neighborhood, walks back to her car and hides her pieces, then she gives her jewelry and Bianchi Milano bag to Carruthers in exchange for Magic Star. And Carruthers comes in here to sell the items. Is that what you think happened?"

"Makes sense to me."

"And how did she think she was going to get away with this?"

"Maybe she didn't think K-Car would sell it so quickly," Luke said. "Or she was too high to think it all the way through." He crossed his arms. "And now we need to go see Ashton Carruthers. He hangs out in Beckman Highlands in the evening when the parents take their kids to soccer practice."

VI

Symanski squinted. "Silver Jaguar?"

Luke nodded. "License plate matches. Where do you think he is?"

"In the house. Doctors don't make house calls anymore, but drug dealers do."

They waited.

"Hey," Luke said, "thanks for kicking my ass earlier."

Symanski looked at him out of the corner of her eyes. "What do you mean?"

"You didn't let me get away treating Zimmer the way I did, and you called me out."

"I snitched on you to Thoreau."

Luke shrugged. "Still. I need to make some changes."

Symanski nodded. "Big Mike is a problem, though. I get why you want to make him look bad. But realize—he ignores the rules everyone else has to follow."

Luke's head snapped up. "There he is."

Ashton Carruthers, in a button-up dress shirt and beige slacks, walked down the driveway to his Jaguar.

Luke jumped out of the cruiser and hurried to the Jaguar, badge in hand. "Mr. Carruthers? A word?"

Carruthers turned, saw the badge, and smirked. Ugh, Luke saw that same smarminess on Big Mike, too. He felt like slapping the smile off Carruthers's face.

"Good afternoon, officer. What can I do for you?"

He wanted to correct him: *Detective.* But he bit his tongue. "We've heard reports that you've been trafficking in stolen goods."

"Stolen?"

"An emerald necklace," Luke said, walking closer. "There's also a diamond-encrusted watch and a Bianchi Milano purse."

Carruthers's smile broadened. "You've been misinformed, Officer. I have sales slips for all three items."

"Maybe you can come down to the station and we can sort this out."

"I don't think so." He folded his arms. "I wonder if you're aware who I am. And what the price you'd have to pay for holding me under false pretenses."

Luke glanced over his shoulder. Symanski had gotten out of the cruiser but was standing next to it. This was Luke's show.

He took another step toward Carruthers. "You've heard by now that one of your former clients was found dead in Lemon Hill Park yesterday morning."

"Don't know who you mean," Carruthers said.

Luke shook his head. "I think you do. We'll uncover his Magic Star use. Rumor is, he was trying to get people to quit. And that affected your business." Yes, Luke knew otherwise, but K-Car might not realize that. "Now maybe you can tell me where you were Tuesday night around midnight."

His smile faltered for a half-second. "I had nothing to do with that."

"I believe you," Luke said, though he didn't. "I believe that you're just in the Magic Star business for the money. You keep your nose clean otherwise, you inform on other dealers when it suits you, and you—"

"Look, I haven't talked to Domino in six months. Maybe longer. He found this recovery program. Yeah, he was trying to sober up some of my clients, but no one was buying it."

"Who was he trying to sober up?"

"You gotta talk to the program," Carruthers said. "They'd know who he pissed off. Me, I'm trying to run a business."

"An illegal business."

"Talk to Paul Broxley and see how many arrests he would've made this year if I hadn't handed the Y-15s to him on a silver platter." The grin was back. "Ask yourself if you really want to push me on the stolen necklace thing."

He turned and got into the Jaguar.

"What program?"

"He tried to recruit me into the healed life," Carruthers said. "Good thing he was so famous in Sacramento or I'd've kicked his ass."

Yeah, Beckman Highlands probably had a tough HOA.

Carruthers pulled the Jaguar's door shut. A moment later, the engine roared to life, and he sped down the street.

VII

Symanski and Luke got the arrest warrant for insurance fraud in a couple of hours and went back to Beckman Highlands to Alannah Zimmer's house. She squawked for a minute about the unfairness of it all, then asked for her lawyer. Her husband was in the house too, and complained bitterly to the arresting officers, but after twenty or thirty minutes, and after seeing the photos of the necklace at Morotto Gems, he went quiet.

At a few minutes past six o'clock, Symanski and Luke got back to the precinct.

"So," Symanski said, sitting at her desk, "we solved the case. And since Alannah Zimmer was the guilty party, your instincts to insult her were on the nose."

"Not really." Luke stood, leaning over his PC and waking it up. "But I appreciate you giving me a little grace."

"Celebratory cocktails?" Symanski asked. "The first in a long road to getting our reputations back on track?"

Luke hesitated.

"Uh oh. You're still stuck on the Pye Domino murder."

"How much headway have Friedman and Damanpour made?"

"I don't know. It's not our case."

"Pye Domino went to a recovery program. Shouldn't we at least see which one?"

"Aren't those supposed to be anonymous?"

"A gray area, legally." Luke hoped so, anyway. "But Domino's dead, and I would think those who lead the programs are just as interested in justice as the rest of us."

Symanski shook her head. "I don't think this is a good idea. Besides, there must be a dozen recovery programs."

Luke clicked on the screen and typed in an online map URL. "We know Domino wanted out of his addiction. And he crashed his private plane in Tahoe late last year."

"He did?"

"Yes—he was lucky. Only broke a couple ribs, saw his life flash before his eyes—"

"How did you find that out?"

"Research." Luke tapped the screen. "Good guess. There are thirteen recovery programs in the greater Sacramento area. But only four of those are near downtown."

"How about near his house?"

Luke shook his head. "No, I bet those neighborhoods are

too posh. They send their drug addicts out into nature." He tapped the screen. "There are two places between downtown, where Domino-Barkley Properties is located, and Beckman Highlands. But look here." He turned his monitor so Symanski could see it, and she leaned forward. Then he tapped the screen.

Symanski grunted. "That's nowhere near Beckman Highlands."

"No. But it's only a block away from Kadema Gardens."

"I don't get it."

"That's where Vesper Montpelier's apartment is. The one Pye Domino paid for."

"Wait—what? Domino is paying for Vesper's apartment? How much research have you done on this murder?"

"Enough," Luke said. "Friedman and Damanpour aren't following up like they should, and I think Big Mike's encouraging them to stay away from Vesper Montpelier. Someone's getting away with murder because of it."

"So what?" Symanski said.

"Do you see the name of the recovery program?"

Symanski squinted. "Healed Life Horizons."

"Carruthers said that Domino tried to get him to join his 'healed life.' Those were the words he used."

Symanski cocked her head. "Any other Healed Life Horizons in the area?"

"Two: one out by Pioneer Mesa, and one in Pineville."

"Those are both at least thirty miles away."

"Precisely." Luke looked up at Symanski. "Care to join me? The Healed Life Horizons group near Kadema Gardens has a meeting tonight."

"It's not our case."

"And Big Mike is purposely tanking it."

Symanski screwed up her mouth. "I bet no one will give us any useful information."

Luke shrugged. "They will if we phrase it right."

VIII

"I'm sorry," Luke said as he opened the door into the church conference room, holding his badge out. "I'm Detective Luke Guillory, and this is my partner, Detective Symanski. We don't mean to intrude, but if anyone has any information about Pye Domino, we'll be waiting outside. We're investigating his murder, and we want to know if he was in trouble, if anyone had been threatening him. No matter how small you think it is. You don't have to give your name—"

A man in a full beard, about six foot two, turned to him. "This is highly inappropriate. These meetings are—"

"Not subject to privacy laws," Luke said, though he wasn't sure if that was true. "And we're trying to balance solving a murder and being respectful. That's all I'll say. Please come out and talk to us if you have any information that could help us. We'll be right by the Welcome sign in the church garden if you want to talk."

He closed the door.

Maybe the bearded man would report Luke to Thoreau. But that would be on Friday morning, and he would magically transport back to Wednesday before he had to face any consequences.

He walked down the hall into the church foyer, out the front doors, and turned right into the garden, where Symanski was waiting for him with two large white paper bags.

"Double Sunny Burger, pepper jack, onion rings," she said, handing one of the bags to him.

"This is better than going out for cocktails, right?" Luke unwrapped his burger.

"No," Symanski said, pulling out a grilled chicken sandwich

from her bag. "I don't know how you can eat like that. You're not nineteen anymore."

"I should worry more about tomorrow." Luke took a big bite. He chewed with difficulty, then swallowed. "I don't think I've had a Sunny Burger in a few years."

"This better be as good as you promised," Symanski said, taking a bite of her chicken sandwich. She chewed, closing her eyes.

"See?" Luke said. "Sunny Burger is where it's at."

They ate for a few moments, with nothing but the sound of them chewing and drinking from their sodas over the sound of the crickets in the garden. They finished eating and Luke took all the trash and threw it away in the cement trash receptacle next to the church entrance.

The door opened as he turned. A man, about five foot seven, with a prominent Roman nose and close-set eyes, stood there with the door open.

"Hi," Luke said. Did the man look familiar?

"You're the one who wanted to talk about Pye?" the man asked.

"That's me."

The man hesitated; Luke waited, doing his best not to appear hurried. If the man were on the fence about giving them information, Luke would need to slow his questioning.

The man's eyes darted across the front of the church, then finally spoke. "You're Detective Luke, right? You're in Lemon Hill Park all the time."

Luke nodded.

The man dug his hands into his pocket and stared at Luke's feet. "You knew my brother Earl."

Ah yes, the nose, the close-set eyes—much like Earl Shent, the vet who'd overdosed in the park three weeks before. "I did," Luke said.

"You helped him out."

"And he helped me. Called a few times when kids were O.D.ing. Saved a couple of them." A pang of regret for Caleb Vargas.

"But he couldn't save himself," Earl's brother said. He kicked halfheartedly at the sidewalk. "Yeah, okay. This is probably nothing."

Luke shrugged. "Maybe not. Earl would say his info was probably nothing, and sometimes he wound up saving a kid's life."

Earl's brother pinched the bridge of his nose. "If he hadn't—" He exhaled loudly. "Earl's the one who got me into a program. I guess I owe him this much." He dropped his hand and looked Luke in the eye. "Pye's been coming to Healed Life for maybe half a year. Had a story about crashing a plane that freaked me the hell out."

"Yeah. I heard about that. Up in Tahoe."

"The first couple of times Pye came, he brought a woman with him."

"His wife?"

The man shook his head. "I don't think so. I thought it was his daughter at first, but the two of them acted more like a couple, you know?"

Luke took his phone out, pulled up a picture of Vesper Montpelier, and showed it to the man.

"Yeah, that's her. Anyway, the third or fourth time they both came, the two of them screamed at each other in the parking lot for ten minutes, maybe. I didn't stick around much after that, so I guess it could have gone on longer. But he didn't show up with her after that."

"Oh. Interesting."

"Except she came with him Tuesday night."

Luke blinked. "Like—two nights ago?"

"Right."

"And how did they treat each other?"

"Another blowup," he said. "And again, I didn't really hear what went on, but I don't think she wanted to be there."

"But he wanted her to be there."

"Yeah." He paused. "They were giving off way different vibes, though."

"Still like they were together?"

The man thought for a moment. "I don't know. Something was off."

"Like they had broken up?"

"I guess that would explain it. But like I said, I didn't hear any of what they were saying."

"Thanks," Luke said. "That's really helpful."

Earl Shent's brother nodded and walked away.

Luke walked back to Symanski.

"Anything?"

Luke nodded. "Tuesday night. Pye was here with Vesper, and they fought. Maybe broke up."

They waited until the meeting attendees left the building, but no one else came to talk with them. The lights in the church turned off. The tall bearded man exited the building, locked the door, and hurried into the parking lot, glaring at Luke.

"I guess that's all the info we're getting tonight." Symanski yawned. "Guess we need to tell Friedman and Damanpour about this tomorrow morning."

"Yep," Luke said. "Tomorrow morning. Thanks for keeping me company."

"No problem. Thanks for the cheap dinner."

"My generosity knows no bounds," Luke said.

CYCLE 5: WEDNESDAY

I

Luke opened his eyes. His heart was pounding, but he took a deep breath and calmed down.

He glanced at the bedside clock. 12:13 AM. Of course it was.

He jumped out of bed, reset his 12:20 alarm for 6:15, and got in the shower. Three minutes—enough to get clean. He toweled off and found the blue and orange swirl shirt. Good enough for the club, even if he was on the older side of their clientele. He grabbed a pair of fitted gray trousers—he hadn't worn those in a couple of years, but they still fit. Barely.

He went into the bathroom and opened the medicine cabinet. Ellie had bought him a pomade for Christmas. The hair goop made him look a little villainous, but he dabbed a little in his hand and ran it through his hair. The slicked-back look was almost off-putting; he didn't look like himself. And with his mustache and goatee, he only needed horns and a tail to look like the devil.

Maybe not a bad look for going clubbing, though.

No time to deal with Ellie. Besides, she would text him in the morning.

He went to his Malibu and typed in *Club Collective* into his map application. Ah—it was in the same location as *Evoke*, the club he and Ellie went to when they were first dating. Six minutes away, if he could find a parking space.

Club Collective was in the middle of a row of warehouses and storefronts on Fruitridge, and he found a parking spot two blocks away. He hurried to the entrance, trying not to look like he was rushing.

A hulking bald man in a black leather jacket stood in front of the door, a thudding beat coming from behind him. He was even bigger than Big Mike. Two people waiting to get in stood in front of him. People a decade younger than him, the man in jeans and coiffed hair, the woman in a short black skirt and a matching halter top. The bald man was checking IDs, taking money. Luke stepped behind the man in jeans and looked at his watch. Twelve forty. Vesper Montpelier was in the club already.

"Hey," Luke said when he got to the bald, hulking man. "What's the cover?"

The bouncer shook his head. "Naw, man. This isn't the club for you."

"I'm meeting friends."

"Too bad. Get out of here."

He glanced past the man into the club. It wasn't crowded.

He'd left his badge in his pocket—he didn't think it would be good to use here, even if it was just to get in the door—and he walked from the club to the sidewalk. He looked to the left; nothing down there. But to the right, an all-night convenience store.

The convenience store had an ATM at the back, and he withdrew three hundred dollars from his account. The stack of twenties went next to the lone ten-dollar-bill in his wallet. He walked back to the club. There was no one in line; Tuesday after midnight wasn't a popular clubbing hour.

"I told you—"

"Fifty?" Luke asked, holding up two twenties and a ten.

The man glared at him a moment. "A hundred," he said.

Luke pulled out another three twenties and handed them to the bouncer. "There you go."

"Cover charge is twenty," he said.

Luke gritted his teeth, but he nodded and handed over another twenty. The bouncer stepped aside and let Luke pass.

The club was dark, with lights over the dance floor and a square bar to the right of the entrance. He asked the bartender for a whiskey and soda, and began pulling his credit card out—but thought better of it. If he'd be arresting anyone today, he didn't want his name to be traced to Club Collective. He handed over a twenty and got three dollars in change, which he left on the bar. Expensive drink, but he should have expected it.

Luke stared at the dance floor and finally saw Vesper. She was dancing with two other women, looking disinterested. She took out her phone and held it at arm's length. A selfie. And her face completely changed: from ennui to effervescence. A smile that lit up the room. For a moment, everything was right with the world.

No wonder Big Mike had been enthralled.

It didn't *look* like she'd come directly from killing her lover in the park. But maybe that's what she was happy about.

He set his drink down—it was rotgut whiskey anyway—and decided to walk toward the dance floor.

But Vesper had other ideas: she fanned herself with her hand and Luke paused. She threaded her way around the other bodies and stepped off the floor, then walked up to the bar—next to Luke.

He turned toward her as the bartender walked up. "Buy you a drink?" he asked over the music.

She looked over at him, appraising his outfit. Luke pushed his sleeve up a few inches. The Von Zeitmann twinkled in the low light of the bar. Her eyes widened. "Sure."

"What are you having?"

"Verity and cranberry." Oof. Top-shelf vodka. The bartender glanced at Luke, who nodded. The bartender stepped away.

"You know, you look familiar," Luke said, then cringed.

"I get that a lot," Vesper said.

"Do you know Mike Moody?"

She frowned. "I do."

"Thought so." Luke nodded. "I work with him."

"Ah. Well, you can tell him I said fuck off."

Luke chuckled. "He and I don't like each other much. I'd pass your message along, except that would mean I'd need to talk to him."

Vesper smiled. The bartender set the drink down in front of her.

"Thirty-five," he said to Luke.

At this rate, he'd need to go back to the ATM. Luke pulled out two more twenties and handed it over. The bartender didn't even pretend he was going to make change.

"So what are you doing here on a Tuesday night?" she asked.

"Couldn't sleep and felt like doing something besides watching TV."

Vesper giggled. But that wasn't a funny statement.

"You here with anyone?" Luke asked.

Vesper shook her head, and a dark cloud passed over her face. "Not tonight," she said, and she leaned forward toward him. "You believe in magic, too?"

Luke blinked. That *had* to be a reference to Magic Star. "I might," he said. "You know anyone with a little magic to share?"

Vesper batted her eyelashes. "Maybe," she said.

He hesitated. Had she left the club to go argue with Pye

Domino more? Maybe Domino had backslid, and she got more Magic Star off him after she killed him?

No, no—though he suspected her, he didn't have any proof.

"If I knew someone who had stuff," Vesper said, putting a hand on Luke's arm, "would you want to get out of here?" Oh, she was starting to slur her words. Luke remembered what Hector had said: Magic Star made some people mellow, some people manic. This must be the mellow version.

Luke blinked. Vesper was a decade younger and *way* out of his league. But—if Pye Domino had told her that he wasn't leaving his wife, maybe she was out for revenge. Or maybe his watch made her think he was looking for a sugar baby.

He looked into Vesper's dilated eyes. She was high, and the vodka cocktail wasn't helping. He glanced at her fingers, wrapped around the forty-dollar cocktail. Despite the low light, he saw the slight magenta discoloration in the skin around her French-manicured fingernails.

Maybe she'd gotten high on Magic Star and hadn't known what she was doing when she went to Lemon Hill Park. He could ask her questions, find out where she'd gone around midnight when she'd gone out of the club.

"Absolutely," he said. "We can definitely get out of here." He offered her his arm and she took it, tottering as she stood from the barstool.

"You know," Vesper said, "my boyfriend just broke up with me."

"That's terrible," Luke said. "He's an idiot."

"Like Big Mike," Vesper said, taking an unsteady step.

They had to get out of the club before Vesper passed out. Luke began walking toward the exit.

"I definitely think Big Mike is an idiot." Luke pointed at the floor. "Watch out, there's a step right here."

"Yeah. I mean, I'm hot, right?"

"Yes, you are."

"Any guy would be lucky to be with me. My boyfriend didn't know how good I could be."

"That's true."

"Do you know," she said, talking to the air in front of her, not to Luke, "he wouldn't leave his wife. I spent a year with him. He told me he was leaving her. I—I liked him, you know?"

"I'm sure you did."

"I'm not some—some toy, right?"

"Right." Maybe she wasn't looking for revenge; maybe she was looking for a therapist. That would be healthier, anyway.

"Serves me right," she mumbled.

Just get her to the door. Maybe put her in a FlashRide and get her home.

No—if she threw up in the hired car, Luke would get stuck with a cleaning bill for hundreds of dollars. Plus, if Vesper *was* the killer, they'd be able to track the FlashRide. They'd know Luke had been with her. He'd get kicked off the case like Big Mike. There had to be another way.

He scratched his goatee with his free hand. He wouldn't feel good about this, but he knew Vesper lived in an apartment in Kadema Gardens. Her address was probably on something she had with her. Maybe a driver's license.

"Your place?" he asked.

"I don't know," she said. "Are you a nice guy?"

"We'll get you home safe," he said.

Vesper tossed her hair, smiling radiantly as if flipping a switch. "Oh, you'll get me home, all right."

Luke glanced around. Had anyone noticed them together? This could so easily go sideways—and Luke could find himself in trouble, no matter how noble his intentions. "What's your address, Vesper?"

Oh, crap. He hadn't asked for Vesper's name during their conversations—he hoped she wouldn't notice. Vesper smiled.

"The building at the corner of 60th and Del Oro. It's a nice place. I hope I get to stay there."

"Apartment number?"

She frowned. "I don't even know your name, and you know where I live."

"Bobby," Luke said, and immediately his stomach dropped. A lie.

She smiled. "Bobby. That's a good name." She closed her eyes. "I bet you're a good guy."

"Yeah, well, I try."

"I try, too, but sometimes things don't work out, you know?"

He had Vesper lean on him, and her steps got less stable with each step. "I'm going to take off your heels, Vesper."

"I bet you want to take off more than that, Bobby."

He ignored that and slid her shoes off—no easy task when she was so out of it. "So you don't fall when we go to the car." Bare feet on the sidewalk and the asphalt crossing the road; she might get a rock in the bottom of her foot, or a splinter, but she'd prefer either to a broken ankle.

He got her to the car, and she leaned against the passenger door as Luke started the engine.

"How long were you at the club?" Luke asked, as casually as he could.

"I don't know what's wrong with me," Vesper said.

"You're just high," Luke said, driving out of his curbside space and onto Fruitvale Avenue. "You took Magic Star, right? Your boyfriend used to take it too, didn't he? Did you see him tonight?"

"I knew it was over," she mumbled, "but he didn't have to be so harsh."

"Did that—" Luke almost blurted out an accusation. "That couldn't have felt good."

"I'm an idiot," she said, and turned and stared out the window.

"Hey, now," Luke said, "sometimes our hearts don't always pick the right people. Doesn't mean you're an idiot."

She turned and sized him up with an unsteady gaze. "He said I needed to forget about him."

"When did he say that? Tonight? You go to the park tonight?" Luke tried to keep his tone casual, light.

"I thought you were taking me to my place."

"No, I—" Luke glanced at her again, but she was staring at her hand, which still rested on his arm. Luke very much wanted to shake her off, get away from her touch. She was zoning out, and besides, she wasn't answering questions. Getting Vesper out of the club might have been a bad idea.

But he still had to get her home safely.

She managed not to throw up in his car, and when he got to her apartment building, he found a parking place on the street half a block away. She leaned on him heavily, and with her draped over his shoulders and her shoes in his hand, he took her to the building.

Nothing she'd said or done either confirmed or denied that she had killed Pye Domino before he'd shown up. But he'd seen killers get falling-down drunk after murdering someone, especially if they hadn't intended to do it when they'd gotten up that morning. He'd seen this a few times before in the addicts he'd investigated. And Vesper Montpelier was at least a heavy user: pills, alcohol, possibly more.

At the cement staircase, he grabbed her purse and pulled her wallet out. Credit card, credit card, credit card—ah, driver's license. Apartment 210. Good; that would only be one flight of stairs.

She leaned on him until he was practically carrying her, and he broke a sweat about halfway up.

"You're a big, strong man," Vesper said. Ugh, whatever she had taken—and Luke assumed it was Magic Star—was relaxing both the muscles in her legs and her inhibitions. What had she done in the club on all the cycles when he *hadn't* been there? Did she have friends who kept her safe? Did she drive home high and drunk?

He rummaged around and found a keyring. The third key he tried worked in the door.

The front door swung open, and Vesper's apartment was a mess. Plates and diet soda cans were stacked on the coffee table. The sofa was strewn with clothing.

"So this is my place," Vesper slurred.

Luke struggled to get Vesper through over the threshold of the bedroom. With his elbow, he flicked on the light. Wow, more clothes on the bed. He gently maneuvered his way to the bed and had Vesper sit down on a mostly clear place on the mattress. Luke let go of her—and she immediately slid sideways, falling onto the floor and sputtering with laughter.

After pushing all the clothes into a pile on the edge of the bed, he pulled the covers down. He grabbed Vesper around her shoulders and pulled her up onto the bed.

"Don't mind if I do," she mumbled.

He put her in bed and turned her on her side. She tried to pull him to her.

"Relax for a few minutes," Luke said, as soothingly as he could.

"Nice and relaxed," she began, and closed her eyes.

A moment later, her breathing turned slow and steady. She'd passed out.

Luke extricated himself from her grasp and exhaled.

He walked into the kitchen. Plates piled in the sink, torn bags of chips on the counter. An open bag of wheat bread. He looked inside briefly for signs of mold, and seeing none, spun the bag closed and set it aside. He opened three cabinets before he found a big mixing bowl, and he went back into the bedroom and nestled the mixing bowl in the crook of Vesper's right arm. Just because she hadn't vomited in the car didn't mean she wouldn't tonight.

He went out to the kitchen again, putting his hands on his hips as he surveyed the disaster of Vesper's apartment. He had an urge to clean it all up, but that would have wasted precious hours.

Vesper was home safely, but she had been too out of it to talk.

He walked around the apartment.

Would she have any evidence in her apartment of what her intentions had been that night? A note in a jacket pocket? A pill bottle from Magic Star?

He went to the bathroom and opened the medicine cabinet. Toothpaste. Birth control pills. Nothing that looked related to Magic Star.

Luke walked out into the kitchen again. Maybe a ripped note in a junk drawer? But while the kitchen was a mess and the junk drawer was full of plastic bags and rubber bands, he found no torn-up restraining orders or signed confessions. Luke closed the drawer, wandered into the living room, then opened the hall closet.

Jackets, mostly. An umbrella. At the back of the closet, under two pairs of high heels and a pair of running shoes, lay a canvas bag with the Domino-Barkley logo. Inside, a paper, the edges crumpled: *Welcome to Your New Apartment.* A flathead screwdriver, a Phillips-head, a cheap hammer, a small jar of wood putty, a two-inch-wide paintbrush.

And a small coil of rope, still in its red-and-black wrapper. Canfield Pro Polymer A.

Luke pulled the rope out of its wrapper, then grabbed the other end. Maybe six feet. He hadn't written it down, but he was pretty sure Canfield was the brand of rope with the unique synthetic fiber that had killed Domino.

Was he holding the murder weapon in his hand?

Probably not. But if she had one hospitality kit with the right kind of rope, she might have had more—especially if the kits were given away as promotional items.

He put the canvas bag back in the closet under the pile of shoes and stood up.

Luke got a sick feeling in the pit of his stomach. He was violating Vesper's fourth amendment rights. Yes, she'd invited him in, kind of, but she wouldn't have let him search through her drawers and closets.

Is this what made him an ineffective detective? Whatever Luke found would be inadmissible in a court of law. Unless, of course, he left it there and found a reason to get a search warrant later. He'd know what to look for.

Still didn't feel good.

Plain sight. Anything he could see that was out in the open —that was fair game. The Supreme Court said so. He took a deep breath. He'd look around for another five or ten minutes, maybe check on Vesper again, then be on his way.

Luke looked around the living room and kitchen.

There on the edge of the counter. A pile of opened mail. Luke walked over, hesitated, then leafed through it.

Credit card bill, over twenty thousand dollars. Another credit card bill, eighteen thousand dollars. Aha—a letter from the Kadema Gardens Management Office.

Dear Miss Montpelier,
Our office received a communication from Domino-Barkley
Properties that their last payment for Unit 210 will be May 1.
If you wish to continue living in the unit, the monthly rent is
$2,300, due and payable the first of every month, starting with
June 1. Please contact us by May 1 if you wish to continue
living at this property.
Sincerely,

Kadema Gardens Management

He rubbed his goatee. So Domino had likely broken up with Vesper and wouldn't keep paying for her apartment. Why had Domino stopped paying? Maybe Angelina had found out. Maybe Pye had really turned over a new leaf after the plane crash and had ended the affair.

Was the breakup enough motive for Vesper Montpelier to kill Domino? Maybe she hadn't intended to do it; if she'd just wanted to get him high to convince him to keep paying for the apartment, maybe he refused. Maybe she had one of those hospitality kits in the trunk of her car. And maybe, just maybe, she'd lost her temper.

II

Luke left Vesper's apartment with her keys. She had a key fob to an Infiniti, and he pushed the lock button as soon as he got down to the parking lot. Nothing.

He rubbed his goatee again. If she'd driven to the club, her car would still be there.

He took his Malibu back to the club and drove around the neighborhood. A lot that said *Parking from $2* was a block east of Club Collective on Bird Avenue. He rolled down the window and pushed the lock button on the Infiniti key fob.

A chirp.

He pulled the Malibu to the curb and walked into the parking lot. Another push, another chirp. There it was: a white sedan in the third row, behind a black SUV.

He held down the bottom button and the trunk popped open.

More clothes. Workout outfits that smelled like stale sweat.

And at the bottom of the trunk, a Domino-Barkley Properties canvas bag.

He thought for a moment, then pulled the sleeves of his blue-and-orange shirt down over his hands. He grabbed the canvas bag—

Empty.

Maybe the rope that had been in the bag was the murder weapon.

III

After putting Vesper's keys back in her apartment, Luke went home. He knew he wouldn't sleep again before sunrise; he was too wired.

Vesper was the most viable suspect Luke had found so far, even if much of the evidence was circumstantial.

He'd have to figure out how to prove the rope from Vesper's canvas bag was the murder weapon—but at least he could connect the type of rope used in the killing to Vesper and how she could have gotten ahold of commercial-grade rope. But motive and opportunity weren't a problem: she was a block away from the murder scene at the right time, with the correct type of rope at her disposal, and Pye Domino had spurned her. No other suspect had everything line up like that. But how could he prove it?

Oh, of course. Write everything down. That was the most important thing. He grabbed the pad of paper in the kitchen drawer.

As he wrote, he focused on everything that had happened since he'd awakened. Other bits and pieces came back, and with every item he wrote down, he remembered more. The name of Solomon Vargas's building material—Vargastic. Hector Corazón taking Domino's phone from his pocket. The name of Calvin Barkley's dinner companion in the gray suit: Gabe Wexler. Brev's majoring in architecture.

Hold on. Calvin Barkley. Assuming he could figure out how to keep the Domino murder out of Big Mike's hands, he and Symanski could go see Barkley and get *him* to connect the canvas bag and the rope to Vesper.

He wrote for another hour and a half.

His phone buzzed.

Who's calling this early? He picked up his phone and saw a message from Ellie.

> I'm not coming home tonight
>
> I'll call you later and we can talk

Ah. Right. Still Wednesday morning. He hadn't picked her up at the airport.

A thought struck him, and he set his pen down.

Vesper would recognize him.

Yes, she'd been drunk and high, so the chances weren't a hundred percent. At least he'd given a fake name—but still.

He rubbed his goatee and thought.

Ah.

He went into the bathroom and dug around in the drawer until he found his beard trimmer. He hadn't cleaned up his mustache and goatee for—well, he wasn't sure. Maybe Sunday, but that seemed like weeks ago.

He plugged the trimmer in, turned it on, and a few minutes later, the remains of his mustache and goatee were littered around the sink. He looked at his face: still heavy stubble, but he could get that with a regular razor. And maybe another shower—he smelled like sweat and alcohol from the bar. He looked at himself in the mirror, his sad eyes, his weak chin, and barely recognized himself.

Beep beep beep.

Oh wow. Six fifteen already.

IV

He got ready for work quickly and left a half hour early. He was relieved he didn't have to deal with the cyclist.

Everyone ignored him in the halls on the way to his desk—like every other Wednesday morning so far. When he'd made it in, that is. Going through the double doors to enter the bullpen, Moody and Babino weren't at their desks.

He looked at his watch. A quarter to eight.

"You're in early."

Luke looked up at Detective Symanski, who sat at her desk. "Good morning, Detective." Her eyes widened slightly. "You shaved."

"Oh. Yeah. I did."

"I figured you'd be a little late. Ellie was coming home last night, right? Did she finally convince you to shave it off?"

Luke rubbed his clean-shaven face. "She liked my vandyke. And the plan was for Ellie to come home last night, but she didn't come to the house after landing in Sacramento."

Symanski cocked her head.

"She's been making excuse after excuse why she had to stay in Boston—and I realized she's going to divorce me."

"What?"

"Mark my words—sometime today, I'll get served divorce papers."

Symanski blinked. "You—you sound so casual about it."

Luke grinned. "Oh, no, I'm a mess. But I figured work would take my mind off it. Not much I can do."

"You can fight for her."

Luke shrugged. "She's getting a promotion, but she'll have

to move to Boston. Or maybe she wants to move to Boston. But anyway, I can't."

"Why not? It can't be the job." Symanski lowered her voice. "They treat you like shit here."

Luke shook his head. "My mom is a forty-minute drive away. I can't move across the country."

Symanski was quiet for a few seconds. "You know, a lot of people live far away from their parents. See them once or twice a year."

Luke cleared his throat. "Well, uh, I'm helping Mom go through the appeals process."

Symanski selected her words carefully. "Some people might say you were choosing your mother over your marriage."

"I'm not sure Ellie gave me a choice." Luke sat down at his desk. "Maybe this was the wake-up call I needed to get my act together." He adjusted his keyboard and mouse a half-inch. "I should get some paperwork taken care of before the day gets rolling."

Symanski stared at Luke for a moment longer, then turned her attention to her computer as Luke started on an online form.

About thirty minutes later, Big Mike and Vince showed up, guffawing and drinking coffee. Behind Symanski, the office door opened, and Captain Thoreau stood in the doorway.

"Listen up, people," they said. "We've got a dead body in Lemon Hill Park."

Symanski and Luke both stood.

"Let me guess—another junkie O.D.'d?" Babino said, chortling. "We should set up a conveyor belt between Lemon Hill Park and the morgue. It'd save time."

"Lucy and her girlfriend can take it," Big Mike said, sitting down.

"Knock it off, Moody," Captain Thoreau said. "You let

anyone hear you and your buddy talk like that, I won't be able to stop the disciplinary committee from getting involved."

"We'll take it," Luke said quickly.

Thoreau nodded. "I'll send you the file. An officer is already onsite." They turned and went back into their office, shutting the door behind them.

"Told you the girls could handle it," Moody said to Babino. "Come on, we gotta talk to that carjacking thug."

Babino, coffee in hand, followed Big Mike out of the bullpen.

"You took that quick," Symanski said.

"Nothing like working a suspicious death to take your mind off personal problems," Luke said. "Now, come on, let's get going."

V

Luke parked the cruiser next to a red curb on Muñoz Way between an old Lincoln and a green Nissan. He and Symanski walked the quarter mile to the covered walkway of junipers.

Pressler stood in the middle of the walkway. "Shit," he muttered. "Sacramento's finest."

Luke put on a pair of latex gloves. "Morning, Officer Pressler."

Pressler flinched.

Luke pointed to the walkway. "The body's in there, correct?"

"Uh, yeah."

Luke held up the police tape and Symanski ducked under, pulling on her gloves too.

"Have you touched the body?" Symanski said.

Pressler shook his head, crossing his arms. "Pretty obvious

overdose. Figured I'd leave the clinical stuff to the professionals."

Luke and Symanski walked another twenty feet farther to the body. Face down, blue jeans, dress shirt. They crouched next to the body. Luke knew what he'd find, but he had to make quick work of this to keep the case and make sure Big Mike didn't take it.

"Look how well he's dressed," Luke said. "Not a typical O.D." He peered at the victim's neck, reached a finger out, and pulled down the collar to review the red ligature marks.

"What is it?" Symanski asked.

"Not an O.D. at all," he said, pointing to the victim's neck. "He was strangled. Garroted, if I'm not mistaken."

"I need to call this in."

"Yes, CSI needs to treat this like a murder scene." He leaned over and peered at Domino's face. "Uh oh."

"What?"

"This is Pye Domino." Was his act convincing?

Symanski hesitated. "Who?"

"I'm sure you've seen the signs all over downtown. Domino-Barkley Properties."

"And you recognize him?"

"Yes. Maybe a *Sacramento Business Monthly* interview. He's the closest we get to a celebrity here."

"Except for, you know, all the internationally recognized politicians."

"Well, yes. Except for them."

Symanski, lower on Domino's body, checked his pockets. "No wallet, no ID, no phone."

Luke set his mouth in a line. "I think I know who has his phone."

"What? Who?"

"The guy who gave us the information that got the heroin dealer arrested. I think he might have it."

"Why would he have it?"

A good question. One Luke couldn't answer, so he stood. "I'm going to get Domino's phone."

Symanski pulled out her phone. "I'll call it in."

Luke hesitated, then shook his head. "Hold off a moment, Detective Symanski."

"Why?"

"Call CSI—that's fine. But a high-profile death like Domino? Big Mike is sure to snatch it out of our hands. Don't say you recognize the victim. And don't say it's a murder yet."

Symanski tilted her head. "And you want a high-profile case like this to, what, resuscitate your career?"

"You could use a good solve too. New detective, partnered with someone no one likes."

Symanski folded her arms.

"Please—hold off on the identification until I get back."

Symanski tapped her foot but nodded.

Luke turned and dipped back under the police tape, swearing at himself quietly. How many times would he have to go through this day before planning ahead? He spent time writing everything down he was supposed to remember, but he didn't have any strategy for how to get all the evidence he'd need to gather to arrest Vesper Montpelier.

Luke made a beeline for the bridge in the center of Lemon Hill Park. Like before, Luke recognized Hector Corazón from the dirty olive trousers and jean jacket.

Oh, right. He'd had a coffee before. Hector seemed to like the coffee more than the twenty dollars. He hesitated. Hector would be here after he got the coffee. Ten minutes and Luke would return.

He made a circular sweep of the park on the way to the coffee shop, trying to avoid the crime scene and any questions Pressler or Symanski might have if they saw him leaving the park.

The line was shorter than the days before—he was in line ten minutes earlier than before. He hesitated a moment before ordering four coffees, then carried the whole tray back to the crime scene.

"What's this?" Pressler said.

"I wanted a coffee to get my witness talking," Luke said. "Figured I'd grab you and the team some." He pointed to the middle of the tray. "Cream and sugar, too. I don't know how you take yours."

"You can't bribe me like your mom bribed—"

"Okay, okay," Luke said. "I'll give yours to Symanski for her witnesses."

He dropped the coffees off with Symanski.

"CSI will be here in fifteen minutes," she said, taking the tray and eying one of the coffees.

"You can take three of them. I got one of 'em for Pressler, but he's too morally upstanding to take it from me."

"Can I call in the identification of the body yet?"

"Not yet. Haven't gotten the phone."

He ducked back under the police tape, holding the coffee, and rushed back to the bridge where Hector was still sleeping. Luke crouched next to him. "Morning, Hector. I got you some coffee. It's the good stuff."

The man stirred.

"I don't mean to startle you," Luke said, "but there's a dead man in the park, and I need you to give me the phone you took."

"What?" the man asked in a thin, wispy crackle. "What are you asking?"

"The phone, Hector. I know you have it."

Hector blinked. "Oh. Detective Luke." He hesitated. "I didn't take nothing."

Luke sighed. "I'm sorry, Hector, but I don't have time for

this. If any other police come and you have a murder victim's phone on you, it won't look good."

"Murder?" Hector pulled himself into a sitting position.

Luke held out the coffee. After a moment, Hector reached out with his trembling left hand and took it. He took a greedy sip.

"That's right," Luke said. "Murder. And you don't want to be involved in that, do you?"

Hector blinked.

"So I need the phone you took. You don't give it to me, and another cop will come take it away from you and pin you as the killer. And he won't give you good coffee." Luke pulled out a twenty-dollar bill. "They might even take the twenty bucks you dropped on the ground."

"I had nothing to do with any murder, man."

"I believe you," Luke said. "So if you have C.D.'s phone, you're going to want to give it to me."

Hector grunted, setting the coffee down on the asphalt. He fished the phone out of his pocket and handed it to Luke, who took it and handed the twenty dollars to Hector, who put the bill in his pocket with a nod of acknowledgement.

"Thanks, Hector," Luke stood. "You might want to get your stuff and go somewhere else. The park's going to be crawling with cops in a few minutes."

He hurried back to the body, where Symanski stood, coffee in hand.

"Well?"

Luke held up the phone.

"Okay. Now—"

He knelt in front of the body, tapped the screen, and held the phone in front of Domino's face.

"What are you—"

"Unlocking his phone," Luke said. "Now, let's go into call history." He tapped the screen. "Okay—Angelina. That's his wife. Just after midnight. Before that, a call to an unknown number." Luke suspected this was Vesper's number. Luke's finger hovered over the number, then he looked over his shoulder.

Pressler was too close. He might hear them. Luke motioned with his head. "Let's go a little further away."

They walked another twenty feet into the covered walkway. That was far enough; the plants would deaden their voices, too. Luke tapped the phone number and put the speakerphone on.

"Hey, come on, that's for—"

The phone rang three, four, five times. Luke hoped for it to go to voicemail—and for the voicemail to say who the phone belonged to, instead of simply announcing the number.

A click.

Vesper's voice, sounding professional. "You have reached Vesper Montpelier at American River Realty. Please leave—"

Luke ended the call.

"So what? Was Domino buying a property?" Symanski took another sip of coffee.

"A fifteen-minute call past eleven at night?" Luke asked. "No. I think Mr. Domino was having an affair." This next part would be tricky. Luke bent forward. "Big Mike dated a woman named Vesper Montpelier."

Symanski cocked an eyebrow.

"And I heard a rumor that Vesper dumped Big Mike for a rich guy in real estate."

"Sacramento is full of real estate millionaires. You'll have to do better than that."

Luke nodded. "Sure. It *is* a hunch, after all." He rubbed his chin. The lack of a goatee felt weird. He opened a browser on his phone, searched for *American River Realty*, then tapped the phone number and turned the speakerphone back on.

A woman's voice answered. "American River Realty, how may I direct your call?"

"Vesper Montpelier, please."

"Speaking."

He paused. He really thought Vesper would be sleeping off a hangover rather than at the reception desk in the office. The resilience of being twenty-four.

"Hi, Vesper," he said, trying not to fumble his words. "This is Detective Lucien Guillory of the Sacramento Police Department—"

"Tell Mike to leave me alone."

Luke glanced up at Symanski; the reaction had surprised her.

"I'm not—" Luke began. He stopped and cleared his throat. "I'm not sure who you're referring to—"

"Michael Moody. I know he had me pulled over last week—"

Ugh. This had the potential to get ugly. "I'm sorry, Ms. Montpelier, but I'm calling about another matter. Did you talk to a man named Pye Domino last night at eleven—"

"I'm reporting you for harassment," Vesper said. "You tell Mike to stop contacting me. I don't belong to him, and I can see whoever I want."

She hung up.

Luke looked up at Symanski.

"All right," Symanski said. "We've got to keep this investigation away from Big Mike."

"And that means keeping ahead of him," Luke said. He paused. "We should call Thoreau."

"And tell them what?"

Luke was already calling.

"Thoreau."

"Captain, it's Guillory and Symanski."

"Everything okay?"

Luke lowered his voice and turned down the speakerphone. "The dead body in Lemon Hill Park is Pye Domino."

A pause. "I recognize that name. Isn't he the property guy?"

"Right."

"I see." A deep sigh. "I hate to do this, Guillory, but—"

"Hold on, Captain. Before you give this case to someone else, we found Domino's phone. He talked to Moody's ex-girlfriend last night, a fifteen-minute call, and when I called her work this morning, she accused Moody of harassing her since their breakup."

"Oh, no," Thoreau said.

"Right. You give this case to Moody and it's a definite conflict of interest."

"This'll be a high-profile case." They paused. "Maybe Friedman and Damanpour—"

"You really think Friedman and Damanpour will be unbiased toward Moody's ex?"

Another sigh. "I take it the two of you want to stay on this case."

"I recognized our victim," Luke said, "and we have his phone. But we don't have to make his identity public yet."

A pause. The gears were turning in Thoreau's head. Luke wanted to say more, but bit his tongue.

"All right, for now," Thoreau said. "We might have to give this to another department altogether, though. I know you and Moody don't get along, but that could compromise the case with bias as much as assigning him to it. Keep your nose clean on this one. Step out of line and it's going to the tenth precinct."

"Thanks, Captain. I'll update you by noon."

"Earlier if you make headway."

"Gotcha."

He ended the call and looked at Symanski.

"Are we equipped for this?" Symanski asked. "Big Mike's going to fight us every step of the way."

"Not if he doesn't know who the victim is," Luke said. "And I hope we can keep it from him for a least a couple of days."

Symanski paused. "You're thinking that Vesper Montpelier dumped Big Mike for Pye Domino?"

"Right."

"So… wouldn't we need to question Big Mike like he's a suspect?"

Luke closed his eyes and exhaled. "In a perfect world."

"And that's going to make things harder on us."

"Let's cross that bridge when we come to it."

"Come on, Guillory. We're already there."

"We have a list of names on the phone to interview first."

"Anyone else on the call history?"

Luke scrolled further. Tuesday during the day, a long call to the office past ten in the morning, forty-three minutes. Two calls of less than a minute each: one to a Blake Yardley, and one to Lincoln Carruthers. That was Ashton's father—was Pye Domino about to blow the whistle on K-Car to his father? Interesting possibilities. But only ten seconds for each call—enough time for short voicemails.

He looked up at Symanski. "Let's get Pressler to canvass the park and we can interview Vesper."

"And the wife. She might have known about Vesper and her husband."

Luke nodded.

VI

They walked back to the cruiser and got in. Luke started the car, and Symanski put her hand on Luke's arm.

"Where are you going?"

"Aren't we going to interview Vesper Montpelier?"

"How do you know her work address?"

"I—" Luke paused. He couldn't very well say he'd been at Vesper's workplace the cycle before, could he? "I know the realty company. Ellie and I interviewed realtors when we bought the house." Technically true. Symanski didn't have to know that they didn't interview Vesper's real estate business.

"Oh."

Luke put the car in gear.

"Wait. We don't know what went on between Big Mike and Vesper, right?"

"No."

"And she already accused you of being Big Mike's minion, right? Harassing her?"

"Uh... yes."

"We need to tread carefully, Detective Guillory. Neither of us needs a lawsuit in our personnel file."

"That's for sure." And even with the shaved beard and a different name, there was still a chance that Vesper would recognize him from the early morning. He'd have to tread carefully indeed.

Although if Vesper recognized Luke, he could start fresh from the next cycle. And he wouldn't be able to exit this day *without* interviewing Vesper, especially if she were the killer. "Let's get CSI to examine the ligature marks," Luke said. "If it's from some kind of rope, let's narrow it down. Length, diameter, that kind of thing. Maybe there are fibers in the wound."

"Could be something like a bungee cord."

"Could be. But I'm thinking the marks look a little rough."

"I didn't look that closely. You think they can tell what kind of rope it might be if any fibers were transferred to the wound?"

"I feel lucky." Luke paused. "You know, I bet realty companies use rope for certain applications."

Symanski paused. "Really?"

"Sure. Must be a ton of problems with houses they're trying to sell."

"Maybe. Not the first thing I think of. But for sure, realtors have contacts for handymen, landscapers, construction companies. All those contacts could have rope."

Luke got a flash of inspiration. "Hey—let's talk to Domino's business partner first."

"The Barkley in Domino-Barkley?"

"That's right. I bet they could tell us about what rope they use."

"So it could have been Domino's own rope?"

Luke thought back to the Domino-Barkley branded canvas bag in Vesper Montpelier's closet. "Maybe." He looked in the rear-view mirror, then scooted out into traffic.

"You know where Domino-Barkley Properties is located, too?"

Luke pressed his lips together. He hadn't looked at the map. "Doesn't everyone know they've got the top floor of the Braley Tower?"

"Well, I didn't."

"You've only been in town a month. You'll know downtown like the back of your hand soon enough."

Symanski narrowed her eyes at Luke.

Luke cleared his throat. "Sorry. That sounded condescending."

A few moments later, Luke pulled next to a curb in a fifteen-minute spot on H Street in the shadow of the twenty-story Braley Tower. They walked through the glass-and-marble lobby, Luke holding out his badge to get past the security guard and into the elevator.

Luke reached out and pushed the *PH* button.

Symanski glanced at Luke. "You act like you own the place."

Luke dropped his hands to his side. "From what I've read,

this guy Barkley is one of your typical entitled, pushy CEO types."

"Give him an inch, he takes a mile?"

"Yeah. But bullies have thin skin. If we push him, he might push back, but it's equally likely he'll back down."

The doors pinged and opened into the reception area. Behind the desk, the young enby with long hair wore a pale blue Oxford dress shirt. Luke had written down their name: Brad? Bev? No, *Brev*.

Symanski and Luke strode to the long reception desk.

"May I help you?" Brev asked.

Symanski flashed her badge. "We'd like to speak to Calvin Barkley."

"Do you have an appointment?"

Luke stepped forward. "We need to speak with him regarding his business partner."

A frown. "Mr. Domino?"

"That's right." Luke raised his head and looked across the open floor to Barkley's glass-encased office. He remembered that he'd been there on Wednesday the last time, and Barkley had met with a man in a shiny gray suit. He searched his mind. Ah, yes, Gabe Wexler.

But the office was empty.

Oh, that's right. Luke had visited later in the day. He and Symanski had taken more time at the park, they'd gone to Angelina Domino's house, and Luke had walked around for an hour or two thinking he was going crazy.

Oh—and in one of the earlier cycles, Luke had asked Brev about the type of rope the company used, and the woman who ordered supplies—Janet? Joanie?—had been in Cancún or Puerto Vallarta or something.

"Mr. Barkley isn't in yet. Neither is Mr. Domino."

"Right," Luke said. "Do you know Mr. Domino well?"

Brev shifted in their seat. "Uh—not really."

"Do you know Vesper Montpelier?"

Brev flinched. "She was the receptionist before me."

"Why did she leave?"

Brev's eyes darted between Symanski and Luke. "I don't know anything for sure."

"But you've heard rumors," Luke pressed.

"I don't want to get anyone in trouble if the rumors aren't true."

Symanski nodded. "I understand. But this is—"

"—a missing persons case," Luke interrupted. Brev had been forthcoming in previous cycles, but had never known that Domino was dead. At least Luke didn't think so. "If Mr. Domino is with Vesper, we need to know."

"Oh." Brev bit their lip. "Well—I heard she and Domino were a thing."

"Like, a romantic thing?" Symanski asked.

"Yeah," they replied. "And I also heard that Vesper had a problem with drugs."

"Magic Star?" Luke asked.

"Uh… I don't know what *kind* of drugs. They caught her sleeping in the utility closet."

Luke leaned forward. "Now, if you took over Vesper's job, and if she'd been fired, you saw quite a few papers and files that Vesper had, right?"

Brev nodded.

"Anything in there that might help us figure out where to find Mr. Domino?"

Brev half-stood from their chair and looked around the office. No one else was paying attention. They sat back down and lowered their voice. "Some emails about Mr. Domino paying for Vesper's apartment in Kadema Gardens. And there was a SugarShack account Vesper was still logged into."

"SugarShack?"

Brev rolled their eyes. "A dating app for rich old people and young hot people."

Luke had missed so much in the dating world since he'd gotten serious with Ellie.

"She and Domino were kind of explicit in their DMs," Brev continued. "I don't think the company knew about that app."

"Can we see the SugarShack account?"

Brev shook their head. "Oh, God, no. I deleted SugarShack as soon as I found it. I had no desire to get blamed for anything, and I sure didn't want Vesper or Mr. Domino finding out that I saw it."

Luke rubbed his newly hairless chin. They might get the Sacramento P.D. tech people to find the app, but there might be an easier way to gain access to Vesper's SugarShack account—or Domino's. "Sorry for all these questions," Luke said, "but I've got another one. Would Vesper have had access to any rope while she was working here?"

"Rope? No, I don't think so."

Luke furrowed his brow. He needed to make this connection. "You sure? You don't have any vendors who give samples out, or any welcome kits or anything?"

"Oh. Well, yeah, we do have these welcome kits we give to our clients when they lease property or buy a building. It's kind of kitschy, but people seem to like it." Brev paused. "Yeah, we put rope in the kit."

"And when Mr. Domino rented the Kadema Gardens apartment to Vesper, did she get a welcome kit?"

Brev shrugged. Of course Brev wouldn't know if Domino gave his on-the-down-low lover a welcome kit with the possible murder weapon in it.

Symanski stepped forward. "Do you know anyone who would want to harm Mr. Domino?"

Brev paused.

"Perhaps a business arrangement that someone was unhappy with?" Symanski continued.

Luke crossed his arms. This wasn't the direction he wanted to go in; Vesper had motive, opportunity, and, with the rope from the welcome bag, means. But he couldn't very well interrupt his partner.

"Solomon Vargas," Brev said.

"What does he have to do with Mr. Domino?"

Brev sighed and crossed their arms. "I thought this place was different. When I started here, the company was working on a project to convert unused office space to low-income housing. Taking action on the unhoused problem, you know?"

Symanski nodded. "And Vargas was involved with this project?"

Brev leaned forward. "He's a civil engineer and designed a process and developed an inexpensive material to do it."

Symanski furrowed her brow.

"Right," Luke said, trying to move things along. "Conversion to residential is a lot more complex and expensive than people think."

Brev nodded enthusiastically at Luke. "And Vargas has patents on three types of materials. A composite—"

"And Domino reneged on the deal?" Luke asked.

Brev pressed their lips together. "Well, I don't think he meant to, but the vote didn't go their way."

Symanski shot a questioning look at Luke.

"The Sutter Block Towers," Luke said.

"7th and D," Symanski said.

"Right. Empty for almost five years now. So Vargas and Domino strike a deal to convert the building using Vargas's cheap conversion methods, but the city council voted down the zoning change."

Brev nodded.

"And Solomon Vargas was upset?" Symanski asked.

Luke stared at Barkley's empty office while Symanski got more information out of Brev. It was everything he'd heard before: the promise to push through the zoning change, Vargas being homeless, Vargas heading up the construction project. Symanski asked about the rope this time, though she didn't know that she was looking for Canfield Pro Polymer A rope. Luke had been wrong: the woman who ordered the rope was *Janice.*

"What did the deal look like?" Symanski asked.

"Vargas gave exclusive rights to his patents to us," Brev said. "In exchange for his company leading the construction project. A win-win for everyone—well, it was supposed to be a win-win."

Symanski questioned Brev for a few more minutes, but Brev had no more information to add. Luke caught Symanski's eye, and Symanski wrapped it up. A few minutes later, they were in the cruiser.

"Where to next?" Symanski said as Luke started the engine.

"Let's get a warrant for Vesper's apartment," Luke said. "With Brev's statement, I think it's enough to search her place—"

"What?" Symanski said. "We haven't done nearly enough work yet. The wife might have known about the affair. We don't have any physical evidence connecting Vesper to the crime."

"We know Vesper got Domino involved with drugs." Luke turned right on 23rd toward the precinct. "We know she had access to the rope."

"Everybody has access to rope."

"Not Canfield Pro Polymer A." Luke soldiered on. "We know she was about to lose the apartment."

Symanski was silent.

Oh no.

"Detective Guillory," Symanski said, using the same tone of

voice Zepherine used with him as a child when he was in trouble, "how do you know Vesper Montpelier is about to lose her apartment? How do you know Vesper got Domino involved in drugs? And how do you know what kind of rope was used in the murder?"

Luke's mind raced. He couldn't tell her that he was repeating these days, could he? She'd taken it okay the last time he'd said something. He blinked. What would Justine Blood tell him to do?

Something came into his head that he hadn't written down: Justine had gotten Big Mike into bed, and he'd told her stuff about Vesper.

"I—I, uh," Luke stammered. How could he get this into words? He stared through the windshield, looking as if the driving was distracting him—then the green light ahead of him went from green to yellow to red. When he stopped, Symanski's eyes were boring into him.

"All right. I heard this stuff from—" He almost said, "Big Mike," but stopped. If it got out that he was getting his information from a relationship that a fellow detective had with a suspect, they might *all* get booted off the case.

Not ideal.

"You won't believe me if I told you," Luke said.

"Try me."

Luke took a deep breath. "I've been repeating the two days after Pye Domino's death. Wednesday and Thursday. This is my fifth or sixth time through these two days. So all the stuff I know? I learned most of it in a previous cycle. And no, I don't know why I'm repeating these two days, and yes, I know it sounds nuts."

The light turned green before he could look at his partner's reaction.

VII

They drove in silence for a minute while Luke pulled the cruiser into the precinct lot. He navigated the car into a parking space and put it in Park.

"You're not kidding?" Symanski asked.

"No. I wish I were."

"Well, you're right. I don't believe it."

Luke nodded. "I don't believe it either. I thought I was going crazy the first couple of forty-eight-hour cycles." He pressed his lips together and turned to her. "During the second cycle, I freaked out. I yelled at everyone that they were trying to trick me. This was in the middle of an interview with Angelina, so it didn't look too good."

"Who?"

"Oh—Angelina Domino, Pye's widow." He rubbed his chin. "She has a whole bunch of that new patented material that Solomon Vargas created in her garage. Pye brought it there a few days ago. She didn't seem to know about his affair, but she could be a good actor."

Symanski cocked her head.

"And before," Luke said, taking care not to lie, "I found a canvas bag in Vesper's closet with a rope in it. And to me, it looked like the same kind of rope that the killer used to garrote Domino."

Symanski furrowed her brow. "And did you have a warrant for searching Vesper's apartment?"

"Well—no. You and I had found a rental agreement with the Kadema Gardens apartment when we searched Pye Domino's study at his house."

Symanski shook her head. "I'm not sure what you're up to—"

"I don't blame you for not believing me." Luke checked his watch—only about a quarter to eleven. "Right around lunchtime, Ellie's best friend Martha is going to walk into the precinct and hand me divorce papers."

"What?"

"I think she hangs around for a while if I'm not there. And she goes to my house later if I don't show up at work."

"I thought—"

"Look, you don't have to believe me. I'll say stuff that happened in previous cycles—"

"Cycles?"

"Well, that's what I call them. Forty-eight-hour periods."

Symanski crossed her arms. "I don't know if I'm being punked, or if you—"

Luke rubbed his eyes. "Well, crap. You believed me before. Or at least you were more willing to go along with me." He paused. "Of course, the first time I told you was after I had a breakdown, so you knew something was up." He smacked the steering wheel. "All right, forget I said anything. Everything I mentioned before? A hunch. A lucky guess, maybe."

"You're having too many lucky guesses."

Luke shrugged. "All right, fine." She wouldn't believe him even when if Martha showed up—she'd think Luke put her up to it.

This day wasn't going well.

Still, getting out of the cycle was a priority.

"I know you don't believe me, but we still can't have Moody take the case from us. He'd arrest the wrong person, and he'd hide Vesper away from the case. She's a viable suspect, and—"

Symanski set her jaw. "That's a big accusation."

"Well—" Luke closed his eyes. "Forget I said anything."

Symanski nodded. "Maybe that's a good idea."

"Tell you what," Luke said. "I'll see if I can get a warrant for Vesper's apartment, and you go interview Angelina. Maybe Solomon Vargas too."

"We're supposed to be partners," Symanski snapped.

"I don't know what to tell you," Luke said quietly. "Vesper is the prime suspect. I've seen it for a while now."

Symanski folded her arms. "Walk me through this. What makes you think she's the prime suspect?"

Luke held up one finger. "She was in a club a few blocks from Lemon Hill Park about twenty minutes after the murder." A second finger went up. "She's a Magic Star user, and she was high last night. If my suspicions are correct, the M.E. will find Magic Star in Pye Domino's system—and Vesper Montpelier could have supplied Domino with enough Magic Star to knock him out." A third finger joined the other two. "She had access to the Canfield Pro Polymer A rope that was used to garrote Domino." Luke popped his pinkie up too. "And Domino not only spurned her, but he was about to stop paying for her apartment." He dropped his hand to his lap. "Means, motive, opportunity."

"Lots of suspects have motive to kill Domino. I bet lots of them also had access to that kind of rope. And we haven't talked to anyone who has a strong alibi."

"That's a lot of unknowns. We *know* Vesper Montpelier was there. We *know* she had access to a possible murder weapon, and a viable way to keep him docile while killing him. We *know* she had motive."

Symanski shook her head. "Yes, Vesper could have done it, but I don't think you've looked closely enough at the other suspects. Have you dug into the wife at all?"

"Some. If she'd killed Domino, though, it wouldn't have been at Lemon Hill Park. She wouldn't go to a dangerous place like that by herself."

"She might if she thought homicide detectives would assume she'd never go there."

Luke rubbed his forehead. "Well, yeah, that's true. People are killed by their intimate partners in over half of all murders."

Symanski frowned. "At the risk of undermining my own point, that's only for women. Half of all female victims are killed by their spouse or partner. For men, it's under ten percent." She held up an index finger and pointed at Luke. "But you haven't done the work to make sure. You're homing in on Vesper Montpelier because you think the pieces all fit. But you haven't taken all the puzzle pieces out of the box yet."

Luke was quiet. He only had two days to get out of this cycle. Yes, each piece of evidence against Vesper Montpelier wasn't compelling by itself, but when all the evidence was taken together? She was a strong suspect.

"And I can't believe you've uncovered this information in 'repeating days'." Symanski opened the door and got out. "I'll see you in there. Maybe you should take a walk. Clear your head. Take a few steps back and see as much of the picture as you can."

She shut the cruiser door, leaving Luke alone.

Okay, well, this was a setback. He shouldn't have said anything, but he was puzzled. Symanski had accepted his crazy story before—was that in the second cycle? Or third? No, the third cycle was when he was in jail. Why hadn't she accepted it this time?

Maybe Symanski was right. Take a walk, clear his head. He'd been laser-focused on assembling the case against Vesper Montpelier so he could escape this cycle. Was that the right thing to do?

He got out of the cruiser. He went inside, checked in and handed the keys over, then exited the way he'd come in, walking through the cruiser lot and getting out onto 23rd Street.

Luke wasn't sure what to do—then the light bulb went on in his head. He took out his wallet and opened the middle section.

Justine Blood's number.

VIII

"Hello?" Her voice was disinterested.

"Detective Blood, it's Luke Guillory."

"Well, how about that? I thought you'd never call. Figured you'd been an idiot and threw away my number."

"Actually, we've talked before. A few times."

"Oh?" She perked up. "Really? How many cycles is this?"

"I think it's five. Might be six."

"Five. How many have we talked in?"

"Uh… well, all but one."

"The first one?"

"No, I talked to you in the first cycle, when I didn't know it was a cycle. I didn't talk to you in the cycle where I was arrested for the murder that I need to solve."

Justine Blood burst out laughing. "Knew too much, huh? Yeah, they tried to do that to me, too, once or twice."

"Well, here's the thing: I think I know who the killer is."

"That's a good step."

"But I don't know how to assemble all the information I need to make it stick. And to get out of this cycle."

Blood smiled. "Yeah, I figured you'd need some help."

"And I did something stupid."

She grinned again. "Figures. What did you do?"

"I confided in Detective Symanski about the cycles repeating."

Blood rolled her eyes. "Of course you'd do that."

"You told me you did that a few times, too. Your ex, your partner—"

"Sure. Whenever I did it, the day always restarted. You and me, we're the only ones alive who know about this little repeating cycle thing. Doesn't bode well for you getting out of the cycle this time, does it?"

"I'll take my chances. Can we meet?"

"Now that I'm back from Pilates, I don't have anything else to do today."

"You do Pilates?"

"Shut up. It's good for my core. Plus, Vineet is a hottie." She cleared her throat. "Blue Oak Tavern?"

"How about some lunch? My treat."

"If you insist."

"What do you want? The world is your oyster."

Justine thought for a moment. "You know that hole-in-the-wall place on 12th and J?"

"Jake Dandy's. I like their Southern Dandy Burger."

She chuckled. "Jeez, Lukey-boy, how many different animals do you eat at one sitting? A little rich for my blood."

"Today isn't real. You'll be resetting in no time. No time for the grease to set up camp in your arteries."

Justine laughed. "Fine. I can be there in half an hour."

IX

Though Luke set out walking at a good clip, Justine still beat him to Jake Dandy's. The same Black woman behind the counter was chatting with Justine. Luke sat next to Detective Blood, and the woman behind the counter stopped talking and stared at him.

"This tall drink of water is with me," Justine said, then narrowed her eyes at Luke. "What happened to your goatee? You look like you sell used Toyotas."

"Long story."

"You've got time, remember?"

"Maybe later."

The woman behind the counter nodded. "Get you a drink?"

"Twin River Stout?"

"How 'bout a menu?"

Luke bobbed his head at Justine. "She order a Southern Dandy?"

"Nope. The Cluck-mazing."

Luke ordered a cheeseburger and fries.

The woman turned back to the grill, and soon the sound of the exhaust fan and the sizzle of the fryer drowned everything else out.

"All right," Justine said to Luke. "Now, what is it you need help with?"

"I caught a case. Originally, they thought it was an overdose in Lemon Hill Park. But it's a murder—a garroting with rope, we think—and the victim is Pye Domino."

"Should I know who that is?"

"Big shot real-estate developer."

Justine raised her eyebrows. "And Big Mike hasn't tried to steal it from you yet?"

"Every other cycle? Yes. And he's succeeded. But his ex-girlfriend, Vesper Montpelier, is my main suspect." He told Justine everything: the club, the search of Vesper's apartment closet resulting in the welcome bag with the rope, the discovery of the apartment manager's letter on the counter.

Blood nodded. "Signs all pointing to her so far. Doesn't sound like you've done a lot to find other suspects, though."

"Not today, no, but in previous cycles, I interviewed the widow, Pye's business partner, and his Magic Star dealer. And there's this guy that Domino screwed over with his last business deal. I guess I should do more work on him."

"And Vesper's the one who jumped out at you?"

"No one else had the same combination of motive, opportunity, and means. I know, landing on Big Mike's ex might be career suicide, but how else am I getting out of the cycle?"

The woman set down two beers: the stout in front of Luke, and an Action Lager in front of Justine. Cheap and skunky. Justine grabbed the beer. "Maybe not," she mused. "If this makes Big Mike look bad, maybe people will stop thinking you're compromised just because of Zepherine." She took a swig.

"I don't think that'll happen."

"How much of the brain and memory exercises have I talked about?"

"A little bit in the last cycle. I've been writing down everything I remember."

"And what do you know so far?"

Luke told her everything he remembered, especially about Vesper Montpelier.

The food came and Luke continued talking while Justine ate and listened thoughtfully.

"How is it?" Luke asked.

"The chicken? Not as good as Southern Cross, but it's not bad."

The small restaurant filled up with both people and chatter, and Luke and Justine leaned in to talk to each other without broadcasting their conversation.

"I'll say it again, Lukey-boy. I'm not hearing that you've eliminated anyone else."

Luke grunted. "That's what Symanski said, too."

"Your partner has a good head on her shoulders."

"Look, I know each piece of evidence by itself isn't compelling, but taken together—"

"That's not the right way to think about it," Justine said. "You passed the detective exam, so you know you need to keep your options open. Not just in the paperwork, but in your head."

"I know."

"You might know that intellectually, but you're sure single-minded on one suspect." Justine tapped her fingers on the counter. "Maybe you're too pissed off at Big Mike and you're hoping his ex is the killer so you can knock him down a peg. But right now, if you hear something that pertains to another suspect, you'll ignore it. You're concentrating too much on one suspect, and your brain's blocking out everything else."

"I hear what you're saying," Luke said carefully, "but like I said, Vesper for sure had means, motive, and opportunity. She had access to the right brand of commercial-grade rope that Domino-Barkley Properties ordered, she was a couple of blocks from Lemon Hill Park when the murder took place, and she was getting kicked out of her apartment because Pye Domino broke things off."

"That's not enough to draw a conclusion, Lukey-boy. No one else had means, motive, and opportunity?"

"Not that I've found, no."

"And she's the only one with access to this brand of rope?"

Luke was quiet.

"Well?"

"I found the rope in a Domino-Barkley 'welcome' bag."

"Ah. So anyone who worked with the victim could have gotten the rope. Hell, the victim could have brought the rope with him." Justine paused. "Where was the wife?"

Luke didn't answer.

"How about the business partner?"

A pause. "They say they were both home alone, asleep."

"And this Vargas guy?"

"Yeah. He's about to lose everything because Domino couldn't get the zoning vote passed."

"You said he used to be homeless?"

"Right."

"So he'd know Lemon Hill Park, right? Where was he?"

"I—I, uh, haven't interviewed him yet."

Justine shook her head. "I just named three other people who had reason to kill Pye Domino, who had access to the same rope in the welcome bag. And you don't know where *any* of them were." She set her mouth in a line. "Let's finish up and go to my place. I've got something to show you."

X

The small house on Cherry Street looked tidy but thoughtless from the front: a few mismatched bushes and plants. Between the porch and the sidewalk, gray pebbles where a lawn had most likely been; not for decorative purposes; more like the house owner couldn't be bothered to take care of a yard.

Justine pulled up into the driveway, and Luke got out of the passenger side. She hurried into the house, Luke racing to follow. She unlocked the door and pushed it open, then rushed through the living room and down a hall on the left.

Luke stood in the living room, unsure of what to do next. He took a few more steps in: the kitchen was tidy, but more from disuse rather than someone who'd kept it clean.

Justine walked into the kitchen with a large cardboard box and set it with difficulty on the floor.

She pulled out a red binder. On the spine: *Cheatham, 2018.*

"Is this what I think it is?"

Justine nodded. "Except it's all the stuff the police didn't get to see." She set the binder on the counter and opened it. She flipped several pages, then clicked the rings open and pulled out a sheaf of paper—no, not a sheaf, a folded page.

She walked over to the kitchen table and unfolded the sheet. It was at least six feet long and almost as wide. Lines, different colored writing. Days of the week across the top.

He bent over at the waist, not touching the table or the paper.

"There are a lot of names on here."

"Yeah, no kidding. This took me hours to do. And after a

while, I needed to complete this pretty much every time I restarted the cycle."

"Oh," Luke said. "Of course. The Cheatham case was one of these multiple-cycle things."

"Not *just* one of those multiple-cycle things," Justine said. "I repeated the cycle over a hundred times. Maybe two hundred. I lost count." She balled her hands into fists. "I couldn't get it. I gave up for a while. Stopped going to work for maybe ten cycles. Forgot everything I'd learned. But there's only so many two-day trips you can take. And so many times you can bang Big Mike." She chortled.

Luke blinked. He didn't like to think about his mentor and tormentor getting it on.

"And," Justine continued, "the case started to eat at me again." She tapped a name near the center of the side. "I followed everyone who knew Derrick Cheatham for a few cycles. And I interviewed them again and again. And I started to mix up my questions. On one of the cycles, Quinton Moore gave me different answers depending on how I asked the questions."

"Oh."

"So he immediately popped out as a suspect. I hadn't thought of him before."

"But he wasn't the killer."

"No, but he had something to hide. He'd been stealing money from Cheatham's daughter's school. And that got me thinking—how had he been able to keep that from me after over a hundred days? So I started making this chart."

Luke studied the chart. A timeline of every person associated with the case, even people no one would have thought of, broken down in fifteen-minute increments.

"You have to train your memory," Justine says. "If I were you, I'd start creating a chart like this. Recreate it by memory every cycle."

Luke blanched.

"Yeah, I know. It's a shit-ton of work, but if you want to get out of this repeating loop, then recreate that chart by memory every time you wake up on Wednesday. Writing all the case facts down helped me to remember facets of the case. Interviews I'd had a dozen cycles before." She exhaled, long and slow. "This murder took me a long, long time to solve. You want to exit the cycles? This is what you have to do."

"How is it helpful to create a chart of where everyone is *after* the murder?"

Justine tapped her temple. "Because where people go, who they see, what they do? Very revealing. Lots of times, they reveal the killer. The son who went to see the girlfriend the dead father hated but didn't take the precautions he normally took. The business partner who made a dinner reservation for three instead of four, even though he hadn't been told of his colleague's death."

Luke slouched his shoulders. This sounded exhausting.

Justine tilted her head. "You need a break? Take all your 'vacation' time in the early cycles. When you wake up and you realize you're starting a new cycle, *that's* the time to screw around. Call in sick, take day trips to the river or Yosemite or San Francisco or wherever you want."

Luke nodded.

"Once you start working," Justine continued, "keep your memory sharp. Anytime it overwhelms you and you feel like taking a couple days off, you risk of forgetting everything you've learned." She folded her arms. "I wound up starting over a few times, no idea what I'd done before. In two days, you can forget a lot you learned, and if you've already been stuck for twenty or thirty cycles, it'll take another ten or twelve cycles to get back to where you were."

Goosebumps crawled over Luke's skin.

"Oh—and for God's sake, keep these charts hidden away. If

my captain had found any of them, I'd have had to answer a lot of uncomfortable questions."

"And it would land you in jail."

"That never happened to me, fortunately." She dropped her arms to her sides. "Well, not outside a cycle, anyway. As soon as I knew the cycle would reset without me arresting the killer, I'd study the chart, rewrite parts of it, and get ready to recreate it the minute the cycle reset."

Luke slumped his shoulders. Justine was right that making this kind of chart would take a lot of work—work that would need to be redone every cycle.

But he didn't want to be stuck in these two days anymore.

XI

Luke called Symanski from the back of the FlashRide on the way back to the precinct.

"Guillory? Where the hell are you?"

"I'm—I'm on my way back."

"I didn't ask you if you're coming back—"

"I went to talk to Detective Blood."

A pause before Symanski asked, tentatively, *"Justine Blood?"*

"Yes."

"She get your head on straight?"

Luke paused. "Look, I know you don't believe me, but Detective Blood had this happen to her too."

Silence.

"And by that," Luke continued, "I mean the repeating-days thing."

"Yeah, I know what you meant." He couldn't tell if Symanski was pissed off or resigned. "So you're saying that if I called Detective Blood—"

"I don't know what she'd say. She doesn't exactly like this getting around."

A deep sigh from the other end of the phone.

"The repeating days thing—that's how she solved the Cheatham case. Took her over a hundred two-day cycles before she figured it out."

Another sigh.

"Okay, you don't have to believe me—"

"I don't," Symanski said quickly.

"Right, but we can still—"

"Since you left and I didn't know where you were, I took the stupid search warrant for Vesper Montpelier's apartment to Judge Bancroft. And he signed it. So do you want to join us?"

"When?"

"We're serving it at a quarter to five."

Vesper would probably still be at work. "Yes." Luke glanced at his watch. Four fifteen. "I'll be at the precinct in ten minutes."

When he arrived at the precinct, Symanski was waiting for him in the lobby. She drove Luke to Vesper's apartment complex, where two other teams of officers—none of whom Luke knew, thankfully—were ready to execute the warrant.

Symanski marched into the apartment's management office, Luke on her heels, and presented the warrant to the property manager. He was a large man in a royal blue *Kadema Gardens* polo shirt, and he paled when he saw the warrant. He went into the back and came out less than a minute later with a key.

All seven of them—four officers, the property manager, Luke, and Symanski—traipsed across the complex to Vesper's building and up the flight of cement stairs to Apartment 210. Symanski and Luke both snapped on their latex gloves, as did all the officers.

The property manager opened the door with his key. Luke checked the time: 4:48 PM.

They took the letter from the property management company from the counter. Luke pointed out the bag in the closet underneath the pile of shoes.

One officer found another coil of Canfield Pro rope in the bottom of Vesper's bedroom closet, under yet another pile of clothes.

Symanski took Vesper's laptop from the coffee table.

They were in and out in seventeen minutes.

XII

The silence in the cruiser back to the precinct was deafening. After three or four minutes—which seemed like hours—Symanski finally spoke.

"How did you know about the welcome package with the rope in it?"

Luke shook his head. "That's not important," he said. "Let's focus on getting this case closed."

"Dr. Koh should be able to match the type of rope to the ligature marks."

Luke shrugged. "The type of rope will be a match. Unique fiber." Luke turned to stare out the window.

"You really think you have to solve the murder in a day?"

"Two days," Luke replied. "Which is crazy, I know."

"Maybe we go some other directions while we wait on Dr. Koh."

Luke nodded. "What first?"

"Wife," Symanski said. "I can already hear the admonishment from Thoreau for not talking to the widow before now."

"And let's make sure we look at the Vargastic."

Symanski paused. "The what?"

"Sorry. That's what Solomon Vargas called his building material—what he uses in the office building retrofit for residential."

They drove in silence for a couple of miles, and the houses grew further apart as the road narrowed.

"Look at this place," Symanski said. She pointed out the window.

A posh café they'd passed in a previous cycle, with an elegant sign reading *This Morning — Crepes, Mimosas, Brunch*. Luke had read the sign correctly before.

"I bet breakfast costs fifty bucks there," Symanski muttered.

"I bet they have better coffee than the precinct."

They turned into the Beckman Highlands neighborhood and, after a few more turns, stopped in front of the palatial Domino residence. Angelina Domino answered the door in her maroon pants and white silk blouse, with the same red-rimmed gray eyes as in previous cycles.

"Angelina Domino?" Symanski said. "I'm Detective Summer Symanski with the Sacramento P.D., and this is my colleague, Detective Lucien Guillory."

"Detectives," Mrs. Domino said, opening the door wider. "Please come in."

"We're sorry for your loss," Luke said. "And please understand, we must ask you these questions. They might seem insulting—well, they *are* insulting—but we have to have these answers to move forward in the investigation."

Angelina nodded.

They proceeded to ask Angelina the same questions as a few cycles before: when was the last time she saw him, was she asleep all night, if she knew about his relationship with Vesper. They walked into the garage and Angelina showed them all the Vargastic building materials stored there.

Fortunately, Big Mike didn't pull into the driveway this cycle.

They assessed the building materials soberly. "Did Mr. Domino say how much this material was worth?" Luke asked.

Angelina shook her head.

"I'm sorry to ask this," Symanski said, "but do you inherit everything from your husband?"

"Everything?"

"Now that he's passed."

"Oh." Angelina blinked, standing in the garage next to her SUV. "I don't think so. Some. I get the house and enough to maintain my, uh, lifestyle. But most of his money is going to charity. He made the change after his plane accident."

"No other beneficiaries? No kids from a previous marriage?"

Angelina shook her head, her eyes wet.

"Did you and Mr. Domino have a prenuptial agreement?"

Angelina frowned. "Yes—but that was years ago. All the terms expired on our twentieth anniversary."

"Life insurance?"

"Oh, he increased his policy after the crash. It's—it's quite sizable, I think, but I don't know the details."

"Do you mind if we look in Mr. Domino's office?" Luke asked.

"I need to make a call," Symanski said. "I'll step outside."

Luke found the same items that he and Symanski had found a few cycles ago: the documents showing Domino paying for Vesper's apartment in the false bottom of the desk drawer; the files for Sutter Block Towers. After ten minutes, Angelina returned.

"How is the real estate business lately?" Luke asked as Angelina watched him from the home office doorway.

"Fine." Angelina hesitated.

"Something wrong?"

"Well, Pye was angry when he came home from the city council meeting Monday night."

"Do you know why?" The city council vote hadn't gone his way, for sure, but had he told Angelina? Or was Domino upset about something else, like an interaction with his mistress? Of course, he wouldn't tell Angelina about that.

"He said something about a broken promise."

"Did he mention Solomon Vargas?"

"I think so, but he was pacing all around the house. I didn't really listen."

"Did anyone else come to the house in the last few days? For business reasons?"

Angelina paused. "Besides Calvin?"

"Oh—was Calvin a frequent visitor?"

Angelina shook her head. "Honestly, not anymore. But he and one of his clients came by."

Luke cocked his head. "Solomon Vargas?"

"Uh, no. I know Solomon. This man was white. In a nice suit. Tall."

"How old?"

"His hair was gray, but not all the way. But who knows—that could be thirty or sixty-five."

"Right," Luke agreed. "Beard? Mustache?"

"No, clean-shaven."

"I see." Luke took out his phone and searched for a picture of *Gabe Wexler* online. He found one on ProfLinks, and he turned the screen toward Angelina. "Is this him?"

Angelina nodded.

"What did they talk about?"

"I didn't listen. They stayed about a half hour."

He turned his attention to Wexler's ProfLinks profile. Not very active, mostly reposting articles. A couple on technology in military applications. Another on temporary military housing in war zones, the need for something strong and stable. He tapped his way back to Wexler's profile. Vice President of Project Management. Company name not made public, and Luke didn't want to spend the $18.99 a month to get that info.

Besides, knowing that Barkley and Wexler visited Domino wasn't useful unless Luke knew the content of the conversation. Maybe he could ask Barkley about it.

Symanski appeared behind Angelina, rocking back and forth on the balls of her feet.

"Off your call?" Luke asked.

"Sure am," Symanski said, a little too brightly. "You ready to go?"

"Yep."

They both wished Angelina Domino well and mentioned again how sorry they were for her loss as they walked through the house and out the front door.

Luke could barely keep up with Symanski as she hurried to the cruiser. As soon as they got in, Luke turned to her. "Well?"

"Well, what?"

"You're clearly dying to tell me what you found out."

"Yeah. That life insurance policy? Angelina is getting over ten million dollars."

"That's quite a bit."

"Angelina was right. When Domino changed his will, he cut her share down significantly and gave the balance to several charities. But he upped his life insurance."

"Did he up his life insurance to more than Angelina would get in a divorce?"

Symanski bobbed her head noncommittally. "I have our forensic accountant looking into that."

"If so," Luke said, "there's a lot more motive for Angelina Domino."

XIII

"Where to now?" Luke asked, turning the ignition.

Symanski picked up her phone and tapped the screen. The speakerphone came on, and the phone rang.

A woman's voice. "Sacramento M.E."

"Good afternoon, Dr. Koh."

A scoff from the other end. "I hope you don't have any more dead bodies. The overtime is killing my budget. Plus, I've got Kings tickets tonight. Last game of the season. I am *not* missing this."

"The body we brought in this morning," Symanski said. "From Lemon Hill Park."

"Yeah. We're processing the fingerprints once the database gets back online. You should have the ID first thing tomorrow."

Luke bit his tongue. Thoreau *had* listened to him and had kept Domino's identity out of the precinct. Big Mike wouldn't try to steal this case until tomorrow, and they'd already established Vesper—Big Mike's ex—as the prime suspect. Even if other suspects were emerging, there'd be no way Big Mike would pry this case away from him now.

"I know you're swamped," Symanski said. "Thanks for everything."

"Hold on, hold on," Koh said, "don't you want to know about the murder weapon?"

Symanski shot a look at Luke out of the corner of her eye. "Of course."

"Fiber transfer from the garroting wound. We've narrowed down the type of rope."

Symanski cleared her throat. "What did you discover?"

"Called a Multi W Braid," Koh replied. "Nylon core, polypropylene cover, and a third braid of a unique fiber. Only one manufacturer—they've patented it."

"Canfield Pro Polymer A," Luke whispered so only Symanski could hear.

"Made by Canfield. This rope is called their 'Pro Polymer A,' and it's only available to commercial organizations. Not something you'll find at Marks-The-Spot. And you're looking for a rope about an eighth-inch thick."

Symanski turned to look at Luke, her eyes wide and a crease down the middle of her forehead. "Good—good," she stuttered after a brief hesitation. "Does it match rope associated with any of our suspects?"

Koh harrumphed. "'Thank you, Dr. Koh,'" she said, imitating Symanski's voice. "'I know how resource and time-intensive it is to analyze fibers from a garroting wound. This type of analysis often takes two to three weeks, so your team working their asses off to get this completed in a matter of hours is nothing short of miraculous.'"

"I'm sorry, Dr. Koh," Symanski said. "Of course, you and your team are fantastic. We'll tell Captain Thoreau how you went above and beyond."

"Now you're kissing my ass," Koh said. "Get us something to compare it to, and we'll see if we have a match. Until then, I'd imagine finding out who ordered that particular brand of rope would be your priority."

"I appreciate it."

Koh's tone softened. "I'll let you know if the fingerprint database comes online before I got home."

"Great, thanks." Symanski ended the call. She cocked an eyebrow at Luke. "So you knew."

"Yeah."

Symanski pursed her lips. "Even if the rope from the apartment is a match, it doesn't mean Vesper did it."

"Right."

"I'll see who's ordered this Canfield Pro rope in the last few months."

"Let's hope that narrows it down," Luke said.

A rumbling sound. Symanski looked down. "Apparently," Symanski said, "I've gotta get some food in my system."

Luke looked at his watch: a few minutes past seven. "Thoreau approving our overtime?"

"I'm pushing two hours already."

"Me too."

"What do we still need to do?" Symanski asked.

"We could interview that one guy who created the building materials. Solomon Vargas."

"But we might want to wait for Koh and the rope results. See if we can tie Vargas to any rope purchases before we go interview him."

Luke nodded. "And we can interview Vesper's dealer."

"Her dealer?"

"Yeah. A guy named Ashton Carruthers. Hangs around Pye Domino's neighborhood."

Symanski narrowed her eyes.

Oh, this was one of those things she thought Luke would say was because of the time loop. Did he want to bring up the repeating cycles up again? Maybe he should take it more slowly.

"Got the name from Aaron. My friend in Vice. The dealer goes by 'K-Car.'"

"All right. I guess I can do one more interview before I eat."

Luke shook his head. "I don't know where he is tonight, but I know he'll be in Beckman Highlands tomorrow morning. He hits 'em after the morning commute on Thursdays." He looked at Symanski. "If you want to strategize, we could grab something. Talk over dinner."

Symanski shook her head. "I appreciate it, but I've got stuff to do."

"Sure." That's right: meeting her book club friend for a run.

"Let's go back to the precinct. Good night's sleep, and we'll get 'em tomorrow."

XIV

Back at the precinct, Symanski packed up and left. Luke was alone in the bullpen; Thoreau's door was closed. Luke called three expensive restaurants; none of them had openings. And Le Bistro Cinq only had that opening at 5:30, which was long past. He stared at his computer for a while, the online map showing several unappetizing chain restaurants.

Maybe this was a good thing: the investigation was starting to circle Vesper Montpelier, and this could be the cycle where he'd make the arrest that would get him out of the cycle.

He zoomed out and found an affordable Jamaican restaurant in the Arden-Arcade neighborhood. A little out of his way, but maybe worth trying.

The crowded restaurant was in a strip mall. He took a seat at the bar, ordered a beer, and asked for a full menu. He took his time ordering, then went over the case as he ate the jerk chicken and fried plantains. Vesper was his prime suspect, and he could *almost* place her at the scene of the murder, and he could *almost* connect her to the murder weapon. And motive wasn't a problem.

He thought about canvassing the neighborhoods along Fruitridge to see if Vesper had gone to Lemon Hill Park. But no—these houses weren't close enough to Lemon Hill Park to prove anything about Vesper's timeline. Plus, he didn't want to find any witnesses who would have seen Luke putting an under-the-influence Vesper into his car. That wouldn't look good.

He finished his last few bites and drained the rest of his beer. He didn't know what to do next.

He opened his wallet to take a credit card out to pay and saw the corner of Justine Blood's business card.

Of course. The chart.

After paying, he drove to Marks-The-Spot. The store was closing at nine—only fifteen minutes—so he hurried to the school supplies section, where he found something that would work: a roll of white craft paper, twenty-four inches wide. That would be plenty. A pack of art markers, too. He could color-code stuff.

As he stood in line to pay, his phone vibrated. A text from Ellie.

> You haven't been home
>
> We need to talk

Ugh. He had a murder to solve if he wanted to get out of this endless time loop cycle, and his wife wanted to serve him divorce papers. He'd been with Justine Blood when Martha had attempted to give him the papers at lunchtime.

Still standing in line, he texted back.

> Yeah, I heard Martha was looking for me
>
> Serving me divorce papers, I suspect
>
> It's okay, it's obvious we were headed that direction
>
> I'm in the middle of an investigation, though
>
> Can you wait until Friday?

"Sir?"

Luke looked up. "Sorry." He bought the butcher paper and the markers, and Ellie didn't text him back.

He cleared off the dining table at home and spread the butcher paper over the top. It was quite a bit smaller than the

Cheatham case chart that Justine Blood had shown him, but it would do. At least for this cycle.

He wrote all the suspects down the left-hand side. Vesper was at the top. Solomon Vargas was next, then Angelina Domino. He put Calvin Barkley next, followed by Gabe Wexler. After hesitating, he wrote Big Mike's name too. Moody might be the best detective in the city after Justine Blood's retirement, but he had motive. And he had an entire police force who'd cover it up.

Luke closed his eyes. He hoped Big Mike wasn't the killer. Maybe arresting Moody would end this time loop, but the ramifications would echo for the rest of his career. He'd have to leave the Sacramento P.D., that was for sure, whether his mother was in Pioneer Mesa Prison or not.

He filled in the time slots. A column for each thirty-minute increment on Wednesday, and one for each half-hour on Thursday.

Oh. Maybe he needed one for Tuesday night as well. That was when the murder had taken place, after all.

If he had to, he could track the movements of each of the suspects on his list. But he was most concerned about Tuesday night. And because the murder had happened just past midnight, almost everyone had been home in bed, mostly alone.

Luke sighed.

He had interacted with most of these people during at least one or two of the cycles. But Luke's interactions sometimes changed what they did or where they went. Where would Vesper have ended up if Luke hadn't been in the club early this morning? He popped the cap off a purple marker and wrote "Club Collective" at 1 AM Wednesday morning.

Some people went to the same places no matter what Luke had done. Calvin Barkley and Gabe Wexler would still be negotiating their deal at dinner tomorrow night. Luke grabbed the blue marker and wrote "Le Bistro Cinq" at 6:30 PM on Thursday in the Barkley row.

He filled in other spaces: Big Mike at the precinct at eight on Wednesday morning, but depending on what Luke did and said, his actions were all over the place.

Vesper had been at work that day—ten thirty, if Luke remembered right.

After identifying her husband's body, Angelina stayed home on Wednesday—he'd interviewed her at the house twice.

He blinked. Nothing for Solomon Vargas: a glaring hole in Luke's investigation.

His chart also didn't have room for things like motive, means, and opportunity. Vesper had all three. Angelina might have had all three, too: she was home alone, she had motive—both her cheating husband and the ten-million-dollar payout, assuming it was more than she'd get in a divorce—and she had as much access to Canfield Pro Polymer A rope as Vesper did as a former employee of Domino-Barkley properties.

After an hour, his eyes felt gummy, and he felt no closer to solving the case than he did before.

But looking at the chart, all the pieces were in place for Vesper Montpelier to be the murderer. Not exactly process of elimination, but Luke felt sure the chart justified her place as his prime suspect.

But the evidence was all circumstantial. Luke ran his hand over his face. He would have liked to work all night and get something concrete, but a wave of exhaustion overtook him.

Maybe he'd have a new idea when he woke up in the morning.

CYCLE 5: THURSDAY

I

Luke pulled his chair out at his desk, and Symanski glanced up and flinched in her chair.

"What?"

Symanski shook her head. "I'm still not used to you without your mustache and goatee."

"Makes me look younger, right?"

Symanski shrugged. "I kind of hate it, to be honest. You look—I don't know. Less serious, I guess. You've always worked better as a facial-hair guy."

"Uh, thanks. I think."

Symanski watched Luke closely.

"What?"

"Do you still think you're repeating the day?"

Luke blinked. That's right—he'd told Symanski about it yesterday. Did she believe him? Did she *want* to believe him? He shrugged. "Doesn't really matter now."

Symanski blinked. "I'd think it matters quite a bit."

"Well—I meant what I said yesterday: forget I mentioned

anything about repeating days." He tapped his watch. "It's eight fifteen. If we want to catch Ashton Carruthers, we need to move."

"Who?"

"Vesper Montpelier's dealer."

Symanski stood, her eyes bright. "I'm ready."

Behind Symanski, Captain Thoreau appeared in the doorway to their office. "Guillory, Symanski?" They turned and went back into their office, and the two detectives followed.

Thoreau stood behind their desk. "Shut the door."

Symanski complied.

"The fingerprints from the victim came back," Thoreau said. "Pye Domino. Now, as soon as Detective Moody finds out, he'll want to take over the case. I understand that his ex-girlfriend is a person of interest, so I can't have him assigned to this case. You two still have the case until further notice." They locked eyes with Luke. "I'm going out on a limb here, Detective Guillory. Please don't make me regret it."

"Understood, Captain."

Ten minutes later, they turned into the Beckman Highlands neighborhood and Luke slowed to ten miles an hour, glancing from left to right.

"What are you looking for?" Symanski asked.

"His Jaguar," Luke said. He drove down a few streets before spotting the Jaguar parked on in a cul-de-sac.

Symanski pointed, and Luke pulled the cruiser behind the silver Jaguar.

He glanced up at the mini-mansions on both sides of the street.

"Now we wait?" Symanski asked.

"Now we wait." Luke rubbed his chin. "Hey—did you catch that there was a mugging last night?"

"Probably a few muggings last night."

"No—I mean from a woman who lives in this neighborhood."

"I haven't heard anything about that."

"No, I guess not."

"Is this one of those things you dreamed about in your—"

Ashton Carruthers appeared on the front porch of the house on the right and hurried toward his car. Saved by the bell.

Luke jumped out of the cruiser, badge in hand. "Mr. Carruthers? Can I talk to you?"

Carruthers lifted his head, saw the badge, and shook his head, a smile on his face.

"Good morning, officer."

"Detective," Luke said. "You've heard by now that one of your clients was found dead in Lemon Hill Park yesterday morning."

"I don't know what you're talking about," Carruthers said.

Luke stood next to the driver's door of the Jaguar. "Pye Domino. Lived right around here. Pretty reliable customer, until about six months ago."

"Must be mistaken."

Luke tilted his head. "I know you've recently sold an emerald necklace, a diamond-encrusted watch and a Bianchi Milano purse. All of which Alannah Zimmer has reported stolen in a robbery on Tuesday night."

Ashton frowned. "I've got sales slips. Those were—"

"But," Luke continued, "maybe we could offer Alannah Zimmer a deal. The name of her Magic Star dealer in exchange for dropping the charges."

Ashton giggled, a high-pitched, churlish sound. "Then I'd never give your friends in Vice any information ever again." He screwed up his mouth. "Besides, Alannah is smart enough to keep my name out of her mouth."

"I don't know," Luke said. "We take murder seriously. I don't know if you can get your daddy to pull enough strings for that."

"Murder?"

"Pye Domino. Your former client. Went by C.D. when he came down to Lemon Hill."

"I didn't have anything to do with any murder."

"You sure about that?"

"Positive."

"Because the victim called your daddy just a few hours before he was killed."

K-Car shrugged. "My dad didn't say anything to me."

Luke studied K-Car's face. No recognition in those eyes. And Lincoln Carruthers hadn't called Pye Domino back, at least not according to Pye's phone call history. So Luke changed tacks. "Maybe you know the person who *was* involved. Someone you sold to on Tuesday night, maybe. Not here, but down by Lemon Hill Park." He paused and nodded at Symanski. "What do you think, Detective? I bet if we pull ATM camera footage from Fruitridge Avenue, we can find a silver Jaguar driving around Lemon Hill right around midnight. Your daddy can protect you from a lot of things, but I'm not sure you want to find out whether that applies to murder."

K-Car's smile faltered slightly.

"So we've got a pretty simple question," Luke said. "Who was your buyer?"

"She didn't have anything to do with this either."

"You don't know that," Luke replied. "I need a name."

Ashton hesitated. "Vesper Montpelier."

"What did she buy?"

Ashton paused again. "Twenty Magic Star."

"Did you sell it to her at Lemon Hill Park?"

"No, man. Parking lot on 35th and Bird."

Right where he'd found Vesper's car. "How did she act? Nervous? Excited? Out of it?"

"Nervous, but I think that was because she was in a bad neighborhood. She wanted to get back to the club." Ashton paused. "And twenty was her usual purchase. Now, if you're looking for someone who bought more than usual, you should try the guy on the corner—"

"Stop changing the subject," Luke said. "She carrying anything? Maybe a canvas bag with the Domino-Barkley logo on it?"

A longer pause this time. "Yeah, maybe."

"Maybe?"

"Yes. Yes, I remember it."

"Don't just tell me what I want to hear, K-Car."

Ashton flinched when Luke said that.

"I want to know if she had anything in her hand. Not maybe, not 'gee, Detective, if you say so.' I want a definitive answer."

Ashton shook his head. "I don't remember. I wasn't paying attention to what she was carrying. She had the money; I had the pills."

"Did you see which way she went? Or where she came from?"

"She said she was going back to the club."

"Did you *see* her go back to the club?"

"Uh—no. She was standing on the corner when I pulled up, then she turned and walked into the parking lot when I was driving away."

"Did you notice the time?"

"When I got back to my car, it was a few minutes before midnight."

Luke rubbed his eyes. "All right, K-Car." He looked at Symanski. "You have any questions?"

Symanski studied Ashton's face for a moment, then shook her head.

Ashton stepped in between Luke and the driver's door. "You

mind? I have an appointment."

Luke took a step back, and Ashton got into the Jaguar. He shut the door quickly, started the engine, and drove away.

He turned to Symanski. "You heard the man. Vesper purchased Magic Star a few blocks away from the park less than half an hour before the murder."

II

Luke got into the cruiser and shut the door. Symanski was on the phone.

"Thanks, Roddy." She ended the call and raised her head at Luke. "Canfield does most of their business online," she said. "And the only company in Sacramento that ordered their Pro Polymer A was Domino-Barkley Properties."

Luke had written down the name of the buyer he'd gotten from Brev: *Janice.* But he'd also written that she was in Mexico on vacation.

"Now what?" Symanski asked.

"Vesper Montpelier had several of those welcome kits with that rope included. And if no other company ordered it, that narrows the scope of the suspects, right?"

Symanski screwed up her mouth. "Only a little."

"But all the evidence so far fits Vesper as the killer. We have proximity to a possible murder weapon—there was a canvas bag with a rope like our murder weapon in the trunk of her car, parked two blocks away from the scene of the murder, and she had motive." Luke pointed to where K-Car's Jaguar had been parked. "K-Car told me he sold Vesper twenty Magic Star pills less than an hour before Domino was killed. I bet she used those pills to drug him so he wouldn't fight when he was garroted." Probably took one or two herself, too—she was high on it at the club.

"Did she trick him into taking the pills?"

Luke shrugged. "Ex-girlfriends can be persuasive."

"She wasn't the only suspect who had access to rope like that," Symanski said. "We've only asked a few people for alibis, and no one can prove where they were."

"But Vesper's the only one we can definitively place at the scene at the right time."

Symanski nodded. "But we can't definitively place any other suspect elsewhere."

"We can't prove a negative." Luke drummed his fingers on the steering wheel. "You know who we *haven't* interviewed?"

Symanski cocked her head. "Domino's client. The one with the building material."

"Exactly. Solomon Vargas."

Symanski turned her head in the passenger seat and studied Luke's face. He could tell she wanted to say something, probably about the time loop. But he didn't want to talk about it. He didn't want Symanski to think he was detached from reality. He cleared his throat and started the cruiser. "Vargas gave up his patents for the promise of work, and after the zoning vote failed, the work is gone. He might lose his home, his business, everything. He might blame Domino for the vote, and that's a decent motive for murder. Can you see where his last known address is? Or if he has a machine shop somewhere?"

III

Vargas lived near ReadiGas Arena, about five miles north of downtown, on the way to the airport. After exiting the freeway and going through a few twists and turns, Luke and Symanski pulled up in front of a small warehouse. Luke got out of the car and squinted; there was a trailer behind the warehouse. A beat-up navy blue pickup truck—probably the one that Angelina had seen Pye and Solomon move the material in—was parked next to the trailer.

He walked across the yard to the trailer, Symanski trailing behind, and knocked on the door.

He heard rummaging around inside and was about to knock again when the door opened.

The man who opened the door was in his early forties, about five foot seven. He had tightly curled black hair, a bushy mustache, and small, intensely dark eyes behind wire-frame glasses. With a barrel chest and broad shoulders, he wore a tweed suit at least three decades out of date.

"Solomon Vargas?" Luke pulled out his badge and showed it to the man in the trailer.

"That's me. What do you want?"

"We need you to answer some questions about Pye Domino."

Vargas paused. "What's this about?"

"When was the last time you saw Mr. Domino?"

"Am I under arrest?"

Luke paused. "No."

Solomon hesitated. "I respectfully refuse to answer any questions upon advice of my lawyer."

Ah. Made sense; Vargas had been homeless, and the cops weren't exactly sympathetic to people who had nowhere to live. Wanted them to move from where they were and get out. Preferably to another city.

Still, Luke didn't want to leave without getting at least some information. "You've got a garage full of your building material at Angelina's house."

No response. Luke waited ten, twenty, thirty seconds, but Vargas's face was blank. Finally:

"Those samples are all his."

"Not anymore they're not." Luke studied his face. Did Solomon know Domino was dead?

"What do you mean? Did Calvin Barkley get you to discuss the building material with me?"

"No, sir," Luke said. "I saw the samples in Pye Domino's garage with my own eyes."

"If he's having an issue with storing the samples, have him contact my lawyer."

"That's not the problem, Mr. Vargas." Luke stared into Solomon's eyes. "Mr. Domino is dead."

Vargas blinked.

Luke couldn't get a read on him, though. Was the blink from surprise or weighing his options?

"That's—that's terrible," Solomon said. He pursed his lips. "You're here to question me about his death?"

"That's right."

"Please contact my lawyer," Solomon said. "If I'm not under arrest, I respectfully request that you vacate my property."

"What was your business arrangement with Domino?"

Solomon smiled and shut the door.

Luke turned to Symanski. "It was worth a shot."

"Now what do you want to do?"

"We go back to the car."

Together they trudged back to the cruiser, but Luke didn't get inside.

"Everything okay?"

"You don't put building material like that together on your own, right?" Luke asked Symanski.

"You'd need a team of people. Engineers, chemists, project managers."

Luke pulled out his phone and tapped on the ProfLinks app. He typed in *Solomon Vargas*.

"What are you doing?"

"Seeing who Vargas worked with." He tapped on Vargas's photo and selected *People Also Searched For*.

"Marcus Rochester, Chief Operations Officer," Luke read. "That sounds promising."

Symanski took out her phone as well. "Does Rochester have a D in it?"

"Uh—no."

Symanski tapped for a minute. "Got it. Sending you his number right now."

Luke's phone vibrated, but then he rubbed his chin. "Maybe this would be better in person."

IV

Rochester lived in the same building, oddly enough, as Vesper Montpelier. Luke's pulse sped up. What if Vesper was here and saw him? Would she remember him from early Tuesday morning?

Another thought: yes, Luke had found Vesper at the club and had made sure she was safe, but what had happened to her in those other time cycles when Luke wasn't there?

They'd interviewed her in another cycle. She'd been safe—alive, anyway. And she'd been at work, too, so he didn't have to worry about running into her here.

After they climbed two flights of stairs and found Rochester's door, they heard jazz coming from inside; Luke didn't recognize the tune, but the music sounded classic, old-school, like an off-shoot four-piece of a Miles Davis project. Symanski reached out and knocked. The volume didn't drop, and after a moment, the song ended. Symanski knocked again. "Mr. Rochester, Sacramento P.D."

The next song started, but the volume went down, and the door opened.

"Marcus Rochester?"

The man nodded. Perhaps six-foot-three, he was Black,

with dark, intense eyes. He wore a Howard University T-shirt and jeans, and his feet were bare. He could have been twenty-five or forty-five.

"You work with Solomon Vargas?" Luke asked.

"I did, until Tuesday."

"What happened on Tuesday?"

Rochester pressed his lips together. "We all got laid off."

"Oh, I'm sorry to hear that." But Luke had expected that answer. "What did you do for him?"

"Project management. I reported directly to him, manufacturing building materials."

"Vargastic, right?"

Rochester nodded.

"How did you come to work for him?"

"Recruited me. I'd worked for Allied Plastics, and he called me up at work one day. Asked me if I wanted to work on something that mattered."

Luke tilted his head.

"He said he was working with this builder who had a, uh, how did he put it? A *vision* for ending homelessness. Starting with Sacramento, but if this pilot project was successful, he was planning to expand to San Francisco."

"This vision—it was about turning unused office buildings into residences?"

Rochester nodded. "It's not as easy as people think—"

"Oh, yeah, I know," Luke said. "I got the lecture on office building conversion already."

Rochester gave Luke a tight-lipped smile.

"Anyway," Luke said. "You came to work for him?"

"Well, yeah. Sacramento is cheaper than L.A., so I moved up here, but Solomon knew I wanted to work on a project that could make a difference. Not just altruism, either. His processes are five years ahead of everyone else, and his building material could revolutionize the construction industry. You know the Sutter Block Towers?"

"Yep. Built a few months before everyone started working from home. It's been empty for years."

"Right. We talked with the management company and signed them up for our first project. We got a couple of federal grants for the project, then a couple from the State of California. Solomon worked with this real estate guy on the permits, and I was able to improve the material to a point where we could use it for load-bearing walls. That was the key—everything started falling into place once we started production." Rochester stared into space. "I've never *wanted* to go to work on Monday morning before this job."

"So what happened?"

"The city council vote. The real estate guy—"

"Was his name Pye Domino?"

"That rings a bell, yeah. Anyway, he promised the votes to re-zone Sutter Block Towers from commercial to mixed-use was in the bag. But the council voted it down on Monday night. On Tuesday, the real estate guy told us we lost our funding, and Solomon laid us all off. At least he's paying us for a couple of weeks."

"What are you going to do?"

"I got a call from a military contractor. Doing the same stuff, mostly, but housing soldiers, not the homeless. I hear they got some new type of building material, too. It'll be okay for a bridge job, but the army's never had trouble finding funding. You know if we took only one-point-three percent of the money we allocate to the military, we could house every single homeless person in the U.S.?"

"I did not know that," Luke said. Sounded like an awfully specific number not to have been researched, but he didn't want the interview to become a TED talk on homelessness. He cleared his throat. "So you're going to take the job?"

Rochester shrugged. "My skill set is limited. I don't want to keep poisoning the environment at the plastics company. There are worse projects in the military-industrial complex than house soldiers, I guess."

"Was Solomon angry with Mr. Domino?"

Rochester shook his head. "He seemed more, like, defeated. He made a couple of phone calls to get a couple of the other employees work. He didn't have connections for me, but that's okay. Seems like a bunch of the team members are headed to the same military contractor. Not many people have experience with new building materials."

"I'm sorry, but we have to ask this," Symanski said. "Where were you on Tuesday night, right around midnight?"

"Here, asleep."

"Can anyone confirm that?"

Rochester thought for a moment. "No, I don't think so, but there are cameras in the parking lot and along a few of the walkways. If building management has the recordings, you should see me drive in Tuesday night, maybe around seven, and not leave."

"You've been here since Tuesday night?"

"That's right. I was putting together my résumé, researching companies to apply to."

"I thought you were going to work for the military industrial complex," Luke said, adding a touch of levity to his voice.

Another tight-lipped smile. "Got my job offer from Keymind-Rowan this afternoon."

Keymind-Rowan. Perhaps the biggest military contractor in the U.S. Luke's uncle had lived in the Bay Area and retired from Keymind. He'd designed some of the missile guidance systems used in the Iraq war. Maybe that's what Rochester meant by working on worse projects for the military.

Luke asked a few more questions of Rochester, but nothing

he answered was helpful or relevant. He was about ready to give up when an idea popped into his head.

"You know Vesper Montpelier?"

A glint of recognition in Rochester's eyes. "Uh, that name sounds familiar. She a friend of Solomon's?"

"She lives in this complex. Apartment 210."

Rochester snapped his fingers. "Right. She worked for that real estate company."

"You and she ever talk?"

"No."

"Really? She lives pretty close."

Rochester screwed up his mouth. "Actually, we did talk once. A few months ago. She and I ran into each other in the parking lot of the real estate company Solomon was working with." He furrowed his brow. "Something like Dominic-Barton."

"Domino-Barkley."

"Right, right. Solomon and I had a meeting with the owner. The Domino guy, I think." He shuffled his feet. "Full disclosure: I, uh, asked Vesper out, but she said she was seeing someone."

That someone was likely her boss.

Wait—that didn't make sense. Pye Domino hadn't contacted Solomon until *after* his near-death experience, and that hadn't been until after Vesper had been let go.

"You sure this was a few months ago? You didn't have some preliminary meeting with Domino-Barkley sooner than that?"

"Nope. I remember it was the day of my niece's birthday. First week of January. My sister was mad I wasn't flying home, but this was a big meeting. And she's only two. I video-called her when I got home."

"And you're sure Vesper Montpelier was in the Domino-Barkley office?"

"She walked out of the building. Where else would she have been?"

. . .

V

Luke followed Symanski back to the cruiser. "So what was Vesper doing at Domino-Barkley Properties after she was fired?" he asked.

"I don't know," Symanski replied. "When we ran her background check, she didn't have any restraining orders against her."

"Was she there to ask for her job back? Picking up personal items she'd left behind?"

"She was still dating Pye Domino at this point, wasn't she? Maybe she was meeting him for a lunch date."

Luke put the car in gear. "We can go to Domino-Barkley Properties and ask. I bet someone there remembers her."

A few moments later, Luke pulled next to a curb in the same fifteen-minute spot on H Street he'd parked in the day before.

Up the elevator to the penthouse, and they walked out into the same sterile reception area. The young enby behind the desk wore a floral shirt; the same one they'd had during the first time cycle Luke had seen them.

Symanski and Luke walked to the long reception desk.

"Oh—detectives." Brev said. "How can I help you?"

Luke glanced toward Barkley's office. The businessman smiled as he spoke, then he tapped his phone and took his earbuds out. Ending the call; he had likely been on the phone with Gabe Wexler. And later that evening—at least in previous cycles—he and Wexler would be at Le Bistro Cinq. That meant Barkley had recently finished the first negotiation call.

Symanski smiled and took a step forward. "I see Mr. Barkley is off the phone. We'll just be a moment."

Brev looked perplexed, but said nothing as Symanski,

followed by Luke, walked between the desks and opened Barkley's glass office door.

"Hello, Mr. Barkley. We missed you yesterday."

He glanced up and frowned. "Who are you?"

Symanski pulled out her ID. "Sacramento P.D. We have a few questions regarding your business partner, Pye Domino, and his relationship with Vesper Montpelier."

Barkley's brows knotted. "Pye hasn't been in. He didn't show up to work yesterday and hasn't been in today, either. He's not in trouble, is he?"

Right; in this cycle, Barkley hadn't been in the office when they came yesterday morning. "That's why we're here, Mr. Barkley," Luke said. "We believe he had some trouble with Miss Montpelier."

Barkley kept frowning.

"She was let go about six months ago, correct?"

"Uh, yes."

"Yet she continued to visit the office after she was let go."

Barkley shifted uncomfortably in her seat. "Well, my understanding is that she and Mr. Domino were still, uh, friends."

"So Vesper would still come to the office?"

"Every so often. A bit awkward, but I tried to stay out of it."

Luke closed his eyes briefly and tried to remember the last conversation with Brev. There had been a SugarShack account Vesper was still logged into, right? "When was the last time Vesper showed up?"

Barkley rubbed his chin. "I believe she came to the building Monday or Tuesday."

"She didn't come inside the office?"

Barkley shook his head. "I gave instructions to security not to let her upstairs."

Luke cocked his head. "Why?"

"Because Pye asked me to. I got the distinct impression that he and Vesper were no longer friends."

Symanski looked out of the corner of her eye at Luke. "What exactly did Mr. Domino say?"

"He asked me not to allow her into our offices anymore. I didn't ask further questions. I valued Pye's privacy."

"Were you aware that Mr. Domino and Ms. Montpelier communicated through a, uh, social media application called SugarShack?"

Barkley raised an eyebrow. "I didn't ask him about his social life, and I certainly didn't ask him about his dating apps."

Luke tried to suppress a sigh. This was getting nowhere, although Barkley's information was underscoring Vesper's being angry about the breakup. He wondered if Pye Domino's phone would still have the SugarShack app on it.

"Did you hear Vesper make threats toward Mr. Domino?"

Barkley crossed his arms. "I don't think so."

"You don't think so?"

Barkley hesitated. "As I said, I valued Pye's—"

"Right, you valued Pye's privacy. But you know something, and this is a—" Luke paused. Had they told anyone at Domino-Barkley Properties that this was a murder investigation? That Pye Domino was dead?

Angelina Domino. She knew. And she could have told Barkley.

Oh—but Barkley had asked if Domino was in trouble.

"This is a serious matter," Luke finished.

Barkley looked down at his desk, then raised his head. "A few days after Pye asked me to keep Vesper out of the building, I was leaving for my lunch break when the two of them walked into the lobby. They didn't see me, but Vesper said, 'You don't want to do this.'"

"Like a threat?"

"I don't know. At the time, I thought she was about to cry. Her voice was catching."

"Did Mr. Domino respond?"

"I left the lobby. I don't traffic in gossip."

"Anything else happen after Vesper was banished from your office?"

"Not that I recall."

Luke nodded and glanced at Symanski. "Do you have any more questions?"

"I have a question," Symanski said. "Are you aware of any bad blood between Solomon Vargas and Mr. Domino?"

"Oh, no. Everything there was smooth."

"Did either of them ever bring up Solomon's nephew, Caleb?"

Barkley blinked. "Caleb?"

"That's right. Mr. Domino had a problem with drugs, he was—he was in Lemon Hill Park on Tuesday night, and Solomon's nephew Caleb died of a drug overdose there about three months ago."

"This is the first I'm hearing of Solomon Vargas having a nephew."

Luke looked at Symanski, who tilted her head.

"Thanks for your time, Mr. Barkley," Symanski said. "We'll see ourselves out."

VI

In the elevator on the way to the ground floor, Luke turned to Symanski. "Any way we can get to that SugarShack account?"

Symanski nodded. "I was on a case last year with someone who arranged the murder of his wife using a SugarShack account. He'd deleted the app from his phone, but he still had an active account. All we had to do is log in."

"You guessed a password?"

Symanski grinned. "He had the password saved in his

phone. So all we had to do was download the app, and it logged in automatically."

Luke tilted his head. "And maybe we could do the same?"

"Maybe."

When they walked into the precinct, the two of them walked straight to the evidence room.

The officer behind the counter glared at them as they walked up. "We'd like to check out the cell phone found on Pye Domino," Luke said.

"Case number?" the officer asked, folding his arms.

This wasn't necessary; everyone in the department knew about the Domino case by now, right? Luke cleared his throat, pulled out his phone, and tapped the screen and scrolled until he found the case number.

The officer grunted and stepped back into the rows of shelves. He was gone for several minutes. Luke stepped back in the hallway in front of the evidence room and leaned against the back wall, closing his eyes. Luke wondered if there was another world or another dimension out there where some version of him was trying to get Hector out of jail. And maybe another version of Luke that was still in jail himself. Another one where he had to defend himself in a lawsuit against the cyclist.

And Symanski finally opened her mouth. "You didn't get this SugarShack app info from the same, uh, day that you found out about the brand of rope, did you?"

Luke chuckled. "The SugarShack app is new information."

The officer returned with the evidence baggie with the cell-phone inside. Luke stepped forward, but Symanski was there first and took the phone from the officer.

She turned the phone over, and on a Post-It was the unlock code. CSI had already done their work on it—or maybe they'd gotten the code from Angelina Domino.

Symanski woke the phone up, entered the code, then swiped and typed.

"No active SugarShack app," she muttered, tapping the App Store icon. "But maybe if we download it again..." She stared intently at the phone, swiped, tapped, held down a button on the side, swiped again, and smiled. "Gotcha."

She held the phone toward Luke. "There you go. More than a hundred messages between Pye Domino and Vesper Montpelier."

Symanski tapped again and the full conversation came up. The last messages, all from Vesper, showed first.

> Don't ignore me

Before that:

> Are you going to pretend I don't exist
>
> I could make things difficult for you

Symanski scrolled with Luke reading over her shoulder. At least a dozen messages from Vesper, stretching out over the past two weeks, with Domino not responding. As the time went earlier, the messages got less accusatory, almost friendly. The "don't ignore me" was the worst of the bunch.

"Not exactly threatening," Luke said.

"But taken with everything else," Symanski said, "it underscores the motive: he dumped her and she was angry. I think we have enough evidence to bring to the district attorney."

What would Detective Blood say about this? Luke paused. "A lot of circumstantial evidence."

Symanski nodded. "I've arrested people with less, and the Fresno ADA convicted."

A ding on Symanski's phone. A text message popped up from Dr. Koh.

> Tox report came back
>
> Drugs in victim's system match Magic Star
>
> Enough to render him unconscious at the time of the murder

"So he was drugged before he was killed," Luke said.

"It would explain how the killer could garrote Domino without signs of a struggle."

"Let's walk through this." Luke rubbed his chin. "We need to tell the D.A. a story that would make sense to a jury. So let's make sure it holds water."

Symanski shrugged. "Girl meets boy, girl gets boy hooked on Magic Star, girl falls in love with boy, boy won't leave his wife, boy has a near-death experience, boy dumps girl, girl is angry and kills boy in a drug-fueled rage."

"A tale as old as time," Luke said.

"That last part's a little sketchy," Symanski said.

"Okay, it wasn't a drug-fueled rage," Luke said, "but everything fits, doesn't it?"

Symanski scratched her temple. "Maybe."

"A few minutes after midnight, Vesper leaves Club Collective and goes to the parking lot to buy Magic Star. We've got the dealer's word on this, for whatever that's worth."

"Right."

"Vesper has a canvas bag from her old job in the trunk of her car with the murder weapon in it—or at least, a strong possibility that the murder weapon was in it. She buys twenty pills of Magic Star from her dealer a couple of blocks from Lemon Hill Park before midnight, then we believe she went to the park to meet Domino, where she drugged him with the pills, garroted him with the rope, and returned to the club."

Symanski held up her index finger. "Motive." A second finger. "Opportunity." A third. "Means."

"There are a bunch of people who work for Domino-Barkley and had access to that rope," Luke said.

"Hey," Symanski said, "I was the one playing devil's advocate when you were trying to convince me Vesper was the prime suspect. You've convinced me, okay?" Symanski blinked. "Hold on. If she got pills from the dealer, where are they?"

"She was high on Magic Star at the club."

"*Maybe* she'd take one or two. She wouldn't take twenty."

"She could have stored them at home."

Symanski shook her head. "The search of her apartment would have turned up any Magic Star she had."

"Maybe she had them at work or on her person."

Symanski nodded. "Maybe. But if she doesn't—if she can't tell us what happened to those pills—giving enough to Pye Domino to knock him unconscious is a very real possibility."

"Yeah," Luke said. "Still circumstantial, but that makes a more believable story for the D.A."

"And it makes me think we're targeting the right person," Symanski said. "We better go to Vesper's work and see if she can produce those pills. Or if she has a story about what she did with them."

"What if she can't?"

"We arrest her."

Luke hesitated. "I should stay at the precinct."

"Why?"

His mind raced. He didn't want to see Vesper—or have Vesper see him. But he couldn't say that. "Comb through the phone. See if there's anything else we can use to tie Vesper to Domino that night."

"You'd miss a chance to arrest the killer?" Symanski asked. "Don't you need to…"

Luke's eyes widened. She almost asked about the rules for escaping the time cycles. He wasn't sure if she believed him or if she were about to make fun of him. Either way, though, he didn't want to go to Vesper's work.

"You go ahead."

"We're partners. I'm not confronting a possible murderer without backup." Symanski crossed her arms. "And we should *both* get credit for this arrest."

Luke couldn't see a way out of it. If Vesper recognized him, he'd get pulled off the case—but if she were arrested, it wouldn't matter. Not to the universe, anyway. He'd get out of this time cycle and deal with the consequences later.

VII

They grabbed a quick lunch from the sandwich shop a block away, then they checked out a cruiser. Symanski was behind the wheel this time, and they drove to the office park of American River Realtors near CalExpo. They went in on the ground floor, and like the previous cycle, Luke had a knee-jerk reaction to the sterile gray carpet and cubicle walls.

Vesper sat behind the reception desk in a beige cardigan, concentrating on her computer screen. Symanski strode to the desk, her badge in her hand. Vesper glanced up, blinking at the badge.

"Vesper Montpelier?" Symanski said, her voice was confident and firm.

"Yes?"

"We need to speak with you."

"I got back from lunch a few minutes ago. I can't leave until my break." Vesper, for the first time, glanced at Luke. No glimmer of recognition.

"I'm afraid it can't wait. We'll give you a minute to find coverage."

Luke startled. They'd been there the cycle before, but it was to discuss how Alannah Zimmer had been robbed.

Like the Thursday in the previous time cycle, it took a few minutes for Vesper to find someone, but shortly, a young man in a shirt and tie walked up to the desk. Symanski took a step forward.

"There's a coffee shop next door," Vesper said. "Let's talk there."

Another awkward walk to Java Jim's, devoid of conversation. Again, Symanski chose a small round table by the glass doors, and Montpelier nervously scanned the shop. Symanski sat across from Vesper, and Luke took a seat to the side. Though Vesper hadn't recognized him at first, there was no reason to tempt fate by sitting directly in her line of sight.

Vesper crossed her arms. "When am I getting my laptop back?"

Symanski blinked. "When our evidence team is done with it."

"When will that be?"

Symanski bobbed her head at Luke. "Why don't you see if the evidence team has an ETA on that?"

Luke nodded.

Symanski turned back to Vesper. "You bought Magic Star when you left the club at midnight on Tuesday."

Vesper's eyes went wide. "You don't have—"

"We have a witness," Symanski said.

Vesper said nothing.

"We also know that you purchased the Magic Star two blocks away from the park where Pye Domino was killed. And we believe he was killed around midnight, maybe fifteen minutes or a half hour after you bought your pills."

Vesper pressed her lips together. She swallowed hard.

"The rope used to kill Mr. Domino is the same brand your previous employer kept in a welcome bag for new tenants,"

Symanski said. "The kind of welcome bags you have in your possession."

"Lots of people have rope."

"This rope has a unique type of fiber. And your previous employer was the only one who ordered it."

"Are you saying I—I'm the one who murdered Pye?"

Symanski tilted her head. "I'm telling you where the evidence is leading us, Vesper. We found a lot of Magic Star in Mr. Domino's bloodstream. Whoever killed him gave him enough Magic Star to knock him out."

"I didn't have anything to do with it." Vesper's voice wavered.

"So tell us where the Magic Star is."

Vesper looked up innocently. "What Magic Star?"

"Don't play dumb. You bought twenty pills of Magic Star Tuesday night. Enough for you to get high for, what, a week? A month?"

Montpelier raised her eyes and looked above Symanski's face, across the room, where the wall met the ceiling.

"Are you telling me that now, less than forty-eight hours later, you don't have *any* of the twenty pills you bought?"

Vesper looked down at the table again and shook her head.

Symanski sighed. "All right." She glanced at Luke. "What do you think?"

"Vesper," Luke said, "if you don't produce those pills, we'll conclude you slipped them to Mr. Domino. When he got loopy or unconscious, you took your rope and strangled him."

Vesper's bottom lip quivered. "I would never do that to Pye."

"And with your motive—"

"Motive?" Vesper's tone was sharp.

"Where are you going to live next month?" Luke said. "Domino wasn't paying for your apartment anymore. He dumped you. You threatened him—in public."

"That doesn't mean—"

Luke glanced at Symanski, who nodded. He stood from his seat. "Would you stand up?" He glanced at Symanski, who nodded almost imperceptibly.

Vesper looked up at Luke and blinked. "What?"

"You need to stand up, Vesper."

"Why?"

"Vesper Montpelier, you are under arrest for the murder of Pye Domino."

"What?" Now Vesper jumped out of her seat, hands clenched into fists at her side.

"You have the right to remain silent—"

"I didn't kill him!" She raised her voice, and the two baristas, who were the only others in the coffee shop, glanced over at them nervously. "This is ridiculous—"

But Luke finished the reading of the Miranda warning, then cuffed Vesper.

The click of the cuffs seemed to trigger the off switch on Vesper's mouth, and she said nothing else.

He and Symanski led her out of the coffee shop and through the parking lot.

Luke assisted Vesper getting into the cruiser. As Vesper turned, she blinked at Luke's face. A flash of realization on Vesper's face, then a shade of confusion. Like she recognized him, but didn't know from where.

But she didn't say anything. Luke almost wished she had; he would have said he worked with Big Mike or something. But she kept quiet, taking her Miranda rights seriously.

The ride back to the precinct was uneventful. Symanski drove, and Luke turned around every so often to look at Vesper. She stared out the window. At one point, he thought he saw a tear run down her cheek, but that could have been a trick of the early afternoon light.

Getting Vesper into booking took a couple of hours;

Symanski collected Vesper's personal information. Luke organized her effects. Vesper refused to give a statement. They handed her over to get fingerprinted and photographed, then they got in the elevator to ride up to the homicide division.

As soon as the doors closed, Symanski exhaled through her mouth, loudly flapping her lips together like a raspberry.

"You can say that again," Luke said.

"Biggest arrest I've ever made," Symanski said.

"Me too."

The elevator doors opened on their floor—and there was Thoreau, standing a few feet away, a big grin on their face.

"Congratulations, both of you," Thoreau said. "This is the highest-profile murder in Sacramento in years, and you solved the case in thirty-six hours. I wanted to tell you both to celebrate this win."

"Not a win until the D.A. thinks there's enough evidence to charge her," Luke said.

"I've reviewed the evidence," Thoreau said. "No case is watertight. But most cases I've overseen have far less evidence than this. You can sleep easy knowing you did solid police work."

"Thanks, Captain," Symanski said.

Luke nodded. "Yes. Thanks."

"Now get started on the paperwork," Thoreau said. "If you hurry, you might get it done by quitting time."

They both sat at their desks, divvied up the work, and started in on the computer forms. After a few minutes, Symanski got up and walked out of the room—probably to the bathroom—and Thoreau came out of their office and stood next to Luke's desk.

"Something I can help you with, Captain?"

"I wasn't sure if I should say this, Detective," Thoreau said, "but I decided I should."

"And what's that?"

"Zepherine would be proud of you for today," Thoreau said. "I know you get a lot of flak for being related to her, but she was a talented investigator, and she'd be proud of you for putting the pieces together on the mistress. Finding the dealer, connecting the dots, discovering the gaps in the story, seeing how the mistress's story didn't fit."

Luke was silent. He was supposed to have seen his mother the day before, and he hadn't even thought about visiting her. Although, he supposed, making an arrest in a big case would assuage any anger she'd have over him missing their visit.

Thoreau continued to stand next to his desk, so he cleared his throat. "Thank you, Captain. That means a lot."

Thoreau hesitated, reached out and clapped Luke on the shoulder, and went back into their office.

VIII

A growl.

Luke glanced up. "Was that your stomach, Detective Symanski?"

"Shut up," Symanski said, a little playfully. "It's only five thirty. I think we can be done in another hour and a half."

"Sounds like you need a dinner break," Luke said.

Symanski pulled herself to her feet. "I guess we can finish the paperwork when we get back."

"A celebratory dinner."

"What do you think? George's Diner?"

"Sure."

Luke drove Symanski over to George's Diner. The sun was low in the sky, making the shadows long, and when Symanski got out of the car, the sun shone behind her, her auburn hair falling over her shoulders.

Luke put on his sunglasses. "Shall we?"

"We shall."

They walked into the air-conditioned restaurant, and the chipper host took them to a table. The menu was full of uninspired burgers, salads, and chicken sandwiches. His stomach clenched at the thought of another burger, so he ordered a salad and an iced tea. A good idea to eat something halfway healthy if he was getting out of the cycle. Symanski got a chicken club and a bourbon-and-ginger-ale.

After they ordered, they stared at each other.

"Can I ask you a personal question?" Symanski said.

Luke smiled. "You can certainly ask. Not sure if I'll answer yet."

"Why are you still working for Sacramento?"

"Ah. That's not a short answer."

Symanski shrugged. "I'm not going anywhere."

Luke paused, not wanting the answer to be as messy as it was. "You know my mother was the first female police chief of Sacramento."

"Right."

"And you've heard everyone thinks I was a nepotism hire."

"Right."

"Well, you can imagine how my reputation sank even further when my mom was arrested."

Symanski nodded. "Front page news all over the state. I was in Fresno, and I couldn't get away from the story. It's all everyone in my precinct was talking about."

"Yeah." A lump in Luke's throat and he forced it away. "After my mom was convicted, anytime someone was assigned to be my partner, they'd put in for a transfer. It got so bad, Captain Thoreau started denying the transfer requests, so they'd quit. Go take other law enforcement jobs. Like I had a big ol' scarlet 'A' around my neck."

"I'm sorry."

The server came and placed the iced tea in front of

Symanski and the bourbon in front of Luke. He pushed the cocktail to her side, and she raised the glass. "Here's to being on the outside looking in," she quipped.

Luke reached for the iced tea and clinked her glass. "And here's to us solving a big case. May this be the first of many."

Symanski took a drink and set the glass down. "You haven't answered the question. Why are you still here?"

"Oh." Luke sipped his iced tea. "Well, that scarlet letter, that was everywhere. You said so yourself—my mother's arrest was all anyone could talk about. Believe me, I tried to get out. I applied for jobs all over California. Sacramento is the only place that will employ me."

"That's it?"

Luke sighed. "Maybe this is stupid, but I've been getting the cases no one wants for years. The sex workers, the drug addicts, the homeless. I give them the attention that people like Big Mike don't. Big Mike doesn't care about the sex worker killed by her pimp. He pushes that off. It doesn't get press."

"It's like that TV show," Symanski said. "Everyone counts, or nobody does."

"Right." Luke stared at his iced tea glass.

The server brought their food, and they ate quickly. Symanski ordered a second drink, but only took a couple of sips. They talked about music for a few minutes: they both loved Chris Ferragamo, his boy-band-style pop music a guilty pleasure. Symanski, when she was seventeen, was pulled over going fifty-one in a thirty mile-per-hour zone but acted so upset about her boyfriend dumping her that the cop let her go with a warning. Luke listened and laughed at her impression of the police officer.

When they finished their food, the server pushed the check in front of them. Luke glanced over his shoulder; the host area was full of people waiting for a table.

"I guess we got here just in time," Luke said, pulling out his credit card. "All right, I guess we better go finish our paperwork."

"You in a hurry to get back?" Symanski put her card on top of the check the moment Luke did; their fingers touched, but neither of them flinched.

"Oh, absolutely. I'm *super* enthusiastic about paperwork?"

Symanski laughed. "Did you see what was next door?"

"The cell phone store?"

Symanski playfully—and lightly—smacked the top of Luke's hand. "No, dummy. Miniature golf."

"Ah," Luke said. "And here I am without my miniature golf cart."

"What do you say? It's not even seven. The paperwork will still be there in an hour."

Luke shrugged. "I'm game."

They paid and walked out of the restaurant. The sunset's dusky fingers spread across the sky.

"I should warn you," Symanski said, "that I'm quite the mini-golf player. Toby Harrison trembles at the mere mention of my name."

"Who's that?"

She grabbed his elbow. "Tell me you're kidding."

"Uh—I'm afraid not."

"Have you heard of a golf event called The Masters?"

"Oh, yeah. Augusta, Georgia. Green jacket. Kind of a big deal, right?"

"Harrison won it last year by eight strokes. One of the most dominant—"

"Oh, oh, right," Luke said. "*Toby* Harrison. I thought you said *Tony* Harrison."

Symanski rolled her eyes. "You don't know who I'm talking about."

"As you can tell, I'm a terrible liar."

Luke was a terrible mini-golfer as well, but they continued

their conversation, Luke paying little attention to his score. Symanski was an excellent player; she was almost twenty strokes ahead of him halfway through the course. She hit the gap in the windmill on the first try, where Luke took four shots; she had a hole-in-one on the split-level hole, where Luke had missed the center ridge and had to three-putt after his initial shot.

They talked about high school: their mutual hatred of geometry but their shared love of algebra. Symanski had been a drama geek, singing the lead in *More and More Amor*. Luke admitted he played clarinet in marching band.

"So we're no strangers to being outcasts," Symanski said, swinging her putter lightly on hole fourteen. Her red ball skittered across the fake grass, bounced off a cement wall, up a volcano-like hill, but hit lightly enough not to fall down the other side, instead landing in the hole in the center. Another hole-in-one.

"You wouldn't have been an outcast with these mad mini-golf skills," Luke said.

"We should've put some money on this," Symanski said.

"I'm really glad we didn't."

After their round was done—they had stopped keeping score after Symanski's hole-in-one on fourteen—the mini-golf counter was closing for the night. They returned their putters and walked back to Luke's car, now the only one left in the George's Diner lot.

"I didn't expect this to go until nine o'clock," Luke said.

"If you had been a better shot…" Symanski began, then started laughing.

Luke chuckled along with her, then kept the smile on his face. "Thanks, Detective. I needed a night like this."

Symanski cocked her head thoughtfully. "How about you call me Summer? After that embarrassing drubbing in mini-golf, we should be on a first-name basis."

"Makes sense to me," Luke said. "Summer."

"Thank you for not throwing a fit, Luke."

He furrowed his brow.

"My ex didn't like losing to a girl," Symanski said.

"Ah. Don't worry, I'm extremely secure in my masculinity."

"No kidding. You order a girly salad, a girly iced tea, and you get destroyed by a girl in mini-golf."

They arrived at Luke's car, and Summer drew a circle on the ground with her foot.

Luke paused. "Even with all this emasculating losing, I want to thank you."

"You want to thank *me*?"

"Yep. My life has been—well, pretty shitty for a while now. And the last month, with Ellie and everything? I needed something away from the office and away from my house." And, Luke thought, away from the Blue Oak Tavern. "Unfinished paperwork notwithstanding, you kept me from going home and seeing Ellie everywhere."

Summer smiled. "Yes. This was good for me, too. Especially kicking your ass in mini-golf."

And she hadn't asked any questions about the repeating two-day cycle. Like she didn't think he was crazy.

Luke broadened his smile into a grin. "Shall we go back to the land of the never-ending red tape?"

IX

They got back to the precinct at nine thirty. Their work area was dark and quiet, and Luke and Symanski worked for another hour and a half.

Symanski looked up. "Did Dr. Koh send you the toxicology report before she left for the day?"

"I don't think so."

A sigh. "I need the tox report for this form. You think she's still here?"

"I think one of her staff might be. They've got someone on graveyard."

"I'll be back." And she stood, walking out of the bullpen.

Like in the morning before eight A.M., the bullpen was silent enough to concentrate. Luke liked it; he got through six or seven forms, though they took a long time to fill out. No one interrupted them for over two hours. Though the forms felt like busy work, Luke could see the light at the end of the tunnel: if he finished tonight, maybe he'd exit the cycle—and he'd have an easy Friday.

Yes, he'd have to live in a world where Detective Symanski knew about Luke's repeating cycles, but that might not be a bad thing. And after the mini-golf excursion, maybe their working relationship would be better.

Luke hadn't had that much fun in a while—with anyone. When had things stopped being fun with Ellie? Was it when his mother was arrested? No, it was before that. Maybe before Ellie had given Luke the Von Zeitmann. The expensive watch was a lot of things, but it wasn't fun.

Luke focused on the form in front of him. He had to check his notes for a few of the entries, and he was glad Justine Blood had told him to write more stuff down.

He looked at the clock on his PC: 12:03 AM. Ten more minutes until he'd find out if Vesper was the killer.

The clearing of a throat next to Luke.

"Oh, hey, was Dr. Koh—" Luke began as he turned.

But it wasn't Summer. It was Big Mike.

Luke tried to drop his shoulders into a more relaxed position. "Oh. Hey, Detective Moody. Something I can help you with?"

The tendons in Big Mike's neck were taut. "You arrested Vesper Montpelier."

"That's right." Luke turned back to his computer.

Big Mike stepped into Luke's line of sight.

Luke raised his head. But he glanced around the office. It was just the two of them. Thoreau was gone. So were the other detectives.

Big Mike leaned forward. "You need to drop the charges."

"On the D.A.'s desk as of two o'clock."

"Well, undo it. Vesper didn't do this."

Luke took a deep breath. Maybe Big Mike was still in love with Vesper; maybe that's why he couldn't let this go. Luke would have to tread carefully. "This is exactly why you weren't lead on this case, Moody. You and she used to have a relationsh—"

"No," Big Mike interrupted. "Listen to what I'm saying. She didn't do it."

"How do you know? Were you with her Tuesday night? Did you go to the club with her? Did you go to the parking lot to buy the pills with her? Did you see where she went after buying the pills?"

"I'm telling you right now." Big Mike gritted his teeth. "Get over to booking and drop the charges."

"Or what, Mike? You'll take my lunch money?"

"I'm serious—"

"You know," Luke interrupted, "you always accuse me of being on the take because my mom got arrested. Now you want me to let your ex-girlfriend go because—"

"Look at my face, Lucy. I'm—"

"Because you don't *think* she did it? Or maybe she's paying—"

Big Mike grabbed Luke by the front of his shirt and pulled him out of his seat.

"Get your hands off—"

But Big Mike was much stronger than Luke. He dragged Luke into a conference room and slammed the door closed, then threw Luke into the conference table. Luke's hip bounced off the edge of the table. That would leave a bruise.

He whirled to face Moody. Luke was a decent fighter, was in good shape, and had fought off a few aggressive addicts in the park. But Big Mike was strong enough to do a lot of damage to Luke—and had at least a fifty-pound advantage.

Moody stood, staring at the floor, breathing heavily, his hands clenched into fists.

"Detective Moody," Luke said, "if Vesper didn't kill Domino, this isn't the way to go about this." He considered his options: a surprise choke hold, a feint if Moody attacked him with all his energy in one direction, even a kick to the crotch.

Moody closed his eyes. Maybe he figured out that he was overplaying his hand. "I'm telling you, Vesper didn't do this, Guillory."

Huh. Using his real name, not trying to feminize him. He must be desperate.

"The evidence points to her, Mike," Luke said, dropping into a defensive crouch. "She bought the Magic Star off her dealer, two blocks away from Lemon Hill Park, less than an hour before Domino was killed. Now she can't produce the pills. Domino had so much Magic Star in his system, he must have been unconscious when he was murdered. If Vesper's Magic Star pills weren't coursing through Domino's system ten minutes after she bought them, where are they?"

Moody was quiet.

"Vesper had access to the right brand of rope—a bag that was *supposed* to contain the rope was in her trunk. I know, I know—a lot of people had access to that kind of rope, but we haven't found any other suspects who were two blocks away from Lemon Hill Park at the time of the murder."

"She didn't do it," Moody said quietly.

"And in terms of motive," Luke said, "Domino wouldn't pay for her apartment anymore. And he wouldn't leave his wife for her." Luke flexed his fingers. "You've arrested people with less evidence. The narrative fits, Mike."

"No!" Moody breathed hard, his nostrils flaring.

Luke straightened, holding his hands in front of him, palms out. "Thoreau says there's more than enough evidence to—"

Big Mike picked up a chair and raised it above his head.

No. This isn't how Luke would end this cycle, not with Moody smashing a chair down on his skull. He rushed Big Mike, decreasing the distance between the two of them and making it almost impossible for Big Mike to bring the chair down on Luke's head. Luke extended his arms and connected his open palm with Big Mike's right elbow.

Big Mike dropped the chair, and it glanced off Luke's shoulder on the way down, taking a chunk out of the wooden conference table, too.

Luke was still holding Big Mike's elbow, and the larger man breathed heavily.

"You're crazy," Big Mike said, dropping his arms to his side.

"Takes one to know one," Luke replied, taking a step back.

Moody didn't move except for his labored breaths, and Luke heard his heart pound in his ears.

After a moment, Moody's shoulders slumped, and he put one hand over his eyes. "I've got the Magic Star."

Luke blinked. "You what?"

"Vesper bought the pills for me. That's why she doesn't have them."

Luke stole a glance at Moody's hands. Magenta fingertips.

Hector's words echoed in Luke's mind: *They call it Magic Star because you never know how it's gonna hit you. Some people, they get happy, some get a ton of energy, other people zone out.*

"I'm not admitting anything," Moody said, "but she didn't give them to Domino. So get your ass down to booking and release her."

If Moody had Vesper's pills, did the whole case fall apart?

Big Mike brought his other hand up; now his face was buried in both his hands.

"Mike—Detective Moody," Luke said, "you're saying you took the pills from Vesper?"

"I'm saying," Moody said, his voice cracking, "that Vesper didn't drug Pye Domino on Tuesday night. She didn't kill him."

Luke pulled a chair out from the conference table and sat, staring at Big Mike, standing six-and-a-half feet tall with his hands covering his face, trying not to break down.

Big Mike's shoulders shuddered. "Vesper gave me the pills yesterday afternoon."

"How many?"

"Eighteen."

Luke rubbed his chin. That would explain why Vesper couldn't produce the pills—and why she didn't want to say where the pills had gone. And Big Mike hadn't talked to K-Car to know there were twenty pills, had he?

So if K-Car had told the truth and sold Vesper twenty pills, and Vesper had taken one, maybe two, then given the rest to Big Mike—that would be eighteen.

Dozens of questions popped into Luke's head. Why did Vesper give him the pills? Did she sell them to Big Mike, or was it in exchange for something? Looking the other way? Were they still sleeping together?

"You need to show me," Luke said.

"Show you?"

"Show me the pills," Luke said. "You show me the pills and Symanski and I will go down to booking right now and drop the charges."

Big Mike folded his arms. "You think I have them here? In the precinct? What am I, an idiot?"

"You think I'll simply take your word for it?" Luke tightened his jaw. "For all I know, you're setting me up."

"I'm a good cop," Big Mike said.

"Highest arrest rate on the force," Luke said. "Show me the pills."

Big Mike took a step forward, and Luke thought he might get a punch in the face.

Instead, the conference room door swung open.

"Detective Moody," Symanski said from the doorway. "Everything okay?"

Moody swiveled his head to the open door, Symanski standing on the threshold.

"Guillory and I were having a conversation," Big Mike said.

"Anything I can help with?"

Big Mike looked from Detective Symanski to Luke and back. "I expect Vesper Montpelier to be released by morning," he said through gritted teeth.

"I'm sorry?" Symanski said.

Moody pushed past Symanski, stomping out to the bullpen, and exiting down the stairwell.

Luke exhaled—he'd thought for sure Big Mike was about to hit him. And that would be a never-ending mess of paperwork.

"What the hell was that?" Symanski asked.

"Big Mike," Luke said, "told me to release Vesper."

"Why?"

"He said he had taken the Magic Star from her. I told him to show me the pills, but he wouldn't do it. Or maybe he went to go get them, I don't know."

Symanski blinked, then pointed to the broken chair. The conference table had a chunk of wood taken out of the corner. "Did Moody do that?"

"Yep."

Symanski cocked her head. "Wait—he said that *he* had Vesper's Magic Star pills?"

"Uh, yeah."

"Wouldn't that undermine our theory of the case?"

"I think that's what Big Mike was hoping for," Luke said. "I think he uses Magic Star, but I don't think he took the pills from Vesper Montpelier. I think he's still in love with her, and he's trying to protect her. She's still the killer."

Because who else could it be? No one else was near Lemon Hill Park that night. No one else had the opportunity—

Luke closed his eyes.

Other people *did* have the opportunity to kill Domino. Everyone said they were home asleep. Vesper had said that too, but she *wasn't* at home asleep; she had been at Club Collective.

Big Mike might have been telling the truth. His magenta fingertips—even if he wasn't high at that moment, Big Mike took Magic Star. And getting the pills from an ex? Stranger things had happened.

Had Big Mike killed Pye Domino? Did he want to murder the guy who had stolen Vesper from him? Maybe Big Mike hadn't gotten the pills from Vesper Wednesday afternoon, but right after she'd bought them. Maybe Big Mike had been the one to slip the Magic Star to Pye Domino and garrote him.

But Big Mike was one of the few people who *didn't* have access to the rope—although he'd know how to get it. Maybe from Vesper. Of course, Mike Moody wouldn't have used pills to knock out a victim; he'd use his fists.

Maybe Luke had been premature to arrest Vesper. Plenty of people connected to Pye Domino had access to rope like the kind that was used to kill him. His wife, his business partner, the new receptionist, Solomon Vargas, maybe others.

He opened his eyes—and the room was strange, like the light was folding in on itself. Detective Symanski's voice in the background, but everything swam out of focus. He blinked, but that didn't help. He took a deep breath…

CYCLE 6: WEDNESDAY

I

A GASP.

Luke sat bolt upright, heart thudding in his ears.

He glanced at the bedside clock. 12:13 AM.

His hand went to his chin. His mustache and goatee were back.

Another time cycle.

Low, guttural. A scream of frustration escaped his lips until his throat hurt.

So. Vesper wasn't the killer.

He smacked the bedside table with his hand. He should have known Big Mike was dirty. Could he remember back to the week before he started repeating days? Was Big Mike high back then? Luke was angry at himself that he couldn't tell.

His alarm went off.

Oh, right; 12:20 AM. He'd intended to pick up Ellie from the airport. She seemed like a faraway memory now. He didn't have to communicate with her to get through the next two days, especially if the cycle would just reset again. Didn't make sense to spend time and energy on Ellie in the next two days.

Despite himself, he grabbed his phone and typed a message.

> Hope you had a good flight, I'll be asleep when you get home. We need to talk tomorrow

He stared at the three-line message before he hit *Send*. He hadn't communicated with Ellie at all in the last cycle, which made him glad he hadn't escaped it. He couldn't save his marriage, but he was sure that the silent treatment—at least as Ellie would perceive it—would be counterproductive to moving forward.

He jumped out of bed. If he was going to be up seven minutes after Pye Domino had been killed, he'd at least see if a suspect or two was coming home from Lemon Hill Park.

II

Angelina lived close to the Fantastic Fifties but lived much closer than Luke did to Lemon Hill Park. If she'd killed Pye, she'd be able to get home, get her car in the garage, and get inside with all the lights off by the time Luke got over there.

But Solomon Vargas was a different story. Luke lived closer to Solomon's trailer than Lemon Hill Park, and if he left in the next few minutes, he might beat Solomon home. Or catch him still awake or trying to hide evidence. He pulled a pair of sweatpants on, grabbed his wallet, badge, and Malibu key, and hurried out of the house.

His Von Zeitmann read 12:26 when he got in the car. Thirteen minutes since Pye Domino had died. And where he died in Lemon Hill Park would have likely been at least two or three minutes back to wherever Solomon had parked. And that's assuming he didn't try to move the body or cover up signs of his involvement.

He started to back out of the driveway, and although he had a ball siren behind the seat, he didn't want to spend the time to grab it—wait, that was dumb. It would save at least five minutes if he used it.

So he took the ninety seconds it took to attach to the top of the Malibu, turned the spinning red and blue light on—no siren, though; no need to wake the neighbors—and sped down 53rd Street to Alcatraz and onto the freeway.

He hit ninety as he got to the interstate going north toward the airport and killed the light when he turned onto the street where Solomon's warehouse stood.

The street was pitch black and quiet. He pulled in front of the warehouse and checked his watch: 12:37. He'd made the nearly fifteen-minute drive in eleven minutes. If he drove into the driveway, he'd alert Solomon. Of course, if Solomon were awake, he'd probably already alerted him.

But the navy blue pickup truck was parked next to the trailer, the same place it had been in the previous cycle when he and Symanski had gone to talk to Solomon.

And the trailer was dark.

He kept the Malibu idling and got out of the car. He wanted to get a closer look, but didn't want to call attention by killing the engine and restarting it. He pushed the car door almost closed and walked across the street—

And a floodlight came on at the front of the warehouse.

Motion sensors.

Luke went back to the Malibu and got inside. He couldn't sneak around with the floodlight on. Fortunately, it was on the other side of the building and shouldn't be too visible from the trailer. Luke looked at his watch. 12:38.

He waited, staring at the watch, looking up at the floodlight.

The light turned off.

12:43.

The floodlight had been on for five minutes.

If Solomon Vargas had gotten home after 12:31, Luke would have seen the floodlight when he was on the street.

Twenty minutes to drive from Lemon Hill Park to Solomon Vargas's trailer.

If Solomon had been the murderer, he'd have had to sprint to his truck after killing Pye Domino and drive well over the speed limit to make it back to his trailer by 12:31. Five minutes later, the floodlight would still be on, and there would likely still be lights on in his trailer.

Maybe Solomon Vargas wasn't home even though his pickup was here. He could have used a work truck. Or been in league with someone else, like Marcus Rochester.

There was no way Luke could check, though. No official business he could use to explain himself.

Luke had an idea. This was a warehouse area. Unlikely to be many neighbors. Maybe a couple others on this block who lived in a trailer on the property. He hated himself a little for what he was about to do.

He walked up the driveway. The floodlight went back on, and he called out. "Hello? Anyone there? Have you seen my dog? Black lab?"

No response. Luke made sure to stay out of the light; he didn't want Solomon to recognize him later if he had to confront him.

"Hello?" Luke called again. "Someone turned the light on. Sorry to bother you, but I thought maybe—"

A creak: the front door of the trailer had opened. Solomon was in the shadows.

"It's one in the morning." A rumbling voice, crackling from sleep, but it was Solomon.

"I know—so sorry, I lost my dog, and they said—oh, hang

on." Luke pulled his phone out and held it to his ear. "Hello? Oh —you did? That's great. I'll be right there." He pulled the phone down. "They found my dog. Sorry to bother you!"

The slam of the door of the trailer closing.

Luke went back to his car. So much for Solomon being the killer.

III

He drove into Beckman Heights and drove past the Dominos' house. It was also quiet, though three of the front lights were on, bathing the yard in a warm glow. He stopped for about thirty seconds, but didn't want to be too conspicuous, so he drove on.

On the corner of Sage Terrace and Beckman Hill Court, he saw what he'd been looking for: a white Lincoln SUV in the driveway, lights on, movement behind the shades in the windows. Too bad the house wasn't Angelina Domino's. Maybe someone else's spouse had arrived on a late flight, and they'd just arrived at home. Had Luke picked Ellie up from the airport and if Ellie had agreed to go home, that's what their house on 53rd Street would look like right now.

Luke wanted to look up the addresses of the other people who could have been suspects, but over an hour had passed since the murder. The killer was probably at home, trying to fall asleep.

Which is what he should be doing.

When he got home, he set his alarm for six o'clock and went to bed. Four hours of sleep would be helpful.

But after an hour of tossing and turning, his mind running in twenty different directions, he sighed loudly, turned on his bedside lamp, and got up. He remembered what Justine Blood had said to him: that he needed to write everything down. Make a table of the whos and whats and wheres.

The dining table was tidy, and a runner and centerpiece were on it, as well as a few pieces of mail. But no paper.

No, of course not, that was last cycle. And he'd bought a big piece of butcher paper at Marks-The-Spot.

He went into Ellie's home office and grabbed a small stack of paper out of the printer. And the tape dispenser.

He stopped. He'd made a "welcome home" sign for Ellie a few cycles ago—he could use those materials.

The cardboard and marker were in the same place he'd found them before. "Good enough for government work," he mumbled, and a smile tugged at the corner of his mouth, because he *was* the government. Luke didn't have multicolor art markers; he'd bought those at Marks-The-Spot too, but the one marker he'd found was better than a ballpoint pen.

Okay. He'd write the suspects' names on the left-hand side. Vesper had been at the top before, followed by Solomon Vargas. But they hadn't done it, so he tapped the pen against his teeth and thought. He put Angelina Domino's name at the top. The spouse was the killer most of the time, right? And though her house didn't look like someone had just come home from committing murder, but she could have still committed the murder.

Luke had to add Michael Moody's name next. If, as Luke was now convinced, Big Mike was still in love with Vesper Montpelier, he'd have motive. And if he'd gotten pills from Vesper on a regular basis, he'd have access to the Magic Star running through Pye Domino's bloodstream. And being in proximity to Vesper meant he had access to the rope, too.

Luke shook his head. Moody would never have drugged Domino first; he'd have wanted to see the look in Domino's eyes as he killed him. But maybe that was an assumption, and

Moody had a much weaker stomach than Luke gave him credit for.

He put Calvin Barkley next, followed by Gabe Wexler. And Brev, too, though Luke didn't know their last name. Maybe Brev wasn't officially their first name, either. Changing one's name and gender markers was easy in California, but expensive.

As he had the cycle before, he filled in the time slots. A column for each thirty-minute increment on Tuesday night, Wednesday, and Thursday.

And without Vesper and Solomon as part of the grid, he had precious little to fill in.

He ran his hand over his face and decided to take a shower. The hot water pounding on his head often helped him think. Or at least that's what he read in articles about the brain and cognition factors.

As he scrubbed his scalp, he only came up with one new thought: Justine Blood.

She'd always helped him before. When did she wake up? She must sleep late most mornings, right?

Hold on—he'd talked to her last cycle. He called her right before lunch, and she'd said that since she'd had her Pilates class that morning, she didn't have anything else to do that day. He gritted his teeth. How could he find out where—

He closed his eyes. She said her instructor was hot. And she'd said his first name, too.

He got out of the shower, dried off, went into the bedroom, and pulled on his clothes. He put on a dress shirt and grabbed his phone. He searched for *Pilates class Wednesday morning Sacramento.*

He dug through five listings before he found it: Vineet Chaudhry, Pilates class at Core Knowledge Studios, Wednesdays at 7:00 AM.

Luke's alarm went off. Six o'clock already.

Justine would likely be waking up. Luke grabbed his keys.

Twenty minutes later, he parked his Malibu in front of Justine Blood's house. He pulled her private number out of his wallet and tapped it into his phone.

An answer on the third ring.

"Who is this?" Justine Blood said.

"Luke Guillory, Detective Blood."

A pause. "Do you know what time it is?"

"About a half hour before the Pilates class with your hot instructor."

A sigh. "I take it this isn't the first time you've talked to me."

"Nope."

"I'm in my sweats. I'm about to head to—"

"Please, Detective Blood. I've only got another forty hours before the cycle resets again."

"Well, I—"

"I thought I had the murderer last cycle, and I didn't. I found out Mike Moody was taking pills from her, and he's one of my top suspects."

A harsh sound: maybe Blood had sucked in air through her teeth.

"Yeah, yeah, you also told me that you and Big Mike, well, you know."

"Oh, Lord," she said.

"Believe me, I didn't want to hear it either. But that's where I am. And I'm stuck. Maybe I need another pair of eyes. Or a fresh perspective."

"Are you asking me to skip Pilates?"

"I brought coffee. The good stuff from Basilica."

A sigh. "You know, Detective Dunbar never helped *me*."

Luke hesitated. "I've noticed there are two kinds of people in this world, Detective Blood. Those who want everyone after them to know the pain of going through the same hardships they went through. And there are those who don't want anyone else to have to experience that pain."

"Well, well, Lukey-boy, you playing armchair shrink this morning?"

Luke was quiet.

A sigh. "All right, fine, but only because you bought me coffee. How soon can you be here?"

"About thirty seconds."

A pause. "Is that you parked across the street?"

IV

"Okay," Luke said, standing with Justine in her kitchen, "so I caught a case. Well, I'll catch it as soon as I go into the office."

"Who's the victim?"

"A big real estate guy. Pye Domino. Garroted with a rope."

Justine raised her eyebrows. "And you don't think Big Mike will take it?"

"Everyone thinks the victim is a homeless guy who overdosed. And yes, in every other cycle, Big Mike takes the case from me when he finds out the victim is rich and well-known. Except last time, I told Captain Thoreau that Big Mike's ex-girlfriend is my main suspect." He paused. "And she was, too, but I arrested her and still ended up repeating the cycle." He again told Justine everything he'd gone through in the last few cycles. And he told her how Vesper had come to be his main suspect, as well as him staking out Solomon Vargas's residence and believing he hadn't left his trailer all night.

"I'm missing something," Luke said. "I've tracked all my main suspects, and Vesper was only a couple blocks away from the park. She had the pills with the same stuff found in Domino's system; she had access to the rope; she was about to lose her free apartment. Everything fit."

"Except she didn't do it," Justine mused.

"Like I said, I've got to be missing something."

"Way too many people have access to that brand of rope, for starters." Justine turned. "But come with me." She took a few steps down the hall.

"Are you getting the Cheatham box?"

She paused. "I showed it to you before?"

"Last cycle. I've already created one on my dining room table. Doesn't look as nice as yours."

Justine returned to the kitchen. "So let's take a look." She grabbed her purse.

V

Ten minutes later, they were standing in Luke's kitchen. Justine stared at the makeshift chart.

"Not bad," she muttered, looking up. "Your wife doesn't mind that we're chatting in the living room at a quarter to seven?"

Luke shook his head. "You don't have to worry about that. Ellie's not here. She's divorcing me."

"Oh." Justine shifted her weight from foot to foot. "I'm sorry to hear that."

"It's okay. Well, not really, but I've had a few cycles for reality to sink in. And it's sunk in. Mostly. Partially. I don't know."

Justine turned her attention back to the chart. "Not very full, is it?"

"No."

"You don't have much on the wife."

"I don't see her as the killer," Luke said. "She wouldn't be caught dead in Lemon Hill Park, first of all. Even if she were trying to cover her tracks from a murder."

"But you still don't have much on her."

"No."

"Something might fall out when you start building background on her," Justine said. "The wife might not be the killer, but something might not fit."

"She's got a whole bunch of Solomon Vargas's building material in her garage. Not enough to retrofit a building, but maybe enough to do an apartment or two."

"What about the victim's business partner?"

"Calvin Barkley? I don't think it's him, either. He's going through this big negotiation with a client right now, and when I ran into them at dinner, the client was mad that Domino wasn't part of the negotiations."

"Look," Justine said, "you've done enough to know that either the murder was because of something personal, which is why you focused on the mistress, or it had to do with his business, which is why you focused on Solomon Vargas. But Pye Domino affected more people with his decisions than those two."

Luke nodded, then reached out and added *Marcus Rochester* to the list on the left side.

"Who's that?"

"He got laid off when Solomon Vargas found out they'd lost the ability to retrofit the Sutter Block Towers. He's already got a new job, but he might not have known that last night."

"Any other people Solomon employed who *haven't* found new jobs?"

"I think Keymind-Rowan hired everyone but Vargas. That's one reason I was focusing on him." He hesitated. "And Caleb Vargas died of a heroin overdose in Lemon Hill Park a few months ago. I wondered if Solomon blamed Domino for his nephew's death."

"But Domino wasn't using heroin. It was Magic Star."

"He was clean by then, too. I haven't been able to establish a connection. As Freud said, 'Sometimes a cigar is just a cigar.'"

"Freud never said that." Justine put her hands on her hips. "I don't know that I have any advice for you except you have to complete your work. If you were only following your Vesper, no wonder you didn't arrest the right person."

Luke rubbed his goatee. Justine was right. He looked up at the digital clock on the stove. "I've got to get to work. Thanks for your help. Sorry I made you miss your class."

Blood grinned. "I'll have to book a private session with Vineet to make up for it."

VI

Luke drove Justine back to her house, then went to the precinct. His chart would have to wait. Driving the different route, he never encountered the cyclist. He got to work a little earlier than he had in previous cycles.

After fifteen minutes, a few minutes before eight, Summer —Detective Symanski walked in. Dinner and mini-golf with Symanski the previous night, a night she wouldn't remember. In this cycle, they weren't on a first-name basis. But he also hadn't confessed that he was going through the cycles either. He'd take the good with the bad.

"You're in early," Symanski said. "Everything okay?"

Luke couldn't tell her they were about to catch a murder case. Oh—of course. "Ellie didn't come home after she landed in Sacramento. She's going to divorce me."

Symanski's face fell. "Oh, Guillory, I'm sorry."

He shrugged. "I should have seen this coming. And I don't think there's anything either of us could do about it. I expect she'll move to Boston to take a new position at her law firm."

"Do you think you should take the day off?"

He sighed and sat down at his desk. "If this had happened a few days ago, I would have said yes. But now, I want to get past it."

Luke wanted to do research on the murder, but there was no way he could justify it before it was assigned to him. He startled—he could finish up the paperwork for that hit-and-run; he was early enough to get it done before the murder came in.

He only took ten minutes to finish the paperwork. After he submitted it, he opened a browser, which automatically loaded the city of Sacramento's web page.

A small link in the right column. *City council meeting minutes.*

That was the meeting where they'd voted down the zoning change for Sutter Block Towers. The meeting where Solomon Vargas's dreams had gone up in smoke.

Surely if it were a link on the default page, no one could accuse him of looking something up before the fact.

Luke clicked on the link, and Monday night's meeting minutes appeared.

He scrolled down a couple of pages in the PDF, and there was the voting on the Sutter Block Towers.

Very quick. A council member named Robert Nehlway made the motion to vote. One of the other council members asked if they'd allow any debate, but Nehlway said the proposal had been open to public comment for two weeks.

The vote was taken and defeated, five to four.

In the record was an objection from an audience member. Was this Solomon Vargas? No—it was Pye Domino.

He was ruled out of order and the meeting went on.

Hmm. That was interesting. Pye Domino had objected to the vote—which implied he wasn't expecting it. Maybe he wasn't expecting the vote to happen when it did, or he wasn't expecting people to vote the way they did.

He scrolled through the rest of the meeting minutes, and the topic didn't return to the Sutter Block Towers again.

Moody and Babino walked in, holding coffee mugs. Babino glared at Luke as he sat at his desk, but didn't say anything. Symanski walked to her desk, directly in front of Luke. "We have to finish up the paperwork on that hit-and-run on Scarsbury and 9th."

"Just submitted it."

"Oh. Thanks."

Behind Symanski, a door opened. Symanski stood, as did Luke, and saw Captain Thoreau.

"Listen up, people," they said. "We've got a dead body in Lemon Hill Park."

"Let me guess—another junkie O.D.'d?" Babino said, then chortled. ""We should set up a conveyor belt—"

"We'll take it," Luke said quickly.

"You keep taking shit cases and wonder why your close rate is in the toilet," Big Mike said, sitting down at his desk.

"You'd rather take it, Moody?" Captain Thoreau said.

Big Mike said nothing.

Thoreau nodded and turned to Luke. "I'll send you and Symanski the file. There's an officer already onsite."

VII

The sense of déjà vu was getting old. They parked in the same spot between the same two cars. They found the body the same way, and Luke told Symanski who the victim was.

Like the previous cycle, Luke took a Basilica coffee to Hector Corazón and again convinced him to give up the phone in exchange for twenty bucks and the coffee.

And again, he walked back to the body, unlocked the phone with Pye Domino's face—much to Symanski's dismay—and looked through the call history. He called the unknown number, got Vesper Montpelier's voicemail.

Ending the call, he turned to Symanski. "That's Big Mike's ex-girlfriend. I need to call Thoreau."

"Before you look through the rest of the call history?"

Luke felt the color rise to his face. "Right." He scrolled. Oh, right, Lincoln Carruthers. Still not sure why Pye Domino would call a state senator. Symanski walked to Luke's side and read the screen over his shoulder.

"Is that the state senator?"

"Sure is. The chair of a couple of committees, from what my friend in Vice says."

Symanski blinked. "And Blake Yardley?"

"Should I know who that is?"

"Used to be an investigative reporter before all the newspaper jobs disappeared. Now he has his own website. Uncovers corruption, mostly government, but sometimes private sector."

"Oh, I know him now. He had that movie come out about the school shooting last year."

"Five years ago. But yeah. Why did our victim call him?"

Luke shrugged his shoulders. "Ten second call. Probably left a voicemail." He continued to scroll: more calls to the office, his wife, and the unknown number that was Vesper Montpelier.

"I'll call Thoreau now."

Symanski nodded, and Luke dialed.

"Thoreau."

"Captain, it's Detective Guillory."

"Everything okay?"

"I'm at the crime scene, and the murder victim is Pye Domino, the real estate mogul."

"Oh. Well, maybe—"

"He had a fifteen-minute call last night with Big Mike's ex-girlfriend, Captain."

Silence.

"Let Symanski and I work on this a little more. I'm seeing a few connections here, and I want to see if I can shake something loose before you hand it off to another team."

"I wouldn't..." Thoreau began.

"It's okay, Captain," Luke said. "I know I've got a terrible close rate, and people in the department don't want to help me. If Symanski and I don't make headway on this by Friday morning—"

"You need to make headway on this today, Guillory," Thoreau said, trying to sound gruff but failing. "Or I'll hand this off to Friedman and Damanpour."

"We have the day?"

A pause. "Let's see where you are at one o'clock."

Thoreau hung up and Luke glanced up at Symanski. "We have the case until this afternoon."

"You sure you want something this high-profile?"

"Yes."

He scrolled through the call log until he came to Monday night. "I was going through the city council minutes from the last meeting—"

"You were what?"

"The link is right on our home page." He thought for a moment. "Sometimes they bring up salary for officers, stuff like that."

"Okay."

"I think I saw our victim's name in the minutes. Right after a vote—he objected to something, but his remark was stricken from the record. I'm not sure he expected the vote to go the way it did."

"And you think this had something to do with the city council vote?"

"It was about zoning for the Sutter Block Towers."

"Oh." Symanski scratched her temple. "That's the big building downtown, right?"

"That's sat empty for a few years and has the big *For Lease* sign on it, and a Domino-Barkley sign on it, too."

Symanski blinked.

"Pure luck that I was looking at the meeting minutes." Luke tapped on Pye Domino's phone. "And look—Domino made a couple of calls right after the meeting. Some guy named Solomon Vargas. He also called his partner, Calvin Barkley." He looked up at Symanski. "While I'm looking through this, could you see who voted to block the rezoning on that Sutter Block Towers project at Monday's city council meeting?"

"Uh, sure." Symanski took her phone out and started tapping and scrolling.

Luke turned back to Domino's call log on Monday after the meeting. The first call he made was to Barkley: forty-six minutes. A long conversation. Maybe asking what had happened, what had gone wrong. A twenty-two-minute call to Solomon Vargas. Enough time to explain to Solomon that disaster had struck. And the next day, Solomon laid off everyone who worked for him. Quite fortunate that most of his people had job offers from the military contractor by…

Luke blinked.

That was *fast.*

Luke closed his eyes. Keymind-Rowan.

He was familiar with Keymind-Rowan because his uncle had worked there. Red tape was their middle name; it took his uncle four months to go through the application process. So how did they provide job offers with a twenty-four-hour turn-around—for *all* of Vargas's employees?

This was no coincidence—this was planned. Keymind-Rowan stole the workers away from Solomon Vargas.

Luke opened his eyes and took out his own phone. He didn't know anyone who worked for Keymind in Sacramento.

Symanski stepped next to Luke. "I've got the five city

council members who voted against the rezoning of Sutter Block Towers."

"Do you know any of the forensic accountants in the Sac P.D.?"

"A couple."

"Anyone who could find a payment to any of these five people?"

"Ah, I get it. If Domino didn't expect to lose the vote, perhaps we should look for bribes—any council member who was previously for the rezoning but voted against it."

"Right."

"Plus," Symanski said, "the election is in November. An unusually large campaign donation would be public record. We wouldn't have to involve forensic accounting."

"Good thinking," Luke said. "We may be uncovering a new motive. Domino-Barkley made a deal to use Solomon Vargas's company to do the retrofitting of Sutter Block Towers. After the city council meeting, Domino had a twenty-minute call with Vargas. Today, some of the employees—maybe all of them—got job offers from Keymind-Rowan."

Symanski blinked. "Wow, when you research something, you don't mess around."

Oh, crap. That was fast. Too fast. He tried not to let the panic show on his face. "The wonders of technology." He cleared his throat. "Aren't you suspicious that Vargas's team got job offers from a big military contractor within twenty-four hours?"

"Ah. Yeah, they take months to hire people."

"So I think someone at Domino-Barkley, or maybe at the city government, was coordinating with someone at Keymind."

"A liftout," Symanski said. "You sometimes see competitors do that in the software industry. A little unusual to do it from a private company to a military contractor, but not unheard of."

"Then undermining Solomon Vargas would have been

deliberate," Luke said. "Was Domino behind the liftout idea? Or was it someone else?"

"What's the motive?"

"Revenge, if Domino betrayed Vargas's company. I can think of a lot of possibilities. Maybe Domino wanted more money from the government contractor and he was killed so he wouldn't talk. Maybe one of the politicians didn't want their bribe getting public. Maybe someone was mad at Domino for going back on his ideals." In those scenarios, Vesper Montpelier likely wouldn't be involved. Luke tapped his ProfLinks app and searched for *Pye Domino*. Then he searched Domino's connections for anyone who worked for Keymind-Rowan. He rubbed his goatee. Domino had more than a thousand connections. This would be a long, excruciating process.

"Found it," Symanski said.

Luke's eyes went wide. "Already? Who's the connection?"

"You ever heard of a guy named Gabe Wexler?"

VIII

Luke and Symanski went back to the precinct and immersed themselves in research. Gabe Wexler was a director of project management at Keymind-Rowan, but he was connected to politicians, venture capitalists, and CEOs of some of the biggest up-and-coming tech companies in the Bay Area.

They worked through the noon hour. Background on Hector Corazón, on Vesper Montpelier, on Angelina Domino. They didn't uncover any new information that Luke hadn't discovered over the last few cycles, but they both kept Thoreau up to speed on the search for a financial motive.

The elevator doors opened, and Martha walked out, manila envelope in her hand. Luke closed his eyes. Of course—he'd forgotten this was coming. He rushed over to meet her so his co-workers wouldn't take notice; the last thing he needed was for Symanski or Thoreau to tell him to go home.

"Hi, Luke," Martha said.

Luke held his hand out.

"I'm really sorry about this."

"Don't worry about it. I figured this was coming. Divorce papers, right? You need to take a picture of me with the envelope?"

Martha took her phone out and took a picture, then stared at her shoes.

"It's fine, Martha. I've had a few weeks to come to terms with it."

"I'm sorry."

"I appreciate your concern. I'll be okay."

Martha nodded and left. Luke walked back to his desk and dumped the envelope in his top drawer.

About twenty minutes later, Thoreau came out, leaned over Luke's chair, and asked how the case was going.

Symanski looked up. "I got something."

"You got what?" Luke said, and Thoreau straightened up.

"Wexler is one of the board members of a political action committee called Technology for a Stronger America."

"Those guys," Thoreau muttered.

"Guess which PAC recently donated $35,000 to Jerry Montgomery's re-election campaign to the Sacramento City Council?"

Thoreau nodded. "Excellent work, Symanski. You two keep going." They went back into their office, leaving the door open, and less than thirty seconds later, Detective Moody, head down and back arched, strode into Thoreau's office and closed the door.

A few moments later, loud voices from behind the door, but Moody came out, glaring at Luke.

They continued to work into the late afternoon. Luke went

out and grabbed sandwiches, and when he returned, Dr. Koh had called with the preliminary analysis of the rope. After Symanski got the Canfield Pro Polymer A brand name, she put Koh on speaker.

"I'm glad you identified him," Koh said. "Our fingerprint database is down."

"What about a tox screen?" Luke asked.

"I'm putting a rush on it, but no promises."

Luke hesitated—could he press for more info without giving himself away? "Any defensive wounds on the victim?"

Koh paused. "No."

"So he didn't put up a fight," Luke said.

"Maybe the killer drugged him first," Symanski said.

"That would make sense," Koh said. "We'll screen for Magic Star and heroin first, then go on to other common street drugs."

An hour later, Luke ran an obstacle. "The liftout seems relevant to Domino's death," Luke said after another lead had resulted in a dead end, "but I can't figure out why someone would want to kill Vargas's project."

Symanski looked up. "I might have something."

"What?"

"Wexler re-posted something on his ProfLinks feed about a month ago," Symanski said. "Temporary military housing in war zones."

Luke got up and walked behind Symanski to look at her monitor. He pointed at the screen. "He's hinting that they found a new building material that's strong, stable, and inexpensive. What does that sound like to you?"

"I don't know."

Luke opened his mouth to remind Symanski of the Vargastic. But during this time cycle, he and Symanski hadn't seen the massive amount of building material in Angelina Domino's garage or interviewed Marcus Rochester.

He went back to his desk, opened a browser, and found Vargastic. He turned his monitor toward Symanski.

"What's that?"

"A new building material that Solomon Vargas's company has been working on for years."

Symanski gave Luke a quizzical look.

"Easy to get material for military housing when the city council kills a project that's supposed to use that material."

Symanski furrowed her brow. "So instead of turning Sutter Block Towers into housing, Wexler tipped the scales so they could get that building material to build military housing?"

"For cheap, too," Luke said. "Maybe they had to force out Solomon for their plan to work."

He picked up the phone and called the Sacramento office of Keymind-Rowan, and after a few times bouncing around, finally put through to Wexler's admin.

"Gabe Wexler's office."

Luke almost introduced himself as a police detective, but thought better of it. "Hey, there. I'm calling from Domino-Barkley."

A pause. "Mr. Wexler is not in; I hope you're not calling to cancel."

"No, no. I'm calling to confirm the meeting time."

"Mr. Wexler will be there at eight."

Luke flashed on the dinner at Le Bistro Cinq he'd had a few cycles before. Did the admin mean eight at night? No, Wexler and Barkley had gotten there before that. Wexler must be meeting Barkley at eight in the morning. He wanted to ask the admin for clarification, but he didn't want to raise any red flags.

"Thank you."

Gabe Wexler hadn't been at the Domino-Barkley offices in the mid-morning on Thursday in previous cycles, so the meeting couldn't have lasted more than an hour or two. Luke had shown up too late.

Around four o'clock, Symanski stretched and excused herself. She turned the corner toward the bathroom.

And suddenly Big Mike Moody was standing over Luke's computer.

Luke remembered the chair raised above Big Mike's head in the last cycle. "Can I help you with something, Detective Moody?"

"You can hand this case over to me."

Luke shook his head. "That won't be happening, Mike."

Moody leaned forward. "You have no idea how miserable—"

"Vesper Montpelier is a suspect, Mike. I know it, Thoreau knows it. You're not getting the case."

Moody was silent.

"I know you've been taking Magic Star from Vesper. I've got proof. You think a defense attorney won't find that out? Won't embarrass you on the stand? You'll look like you're protecting your ex-girlfriend. A killer could go free." Luke chanced a glance at his face; Moody's mouth was turned down into a scowl. "You might have a great arrest rate, but your Magic Star use could be made public, Mike. You don't want that. It's a career-ender. I'm doing you a favor."

Moody straightened up.

"You don't want me to botch this case, either," Luke said. "You want to look like a good team player, because if I screw this up and you look like you're protecting your ex, that'll make you look foolish—maybe even dirty." He paused. "I won't say anything about the Magic Star, but if another detective sees your magenta fingertips, they'll put two and two together."

Moody's mouth opened and closed like a fish, then he turned and walked back to his desk.

Luke breathed a sigh of relief.

. . .

IX

Luke stood from his desk. Gabe Wexler had his fingers in many different pies, all with varying degrees of subterfuge. Three political action committees, a couple of charities of questionable merit, an S Corp with a generic name that sounded like a shell company.

Still no link to Magic Star directly from Wexler, but four of Wexler's first-level connections on ProfLinks lived within a half mile of Beckman Highlands. That would be good enough for the D.A. to infer Wexler's purchase of Magic Star from K-Car.

And Wexler had been in Domino-Barkley's offices enough where the rope would have been within easy reach. Maybe Barkley had given Wexler a free welcome kit as part of the original discussions or negotiations.

"We don't have a lot of concrete evidence for Wexler," Symanski said. She stood and stretched. It was nearly seven. "And I don't think I can go any more. My brain is full."

Luke grinned. "This was good. I know we spent most of the day at our computers crunching numbers and searching for connections, but we almost had fun."

"Almost," Symanski said.

Luke opened his mouth to ask Symanski out to dinner—but no. She had plans with her book club friend. Plus, now wasn't the right time. Not when he was so close to getting out of the time loop.

"I think Wexler's going to see Calvin Barkley tomorrow first thing," he said. "Want to meet here a little early and go see what he has to say?"

"At Domino's office?"

"He might be taken a little off guard. Won't be on his home turf."

"I could do that. Seven thirty?"

"I'll be here."

"With good coffee?"

Luke grinned.

Symanski smiled back, locked her computer, grabbed her purse, and left the office.

Luke leaned back in his chair. Visiting hours would soon be over at Pioneer Mesa; he couldn't go see his mother today. But he thought maybe she'd be proud of him for this.

She'd be prouder once he made an arrest.

CYCLE 6: THURSDAY

I

Luke's heart was beating fast as Symanski drove the cruiser to Domino-Barkley Properties. The clock on the dash read 7:53.

They pulled up to the loading zone, got out, showed their badges to get past the security guard, and got in the elevator. Luke checked his watch. 7:57 AM.

Symanski pushed the *PH* button, then glanced over at Luke. "Can I ask you a question?"

"Sure."

"That watch."

"Right, yeah. This was a one-year anniversary gift from Ellie."

Symanski was quiet. "Detective Guillory, do you know how much that watch is worth?"

"A few thousand? Way more than *I* would spend on a watch, that's for sure."

Symanski laughed.

"What, is it a fake?"

"No, you idiot," she said, smiling. "I'd be shocked if it cost less than fifty thousand."

"Fifty thousand?" Then Luke relaxed. "Hilarious, Symanski. You had me going there."

"Luke, I'm not kidding. You're walking around the precinct with a watch that costs more than most people's cars."

The color drained from Luke's face. "Seriously?"

"Seriously."

Luke swallowed hard.

II

The elevator door opened into the same sterile reception area. The young enby behind the desk—Brev—wore a floral shirt. Luke now thought of it as Brev's Thursday shirt.

"May I help you?" Brev said, and Luke's gaze traveled through the open floor to the glass-encased office of Calvin Barkley.

Empty.

"Mr. Barkley isn't in?"

"No, I'm sorry."

Luke swore under his breath. Maybe when he'd confirmed with Wexler's admin, he *should* have specified if it was morning or evening.

"I thought he had a meeting this morning," Luke said.

Brev blinked. "Well, uh, he has a breakfast meeting. But not in the office."

"I see," Luke said. "Can you tell us where he is?"

Brev screwed up their mouth. "I don't know," they said, "but I'm not sure I'm allowed to give out that information even if I knew."

"Of course, of course," Luke said. No point in arguing. If

they'd known, that would be a different story, but he couldn't get blood from a turnip.

Luke turned and stepped away from the reception area. Eight o'clock already. The breakfast meeting had started. They had half an hour, maybe forty-five minutes before the meeting was over.

Symanski followed Luke, bent close to his ear, and talked quietly. "So now what? We drive around all the breakfast places in the area?"

"I think we can rule out Pancake Palace," Luke replied.

"Bourgeois places only. Got it."

Luke squeezed his eyes shut. Something was scratching at the dog door of his brain. "Hang on, Wexler said something..."

"When did you hear from Wexler?"

He didn't have a reasonable response for Symanski, so he dug deeper into his mind. At Le Bistro Cinq, maybe four or five cycles before, Luke had been sitting next to Gabe and Calvin at the bar. Wexler was all business, but Barkley had said *We've gotta eat, right?* Or something like that. And Wexler had talked about how the breakfast place was crowded. He frowned. Why couldn't he have remembered that before now? That would have saved them a trip to Braley Tower.

Wait a second.

Wexler hadn't said the breakfast place was crowded.

He'd said *This Morning was crowded.*

Wexler hadn't been referring to the time they'd eaten breakfast. He'd been referring to the brunch and mimosas place near Beckman Highlands.

Luke opened his eyes. "Detective Symanski," he said. "Does Wexler live in Beckman Highlands?"

"I can check."

"Okay. I think I know where they're having their breakfast meeting."

III

Symanski called one of the researchers in the precinct to get Wexler's current address while Luke drove. She pulled the phone away from her ear to ask, "Do you want Barkley's home address, too?"

Luke ran his tongue over his teeth. "Couldn't hurt, I guess. Not if it takes a long time, though."

They arrived at This Morning ten minutes after leaving Braley Tower. The maître-d' asked if they had a reservation, but Symanski's badge made him lose his attitude.

"Looking for a table for Calvin Barkley, or perhaps Gabe Wexler."

The maître-d' nodded. "If I could make a small request."

"Sure."

"If you have anything that you suspect could cause a scene—"

"Take it outside?" Symanski finished.

"Our other patrons wish to finish their meals without interruption."

"We'll do everything we can," Luke said, following the maître-d' through the dining room. He glanced at the food on the tables: heavy sauces, lots of garnishes. Very little he recognized as breakfast food.

They turned a corner, then around a folding wall partition, and there, at a round table with a white tablecloth, sitting in leather armchairs that looked ridiculous at a dining table, sat Gabe Wexler and Calvin Barkley. Wexler was in the seat between the table and the wall, with the divider on the right. Nowhere for him to escape if Luke sat on his left.

Which he did.

Barkley sat across the table from Wexler, on Luke's left.

"Thank you," Symanski said to the maître-d'.

"What's the meaning of this?" Barkley said. "We're discussing a business deal that—"

Luke showed the dining duo his badge. "I apologize for interrupting your meal," he said, casting a quick glance down at the fancy food on their plates. "We're in the middle of a murder investigation, and your name has come up repeatedly."

"I assure you, we have nothing to do—" Barkley began.

"Not you," Luke said, turning to Wexler, who straightened in his chair so much that Luke was surprised military medals didn't pop out of his chest. "You, Mr. Wexler."

"Me?"

"You're involved in a political action committee, correct? Technology for a Stronger America?"

"That's right." Wexler cleared his throat.

"About a week ago," Luke continued, "Jerry Montgomery said he'd be voting to rezone the Sutter Block Towers into mixed-use, which includes residential space."

Wexler blinked. "If you say so."

"But after your PAC donated over thirty thousand dollars to his campaign, he suddenly voted against it."

"Again, if you say so." Wexler looked from Luke to Symanski. "What does this have to do with a murder investigation?"

"Did you authorize those payments, Mr. Wexler?"

"We authorize many donations to political campaigns of all sizes."

"Seems like a large sum for a city council re-election."

"You'd be surprised at a lot of the details in today's politics." Wexler shook his head, and a smile quirked the corner of his mouth. "You're not accusing me of buying votes, are you?"

"I'm not sure it was illegal," Luke said. "But those votes meant that Solomon Vargas's company lost the building project. And he had to lay off his employees—most of whom are getting job offers from you."

Wexler's eyebrows furrowed, and he glanced over at

Barkley, who shifted in his seat uncomfortably. "Is this the liftout we talked about?"

Barkley tapped his fingers on the table. "We can discuss this later."

"The liftout was *your* idea?" Symanski said, turning to Barkley.

Barkley glanced at Wexler, who set down his fork. "This is neither the time nor the—"

"We need to discuss Sutter Block Towers," Luke interrupted. "Mr. Domino had a deal to buy the building material from Solomon Vargas. But not after the city council voted against rezoning."

Wexler frowned, leaning toward Barkley. "You told me the building material was ours."

"This is just a misunderstanding," Barkley sputtered. "I assure you, as soon as you sign the contract, the material is all yours."

Luke studied Barkley's face for a moment, then he turned to Wexler. "So *you* thought you were buying all the Vargastic building materials from Solomon Vargas?"

"From Vargas?" Wexler blinked. "No. I'm negotiating with Domino-Barkley."

Luke turned toward Barkley. "I thought Pye Domino was working on a deal with Vargas."

"Domino-Barkley already purchased all the Vargastic, as well as an exclusive license for the patent." Barkley straightened up in his seat. "And now we're reselling it for Mr. Wexler's project. It's all above board, I assure you."

Luke saw Pye Domino's phone in his head. He'd talked to Barkley for three-quarters of an hour on Monday night. And on Tuesday, a couple of numbers he hadn't known: Blake Yardley, the independent investigative reporter, and Lincoln Carruthers, the chair of the military and housing committees. But only voicemails to both. "You got the deal for the building material," Luke said, "only because the Sutter Block Towers retrofit got voted down."

Barkley glared at Luke. "One man's downfall is another man's windfall."

"You had your thumb on the scales," Luke said. "You two engineered the vote."

Wexler was quiet, but his eyes shot daggers at Barkley.

"I think Domino figured out what the two of you did," Luke said, "and he called you to put a stop to it."

Symanski's phone dinged. She pulled it out, glanced at it, started to put it away—then blinked. "You don't live around here, Mr. Wexler, do you?" she asked.

"Not too far. Half an hour."

"So why are you at this restaurant?"

"At Calvin's suggestion."

Luke's head swiveled to Calvin Barkley. "Wait—you're the one who lives close?"

Barkley bristled. "So what?"

Luke shut his eyes briefly as the pieces slid together in his head, then he looked at his partner. "Symanski, I bet you just got Barkley's address in that text. He lives in Beckman Highlands, doesn't he?"

"Good guess."

Luke turned back to Barkley. "On the corner of Sage Terrace and Beckman Hill Court?"

Barkley blinked. "Well, yes."

Everything snapped into place. This morning, Luke had driven by the house on the corner of Sage Terrace and Beckman Hill Court: the white Lincoln SUV in the driveway, the lights on, the movement inside.

"You," Luke said.

Barkley flinched. "What?"

"You engineered the vote. You got Wexler to donate to Montgomery's campaign. To change his vote."

Wexler half-stood. "We don't condone that kind of behavior."

"You might not have known you were buying a rezoning vote," Luke said, "but that's exactly what Mr. Barkley wanted. He pulled the rug out from under Pye Domino's pet project. Instead of retrofitting Sutter Block Towers to house the homeless, Keymind will pay Domino-Barkley to manage the military housing project for years to come. I bet we're talking billions of dollars."

Wexler sat back down and put one hand over his mouth.

"Solomon sold the material at cost to Domino-Barkley," Luke continued, "because he wanted his company to manage the Sutter Block housing project. The two of you screwed him over. And Domino, too."

Barkley shrank in his chair.

"Domino threatened to call an investigative reporter," Luke said. "And he called the chair of the state senate housing and military committee. You must have been scared he'd get Keymind-Rowan to back out of the deal."

"No laws were broken," Barkley said.

"But that wouldn't stop bad P.R.," Luke said. "Keymind-Rowan doesn't need allegations of buying votes from anyone—and you didn't want to give Wexler a reason to back out. You tried to reason with Domino, didn't you? But he was too stubborn."

Barkley stared at his half-empty plate.

"I bet we'll find ATM footage or a red-light camera that'll show your white Lincoln SUV near Lemon Hill Park." K-Car's words ran through in Luke's head: *The guy on the corner, he bought more than usual.* K-Car wasn't talking about the corner of the street, or the corner of the park. He was talking about the rich guy who lived on the corner of Sage Terrace and Beckman Hill Court—Calvin Barkley.

"We can prove you bought a lot more Magic Star Tuesday

night than you usually get," Luke said casually. "I have a few ideas about how you got Pye to come to the park. Did you tell him Vesper was still using? Did you tell him she'd be there, buying pills?"

"Do I need to contact my lawyer?"

"Domino drank a lot of diet cola, right? I saw cases of it in his office. I bet you brought him an ice-cold bottle—with a bunch of crushed-up Magic Star in it."

"You can't prove any of this." Barkley's eyes darted between Luke and Wexler.

"Then all you had to do was take the rope out of one of your hospitality gift bags and—"

Barkley picked up his plate and heaved it toward Luke's face, leapt up from his chair, knocking down the partition, and raced toward the exit.

The sauce and eggs splashed on Luke's chest and shoulders, splattering everywhere, but he was up from the chair like a shot. Symanski's face registered shock for a split second, then she started sprinting right behind Luke.

They raced past the shocked maître-d' and Barkley ducked around a woman entering as his shoulder smacked against the frame of the front door.

Luke crashed into Barkley, taking him down, head and shoulders on the sidewalk outside, and torso and legs in the restaurant.

"You're under arrest," Luke said.

Symanski appeared above them, handcuffs in hand.

IV

Back at the precinct, they processed Barkley, then Luke and Symanski did their paperwork and gathered all the evidence: the phone calls and the paper trail of the payments between

Wexler's PAC and the re-election campaigns. They applied for warrants for the recorded voicemails left for Lincoln Carruthers and Blake Yardley.

Aaron Rasmussen dragged K-Cal into the precinct, where the drug dealer swore in an affidavit that he'd sold drugs to Barkley—twice his usual ten pills.

They left after lunch and brought Vesper Montpelier in for an interview, with Luke getting glares from Big Mike when he led her into the interrogation room. She admitted everything she had in previous cycles, and Luke didn't have to worry about her recognizing him. Or about searching her closet and car without a warrant.

More reports from the M.E., confirming what Luke already knew: enough Magic Star in Domino's system to render him unconscious, and a garroting wound that matched the rope from Domino-Barkley's welcome kits.

When Symanski went to the vending machine for a soda, Big Mike got up from his desk and stood over Luke.

"What do you want, Moody?"

"Vesper's name gets mixed up in this, you and I are going to become enemies real fast."

Luke blinked, not making eye contact, and chose his words carefully, Earl Shent appearing in his mind. "There's a program downtown for people who have a problem, Mike. Healing Life Horizons. I heard it works."

"Why are you telling me, Lucy?"

"I don't want anyone beholden to drugs, Moody." *Especially cops with good arrest records.* But he didn't say that. "I'm telling you I've heard the program works. That's all."

Big Mike glared at Luke, not knowing if Luke was offering the recommendation to Vesper or to Big Mike himself. After a tense moment, Moody took a step back and returned to his desk.

Twenty minutes later, Officer Pressler found both the rope

and a half-consumed bottle of diet cola in Barkley's trash at his home in Beckman Highlands. The rope had blood on it that, Luke hoped, would match Pye Domino's DNA.

At three o'clock, the captain's door opened, and Thoreau stepped out. Both Symanski and Luke raised their heads.

"Excellent work this week," Thoreau said. "Solid and quick. I gotta tell you…" Then they trailed off.

Luke knew what was on the other side of the unsaid sentence: Thoreau never thought Luke and Symanski would solve the case. And certainly not so quickly.

And Luke hadn't solved the murder in two days. Maybe twelve days—or was it fourteen?

"Anyway," Thoreau said, "enjoy the win. This is a good one. Knock off a couple hours early. The paperwork can wait until tomorrow." A glint in their eye. "I know a certain former police chief who might want to get a visit from her son."

They clapped Luke on the shoulder and went back to their office, shutting the door.

Luke stared at his watch. Fifty thousand dollars. It didn't look like it cost that much. How did Ellie think it was okay to spend that much on a watch?

Ugh, he'd have to stop wearing it. Maybe he'd give it back to Ellie.

He shook his head. No way. He could convert the Von Zeitmann into a new car, or maybe a down payment on a condo.

Or maybe pay for the lawyer to prove his mother's innocence.

He looked across the desk at Symanski.

"You heard the captain," he said. "We should knock off early."

Symanski blinked. "Thank God. I'm exhausted."

Luke paused. "No celebration tonight?"

"No way. Maybe some takeout and a glass of wine before I go to bed early."

No dinner and mini-golf, then. Probably a good thing.

V

Luke sat at the beige plastic picnic table when the door opened and Zepherine Guillory walked in, led by a guard.

"Outside of visiting hours, Lucien?" Zepherine took a seat, and Luke nodded at the guard, who stepped away. She steepled her hands and looked Luke in the face. "Of course, you've never missed a Wednesday visit before."

"I caught a killer, Mom," Luke said, and couldn't help the pride from seeping into his voice. "And I'm getting credit for it this time."

Zepherine's eyes widened.

Luke related the highlights of this time cycle as the smile that spread across his mother's face grew wider and wider.

"Corruption," Zepherine said, after Luke told her about Keymind-Rowan's liftout. "The system is set up to reward trickery and thievery, and I'm afraid we're too far gone to return to normal." She looked into Luke's eyes. "But every time you stop a crime like this, you slow the corruption machine down." She blinked several times. "I knew you had it in you."

Luke leaned forward. "And every time you decline to work with your lawyer on your appeal, you let the corruption machine win."

Zepherine shook her head. "Now, Luke, I can fight the good fight. But I know a hopeless situation when I see one. My career in law enforcement is over, but when I get out, I'll get work as a consultant or a background investigator. Don't worry about me."

Luke folded his arms. "You have me on your side. And Justine Blood needs something to keep her occupied. What do you expect her to do in her retirement, start selling artisan candles?"

Zepherine stared down at the table. "I'm proud of you, Luke, and I'm glad you're getting the fire back in your belly. But you need to leave this alone."

Luke opened his mouth, but his mom's tone stopped him from speaking.

He puzzled for a few seconds before the answer came. Something he'd not heard in her voice before: fear.

VI

Luke stood on the porch of the small house on Cherry Street, a bucket of chicken in one hand and the bottle of Plum Luck Ruby Cask in the other.

The door opened.

"You call out of the blue at oh-dark-thirty yesterday, and now you're showing up on my doorstep?"

"Dinner and drinks." Luke held up the bucket and the bottle. "It's a celebration."

"You caught the killer?"

"For real this time."

"I recognize that." Justine pointed at the bucket. "Fried chicken from Southern Cross."

"Yes, it is."

"How did you know—"

"In a previous cycle, we had lunch at Jack Dandy's. You ordered the Cluck-mazing and said it was nowhere near as good as Southern Cross. Now, can I come in?"

They ate at Blood's kitchen table and drank the whiskey. Luke planned to stop at one shot. Justine had three, then poured herself a fourth, and Luke found himself joining her for a second shot, though he barely touched it. And the Southern Cross chicken was fantastic—spicy without being too salty, juicy and perfectly cooked. As good as anything at Le Bistro Cinq.

Luke filled her in on everything she'd told him over the last few cycles.

Well, almost everything. He left her confessions about Big Mike Moody out of the conversation.

Justine set the drumstick down with a suppressed but satisfied belch. "Well, Guillory, you might have actually gotten to know me over these last two days."

"Yeah." Luke grinned. "Turns out, you're not as much of an asshole as everyone thinks."

"You better not tell anyone." Justine grabbed the glass of bourbon, now on the rocks instead of neat, and took a sip. "And you have some pretty good taste in bourbon."

"Yes, I do."

They talked for another couple of hours, the darkness hanging over the windows.

"If you don't mind, maybe we could hang out even when I'm not asking for help solving a murder."

"I don't know about that," Justine said, a smile touching the corner of her mouth. "If you say something dumb, you won't be able to reset the cycle."

He paused, staring at the top of the table.

"Uh oh," Justine said. "I recognize that look."

"What?"

"That's the look I used to get when something Roscoe Dunbar said in one of the previous cycles bugged me. He was the—"

"Yeah, the detective who had 'the gift' before you." Luke sighed. "You think my mother is innocent."

Justine nodded. "Zepherine Guillory is one of the best cops

I know. I summarily reject that she did anything illegal. She didn't even get parking tickets."

He nodded. "Right. But she doesn't want to fight anymore. She doesn't even want to help her lawyer with the appeal."

Justine tilted her head. "Don't tell me you're planning to prove her innocence."

Luke locked eyes with Justine.

"Oh," she said. "You think *we'll* prove her innocence."

"We both know she isn't guilty."

"If she's not helping her own case," Justine said thoughtfully, "that either means she's guilty or is too prideful to tell you."

"Or she's scared."

Justine studied Luke's face. "Worrell Dyson was gunning for her," Justine said. "Jumped on the bribery charges immediately. And now he's chief. Proving Zeph's innocence won't be easy." She picked up her glass of whiskey. "Let me think about it."

The two-mile walk home from the house on Cherry Street sobered him up. He'd have to go back to Justine's the next day and pick up the Malibu.

He got home just before midnight and looked in the garage before going in the house. As before, no Mercedes E-class. Half of Ellie's clothes gone, too. Oh—and Luke had left the divorce papers, still in the same manila envelope, at the precinct. Maybe in the top drawer.

His life was changing, and not just because of the time cycles. He wouldn't stay in the house on 53rd Street after the divorce. He'd start working to get his mother exonerated.

Luke tapped his phone, searched for *Zepherine Guillory evidence*, and saw a few op-eds in The Sacramento Globe's online edition. The stories didn't mention evidence at all.

He closed his eyes and pictured Symanski standing over the mini-golf green, her golf ball in the cup, laughing, her eyes dancing.

He sighed, stood up, and took off his watch. Setting the Von Zeitmann on the kitchen table, he saw the time.

12:19 AM.

Friday. It was finally, finally Friday.

CAST OF CHARACTERS

- **Lucien "Luke" Guillory**: A robbery and homicide detective in his mid-thirties, he's a pariah in his department since his mother's the arrest of his mother. Struggling to fight for her innocence, he has few friends and a marriage that's falling apart.

LUKE'S FAMILY, FRIENDS, AND CO-WORKERS

- **Summer Symanski**: A new addition to the Sacramento P.D., she's Luke's new partner—with a past that's almost as problematic as Luke's.
- **Nims Thoreau**: The captain of the robbery and homicide division at their precinct, they're often challenged balancing justice and politics.
- **Ellie Kaplan**: Luke's wife is a high-powered lawyer on her way up at her firm. She just spent a month in Boston, away from Luke, working on cases and seeing her mother.

- **Justine Blood**: A retiring detective with an otherworldly close rate and a no-nonsense attitude, she's friends with Luke's mother—and convinced of her innocence. She also finds herself taking Luke under her wing.
- **Michael Moody**: A brash, bullying detective, built like a mountain of muscle, who has the highest arrest rate in the department now that Detective Blood is retired—and he's Luke's nemesis.
- **Vince Babino**: Moody's partner, shorter by a foot and older by a decade, but worships the ground Moody walks on.
- **Aaron Rasmussen**: A detective who works in Vice, he's one of Luke's few friends on the force.
- **Zepherine Guillory**: The first female police chief in Sacramento's history, she was arrested and convicted for bribery and extortion about six months ago.
- **James Pressler**: A young officer who believes the stories about Luke being a nepo-baby—and maybe on the take, too.
- **Dr. Anna Koh**: The snarky medical examiner for Sacramento County.
- **Jason Renfrow**: A robbery and homicide detective from a neighboring precinct.
- **Worrell Dyson**: The police chief who replaced Zepherine Guillory after her arrest.
- **Kyle McCall**: The bartender at the Blue Oak Tavern, a cop bar a few blocks away from Luke's house.

THE CASE

- **Pye Domino**: Found dead in Lemon Hill Park, a

location known for drug activity—and the site of several recent overdose deaths.
- **Hector Corazón:** An unhoused man who often spends his nights under a bridge in Lemon Hill Park.
- **Angelina Domino:** Pye's widow, she lives in a wealthy Sacramento neighborhood and turned a blind eye to Pye's checkered past.
- **Calvin Barkley:** Pye's business partner at Domino-Barkley Properties.
- **Gabe Wexler:** A client of Domino-Barkley who may have more power than he seems.
- **Vesper Montpelier:** A former admin assistant at Domino-Barkley.
- **Brev Berriman**: The current admin assistant at Domino-Barkley.
- **Solomon Vargas**: A client of Domino-Barkley who has a way to revolutionize housing.
- **Marcus Rochester**: A former employee of Solomon Vargas who has a new job offer.
- **Alannah Zimmer**: A mugging victim, robbed in the same neighborhood as the murder.
- **K-Car**: A well-connected drug dealer who sometimes uses the police to eliminate his competition.

MORE BY PAUL AUSTIN ARDOIN

The Time Loop Detective
Book One: A Time for Murder

The Fenway Stevenson Mysteries
Book One: The Reluctant Coroner
Book Two: The Incumbent Coroner
Book Three: The Candidate Coroner
Book Four: The Upstaged Coroner
Book Five: The Courtroom Coroner
Novella: The Christmas Coroner
Book Six: The Watchful Coroner
Book Seven: The Accused Coroner
Novella: The Clandestine Coroner
Book Eight: The Offside Coroner
Book Nine: The Warehouse Coroner
Book Ten: The Digital Coroner

The Woodhead & Becker Mysteries
Book One: The Winterstone Murder
Book Two: The Bridegroom Murder

Book Three: The Trailer Park Murder
Book Four: The Executive Murder

Dez Roubideaux
Bad Weather

Collections
Books 1–3 of The Fenway Stevenson Mysteries
Books 4-6 of The Fenway Stevenson Mysteries
Fenway Stevenson: Rookie Year

Non-fiction
From Zero to Four Figures:
Making $1,000 a Month Self-Publishing Fiction

Sign up for *The Coroner's Report,*
Paul Austin Ardoin's fortnightly newsletter:
http://www.paulaustinardoin.com

I hope you enjoyed reading this book as much as I enjoyed writing it. If you did, I'd sincerely appreciate a review on your favorite book retailer's website, Goodreads, and BookBub. Reviews are crucial for any author, and even just a line or two can make a huge difference.

ACKNOWLEDGMENTS

Many thanks to my cover designer Ziad Ezzat of Feral Creative, and to my early readers, including the Wordforge Novelists group in Sacramento, Dana Luco, Dr. Christina Bellinger, Gavin Ralph, Blair Semple, Charlie Lemoine, Nicole Prewitt, Monique Koll, DeAnna Hart, Genesis Hansen, Rebecca Davis, Ross Hightower, Christian Horst, Zander Strommen, and Safire Fornell. Special thanks to Michelle Damiani and Christine Welman, who went above and beyond with their insights and feedback.

Jamie Sanfelippo has been invaluable creating, organizing, and maintaining my author newsletter, website, reader teams, promotions, and a million other items.

To my wife and children, I'm deeply grateful for your encouragement and support.

Made in the USA
Las Vegas, NV
14 April 2025